Talk to the Moon

By
Katlynn Brooke

Text copyright © Katlynn Brooke
All Rights Reserved
The characters and events in this book are fictitious; any resemblance to persons living or dead is entirely coincidental.

Acknowledgements

Many thanks to my husband Charles who has supported me in more ways than I can say, and in loving memory of my mother Bertha who inspired this book. I would also like to express my gratitude to Kathy Lake, my sister, for her tireless assistance with quality control and fact checking; her husband, Trevor Lake for his knowledge of tobacco planting; my friends Dana B. and Pam B. for their feedback and support. I appreciate the contributions made by all and could not have done it without you.

Table of Contents

CHAPTER 1 1

CHAPTER 2 6

CHAPTER 3 8

CHAPTER 4 13

CHAPTER 5 17

CHAPTER 6 25

CHAPTER 7 33

CHAPTER 8 39

CHAPTER 9 42

CHAPTER 10 53

CHAPTER 11 56

CHAPTER 12 68

CHAPTER 13 76

CHAPTER 14 79

CHAPTER 15 86

CHAPTER 16 94

CHAPTER 17 99

CHAPTER 18 110

CHAPTER 19 118

CHAPTER 20	127
CHAPTER 21	138
CHAPTER 22	149
CHAPTER 23	150
CHAPTER 24	159
CHAPTER 25	170
CHAPTER 26	176
CHAPTER 27	181
CHAPTER 28	184
CHAPTER 29	197
CHAPTER 30	207
CHAPTER 31	217
CHAPTER 32	227
CHAPTER 33	230
CHAPTER 34	232
CHAPTER 35	237
Glossary	247
About the Author	251

CHAPTER 1

Gabe

Zimbabwe, 1992

Gabe watched the bandit-masked bird plunge to the top of the tall kapok tree; the rapid movement of its hooked beak delivering a furious death blow to its unsuspecting prey. He couldn't tell what the shrike had caught, but it must have been a small bird—a quelea, perhaps. There had been flocks of them blackening the skies just a short while ago.

Maman had seen it too. Her eyes locked onto the higher branches of the tree, but then he looked closer and they were blank again: dark depths that revealed nothing. In the old days, she would have admired the tiny raptor for its agility and utter ruthlessness, but the snake eagle had been a bird more to her liking. He remembered the time—it felt so long ago now—when she had sat by the pool, tanned legs dangling in aqua water as the eagle circled overhead.

"There's a snake around here somewhere," she laughed. "The bird will get it." His sisters ran shrieking into the house but he stayed and they were rewarded with the sight of the eagle arrow-diving to the ground and rising awkwardly into the sky with a writhing cobra in its talons. *Maman* had said it was a cobra but he hadn't been able to tell one snake from another at that distance. She remained as cool and unruffled as the water in the pool, her white throat arching back to catch a last, fascinated glimpse as the eagle flew away.

There was no sign of any interest in the raptor as she sat, old and hunched, in her wheelchair. Today, the once graceful neck was hidden by a scarf that she would not have been caught dead in before—before this terrible thing had happened. The scars on her cheeks were still purple and puckered. Slim artistic hands lay on the blanket like those of a sculpted alabaster goddess and a small trickle of saliva ran down one side of her mouth. He reached for the bath towel they always kept nearby and patted it dry.

A gust of early evening air cooled his cheek as he rang the small brass bell on the garden table in front of him. He remembered how *Maman* always shook the bell with such authority. His, by comparison, was an apologetic tinkle, but Violetta appeared almost immediately. She rarely left her mistress' side. He suspected she lurked nearby in the shadows of the frangipani, afraid if she didn't keep vigil he would kill her mistress with his neglect. She must be the only person still living who remained faithful to his mother, he thought. He had been a faithful son but only until a few days ago. The act of betrayal he had committed made him quiver inside, again. He had barely slept in the last week, tossing and turning in the cool night air as the days of horror ran on a closed circuit inside his head. He wished he had never read those diaries. Wished he had never even seen them. Why had he not gone with his instincts and handed them back to their rightful owner, unread? He would have given every possession he owned not to know what he now knew. If he could only erase every word from his mind happiness would once more be within his grasp, as it had been a week ago.

Would he tell his sisters? He would have to. It wouldn't be as bad for them, he thought. *Maman* hadn't cared for them the way she had cared for him. He had always been her favorite and his sisters had known that. They often hinted to him of dark things they had heard, or of things that she had done to them, and he always silenced them with a look he had learned from *Maman*—a look that could freeze a leopard in its tracks.

Gossip about his mother was common; like confetti around a bride, it stuck. Years later a piece of it would resurface, and he would dutifully sweep it away. He always made things better for *Maman* and the family.

He watched Violetta wheel his mother over the grass back to the house. Greystones was his life-long home, but now it was a home that harbored slithery, dark shadows. Shadows he had never noticed—until now.

He sipped from the glass of Scotch he'd been nursing all day, but he was tiring of the taste. He preferred to drink in the beauty of the African sunset, its dying rays caressing the water of the pool as a frog chorus sang, oblivious to his nightmare. It had been a bright, beautiful day after a week of non-stop rain and he inhaled the rejuvenated air.

He felt a great sadness over the death of his godmother, but his own mother was old and ill and he didn't have time to grieve. For years he worked from sun-up to sun down to keep Greystones from returning to the savannah it once had been. Rhodesia had not existed for many years, and the country that now called itself Zimbabwe was fast becoming a

Talk to the Moon

place he no longer recognized. The old lifestyle he had grown up with would never return. The post-war rebuilding of the 1980's had emerged into yet another fight to keep his tobacco farm solvent. He couldn't afford the luxury of self-pity.

His thoughts went back, as they all too often did, to the day he had seen the diaries for the first time. Was it only a week ago? It had been after the funeral when he met Allegra at Aunt Holly's house. She was cleaning out the small place and there were some things she thought he ought to see. He couldn't imagine what they were. His godmother had always kept a lot of mementos; it was natural she'd want him to take a few out of sentimentality. He thought he'd go: out of politeness.

He greeted Allegra as she came to the door and he followed her inside. It felt strange to see the now almost empty room—a room that had always overflowed with happiness and warmth reduced to a bare box and stripped of memories. He wished he'd come to see Aunt Holly more often. He had loved her nearly as much as his own mother and so had his sisters. Even though Aunt Holly was not related to him by blood, she had been a close friend of *Maman's* at one time, and also his godmother. Her family felt like his family. The rumors of problems between the families remained just that: rumors.

He recalled how Allegra had come straight to the point.

"Gabe, I found these just before Mom died," she said, leading him over to a box of old, yellowing notebooks, typed sheets of paper bound together, spiral pads and stained yellow legal pads hand written in faded pencil and browned ink. "She asked me to read them while I sat vigil next to her bed. They are interesting to say the least. I have no idea what I should do. I thought you should read them too then you can decide what—if anything—should be done."

Gabe was mystified. What could she have known that he should know? He thought the two families knew everything there was to know about each other, and he couldn't imagine the sweet woman he had known all his life having any deep, dark secrets. Surely this was a matter for her family, not him? He felt uncomfortable reading someone's diaries, for that is what they were, he thought, as he thumbed through a few notebooks. It was too personal.

He voiced his concerns.

"Don't worry, Gabe, she's gone now and I think this is what she would have wanted me to do. I know you love your mother and that's why I didn't give them to your sisters. They are not as fair as you are. You would do the right thing, whatever that may be."

He looked up. What had any of this to do with *Maman*?

"If you decide you want to burn them, I won't say a word about them to anyone. I promise. But I didn't want to go to my own grave knowing these things and keeping quiet about them as my own mother did. I felt someone—someone responsible—should know too. I'm so sorry to place this burden on you. I could have gone to the authorities myself, but it wasn't my place to do so. Mom thought so too. She had no proof you know, nothing at all: just some well-founded suspicions. She never breathed a word of them her whole life. I wanted you to know what the true situation was. Perhaps some wrongs can be righted. I don't know."

"What does any of this have to do with my family or me?" he finally asked. A rising panic welled up through his attempt to keep a cool exterior. "*Maman* is very sick, and old. She may not live long. Is this old stuff between them that shouldn't be dug up now? I know our mothers haven't always been the best of friends. If its old business, I think we should just put it to rest. What can it matter now?"

"Well, it's not stuff that can be put to rest. That's why I'm giving it to you. I would like you to read only these diaries, not all of them." She smiled, noticing his look of relief. She pulled out a separate box of spiral bound notebooks. "These are the books from 1945 to 1947. Two years. They will give you enough background to know why my mother wrote what she did and why she believed what she did. You can sit here and read them, if you like, or you can take them home with you."

He had decided to take them home. A day or two later he found the time—and the courage—to look at them. That day he would always remember as the last day he'd know any peace of mind.

He'd sat on the verandah as *Maman* took her afternoon nap in her bedroom and picked up the first book. The penciled entries were faded and difficult to read, at first, but he understood there was information to be mined from these diaries, information his parents never shared with him. He didn't want to miss anything through laziness or lack of focus.

As he read, it became easier to make out the scribbles and abbreviations scattered throughout. The cursive script flowed with clear descriptions of everything his godmother saw and felt; details that enabled even his unimaginative farmer's mind to see and feel what she must have felt and seen on that January day back in 1945.

Talk to the Moon

He began to read.

CHAPTER 2

Holly and Eva

Cape Town, South Africa
Sunday, 21st January, 1945

Eva and I are on the train. I feel like a war orphan as a forlorn faced Mom and Dad slowly wilt on the platform. Mom's given up on the pre-trip instructions and I can tell Dad just wants to go home and retrieve the silver flask he hid in the toilet tank this morning. He forgets he uses that place every time and Mom will always find it. He is sober now, Mom saw to that, but Eva and I both know how long that will last.

Eva can find more ways to annoy me than a mosquito. Now she is asking why I am scribbling in this book instead of shouting out to Mom and Dad from the window that we love them and are sad to be leaving.

Quite the contrary, dear sister: I feel relief and joy. But, if it makes you feel any better my joy at leaving is overshadowed by guilt and fear. She acts as if we're going on a long holiday instead of leaving for a strange country and a new job at a church mission, which, if she will stop and think for a moment, neither one of us know anything about.

I already miss our college on the slopes of the Jonkershoek Mountains, my friends, and perhaps even Mom. I'll definitely miss Dad, but it's the old Dad I'll miss, not this one.

I can only imagine the scene tonight. This time I won't be there to comfort Mom as she begs me to pray with her behind a locked bedroom door while Dad stumbles around the house with his loaded rifle; cursing and blaming Mom for what he has become before passing out on the *karos* covered settee.

I will miss that old *karos*. Strange how one can miss something so mouldy but it was there for me during my teenage years. The tears I shed into it are still there. It's seen a lot for a rabbit skin blanket; more than most people have.

I remember when Mom and Dad were wonderful to be around. Dad wasn't like this all the time. He used to be full of jokes and laughter and

Talk to the Moon

Mom was a much happier person too. It was when she lost our little brother to pneumonia and she got religion. That was when Dad started drinking more than usual.

The train has started moving now. I can still see Mom's black straw hat on the platform. I must go wave goodbye; pretend I am sad at leaving them. Eva's eyes sparkle as she laughs and yells goodbye out of the window. She can be so undignified.

Later:

We are on our way. Eva is snoring like a penny trumpet while sitting upright on the cold leather seat. She's not interested in seeing the Cape scenery for perhaps the last time. We may never return. I want to stay awake so I can write everything down: how the vineyards look as they rush helter-skelter past us, rows tumbling by so fast they make me dizzy; how the setting sun turns the peaks of the Witsenberg Mountains a brilliant orange as we approach the Land van Waveren where Mom's Huguenot ancestors settled in the early eighteenth century and where our grandparents still farm.

Its twilight now and we have just emerged from the last tunnel of the Little Karoo into the stunning flatness and desolation of the Greater Karoo. There is a sense of shock—as if I have been slapped in the face—to see how it spreads out so abruptly from the foot of the mountain, like an invisible chalk line drawn on the ground. There is still enough light to see a scrubby Karoo bush dotted here and there in a landscape as empty as the amethyst sky above.

I keep my eyes on the fire-glow of the western horizon and every once in a while a lonely, lamp lit farmhouse or windmill appears and like a phantom mirage quickly disappears backwards into a time long past.

CHAPTER 3

Faye and Gerald

Tuesday, 23rd January

We arrived in Bulawayo just after 2:00 p.m. There weren't many people on the platform and it was hard to tell from the few that were milling around just who had been sent to meet us. Fortunately, we were not left in doubt for long. A klaxon-like voice blared out from somewhere on the platform:

"*Miss Morgan*! *Hello?*"

I wondered if Father Christmas knew he had lost an elf. A diminutive munchkin, barely five feet high, stood on the platform. As we stepped off the train she roared, "God, I thought I met the wrong bloody train! Where were you girls hiding?

"You must be Holly, then. I'm Faye Johnson. Let's get your bags—I hope you don't have a ton of luggage. My car's not terribly big."

The rust colored Austin was not only minute, the front passenger seat was loose and kept sliding back and forth as we careened through the extraordinarily wide streets of Bulawayo. I sat in the front seat and I wished I had allowed Eva the privilege. I had to keep grabbing hold of the dashboard to prevent a terminal slide backwards which would surely pin Eva's legs between the front and back seats.

"How do you drive with seats like this?" I asked.

"Oh! You don't drive with the seats, silly—you use the steering wheel! But don't worry; you'll get used to it—hey! Watch it you…" she yelled at an unfortunate pedestrian who mistakenly thought he had the right of way.

I noticed that when Faye—who had not stopped talking since our arrival—looked at me there was one eye that seemed odd.

"Don't let this old eye of mine bother you. I had an accident as a child and lost one eye, so this thing here is glass. I can't see worth a damn sometimes, but I get by."

Talk to the Moon

I felt cold and hot all at the same time. It was embarrassing to be caught staring but the news did not make me feel better. I hoped we would live to see the mission.

We finally turned off the strip road and the next road, something that resembled one of Mom's old washboards, made the asphalt strips feel like a boulevard. The car bounced over each rut and hole like a demented bull at a rodeo. Faye must have been in a hurry. She did not slow down one iota. Red dust clouds rose up from rusted out holes in the floorboards in choking surges, causing us to cough as tears ran down our dirt streaked faces. Faye laughed.

"Just wait 'til it rains again—which should be any day now—and then we'll have water instead of dust!"

After an eternity, or so it seemed, the Mission gates loomed up in the dust clouds. A copper plate on one of the pillars read "King's Kraal Mission".

The inside of the mission compound was like an oasis—after all we had been through the scene that greeted us was its antithesis. A long, shady gravel driveway lined with feathery Jacaranda trees led up to a low white building with a thatched roof.

Faye cut off the engine in a silence that seemed almost unnatural. Tall, cool cedars cast long shadows across well-tended lawns.

"I'll take you to your quarters soon," said Faye. "I want you to first see the offices where you girls will be working."

The frosted glass double doors opened up into an inviting lobby and through a door on the right there was a long corridor with offices on each side. So this was where we would work! My spirits lifted and I felt a thrill of excitement and anticipation.

A man strode out of one of the doors. He flushed a deep scarlet when he noticed us and looked as if he wanted to turn around and run in the other direction, but he had already committed himself; he barely faltered as he continued towards us with his hand stuck out.

"Hello," he squeaked, "I'm Ger. Gerald Darke."

Faye introduced us and he flushed even deeper and he looked down at his shoes as he shook our hands.

"Gerald is our Administrative Clerk. He takes care of most of the paper work for our patients."

I noticed Eva looking at Gerald as if he were Clark Gable instead of an owlish man in horn rimmed spectacles. She falls in love as regularly as the sun rises in the morning.

"Mr. Parrish isn't in today; he had to go into Bulawayo on some business." Clark—I mean Gerald—had followed us. "This is your office, Holly." A windowless room with a desk, file cabinet and a shabby upholstered mustard chair.

"Where's my office?" asked Eva. Gerald looked at her as if he had never seen her before.

"You're going to work here too?"

When Eva told him she was the new secretary, he led us back into the corridor into an even smaller office with a portly African lady who looked none too pleased at getting another person in her office. A ceiling fan stirred the warm air. She was introduced as Mrs. Ncube, and the other lady, almost hidden behind a large cabinet was introduced as Miss Ayesha Ghosh. She looked Indian but wore fashionable western clothes. She was quite attractive, I thought, but she looked shy and didn't say much.

I was aware of how Eva and I must have looked: our faces were still streaked with the red Bulawayo dust and probably some train soot, too. I felt grimy and wished I could take a long hot bath. But Faye was not done with us yet.

There were four patient wards, one OR, an Emergency Room, and a laboratory. All the patients were African. Faye explained that the hospital subsisted on donations and, except for the permanent staff such as themselves, there were also doctors from other hospitals and practices who frequently volunteered their services; a few African doctors and nurses, and Mrs. Ncube and Mattie, but the Mission was essentially run by white people.

"In 1889 this area of Matabeleland was ruled by King Lobengula," Faye told us. "Lobengula was persuaded by Robert Moffat, the Scottish explorer and missionary, to allow a mission to be built at Inyati. Since Lobengula suffered from gout, and he had often been relieved by white doctor's medicines, he allowed unlimited missionary access to his kingdom. That is how the mission arrived and how it got the name *Kings Kraal*."

Eva was now fidgeting restlessly so Faye cut the history lesson short and we went back to the car. Faye drove quite sedately down a smaller lane, past a small, thatched-roof white church.

Talk to the Moon

"This church was built at the same time the mission was founded. It's much too small and old for our present needs, so we'll be building a new one soon, next to it." Several modest brick homes came into view around the next bend. "These are our married quarters. Mr. Parrish and his wife and family live in that one, and next door to that is where Dr. Blanchard and Gerald live. A few of the African staff live on the mission compound, but they mostly live in kraals on the adjoining Native Reserve. Some of them live in the Township nearer to Bulawayo. You and Eva'll be sharing a room, and Avril and I share a room. You'll love Avril!" she brayed suddenly. "She knows what's what and she'll show you how to have a good time, I can guarantee that! There's never a dull moment with Avril."

I really can't wait to meet this Avril. She sounds quite refreshing. I had been afraid all the girls at the mission would have earnest expressions and thick spectacles on their noses and would spend all their time praying, like nuns. So far, I have already been proved wrong, although Faye does possess the spectacles.

At the end of the road the female single quarters came into view: a round kraal-like structure which was to be our home.

Now we are alone. Faye left after making sure every piece of luggage had been unloaded and carried into our room. Eva's snoring softly in her bed while I sit at the desk, writing. Everything here is so beautiful and different to anything I have ever lived in. We are in one of five rondavels—large round, thatched roof bungalows with mud and pole walls that are called *daga*, whitewashed to a gleaming finish both inside and out. Avril and Faye share the adjoining rondavel. The three other rondavels consist of a common kitchen, dining room, living room and bathroom. They are all joined together by a white stucco wall forming an enclosed compound.

In the center courtyard a delightful grove of papaya, orange and lemon trees and colorful flowerbeds are arranged around a green, manicured lawn. Around the interior of the courtyard a thatched roof stoop protects the inner rondavel doorways. Bright flowered creepers grow up trellises shading the stoop.

I wonder now why I was so afraid of coming here. It's delightful. I have not even thought of Mom or Dad since getting here. I am determined to write as much as I can about this strange new country. One day, I will reread it to my grandchildren and tell them about it all as if it just happened yesterday. I hope there'll be some things I'll not tell anyone about: interesting things. Things that shouldn't be for children's ears! But I'll write it all down here. Everything.

CHAPTER 4

Avril and Tootie

Wednesday evening, 24th January
Oh, what a day it's been. Things here are not at all what I expected. I woke up this morning with a strange, disconnected feeling. I had no idea where I was. I could barely remember who I was. I looked around and didn't recognize anything. What was that white netting over the bed? A moment of panic set in, and then just as quickly, cleared. It was my mosquito net! With a huge sigh of relief and happiness I remembered everything. Eva was still asleep so I thought I'd get to the bathroom first.

Putting on my robe and slippers I gathered up my toilette bag and towel and headed for Number Three. It was a beautiful day. Birds sang in the nearby trees and garden and I noticed one particularly beautiful bird sitting on a yellow flowered creeper just outside our room. It was a small black bird with a brilliant red breast and metallic green crown. The bill was long, slender and curved. Awed, I stood and watched it for a few minutes until a noise behind me startled us both.

The door to Number Two opened. The bird flew away, and I turned around.

A woman stood there looking at me—boldly assessing. She was tall and svelte, clad in a peachy silk robe I would have given a month's salary to own. Even though the woman had obviously just woken up there was none of the pale and tousled sleepy look that I always wake up with. She gave me a crooked, humorless smile.

"Sorry, kid. At seven, the bathroom's mine. You'd better get up earlier in the future." With that she strode to the bathroom door, swung it open and closed it firmly behind her, just barely short of a slam. I felt as if all the air had been sucked out of my lungs. I turned around and slunk back into our room.

We didn't have to work today. It was meant to be an orientation day which, since Faye had to work, would be handled by someone else. I hoped that someone else was not Avril. Surely, that was the woman who had been so rude. It couldn't have been anyone else.

After we both dressed we went into the dining room in Number Four. A portion of our salaries goes towards the meals and also pays for Merry, the Ndebele cook and housekeeper for our compound. Merry is a misnomer. She is a stern looking woman who reminds me of Mom. Her crisp white dress is starched and pressed to military perfection, her blue apron spotless, and the white cap on her shiny black coif as stiff as a board with starch. She's not a large woman but she could hold her ground in a rugby scrum and tackle. I hope to stay on her good side. She served the breakfast, silent and efficient.

We had just finished eating and were sitting on the grass soaking up the sun in the courtyard when a one-woman panzer division wearing riding jodhpurs barreled through the entrance. She slapped a crop rhythmically in her left hand and bellowed:

"So you're up, are you? Good! I thought you might be like your no-good, lazy predecessors. Sleep all morning, they could. Been out riding already I have. Since six this morning. Thought I'd let you sleep in. Which one of you is Holly? You? My husband is the Administrator here. And this one must be Eva. I'm Mrs. Parrish—Tootie Parrish. Call me Tootie. Do you ride? No? Have a couple of horses here if you're interested."

Tootie speaks as if she is sending Morse code—short, and to the point. Energy radiates from her core, powerful and ill contained, but nevertheless a power that could easily disintegrate anyone foolish enough to stand in her way.

Eva asked Tootie about the horses, and, much to my relief I was all but forgotten as the three of us jolted our way around the mission in Tootie's Land Rover.

The mission grounds are large—one hundred and thirty seven acres—containing not only the hospital, a church and hall, a stable for Tootie's horses, various housing and compounds for mission employees and fields where vegetables for mission consumption were grown. There is a large generator room that supplies power for the whole mission. Water is supplied by a borehole and several rain-water collecting boilers that attach to each of the living quarter's bathroom and the hospital. I had no idea that it took so much work to live this far from a city.

Talk to the Moon

We had another tour of the hospital—not daring to tell Tootie we had already seen most of it. We love the hospital courtyard: a grassy area shaded by ornamental date palms. Patients sit on benches scattered here and there and I hope that we can eat our lunches out here on sunny days.

I am surprised and impressed that Faye is the Matron of the hospital. I had no idea—she looks so young! I got the impression Faye rarely uses her office. It seems to be a repository of books, papers and dust. Today, Faye was in the wards. We could hear her through two doors. Tootie barely paused at the door with a sign on that said: Laboratory—Staff Only, and flung it open with an authoritative flourish. It was then that I wanted to turn and run but Tootie was already pushing us in.

"And this is our dear Miss St. Aubin!" Tootie gushed. Her face, as she looked at the woman standing behind a table with a row of microscopes and flasks, was as tender as that of a mother looking at her newborn infant.

"Avril will be an inspiration to you girls, she will! A true Christian."

It seemed to me as if Avril smirked, but perhaps it was just a fleeting smile. She was dressed in a white lab coat, her hair gathered in a smooth chignon at the nape of her long, graceful neck. This woman couldn't look bad in any get-up at any time of day.

"Oh, Tootie, *Ma Cherie*, you are such a charmer!" Avril laughed; a delightful, tinkling laugh. Her eyes twinkled, impish, as she came towards us. A faint whiff of perfume accompanied her as she grasped my hands first and squeezed them, and then Eva's.

"Don't let this old dame scare you," she said, with mock severity, "She's really a harmless old bat."

Tootie giggled and turned even redder with delight.

"Now, which one of you is Holly, and which one is Eva?" asked Avril, smiling lovingly at each one of us in turn. No reference was made to our first brief meeting outside the bathroom door that morning. If I hadn't still felt the sting of it I would have thought it all a bad dream. This woman was—is, angelic.

In a soft and gentle voice she explained every aspect of her job, and what each instrument was for, and how to use it. Eva, of course, looked awestruck, and Tootie beamed.

We stopped by the offices again and this time we met Robert Parrish. He is a compact man about half Tootie's size with a pursed, fuss-budget mouth. He welcomed us both to King's Kraal, and said he looked forward to working with us the next day, and then began to fidget as if he had some really important matters to attend to elsewhere. I noticed Eva looking around hopefully, but Gerald was nowhere to be seen. I hoped Eva wasn't going to make a fool of herself over Gerald. She can be so naïve!

CHAPTER 5

Tony, Eric and Neil

Thursday, 25th January

Rhodesia has two seasons—one wet and the other dry. Today there is no doubt which season it is. We have never seen such rain before. We were both soaked through before we got to work. The single umbrella we shared was useless. We squelched over the shiny green, polished floor of the lobby—our mud-encrusted shoes leaving tell-tale tracks—as if we had just crawled from some slimy, primordial swamp. I wanted to cry, but Eva was laughing.

"*Damn*, we're wet; doesn't rain like this in Cape Town!"

"You're trying to sound like Faye. Who're you going to imitate next *ma cherie*? Avril?"

"What's wrong with Faye or Avril? They're just fine. You've been acting strangely ever since we got here. Maybe I'll go to hell for it, but I'll have plenty of good company." She strode, huffy, towards her office while I slunk to mine. Eva was right. I have been acting strangely; reacting just like Mom would have. If I ever got like Mom…

My thoughts were interrupted by a reedy voice.

"I thought I'd just get a few things in order for you before you got to work!"

It was Gerald. He sat at my desk, beaming at me through a neon-red blush. He had organized all the files I would be working with on a shelf behind my desk, and he had sorted all the papers in the in-tray into different piles.

"This is the invoice stack, and here are your statements, purchase orders…"

I sighed and sat down in the mustard chair. I need help and Gerald is better than…well, better than nothing. I still feel scared and I hardly slept last night. This is my first job, and I have never done bookkeeping—real bookkeeping—before. I will get no grades here, just a one-way train ticket back home if I fail.

The day passed quickly and uneventfully. Tootie's gargoyle-like head appeared briefly around my door to let me know that Eva and I had been invited to dinner at the Parrish residence that evening—at six sharp. Gerald looked deflated when it was obvious the invitation did not extend to him. Tootie looked at him as if he was a new species of insect and the head disappeared.

I wondered who else would be receiving the royal summons. I was almost certain Avril would be there. I thought Gerald would have been the better choice. I feel myself warming up to him—slightly. He really isn't that bad once you get used to him. I wonder if I'm like Mom who often makes people feel uncomfortable. I need to treat him better and put him more at ease.

I didn't see much of my boss today. When he isn't out of his office he sits in it with his door closed. He rarely speaks to me, and when he does, it's terse and businesslike. I notice he behaves that way with all the employees so I don't feel as if I have incurred his disfavor in any way. At least he's not a tyrant. He doesn't yell and scream as I've heard so many bosses do. He's so quiet one hardly knows he's there. When I left for the evening, he gave a forced smile, as if it was the expected thing for him to do, and muttered "'Night!" Did he know Eva and I would be having dinner in his home tonight? I was nervous. What if Tootie hadn't told him and it would be an unpleasant surprise?

It was still raining outside, but not quite as hard as the morning showers. We sloshed through the puddles and mud on the dirt road that led to the compound and laughed and talked about our first day of work. Eva hadn't fared too badly. She liked both her coworkers and, she thought, in spite of the cramped quarters, she'd be happy there. We were both looking forward to a wash-up and a change of clothes. Hearing the growl of an approaching car behind us we stepped off the narrow road. A sporty red MG with its cloth top up sped past without slowing; sending a spatter of brown, muddy water spraying over us. Eva gasped.

"Oh! Just look at that! I wonder who could do a thing like that. They could've at least slowed down!"

I felt I knew who it was, but I wasn't going to say anything. Eva would have to find out for herself. I do admit to having felt a warm smugness in my chest: vindication, at last.

Talk to the Moon

We had little time to shower and change before there was a knock at the door. It was Avril. She must have taken a shower before we got back, having beaten us by at least ten minutes.

She looked like a fashion model. Her dark hair hung to her shoulders in a smooth page bob, and she wore a cream linen suit with a toffee colored silk blouse.

I felt under dressed in my cotton gingham print and my cheap leather shoes pinched my stocking-less feet. Eva and I hadn't had time to iron our clothes. Our dresses were creased and crumpled and our hair was still wet. Eva's dark hair tends to frizz out in humid weather, and instead of getting flat and stringy like my carroty mop, it erupts around her moon face like a cloud of angry bees.

Avril smiled.

"Well, would you two like a lift to the Parrish's?" she purred. "I think I can just squeeze you both in. I unfortunately have such a tiny car. It's a good thing it's not too far, but I just couldn't let you poor things walk in this rain!"

"You didn't have much of a problem when you passed us earlier!"

So Eva had known who it was.

"Oh, yes, I'm so sorry about that. I didn't see you girls until it was too late, and then I didn't want to stop. I had to get to the bathroom quick, if you know what I mean!" She gave a conspiratorial 'it's just us girls' laugh and winked. Eva snorted, but picked up her handbag and followed Avril out. So that was the big hurry. To get to use the bathroom before we got back. We somehow managed to squeeze into Avril's car; Eva sitting on my lap.

Lucky for us, the drive wasn't long to the Parrish house. We staggered out of the car, stiff and even more crumpled than when we had left.

Tootie met us at the door and ushered us in. It's a relief that Tootie is not a fashion plate. A huge, overweight dog, the approximate size of a Shetland pony, lumbered towards us and promptly stuck its nose up my dress. Tootie ignored this breach of social interaction.

"Rob-hert! Get these ladies a drink, will you! Don't mind Brutis. He won't bite. He's been too sick lately. Here, Brutis!" The dog lost interest in my crotch and waddled off to lie in a corner.

Other than Robert Parrish, there were three other people present, and I knew at a glance this was a set-up. The three guests were male, and had a look about them that said unattached. The man in the Air Force uniform caught my eye. My heart did several somersaults and turned inside-out. My legs felt weak as he stood up smartly and all but saluted as we walked in. I noticed his gaze flicker briefly over the three of us as we walked in, and to my delight, they came back to me and lingered. Tootie introduced him as "Lieutenant Anthony Swann." He grasped my hand first.

"Call me Tony," he said. His voice was deep and it seemed he held my hand a second too long, and then he shook Avril's hand and then Eva's. He had not taken his eyes off me once.

The second man who stepped forward was the odd fellow. He was shorter, squarely built, and his bullet head was almost shaved. I was surprised, therefore, to hear him being introduced as Eric Swann, Tony's brother. He shook hands perfunctorily with a meaty paw, and quickly sat down again.

And the older man, who looked to be in his mid-forties, was introduced as Doctor Neil Blanchard. Avril needed no introduction. She smiled and said, "Oh, we know each other, of course!" She looked pleased to see him. (I hope that this means Avril is not interested in Tony).

Mr. Parrish had just handed us each a drink when there was another knock on the door. A man and a woman were ushered in—the woman frantically trying to push Brutis away from her crotch. Eva giggled, embarrassed, and everyone else except Tootie looked uncomfortable.

They were introduced as Pastor and Mrs. van Breda. They were a young couple, in their late 20's. He was affable and shook everyone's hands heartily while his wife looked as if all she wanted was for the floor to open up and swallow her. Tootie explained to Eva and I that Pastor van Breda had just arrived at King's Kraal not too long ago himself, from South Africa.

Avril and Tony stood out from the group like peacocks in a gaggle of geese but Avril was sitting next to Neil Blanchard—hanging onto his every word with rapt fascination. Tony was talking to Pastor van Breda and Robert Parrish—I wished I could overhear what he was saying—and Tootie and Eva were discussing dogs.

Eric sat, awkward, in a large stuffed chair in the corner holding his drink with two hands. He looked bored. On a small table next to him was a worn and oil-stained brown felt hat. The skin on his knees, arms and neck were rough and reddened from the sun, and his hands were obviously accustomed to hard work. I wondered what he did for a living.

Talk to the Moon

Tony, by contrast, had smooth hands, and his skin was a delightful tan. When he smiled, which was often, it was dazzling, whereas Eric looked as if he never smiled.

"Dinner's on the table!" yelled Tootie. "Come along! Come along!"

The dinner was quite a spread. Several different casseroles were served by a smartly uniformed houseboy and maid. We had never experienced service like this before. Our meals at home are dished up out of pots straight off the stove.

The maid and houseboy stood behind each person in turn, holding a platter so that we could serve ourselves from it. My hand shook. I knew I was going to drop peas and carrots all over the snowy white linen table cloth. Eva looked just as terrified, and I knew she would drop something. I was right. She clumsily scooped up a serving of mash potatoes that never made it to her plate. Sliding from the ladle in slow motion, it plopped wetly onto the floor. There was a palpable silence at the table while the houseboy moved on to the next person, who was Eric. Eva looked as if she was going to cry. I felt tears of sympathy stinging at my own eyes, and then I noticed that Eric had taken the ladle and dished up two servings of potatoes, one for Eva and one for himself. He smiled at Eva, and his face transformed into something quite human. Conversation resumed again and the crisis was over.

Nervously, I began to eat. There was another heavy silence. I looked up. No-one else was eating, and Robert Parrish cleared his throat at the head of the table.

"Will Pastor van Breda please do us the honor of saying the blessing?"

I flushed crimson, dropping my fork with a clatter. Mom never allowed us to eat without saying a blessing first. Why had I forgotten? I looked at Tony. He wasn't looking at me but had his head bowed and his hands folded. Avril had her hands folded too, but she looked up from beneath a wing of satiny hair and smiled. I felt as if an ice pick had penetrated my soul.

Dinner conversation revolved around the war and mission business. Tony is interesting. He is stationed at the RAF training field near Salisbury. He has a weekend pass, and he and his brother had come to Bulawayo to stay with an old family friend, Dr. Blanchard. Eric lived in the Province of Victoria near the town of Fort Victoria and is running the family farm.

"What kind of farm is it, Eric?" asked Eva.

"Cattle, mostly. And *mealies*." He continued eating. His face was almost in his plate and he shoveled food into his mouth as if he were baling hay.

"Do you have horses?" Eva persisted.

"Uh-huh." He nodded, cheeks bulging with peas and carrots. He gestured with his fork and a piece of carrot flew into the flower centerpiece. "I have six at the moment." He ducked his head down once more and swept another forkful into his mouth. Tony seemed to blush but he swiftly changed the subject back to his squadron and his year in the RAF in England in '42.

By the time dessert arrived the conversation shifted to Dr. Blanchard and Rhodesian politics. I felt embarrassed to admit that I didn't know who the Prime Minister was.

"Sir Godfrey Huggins," Dr. Blanchard expounded, "has been our Prime Minister since 1933, and the leader of the United Party. He is also a doctor, so you can say—he—I'm somewhat partial to him. He's efficient I suppose: pragmatic. Our Governor is…"

"Sir John Kennedy!" crowed Avril. "I met him once, you know."

"If present company will just bear with me for a few minutes, I will explain the political climate briefly." He was rather pompous, I thought.

And he did. It took at least twenty minutes but I was grateful. At least I was spared from being forced to make conversation and risk appearing a fool in front of Tony. Dr. Blanchard explained how the country had been self-governing since 1923, run on a Parliamentary system similar to that of Britain yet administered by a Dominion's Office in Whitehall.

"So this is a Dominion, and not a Colony?"

"Yes, although we remain subjects of King George."

I felt relieved. I like the Royal Family. Eva and I are close to the young princesses in age—I am only two years older than Princess Elizabeth. We had often fantasized that we were the princesses. We'd always read every publication avidly for news on the Royal Family. It had been only a few years ago that I'd wished so desperately King George the Sixth had been my father, and Lady Elizabeth my mother. Of course, I wouldn't change my parents, but at that time…

Dr. Blanchard was still talking.

"…London's just a little concerned about the way things are looking in South Africa, if you ask me. They consider Smuts a friend, but this

Talk to the Moon

Malan fellow looks as if he is in bed..." He flushed crimson and cleared his throat in embarrassment since he had forgotten there were ladies present—"... with the Germans. Their racial policies are disturbing to say the least."

"Don't we have racist policies in this country too?" asked Avril.

Blanchard cleared his throat noisily, again.

"Yes, we do have the Land Apportionment Act..."

"What is that?" I asked, feeling ignorant.

"Under the Land Apportionment Act all Africans on European farms who were not laborers were placed on reserves. They could not own land set aside for white development."

"Faye told us that Africans don't own land anyway," said Eva. "They own cattle, wives and their huts but land ownership has never been a part of their culture."

"Exactly," said Tootie. "Then they shouldn't be upset by the farmers taking the land, should they?"

Blanchard continued:

"Those Africans who didn't go into reserves crowded into the cities, mainly Bulawayo and Salisbury, so the government built locations. The problem with the locations is that they're over-crowded and crime infested. The traditional family values of the African are breaking down. The family is often unable to relocate with the bread winner and dissolution of traditional values is the inevitable result. However, on the bright side, which is the point I was getting to, Rhodesia still has much more in the way of social services to offer the natives than either South Africa or Northern Rhodesia."

"*Ja*, we seem to be doing a tremendous job right here, offering much needed health services and bringing Jesus to the native population," said Pastor van Breda. I wanted to ask if, as long as one brought Jesus and medical services to these people, it was alright to help oneself to whatever one wanted. But I didn't. I too am one of the invaders, descended from a long line of European colonists.

The conversation continued about the problems of South Africa for a while before we all adjourned to the living room for cups of rather insipid *Rooibos* tea. Mom is a believer in *Rooibos* tea, and she always has a kettle brewing on the stove; but hers is much better. It has body and flavor to it. This had not been brewed long. Reputedly, this African grown herbal tea that translates to red bush can cure many ailments, but it has obviously done nothing for Mom: Anna Morgan suffers from more illnesses, real and imaginary, than I can name.

The evening ended much too soon. I hated Dr. Blanchard for taking Tony away in his black Wolsely, back to Bulawayo, leaving Eva and I to return with Avril. I told Avril and Eva to go on without me. I'd rather like to walk back. Avril said, "As you please. Watch out for the snakes!" before driving off.

It had stopped raining—a large, soap bubble moon bobbled in a dark and sudsy sky. I could feel a cool breeze on my face as I walked down the gravel road towards the compound. I looked up at the stars and wondered if Tony was looking up at the sky this minute, thinking about me, perhaps? No, of course not: why would he? He had just met me and men never fell much for me anyway. At least the boys at school never did.

The road was on a slight rise, and I could see the lights of the hospital winking through a grove of tall eucalyptus trees about half a mile to my left. On my right there was a grassy expanse with scattered trees and in the distance I could see the flickering fires of the servants' quarters which had been pointed out to us the previous day by Tootie. The smell of burning wood and…what was that smell? It was delicious. I thought it was meat cooking over an open fire. I could hear voices too, happy, mellifluous voices, laughing and chattering. I wished I could go and join them, but I couldn't do that. Perhaps one day, but not now. I had to get back to my rondavel.

CHAPTER 6

Merry, Martha and the Swanns

Saturday, 27th January

Once again it has been a near perfect day, and it is not yet over. I am sitting uncomfortably on a hard rock, writing quickly, before the last rays of the dying sun make it too difficult to write. I have so much to write about and not enough time.

Eva and Faye are sitting a short distance away on a rocky ledge overlooking the valley and even their chattering is stilled—the silence of the veldt disturbed only by a soft chorus of frogs, and the lonely, chirring call of an awakening night bird. From our vantage point on the kopje we can see the veldt stretching to the horizon, scrubby thorn trees and dark-silhouetted kopjes slashed with a paintbrush of blazing fire.

I went into the office early this morning, needing to finish up some projects I had begun the day before. Mr. Parrish and Gerald had both been there but I closed the door to my office and no one bothered me. Eva had awakened before me, and gone for her first horseback riding lesson with Tootie. She talked about it non-stop during lunch, Avril and Faye listening to her monologue with a great deal of patience. I didn't know that Avril had it in her but she seems to like Eva. They listened quietly as Eva progressed from mounting the horse—she had been given the oldest nag in the stable—to the correct way to hold the reins and put one's feet in the stirrups.

"Did you know you can put your foot in too far and get dragged if you fall off?"

Tootie had shown her how to hold the crop and explained to her when it was necessary to use it. Eva said she hated the crop, and was determined not to use it. Next week, she would progress to a trot.

"Oh, the crop doesn't hurt them," said Avril. "I've been riding since I was this high—she motioned with her hand—and it's all I ever used. It's the only language those stubborn horses understand!"

"Well, you use it if you want to. I will not. If the horse doesn't understand me, then I must be doing something wrong."

Avril shrugged. "Anyway, you'll soon be riding with me and Tootie into the bush. That's a lot of fun! How about you, Holly, aren't you going to learn too?"

I hadn't given it any thought. Weren't horses dangerous? I had never been allowed near one. I couldn't imagine myself galloping off like Dale Evans into the sunset. They made it look easy, of course, but bouncing around on the back of a huge beast with nothing but a few leather straps to hold onto was insanity.

"Tony rides," said Avril, with what looked to me like a slight sneer. I glared at her and Eva giggled. I wanted to slap her.

"So?"

"So he has a farm, and horses too. He would certainly expect you to ride if you visited him there. Everyone knows how to ride!"

"Well, I doubt that I would be going near his farm, then," I said, in a "so there!" tone of voice, that I hoped would leave no doubt that I had no interest in visiting Tony, his farm, or his horses.

"Oh, shut up, Avril," said Faye. "I hate horses. If we are ever invited to Tony's farm, Holly and I will have other things to do, you can be sure of that. Horses aren't the only amusements on a farm." I looked at Faye, grateful, and Faye winked at me with her good eye. "Avril, would you like to walk to the top of the kopje with us this afternoon? We're going on a nature hike."

Avril made a face.

"I have to wash my hair today, but thanks anyway." She looked at her hands. "My nails are a mess too."

I wasn't surprised to note that Avril's nails were perfect. My own were rather ragged, and perhaps I should stay in and take care of them, and I had some personal laundry to do, and yes, my own hair was still stringy and dull…but the nature walk sounded like so much fun. I could do all the other stuff later. Tonight. I wondered if Tony would come on the walk with us. I wanted to broach the subject but the words wouldn't come out. How could I possibly ask? Avril would smirk and Eva would giggle again. No, I would just have to keep quiet and hope a miracle would occur. Maybe we would accidentally bump into him on our way and he would ask where we were going…

Talk to the Moon

We left the mission grounds at 2:00 p.m. sharp. There was no sign of Tony. We didn't see anyone at all as we walked up the dirt road out of King's Kraal. The sun was almost directly overhead and the tall blue-gum trees at the side of the road cast little shade. There had been no rain since last night and the puddles had dried up into caked mud wafers under the scorching sun. We stepped on them and they made a crunching sound underneath our rubber-soled shoes. Faye had told us to wear comfortable shoes suitable for rock climbing. We both do a lot of walking and climbing in the Cape mountains so our shoes are more than adequate for kopjes.

Faye brought bottled water and I brought my notebook and a pencil, and Eva carried a box to hold the flowers and leaves she would press later.

Faye led us down the road about half a mile, before we abruptly turned off into the trees and onto an almost invisible dirt path that was no more than a track. It had been made by animals first, said Faye, and then later adapted by humans. Faye was born and raised in the Bulawayo area and knows the bush intimately. She showed us small hoof prints in the mud that had been made by the bush pig. She told us to always be careful in the bush because it was almost certain that something was watching you.

Faye said it was particularly dangerous to walk under large trees carelessly because leopards liked to sit up in trees and keep an eye open for prey. However, since it was broad daylight, we were probably safe as leopards preferred to hunt at night. Eva looked hopefully up at every tree we went by. Soon we left the tall gum trees behind and emerged into a wide-open plain of low grass, shrubby mopanis, thorn trees, and scattered kopjes.

I have seen kopjes from the mission, but this is the first time I have seen one up close. As we drew nearer the rock monolith I felt a sense of awe and wonder. Granite walls rose abruptly, like a monstrous carapace, from the veldt. I have seen photos in magazines of Ayer's Rock in Australia and these rocky hills were of a similar shape but not nearly as immense. This was a small hill. Although the rock seemed to be one solid mass, it was not uniformly distributed—rocky outcrops and small clumps of trees and grass broke the monotony of the rock walls, rounding off at the top to a boulder-strewn summit.

Faye led us to a place where the granite walls fell to the veldt in gentle folds and ridges. Damp rivulets of rain run-off turned the rock faces into gleaming mirrors and collected in pools in the niches and hollows. A splash of vivid lichens and mosses scumbled over dappled boulders in the shady copses that sprung out of the rock cracks and here and there a small crack widened into a deep gully of brush and boulder-rubbled blackness. It was cool and dark at the bottom where the sun was blocked for most of the day and we could see at the deeper end a narrow slit that disappeared darkly into the granite wall. We picked our way over dry leaves, dead wood and slippery, wet rocks, and soon were at the mouth of the cave.

Faye reached into her tote bag and pulled out a flashlight. The cave was dark, but enough light came in so that we could see it was shallow and taller than it was deeper. The bottom of the cave was covered in pebbles and dirt. Faye turned on her flashlight and shone it onto the back wall and we gasped in surprise. There were paintings on the wall. They were faded but the colors were still intense enough so we could make out the ochre's, sienna's, umber's, vermilion's and white pigments of the ancient tribesmen. The figures of men with spears in loincloths and masks and the antelopes they hunted danced and skittered across the wall in the sudden flare of light.

As we examined the beautiful rock paintings Faye told us she didn't know how old they were but that they predated the occupying tribes of Ndebele, and were painted by the original San, or Bushmen, inhabitants.

"What happened to the Bushmen?" asked Eva.

"The Bushmen, or San, were smaller in stature than the other tribes that gradually moved into the interior of the country from the south. They were a stone-age culture so they weren't equipped to deal with the more warlike tribes who gradually replaced them. They probably went back to the Kalahari."

"Do you think the other tribes could have painted this?"

"Maybe. They did share the land with them for a while but that would make them only a few hundred years old at the most. These look much older and are typical of the San style."

"Who owns this land?"

"Outside of the mission this is all Native Reserve so that means that the Government owns it all. The Africans who live on this land do not own it, but are allowed to live on it under the auspices of the Native Department." Faye sighed, and then gave one of her barking laughs. "I see

Talk to the Moon

I'm about to climb on my favorite soapbox again! I get angry when I see the greed and self-interest which allows one and a half million Africans to live on just over a quarter of the total land, while less than one million Europeans—far less—are allocated nearly half the land—the best—for development and farming. The African has always been dependent on his cattle for his wealth and livelihood. With less land, and especially since what there is, is of such inferior quality, overgrazing will become a problem—it already has—and since they're regarded as migrant workers in the cities, they have no choice but to stay where they are."

I felt uncomfortable again as I often did when the subject came around to politics. I am not sure if I agree with Faye's sentiments. I can understand them but I don't think that getting angry and upset would be of any help. What could I do about it? It was the same way in South Africa: worse, in fact. I do not dislike black people or people of any other race for that matter but I feel I can't do anything about their predicament. It makes me feel helpless or scared, and maybe even quite a bit guilty. Eva was looking thoughtful and I couldn't tell how she felt about Faye's outburst.

"People shouldn't be herded like animals," said Eva, as if I had spoken out loud. "If I had been born a black person I would be angry indeed."

Faye smile looked sad.

"The anger will come. And the white people will blame the black man and say he is ungrateful for everything we have done for him."

"I don't want to be here when that happens."

"Oh, you will be. Enough of this talk, let's go find a scenic spot and have our picnic and talk of other things."

"Like cabbages and kings?" laughed Eva, as we clambered out of the gully.

I remembered the colorful bird I had seen outside the bathroom door where I first encountered Avril. I described it to Faye—the black bird with the long, curved beak, brilliant red breast and green crown, and Faye said it had to be a Scarlet-Breasted Sunbird. Faye regaled us with tales of the San Bushmen, the legends that included many animals and birds and how the universe had begun by a woman throwing ashes into the sky which became the milky-way; and how the stars showed the sun the way; and how the moon was much like a person who was healthy and fat at birth but slowly became old and shrank in size.

"Never talk to the stars," said Faye. "You can talk to the moon, but not the stars. That is what the Bushmen believe." It made sense to me. Stars seemed aloof, cold, somehow; too far away. The moon was closer and one could see it most of the time. It's a lot easier to talk to the moon, I think.

Later, that same evening:
This has been an evening I will never forget.

It was already dark when we reached the compound. We washed and changed from our sweaty thorn covered clothing—Faye called the sticky thorns *black jacks*—into crumpled but clean dresses. I do wonder when we will have clothes to wear again that do not look as if they have just come out of a suitcase. Perhaps we will have to do what Faye has recommended—hire a personal maid.

Merry's domain is limited to the kitchen and communal living area. The personal room and clothing are the responsibility of the individual. Avril and Faye's maid, Martha, takes care of all their laundry, including their bath and bed linens—washing them by hand in the bath tub once a week, hanging them on the clothes lines behind the compound to dry, and then ironing them with a series of flat irons placed on top of the old wood stove in the kitchen to heat. Perhaps Martha would appreciate some extra money. We will ask her on Monday.

After dinner, we left with Faye for the church. There was to be a short service—a Prayer Service—followed by a communal get-together in the church hall. This was the first time we had been inside the church, and it is the strangest looking church I have ever seen. A rectangular thatched roof bungalow, the walls made out of the same material—whitewashed pole and *daga*—as our rondavels, huge wooden beam roof supports, and large ceiling fans which slowly rotate from the center of each beam. Low candlepower light bulbs hang from the beams in a twilit dimness and wooden pews spilling over with people squatting on the hard polished concrete floor. Faye led us over to the three front rows behind the children, which she said were reserved for the *Nkosis'* and *Nkosikasis'*—white people in the Ndebele language.

Gerald was sitting in the front row, as was Mr. Parrish, Pastor and Mrs. van Breda, two small children, Eric, a white haired older lady who looked like a badly preserved mummy, and Avril…but no sign of Tony. Tootie sat at the organ in the front of the church with her back to the congregation. The organ was an ancient foot pump model that she

Talk to the Moon

pumped vigorously with one foot while simultaneously working the foot pedals with the other. This did not look easy but Tootie was up to the challenge: wheezing notes of *Shall We Gather at the River* swelled asthmatically but distinctly to the rafters. The loud pedal was getting all the work and it didn't help that each note was played a beat too slow—a sepulchral, tolling bell beat. After a crashing crescendo the end arrived and an expectant silence descended on the pews.

A sudden movement from behind the large, wooden pulpit startled me, and I jumped. A small, crow-like man had sprung up like a jack-in-the-box; a face like a desiccated brown apple with raisin eyes that regarded us in silence for what seemed like an unnecessarily long time.

"That's Tony and Eric's father, old man Swann," whispered Faye. "He often comes from Bulawayo where he is the assistant Pastor to conduct services here. That's his wife—we call her Aunt Lalie—next to Eric." She nodded her head at the white haired mummy.

"I thought they farmed?"

"They did, but they gave it up some time ago when it got too much for them. Eric has taken over the farming now. They say the old man always did preach better than he farmed."

And he did: like a thunderclap from Mount Sinai. His words rattled and crashed through the pews like artillery fire and the smell of sulfur and brimstone hung in the air like a fog. The congregation whistled, hooted and jumped to their feet, yelling *"Ye-bo! Ye-bo!"* in a vigorous underscoring of key words. They clapped their hands joyfully, laughing in delight when Satan and Hitler, who were interchangeable, had been finally committed to the bottomless pit. I wondered if they were always this enthusiastic. It would discourage anyone from nodding off. The congregation then all rose while Tootie pounded out her interpretation of *All Things Bright and Beautiful* on the organ. The congregation does a masterful job of making it sound melodious, but also rather melancholy.

Closing prayers were fatiguing and nearly unendurable. Kneeling on the concrete floor, the congregation became twitchy and restless after ten minutes, but old man Swann continued to pray without letup. My knees hurt and the circulation in my legs felt as if it had been cut off. After twenty minutes of beseeching, imploring, sighing and pressuring God to grant special dispensations to his flock old man Swann ended the ordeal with a self-satisfied Amen and the congregation rose creakily to its feet.

After the prayer service the small group of white people and a handful of Africans—I recognized Mrs. Ncube and Mattie Kumalo—walked down a dirt path to the small pole and *daga* hall situated a few yards from the church. The rest of the Africans dispersed; some by bicycle and some walking. Stacks of metal chairs piled on top of each other lined the walls leaving a small open space in the middle of the hall.

Then I saw him. He was standing against the back wall. Dressed in civvies, he looked just as handsome as the last time I had seen him. Had it only been last night? He looked at me and winked. I felt intoxicated with delight but a familiar warmth crept up my neck. I knew I must be blushing again. I was sure that everyone was looking at me so I looked down and turned my back to Tony. When I looked up again I realized that no-one had seen the wink or the blush. They were all busy pulling chairs out and putting them in a circle.

Gerald was looking at me. He didn't look happy. An animated Eva had gone up to him, and was talking to him, but he didn't appear to hear what she was saying. Embarrassed, I turned and walked over to the circle of chairs. I sat down. The decrepit thatch roof could have fallen in for all I cared. I was happy—happier than I have ever been. For the first time in my life I felt as if I didn't care what other people thought about me. I am in love!

How could I describe that evening? A giddy carousel of color and impressions: all my senses fine-tuned to one person only—Tony. The others passed by in a blur of movement and noise, their laughter and chatter a background to the only reality—myself and Tony.

I did remember the games we played: *Postman's Knock, Telephone,* and *Charades.*

The evening ended way too soon. At eleven p.m. they put the chairs back, turned out the lights, and Tony grasped my hand, looked into my eyes, and with a soft 'Goodnight,' he left. And here I am now, sitting at the desk trying to write about I feel. I feel ebullient but at the same time agitated. I won't be able to sleep tonight, I just know it. Eva is softly snoring in bed having returned to the compound in an uncharacteristically quiet mood. There is a distant peal of thunder. It is going to rain again.

CHAPTER 7
Tony

Sunday evening
The storm that had begun last night sent crashing, booming roars of thunder reverberating overhead, rattling the windows and keeping me awake for most of the night. The lightning lit up the room like daylight and the wind howled and clutched at the rondavel roof. I blessed the builders: the roof held intact and not a drop of rain penetrated the thick grass thatch. Eva did not seem to have trouble sleeping through the cacophony.

I awoke at nine a.m. and realized that I had overslept. The gray light made it seem earlier than it was. I leaped out of bed, the night's memories surging back into my mind like a tsunami. Eva was still sleeping and I woke her up and we hurriedly dressed for church. The service was to start at ten, and we were going to be late! We ran to the dining room just as Merry was clearing the breakfast table. She looked at us sternly.

"Breakfast on Sundays until nine. No later!"

But she relented and fixed us each a slice of toast and some milk. She was dressed in her Sunday best: a blue print shirtwaist dress and a bright turban worn around her head of matching material.

The service was similar to the previous nights, except that Pastor van Breda conducted the service. His sermon was light and inoffensive, invoking no spectacles of hellfire and damnation. The congregation was mute today, with only a few quiet "*Ye-bo's*" to be heard.

Old man Swann sat behind the pulpit with Pastor van Breda acting as Deacon and general back-up. Much to my dismay he once again led the closing prayer. Tony was sitting in the pew in front of me. He had arrived too late to sit next to me. By this time, it was almost lunch, and I was acutely aware of the lack of a substantial breakfast. My stomach was snarling and growling like a mad dog. I wished old man Swann would shut up. He droned on and on; an endless repertoire of pestilence and sorrow. Coughs and throat clearings did not faze him from his self-appointed role as mediator between man and God.

I looked up once and I caught Tony slyly peeking at me from beneath his cap. He wore full dress uniform today, and my heart did more flip-flops. His blue eyes twinkled and he winked at me again before turning his head. I thought then that old man Swann could pray forever if he wanted to: just as long as Tony was there.

Gerald and Dr. Blanchard sat behind us, and Avril sat next to Neil Blanchard. Gerald flushed when I caught him looking at me—I had felt eyes on the back of my neck—and he looked down. I noticed that Avril was stunning today. Once again I felt inadequate even though I was dressed in the best outfit I possessed, thanks to Anna's sewing skills: a navy blue and white cotton print with puff sleeves. Although I loved the outfit when Mom first made it, next to Avril I looked like Dorothy in the *Wizard of Oz* looking for a yellow brick road, and my white, wide brimmed straw hat just looked silly.

The prayer came to an end with a relieved "Amen" from the congregation and we all rose. As we filed out of the church, I felt Tony's arm on my elbow, and when we got outside he turned me around to face him.

I have to leave for Salisbury this afternoon," he said. "I need to be back on base tonight. But I want to know before I leave if you will be interested in seeing me the next time I come to Bulawayo for a weekend."

I felt breathless and, for a moment, was torn between two emotions. I had completely forgotten that he would not be staying! But he did want to see me again, and that made me deliriously happy.

"Of course I want to see you again, Tony. When do you think you will be up here again?"

"In about two weeks, I think. I will telephone you at the office and let you know for certain. Maybe we can go to the flicks and have dinner. But first, I want to introduce you to my parents."

He led me over to Aunt Lalie and old man Swann. Aunt Lalie was just as shrunken and desiccated as her husband—as if they had both been left out in the sun like old skulls—Aunt Lalie's white hair making her look even more bleached than her husband. They must have had children late in life. They surely weren't a day under sixty-five. Aunt Lalie held out a frail, liver spotted claw and its grip was surprisingly firm.

Talk to the Moon

"You and your sister must come and visit us in Bulawayo, my dear. We need more young people in the congregation there although the Mission is truly blessed to have you. We try to do the Lord's work at both places. My husband enjoys the Mission and bringing the gospel to the Natives as much as he does to the Europeans in town."

"Yes," chimed in old man Swann. "My wife and I are so happy to meet you and your sister Eva. There's a real lack of ladies in these parts..." I noticed a fugitive glance towards Avril and Faye who were standing nearby, "...But it is evident you girls have been raised in a Christian environment."

I wondered what he would say if he could see a typical Saturday night in the Morgan home. Perhaps Avril and Faye would look better by comparison. Neither one of the senior Swanns' look anything like their sons. Maybe they're adopted? Tony seemed discomfited at the direction the conversation was heading, and he abruptly muttered an excuse to his parents and led me away. I looked back and noticed they were still looking at me, shrunken heads bobbing up and down approvingly, as if I had passed some unspoken test. I felt pleased. Tony wouldn't have bothered introducing me to his parents if he didn't think highly of me, now would he? And they liked me! A golden warmth spread across my chest and made its way to my head, making me giddy.

We spoke for a few more minutes but the time arrived—as it always did—when we had to part. I watched him walk away and it was all I could do to fight back tears. I was aware of a movement at my side and I turned around to find Gerald lurking just within earshot. What had he heard? It was none of his business!

"Are...are you going into town this afternoon?" he asked.

So he had been eavesdropping! I had told Tony we were going into the city with Faye today.

"Yes, Gerald, we are. Why?"

"I was just wondering if you would like some company." A feeling of relief swept over me. I wouldn't have to lie.

"Well, we are going with Faye. You would have to ask her if you can ride in with us." I was certain Faye would veto that plan. The afternoon had been planned with just the three of us in mind. Of course, if it had been Tony who had asked, that would have been different. But it wasn't. Gerald hustled over to where Faye and Eva were talking to a group of people whom I did not know. I smiled and walked over as well. I wanted to hear this! Faye noticed Gerald shifting around from one foot to another.

"What is it, Ger?"

"Holly told me you're going in to town today. Can I get a ride with you?" I gasped. He had made it sound as if it had been my idea! Before I could say something, Eva piped up.

"Oh, Faye, do you think we could squeeze him in? I wouldn't mind making room in the back seat for Gerald!"

"You're welcome to join us Gerald. Be ready to leave at 2:00 p.m."

I felt betrayed. How could Faye do this? Why had Eva gone and opened her big mouth? The day had started off so well and now it was ruined. First Tony leaving and now Gerald foisting himself on us. He had no right…! I turned on my heel and marched off down the road to the compound. It had stopped raining and looked as if the sun wanted to come out. I suddenly wanted it to rain. It should be raining. The sun had no business coming out now. I was going to change into the most comfortable, but ugliest outfit I possessed. Why waste a good dress on Gerald?

We cruised down lush, broad tree lined boulevards, shaded by feathery jacaranda trees. The traffic was light since it was a Sunday afternoon and the business district was almost completely deserted. Shops were shuttered and, just as in South Africa, everything closes from noon on Saturdays until Monday morning. We parked on a wide boulevard in the center of the city and got out of the car.

"Do you know why the streets are so wide?" asked Faye rhetorically. "So that in the old days a team of sixteen oxen could make a full turn!" One and two story buildings with overhanging roofs, white colonnades and green striped canvas awnings, jutted out over the pavement providing shade to the sedate couples and families on their Sunday afternoon strolls. "Since nothing opens here on a Sunday, this is how we entertain ourselves—window shopping," said Faye.

"I can't imagine what it would be like to be in the middle of a war," I said. "Over here, everything is so peaceful and 'business as usual' that it seems almost inconceivable that there's a war going on!"

"We're lucky, I hear the Dutch are starving and eating their tulips. Acorns have become a staple in Europe."

"I heard in some places in Europe they're smoking nettles," said Eva. "I'd give up the habit before I did that!"

Talk to the Moon

"With the Red Army in Warsaw and the Hungarians signing the armistice it's just a matter of time now and it's over."

"I hear there's going to be a conference in Yalta," said Gerald.

"But first in Malta, in Malta!" sung Eva, doing a dance.

"You have a beautiful voice, Eva," said Gerald, "You should join our choir!"

"I didn't know there was a choir at the mission?" I said, because Eva was struck speechless, her face glowing with happiness.

"I, well, not really. I mean, not yet. I want to start one but haven't got around to it yet."

Eva found her voice. "I want to join. Gerald, I'll help you start one up. I know Avril can sing. I've heard her, and Faye and Holly…"

"That's a damn good idea, Gerald," yelled Faye. "I know many Africans in our congregation and in the hospital who love to sing. Before we know it, we'll have the best choir in Bulawayo!"

We talked eagerly of the choir until we arrived at the next destination, City Hall. Flower sellers, bead and basket workers and artists lined the pavement around City Hall, their wares spread out on blankets so that one had to step off the sidewalk to get anywhere. I found myself admiring the wooden sculptures of animals and the carved soapstone heads and figurines.

Eva was studying the crochet doilies and I hoped she wouldn't buy any. Crochet work always reminded me of Mom whose house was blanketed with her own handiwork. Crochet doilies on the milk jugs, crochet runners on the furniture and tables, crochet antimacassars on every chair, and she had even made crochet hats and gloves for us while we were at school. I was sick of crochet. Well, we didn't have much money anyway so we couldn't waste what we had on frivolities.

Mom and Dad had given us each ten pounds: an amount they could not possibly have afforded to give lightly. We won't get paid much either since we arrived at the end of the month and only earned a few days salary. I wonder how we are going to make it until the end of February?

We drove to the city's central park. The park grounds were enormous, straddling many blocks with shaded lawns and picturesque walks. Right in the middle of the park was a gazebo with a brass band. We sang all the band songs we knew the words to and tapped our feet to the rhythm. A group of old ladies sitting on a nearby shady bench smiled and laughed. I was happy, but I felt an acute sense of something missing. I had almost forgotten—I felt like a traitor. How could I pass one minute of the day not thinking about Tony? I supposed I had just been too busy thinking of other things. Well, that is the solution then. I will have to stay busy from now on or go mad.

CHAPTER 8

"Gloria" and Esther

7th February, 1945
These past two weeks have alternately crawled and flown by. Eva has settled down and I have been working long hours. I reorganized my office, sorting out piles of work into a more efficient system. I wrote letters home, keeping them short and factual. We received a letter from Mom. It reads like the Book of Job but not as cheerful:
"Dad has been drinking..." what else? "... and money is tight. He has lost his job again and is having trouble finding another one." Mom made references to the Lord taking care of them since "*sparrows toiled not and neither did they spin.*"

I wonder how God must feel every time Mom gets on the blower to him. Otherwise, it was the same old story. Not a thing has changed since we left. Mom mentioned that she had a visit from Pastor Wendt, and how thrilled she was to have his undivided attention.

I remember the weekly visits from Pastor Wendt, the poor man held captive by Anna, two hours a week gone forever from his life. The man is a saint: he never complains, he always listens, and he never misses a week

When I stopped by Eva's office to give her the letter, I bumped into Gerald, or "Ger", as he likes to be called. He has become my shadow. I can't seem to escape him, and every opportunity he gets, he asks me to go out with him. I always know when it's coming: his face gets redder—which makes his pimples glow—and he begins to wring his hands as he mutters something about "going to the flicks". I wish Tony would ask me out so he can see I am dating someone else. At the moment, he thinks I am available.

Tony is coming to Bulawayo this weekend so I told him I have plans. I hope it's true! I also asked him why he does not ask Eva, who would be happy to go to the flicks with him. His response:

"Oh. Well, okay then. I'll ask her. What about next weekend?"
Friday, 9th February

I have not heard a thing from Tony for weeks. I was beginning to think I had misunderstood him when it happened. Just as I was leaving work the phone rang.

"Holly?"

I croaked like a fool, "Tony, is that you?"

"Holly, I was hoping you'd still be there. I know you close at five and this is the first chance I've had to call. I've had to fight all week to put a call through to Bulawayo. I keep getting cut off and then someone else wants to use the phone. Anyway, I'm glad I finally got through to you. I've bought a motor bike and I'm driving it down to Bulawayo tomorrow morning. I'll probably get to the Mission before lunch. Maybe we can do something when I get there? Perhaps you'd like a spin on the bike?"

I could still barely speak as I whispered "Oh—Oh, yes—definitely. I'd love a spin on the bike! I am so glad you'll be able to make it, Tony. I was beginning to think you weren't coming."

"Well, I wasn't sure myself until just a few hours ago. But things worked out and they delivered the motorbike this afternoon. It takes so long to get these things during war time, you know."

"Oh yes, Tony, I know. The funny thing is…"

I was going to tell him about the bicycles Eva and I had just bought, but he began talking again.

"She's a real beaut. Second hand, but a beaut. You should see her! A '38 Norton, with a 490cc engine, overhead valves…." I didn't care. I didn't understand any of it and just hearing his voice was wonderful and if he had been reading the Bulawayo phone book to me it would sound just as sweet. I will never forget sitting on the edge of my desk as he spoke, looking out the window at the tangerine tinted clouds that floated in a cerulean sky and the golden light on the topmost fronds of the sun-kissed palm trees in the courtyard. The air looked fresh and sparkling and I wanted to fill my lungs with this champagne elixir.

"Well, I've got to hang up now, love…

He called me love!

"…But I'll see you in the morning. Sleep tight and…" His final words were cut off. He must have been calling from a pay phone. Oh well. But at least he called. I wondered what he had said that I hadn't heard.

This week Tootie found us a maid and not a moment too soon. Our room was beginning to look like a mushroom farm, or at least on Eva's side. I am almost fanatical when it comes to neatness. Mom did a good job on me, but Eva cannot concentrate long enough to clean up her side of the room. She will start picking up clothes—which are draped over every surface—and something else will catch her eye and she'll be off on a tangent, cleaning project forgotten. I am tired of nagging and complaining. It doesn't help anyway, Eva will just laugh and promise it would all be picked up by that night, but by bedtime nothing ever looks different.

It was Monday when Tootie brought the candidate from the Native Reserve around to the compound along with Martha, the girl's sister who works for Faye and Avril. The girl speaks excellent English. She learned it at the government run school which she has just left. She looks no older than fifteen. Her name is Esther and she is shy and soft-spoken. We took to her immediately, and Martha has promised to teach Esther everything about being a personal maid. We are sure Martha and Esther will exceed our expectations, and already we are dressing better in pressed clothing and shined shoes. Now I will have time to take care of myself and will not have to feel ashamed of how we—or our room—look.

Yes, the bicycles! We found the store close to the mission that Ayesha's parents run and her mother, Mrs. Ghosh, sold them to us cheap. We are now each the proud owners of a shiny new bike. We have never ridden bicycles before but Faye and Avril showed us how and after an hour or so we felt as if we have been riding bicycles all our lives, Martha, Merry and Esther freely lending advice and admonitions, standing by in case of disaster. They laughed loudly and unabashedly when I had my first run in with the wall but I did not fall off. Merry chuckled and clucked and told me to remember to use the brake!

This evening, after Tony called, I wondered if Gerald had asked Eva out. She did not look as happy as I was, so I did not think he had. Eva doesn't need someone who has been pressured into asking her out, so maybe it's a good thing.

CHAPTER 9

Avril

Late Saturday Evening, 10th February

Another memorable day: my first date with Tony. Much to my dismay, when we woke up this morning it was raining. Why does it rain nearly every weekend? I hoped it would be gone by this afternoon. Eva was upset too. She wanted to get an early morning horse ride in with Tootie.

I attempted to put my hair up in rolls but my hair was still damp and the pins would not stay in. The rolls did not look the way they were supposed to. I knew that Avril owned a curling iron. I didn't want to ask her for it but unless I wanted to look a sight I would have to forget about my pride.

Avril was sitting at the breakfast table reading a book. She nodded a good morning and continued to read. Not a good sign.

"Avril, do you have a curling iron?" I knew she had, but I didn't know how else to broach the subject.

"Yes, why?"

"May I borrow it, please?"

Avril closed her book and looked up with a frown.

"I don't usually lend my stuff out. A curling iron is something personal. But I'll tell you what; if you come to my room I will do your hair for you. What do you say to that?"

I had been expecting a flat "no." I didn't know what to say, but what choice did I have? I had never used a curling iron before and it would not be a good idea to start practicing now.

"Okay, thanks Avril. When should I come?"

"How about right after breakfast? I'm going into Bulawayo today with Neil so the sooner we get started the better." She got up and left the table without another word.

"Gee," said Eva, when I told her. "It sounds as if Avril and Neil are an item!"

Talk to the Moon

We discussed this subject for a while and speculated on whether or not they would get married.

"He's too old for her."

"I don't think so," countered Eva. "Avril needs someone who is already well established in life, someone who is not threatened by her intelligence and independence."

It was then that I gathered up the nerve to ask Eva if Gerald had asked her out yet.

"No," she said, her face turning sad again. "I don't think he likes me much. I don't know why I like him, either. He's not good looking. Not like Tony. There's just something about him…he needs mothering. I want to mother him."

I felt surprised that Eva could acknowledge this. She has some good insights into matters and few illusions. I sometimes feel as if I am the one with the illusions, the younger and more naïve one, rather than Eva.

Straight after breakfast we went to Avril's room. This was the first time we had seen Avril and Faye's room. Faye's side is Spartan, the bed made with military precision and the only decorations hang on the wall next to her bed, several framed nursing certificates from the Bulawayo Nurse's Training Hospital.

Avril's half is a riot of color and confusion—ceramic knick-knacks, glass vials and colorful perfume bottles that litter the top of the dresser between make-up trays crammed with brushes, lipsticks, powder puffs and hairbrushes. Small, original gilt framed paintings and photographs of Paris and London hang on the wall.

I gaped while Eva cooed in delight.

"Sit over here," said Avril, pulling out a chair. "I've heated up the curling iron, so we can begin. What did you do to your hair? It looks like a mouse chewed on it during the night." Eva and Avril laughed, but I felt humiliated. "You could use a good cut. I'll give you the name of my hair stylist in Bulawayo. She's wonderful. Please go and see her next time you go into town."

I was glad I hadn't been loaned the iron. I would have been terrified of it. As it was, I hoped my hair wouldn't fall out in charred handfuls later, but Avril was deft and skilled in its use. She didn't even burn my ears, although she seemed to come close several times, her smile sardonic as the hot iron approached bare skin.

I had brought my own brush and comb with me, and Avril used the brush vigorously until my hair stood out in a coppery cloud around my face. Then she took separate strands and shaped them into soft curls, rolls and waves so that they framed what Avril referred to as my heart shaped face. I could not believe my hair could look so—so stylish! I would never be able to get my hair to look like that again.

"So what are you doing today that justifies the hair panic?"

"She's going out with Tony!" piped up Eva, and I wanted to kick her, but my foot couldn't reach that far. I would have said, 'Nothing.'

"Oh!" Avril smiled and raised one eyebrow. "Doing what?"

"He's got a new motorbike." I muttered.

"Oh. Oh dear. I wish you'd told me. We would have picked a different style for you. This won't do at all!" She looked genuinely distressed, and I reassured her it wouldn't matter.

"I'll wear a scarf."

"Well, okay then. But I can put it up for you and pin it."

"No, Avril, please don't bother. You've done enough already. I'm really happy with this style, and even if it lasts for only a few hours, it will be enough…"

"A few hours, *Mon Dieu*! A few seconds, more like it. Well, okay then, if you're sure. Tie that scarf around your head well. Let's hope it will hold. Now," looking at her watch, "I've got to run."

It took me the rest of the morning, with Eva's help, to decide what I was going to wear. Since I was sure that whatever we did it would include the motorcycle I at last opted for my dressy pleated pants. The only other pair of pants I own make me look as though I ought to be under a car changing oil.

Eva looked almost as happy as me, as though she was personally responsible for my Cinderella transformation and good fortune. She fussed over me as if she were my fairy godmother, dabbing powder on my shiny nose, pinching my cheeks and brushing what was left of the one lipstick we shared over my lips.

"Aren't you going to tell me to be home by midnight or I'll turn into a pumpkin?"

"I certainly hope you'll be home long before then. I'll send Merry out looking for you if you aren't home by ten!"

"Okay, Mom!"

Our laughter was interrupted by a knock on the door.

Talk to the Moon

"Oh, Gerald! Hello!"

"Hello Eva. I was going into Bulawayo this afternoon and thought I'd go see a flick. I'm sorry about the short notice, but I was wondering if you'd like to go in with me?"

He sounded rather ungracious, making it clear that asking Eva out was an afterthought.

"I'll go. What's showing?" Eva looked flushed.

"I don't know. We'll just take a chance and see."

"Okay, then give me a few minutes to get ready. How are we getting there?"

"Neil loaned me his Wolseley. He's gone off with Avril in her car."

"Oh, wow! We'll be driving in style, then!" Eva laughed. "What can I wear that will do justice to a Wolseley, Holly?"

Gerald disappeared, saying he'd be back in an hour, and now it was my turn to play fairy godmother. We searched Eva's wardrobe, looking for something that wasn't too frumpy. I offered her a felt hat with a small feather in the band that I had never worn. I tried to brush Eva's curls the same way Avril had brushed my hair, but the curls would not obey the laws of gravity and Eva flatly refused to wear the hat, saying that, on her head, it made her look like Groucho Marx, and with the green dress, she felt like a Tyrolean yodeler. I tried tying her hair back with a white ribbon, but it was even worse.

"Now I look like little orphan Annie!"

We went back and forth in this manner, until there was another knock on the door. I was still telling Eva she needed to try the ribbon again when I flung open the door, thinking it was Gerald.

It was Tony.

"Well, you look like a million dollars, as they say in the flicks!"

"And so do you!" He wasn't in uniform, but was dressed in a leather bomber jacket and leather motorcycle helmet.

"Come and see my bike. It's parked outside." We hadn't heard it arrive; we had been too busy arguing. Tony presented Gloria to us as if she were his debutante girlfriend at a coming out ball.

Gloria looked like any other motorcycle, maybe even plainer. Just in case we failed to notice, he began pointing out Gloria's main attractions—mostly shiny chrome whatsits—and a mile by mile description of her performance on the long trip from Salisbury. He jumped on the bike and kick started it so we could hear the rich roar of Gloria's engine. Our smiles became fixed as we were enveloped in a blue cloud of noxious exhaust fumes and after several minutes of listening to repeated noisy revvings of the engine my smile became positively frozen. But he didn't appear to notice and finally he shut off the engine. I had gone deaf and didn't hear Gerald pull up in the Wolsely. He was well mannered towards Eva, holding the car door for her as she got in, and civil to Tony.

And then it was our turn.

We flew out of the mission like a stone from a slingshot leaving Avril's handiwork and scarf somewhere near the mission gates. I closed my eyes in terror, the ground flashing by inches from my feet. Tony had given me goggles that pinched my face but my hands had a death grip on him and I couldn't remove the goggles.

Tony stopped the motorcycle on Main Street and I gingerly removed my fingernails from his back. He asked if I was hungry. I was, and he suggested we eat at a café he knew about around the corner. I climbed, legs shaky, off the bike and realized my hair must look terrible. I tried smoothing it down with my hands but there didn't seem to be much I could do. I hadn't brought a comb with me either. Then I realized something else.

"Tony, I didn't bring money with me." I felt embarrassed because I had never been on a real date before and didn't know what I was supposed to do. I knew women weren't expected to pay but I still felt as if I ought to be paying for my food. What if I insulted him by even mentioning it?

"Don't worry, Holly. Leave it all to me." He smiled. "Lieutenants aren't rolling in money, so it will be a cheap lunch but I'd insist on paying whether or not you brought money." I was so gauche. Avril would have known exactly what to bring.

I wonder, not for the first time, what Tony sees in me and why he isn't attracted to Avril instead. In fact, I wonder why every man on the Mission is not beating down Avril's door. To me, Avril seems the classic vamp, a heartbreaker. Yet this is not the case. Certainly, Neil seems to like her, but it's hard to tell with Neil. He is such a stuffed shirt.

The café was owned by Greeks. Tony introduced them to me as Nick and Pete. They were Cypriots, he said, and they made the best and cheapest food in Bulawayo. The front of the café displayed a variety of foods and goods for sale and small tables with red and white checkered tablecloths in the rear. We sat down at one of these and Nick brought over

Talk to the Moon

a menu. None of the dishes looked familiar to me, and although they were written in English they may as well have been in Greek. I had never eaten at a restaurant before—Mom and Dad had occasionally treated us to a meal at the Gladstone Hotel but the menu had been fixed—the food standard and predictable. One never ordered from an *a la carte* menu at the Gladstone.

"You do eat meat, don't you?" asked Tony, seeing the consternation on my face.

"Oh yes, it's not that. I just don't know what to order!"

He laughed with delight and told me to leave it up to him. He would order everything. My nervousness faded and I relaxed.

"The usual, Nick, make it two!"

I remembered my hair. I must have looked quite a sight. No wonder Nick had smiled. I excused myself but when I looked into the mirror I nearly wept. I hadn't overestimated just how bad it was. My hair hung straight and stiff to my shoulders. Every curl was out and it looked dull and lifeless. That wasn't all. The goggles had given me two red, panda-like rings around the eyes. Desperate, I combed through the hair using my fingers, but it didn't seem to do much good. I rubbed at the panda rings with damp toilet paper and my eyes now just looked red. Why hadn't I listened to Avril?

As I sat down, I noticed a black streak on my slacks. Oil! The food arrived, and the aromas of eggplant, minced lamb and potatoes with spicy overtones made me realize just how hungry I was. Then I noticed something else. Tony was drinking wine. A bottle of red South African wine stood on the table, and two glasses. They were both full.

"Tony, I'm afraid I don't drink. Could I have some tea instead?"

"Sorry love, they don't have *rooibos* tea here," he said, deliberately misunderstanding. "We're not on the mission now. Why don't you try some wine? It really won't hurt, you know. Those old sackcloth and hair-shirts in the church would start Prohibition here too if they had their way. It didn't work in America, and it won't work here. One thing they always try to cover up is that Jesus drank wine. Don't you remember the feast at Cana?"

"Well, I don't drink for reasons that have nothing to do with religion."

The last thing I wanted was to become my father, and besides, the one drink I'd had at my grandparents table had given me a bad headache. "But if you want to drink the wine, I won't object." I felt surprised. I could not

47

believe I was not giving in to Tony on this matter. He smiled. "Okay, I'll drink it all, then. *Cheers!*" and he raised his glass and took a long swallow. "Mmm…its good stuff. From the Cape you know. Nick! Bring a pot of tea over here, will you! Looks like we're beginning to see a bit of the redhead in you coming out."

I felt irritation. I hate being labeled because of my hair—I am about as far from the stereotypical redhead as one can get, but I smiled and continued to eat.

After lunch we got back on Gloria, found a petrol station that was not closed, and using several of Tony's ration coupons filled up Gloria's tank and headed south, towards the Matopos. Tony seemed no worse for wear from the bottle of wine. He negotiated the curves and hills with skill. We saw some antelope and baboons although Tony said it was better to see the animals during the winter months when the foliage had thinned out. It was starting to get dark when we left the hills and returned to Bulawayo. Tony asked if I wanted to get a bite to eat at the Greek café but I said I felt so windblown I would rather go back to the mission and raid the kitchen.

I fixed some sandwiches and we sat out on the grass in the compound and ate.

There was no moon so we could see the stars clearly. The Milky Way did look like ashes and I told Tony the story Faye had told us of the Bushman legend. Tony mentioned that in the northern hemisphere the stars were never as bright as those of the southern skies.

I wondered where Eva was. There had been a service in the church tonight so perhaps she was there. There was no sign of Avril or Faye either. We had the whole garden and compound to ourselves and I felt relaxed and happy. We talked and laughed, and for the first time, I felt as if I was at last getting to know Tony. He told me of his life growing up on the farm near Fort Victoria. He also mentioned that the Swann's were not in fact his parents, as I had suspected, but were his grandparents. He said his parents had died when he and Eric were young, in an accident, and their mother's parents had adopted them.

"Where are your father's parents?"

"I heard they were in South Africa, somewhere, but we were told they had passed away too."

At least I still had both my parents and grandparents. Mom's parents lived on a farm, and Dad's mother was still alive, in a nursing home in

Talk to the Moon

Cape Town. We visited her occasionally but she never recognized anyone.

Tony told me that he didn't care for farming.

"Eric is the farmer in the family," he said, "and as far as I'm concerned, he can have it all. As soon as this war is over I am going to sell my share of the farm to him. He wants it, and he's doing a great job and can afford to buy me out."

"What will you do after the war, Tony?"

"I want to open my own business somewhere. I don't want anything where I'll need to get my hands in the dirt or get up with the chickens every day. I don't want to scrape for a living. There must be something out there I can do which doesn't take too much effort and will make me some money."

"I suppose you aren't staying in the Air Force, then?"

"Not in a million years. In the beginning it was something to do that didn't involve farming and I thought the war was going to last six months. It hasn't been bad but it's not my idea of a career. I would farm if I could be a gentleman farmer. Like Neil, for example…"

"I didn't know Neil was a farmer? He's a doctor."

"Yes, he is, and like me, he hates farming. His father actually farms—a huge old tobacco farm near Salisbury. That really bothers Neil, being a doctor and non-smoking Christian and all, but that farm makes so much money they can't spend it all. The old man is on his last legs so Neil will inherit the farm when he kicks the bucket. I wonder what he'll do with it."

"Won't his mother keep it?"

"His mother died years ago. No, it's just him and the old man. No brothers, no sisters. *Yep*, a tobacco farm would be right up my alley. Hire as many *kaffirs* as you can to pick and do the work, and you're made. Sit on the verandah all day and drink gin and tonics."

I felt as if an electric shock had gone through me. In America, I hear some call black people a derogatory name my parents would never allow us to use, and here in Southern Africa, it is *kaffirs*, which many whites justify using by saying it is an old Arabic word meaning "non-believer", but the sentiment is the same no matter the original meaning of the word. I wanted to tell him I don't want him to use that word around me but just as the thought formed a "*Yoohoo!*" came from the compound entrance. It was Eva. She looked radiant.

"So you're home! I was starting to get worried about you but I see you didn't fall off the motorbike. When we last saw you, you were hanging on so tight I thought Tony would have to pry you loose with a crowbar!"

"He almost had to! Well, I was worrying about you too, but I suppose you went to church tonight?"

"Yes, Ger and I went, and guess what? We started our choir list already."

"Well, that's wonderful, Eva! How many people have you got? You can count me in, by the way."

"Not me," grinned Tony. "I can't carry a tune in a bucket. I'll be glad to attend though and offer my opinions."

"We probably won't need you. We already have half the congregation volunteering so we will have to be choosy about whom we pick. We don't want it to get out of hand. And then there's Faye, me and Ger, and of course, you Holly. We haven't asked Avril yet. But that's not the most exciting thing. Ger can actually play the guitar! We're not having the organ…oh; I don't know how we're going to break the news to Tootie. But we need to spice up the music, and let's face it, that old organ can't do the job."

"Hmm, yes, it's going to be a problem. Tootie seems to enjoy that old thing but it does sound quite awful. And slow."

"I see moths fly out of it every time she pumps," said Eva, "And I wouldn't be surprised if there's a rat's nest in there too."

"The gorgon on the organ," muttered Tony. "I don't think she's going to give it up without some bloodshed."

"Perhaps we can sabotage it."

"I'll see what I can do about finding us some hand grenades."

"Too obvious," said Eva, "They'll know who did it. We need something more subtle, more natural…"

"How about killer termites? Do you think you could locate a source, Tony?"

We were laughing so hard we didn't hear Faye walking up behind them.

"Well, are you going to let me in on the joke, too?"

We did, and she joined in. The stars wheeled overhead as our chattering laughter filled the night air. Frogs croaked and crickets chirped, and every now and then a hyena's cackle came from far across the veldt— a mocking echo of our merry-making.

Talk to the Moon

Tony looked at his watch.

"I have to go," he said. "I'm staying with the folks tonight so that means I've got to go back to Bulawayo. I'll be back tomorrow so will see you in church."

Eva and Faye excused themselves and said goodnight to Tony and we were alone again. I wondered if he would try and kiss me goodnight. I wasn't sure if I should let him. What did one do? I didn't want to seem easy, but at the same time I wanted him to kiss me. What if he didn't even try? Would that mean that he didn't want to kiss me or would it only mean that he was being a gentleman and respected me? Mom always told me that a man had no respect for a woman if he kissed her on the first date. Nothing had ever been discussed about what could possibly transpire after the kiss. I had to learn that from my friends at school.

We walked out to where he had left the motorcycle and talked a while longer. I thanked him for the wonderful day and thought "Well, it's now or never." He made a move towards me and I felt my heart begin to race, but it was only to take my hands in his own as he gazed deep into my eyes, and say, "Holly, I enjoyed today more than you will know. I hope we can do it again soon," and then he got on his motorbike and roared into the night.

I stood in the dark for a while, collecting my thoughts, before returning to the rondavel. I told myself that it was relief that I felt—relief that he hadn't kissed me yet. I would still have something to look forward to and I knew he must respect me. I have never been kissed before by a man. I walked slowly back to the room and opened the door. Eva had just returned from the bathroom and her hair was wet from the shower.

"Mom would have a fit if she could see me now," giggled Eva. "You know how she is about wet hair at night!"

"Yes, it's a good thing she doesn't know how many times we've both narrowly escaped some terrible fate from a nocturnal hair washing. How was your afternoon, Eva?"

Eva sat down on the bed and hugged herself.

"It was wonderful! We went to see *Rebecca* with Olivia de Havilland. Do you remember reading the book…?"

"Yes, I loved that book. I wish that Tony and I had gone with you. I don't know how long the films stay here before changing. I may never get to see it!"

"I cried all the way through it, and Ger didn't seem at all embarrassed by my snuffling. He even loaned me his hankie!"

"That was sweet of him! I read *Frenchman's Creek* last year. That is so romantic, full of highwaymen, moonlit moors…I would love to go to Cornwall and see the places she writes about. What else did you do?"

"Not much. We stopped in at a tea room—I forget the name—and had some tea and scones. Ger eats like a bird. I had to eat half his scones."

"And then you came home?"

"Oh yes. There wasn't much else to do. But we spent the rest of the afternoon discussing the choir…how we were going to organize it, and Ger showed me his guitar, and played it for me. He's really quite good, you know."

I told Eva about my day and we laughed about the panda eyes.

I am so happy for Eva. She and Gerald seem perfect for each other. She is the door and he is the post. Together, they'll make a great team.

CHAPTER 10

The Stranger

22nd February
Work has begun on the new church site behind the hall. Eva and I stopped by one day on our way home from work to take a look at the progress. It wasn't that exciting. The workmen have begun to lay down string line markers where the foundations would be dug.

There was a white man who was supervising the workers, shouting directions as he consulted a blueprint. It is difficult to tell just how big the new church is going to be and the workers all looked too busy to talk so we didn't stay.

Each day we passed by the site and each day nothing much had changed. Trucks loaded with bricks—they were using brick this time, thank God—came and left, leaving deep ruts behind in the red clay. A large cement mixer stood idle off to one side as if it were waiting for the foundations to be dug, Large, gray bags of cement were neatly stacked in a nearby tin shed.

"Well at least they're not leaving the cement out in the rain," said Eva. "A good sign!"

"Who is the contractor?"

"Barton Construction. That must be him over there." There was a man leaning against the cement shed door drinking tea from a white china cup.

"Civilized to the core, I see. What do you say he's got a man whose sole function is to make tea?" We snorted with laughter, and the man looked up, his brief gaze flickering disinterested over us, as if we were a couple of *mombies*—African cattle—that had wandered in from the reserve. From this distance I couldn't tell if he was young or old. He was tall and thin but his face was in shadow under the brim of his battered fedora. He wore what Eva and I have come to consider the Rhodesian male standard wear: khaki shirt and shorts, hat, knee length socks and *veldskoen*. We cycled away, still laughing.

"Don't let me marry a man whose hat is glued to his head, and who wears khaki shorts, Eva!"

"I'll commit you myself. I'll bet they never take their hats off, even in bed. I wonder why they think hairy legs and knobby knees are so attractive."

"Thank God Tony doesn't wear shorts—although he'd look good in them. His legs are muscular. He always looks well dressed, but Eric…you never see him in anything else, and he always has that old battered hat on!"

"I wish I had a camera. That tea service was priceless—out in the middle of nowhere—white china! I'm just surprised we didn't see a tea cozy too."

"Well, the milk jug had a beaded doily over it. Didn't you notice?"

Saturday, 24th February

Tony called me to say that he could not get a weekend pass but he would try and make it the following weekend. I live for his visits, and when he doesn't come, it feels as if I have been sentenced to a year of hard labor. All the color drains from my life and my senses are dull and heavy. Soon after the news I had my first bad migraine since arriving at the mission—a jackhammer rattling in the skull which forced me to miss a day of work and lie in my darkened room with a wet washcloth—Mom's remedy—on my head.

Neil insists that all mission personnel take malaria prophylactics so we have started a daily regimen of quinine. If one doesn't swallow it all down at once, it leaves a bitter taste in the mouth, so bad that Eva retched the first time a pill got lodged in her mouth. Water cannot wash the taste away. Malaria is endemic at this time of year. Mosquitoes breed in puddles, old tires and tin cans left out in the rain. Our mosquito netting helps but we cannot be under it constantly. As soon as the sun sets the tiny, whiny *mozzies* make their appearance.

Neil told us that it isn't the whiners we need to worry about; it is the female mosquito—the *Anopholes*—that strikes in silence, the deadly parasite it carries hitting your bloodstream before you even know you have been bitten. The hospital was full of malaria cases, he said, and there were different varieties of the disease. Some were mild, while others attacked the brain, death the only cure.

Neil and Avril are now seen everywhere together. The whole mission knows they're an item and talk about it constantly. Tootie is thrilled—a mission wedding is her heart's desire, and even though nothing has been announced yet, her conversations are peppered with the phrase, "when Avril and Neil get married…."

We are genuinely happy for Avril. I don't want to think I am only happy because it means Avril is not a contender for the Mrs. Anthony Swann title; it is rather that Avril is now a better person. She's by far the sweetest angel on the mission, going out of her way to be helpful to me and Eva and even offering us the use of her car occasionally. I have declined. I can't drive, and anyway I wouldn't want to be responsible for a car that isn't my own.

CHAPTER 11

Josh

Saturday, 3rd March
The announcement was made this week. Avril and Neil are engaged! A church pot-luck supper evening was held in the hall tonight. Car loads of people arrived bearing huge dishes and platters of food and Eva and I shanghaied Merry's kitchen to bake brownies. They had come out burned and crispy around the edges, but we sampled a few and, although crunchy, they didn't taste that bad.

"We'll just bury them amongst the other desserts and maybe no-one will ask who baked them." said Eva.

"Absolutely. I don't want Tony thinking this is how I cook all the time."

"It is how you cook all the time. No, you better not own up to it. Let him find out when it's too late."

"What do you mean? You were the one who was supposed to time them…" But neither one of us had a heart to pursue the argument. We were both looking forward to the supper and meeting new people.

The Bulawayo congregation seemed to be swarming with young people our own age. There were many older folks and families but the younger generation had turned out in force. Tony and Eric arrived in the car with their parents.

"I couldn't get all of them on the back pillion," Tony joked, "So I was forced to take the car." Aunt Lalie and old man Swann seemed delighted to see me again, and Aunt Lalie hooked her dry, twig-like arm around mine.

"You must come and sit with us, my dear." I didn't want to sit with the senior Swann's, but I allowed myself to be pulled towards a group of chairs that Eric was arranging in a small circle. To my chagrin I noticed that Tony had wandered off and was talking to a man I didn't know. Well, I couldn't be rude to his folks now, could I? I would have plenty of time to meet people later. Eva was already talking to a plump blonde girl who looked about her age, and they were both laughing loudly while they hovered near the food table.

"So tell me about your family, dearie. I hear you're from Cape Town?"

I hadn't told anyone about my family yet and Aunt Lalie was the last person I wanted to say anything to. I decided to keep it neutral. Old man Swann leaned forward, raisin eyes shining with undisguised curiosity. Eric looked bored and pretended he wasn't listening. I told them that my father, Leolin, was currently between jobs and that he had been born in Wales. My mother, I said, came from a farming family.

"What did they farm?" asked old man Swann.

"Wheat and sheep, mostly. There were some cattle, horses, and at one time even some ostriches, but sheep are the main stock. My ancestors grew grapes as well but my grandfather only grows them for personal use now." I felt I was on safe ground. Talking about my grandparents would not raise any grotesque specters. They are...well, normal people. People who could have wine with their dinner and not find it necessary to yell and scream at each other afterwards.

Grandfather—*Oupa*— is a stern and uncompromising man, even stubborn and tactless, but he loves us and spoils us when we visit. Unfortunately, we had not been to *Mirebeau* in a long time. With every past visit Mom and *Oupa* battled. He would ask her if she was still raising her children in that *God verdamt* church and then berate her for marrying an *Outlander* who was forever drunk. The Boer War was fought over and over again, between them.

The de Villier's have never forgiven her for marrying an Englishman. They cannot—or will not—see any difference between the Welsh and the English; the final blow descending when Mom abandoned the faith of her forefathers for a strange and foreign religious sect.

Oupa had wanted to teach us how to ride horses, take care of livestock, and in general, be able to think of *Mirebeau* as our inheritance, but Mom will not hear of us girls being involved with farm animals. She has a phobia for all animals and regards them as dangerous and disease carrying.

Eric had quickly lost his undisguised boredom and pulled his chair closer when I mentioned the farm. He asked questions about the cattle, the sheep, and the horses, but I didn't know the answers. I didn't know how many head of cattle there were, or what type of sheep there were—sheep are sheep, aren't they? They all look the same to me.

Eric lost interest once more and went back to contemplating the floor. He was still wearing his hat. No-one had asked him to remove it, and people seem to accept the hat as a biological part of Eric.

He had the 'uniform' on—the khaki shorts and knee socks and the same *veldskoen* he had worn before. I thought again of the contractor. I wondered if he would be here tonight. Surely someone would have invited him? I was curious. Was he young? Was he married? Was he a church member? I wanted Eva to meet more men.

Just then, the air in the hall became electrified and there was a collective intake of breath. The royal couple had arrived. Avril looked enchanting, as usual, and Neil appeared unusually animated—his dour, inscrutable face betraying an imperceptible twitch at the corner of his mouth. A glowing Avril greeted us all with a kiss—on both cheeks—and a clasp of the hands, as if we were long-lost friends who had suddenly reappeared after many years absence. Her silvery laughter rose above the excited chatter as she slithered through the crowd, Neil following on her heels like a well-trained dog.

"Strumpet!"

I jumped, startled.

"Excuse me?"

"Strumpet, I said!" hissed Aunt Lalie. "She's the devil's daughter, she is. Look at them all. They think butter wouldn't melt in her mouth. Well, let me tell you something. I knew her when she was this high," Aunt Lalie motioned with her hand around her knees, "And I can tell you she's a treacherous one, she is! I wonder what kind of misery she will put our dear Neil through."

I was astounded at the venom in Aunt Lalie's voice, and also by the statement that she had known Avril since she was a child. Tony had never mentioned anything like that to me! One could hardly ignore a childhood friend…that night at the Parrish house…acting as if they were virtual strangers…. What was going on here?

"I…I thought Avril was French…from Paris…? I didn't know she grew up here?"

"She grew up here, alright. Her parents, now they're French. Rich as Midas! Had a sugar farm in Mauritius and a cattle ranch in the Lowveld—that's in the southeastern part of the country, my dear—and ran it straight

Talk to the Moon

into the ground." Aunt Lalie's cackle was malicious. "Ran both of them into the ground! They blamed the stock market crash and the depression years, but let me tell you, the way they spent money, nothing would have lasted!" She nodded her head. A small, self-satisfied smile played around her mouth.

"Now, Lalie, we shouldn't be talking about other people to Holly. What will she think of us?" Old man Swann's face maneuvered itself awkwardly into a humble expression of charitable virtuosity. "But Lalie is right," he continued, nevertheless. "We have been acquainted with the girl for many years—and whatever people may say about her—her parents were faithful church-goers and tried their best with that girl."

"They sent her to the finest schools! That girl's school in Salisbury—where the daughters of all the wealthy go—oh, I forget the name, but you know which one I mean, Malachi?"

Another surprise: the old man's name is Malachi. I had thought it would be something biblical; although he seems much better suited to Job or Elijah—something apocalyptic.

"They always talked about sending her to a finishing school in Switzerland, but by then the war had already broken out."

"Oh Malachi, you know that by then they were stone broke! They didn't have two pennies to rub together. War had nothing to do with it. Switzerland is neutral. She went to the Tech in South Africa instead. That's where she got her certificate, or whatever you call it."

"Where are her parents now?" I asked, curious in spite of myself.

Aunt Lalie looked vague, and rolled her eyes. "Last I heard, somewhere in South Africa."

"Haven't seen or heard from them since before the war, right Lalie?"

"They sold up everything here: ranch on the auction block, cars...oh, do you remember those cars they had? My, what a collection; I think Avril kept one of them. He even had a yellow airplane!"

I felt a hand on my shoulder. It was Tony. He had come to rescue me at last but now I didn't need rescuing. The conversation was getting interesting. I needed to find out why Aunt Lalie had called Avril a 'strumpet.' Did it have anything to do with Tony? I wasn't sure that I wanted to find out, but the urge to do so was overwhelming.

"I hope my folks aren't boring you to tears. There's a few people here I want you to meet. Mom and Dad, go get some food. We'll join you later." As they walked away, he said, "You shouldn't let them monopolize you like that."

"Well what could I do, Tony? They're your parents. I can't be impolite if they want to talk to me. Anyhow, we were having quite an interesting conversation."

"I know my mother. She loves to gossip. Be careful what you say to her. She will repeat it to everyone in Bulawayo. Who was she talking about this time?"

"Avril." I looked carefully at Tony's face as I said this, but he betrayed no emotion. Not even a flicker. His expression remained quite neutral.

"She's always hated Avril. I don't know why, she's a good sort."

"Tony, you never told me you knew Avril from way back."

Tony looked surprised.

"I didn't? Gosh, I'm sorry. Yes, we've known each other for…well, ever since we were kids. We used to play together sometimes, but you know, she was a girl, and we went to different schools and so on, so I never really got to know her that well."

"I just had the impression, when I first met you, that you didn't know her."

"Oh, that! So that's what's bothering you? No, that's just a joke we share. You wouldn't understand. I didn't even think anyone would notice."

I felt irritated. I hated to be told I 'wouldn't understand.' It's insulting, as if I am too stupid to get the joke, or worse, a not so subtle way of saying I am an outsider and would always be one.

Before I could think of a snappy retort the young man I saw Tony talking to earlier was standing in front of us. He was introduced as Josh Barton.

So he was the contractor, Barton? Well, he looked spiffier tonight. He wore long khaki pants and a white shirt, still not cutting a dashing and debonair figure, but a definite improvement on the shorts.

"So you are building our new church? I have been dying to talk to you ever since you started. Now I have you cornered you must tell me all about it. How long is it going to take?"

Josh's face brightened.

"It'll take about three or four months, tops, I'm reckoning. If the weather holds and we don't get too much rain. I can dig the foundations

Talk to the Moon

but pouring the concrete is tricky so we may be held up a few weeks until the rainy season subsides. That shouldn't be too much longer now. I think I've seen you on your bicycle, with another girl?"

"Yes, that's my sister Eva."

I felt embarrassed and wondered if he had noticed us laughing at him.

"Well, let's get something to eat and find a place to sit," said Tony. "I'm so hungry I could eat a missionary!"

During the meal Josh and I talked almost nonstop. Tony watched us with amusement. We talked about learning African languages and his stints in the bush. It appeared that he knew as much about the bundu and animals, folklore and legend as Faye. Tony and Josh didn't say much to each other except to exchange a pleasantry every now and again or to make a comment about the food. I thought they were both such different men and wondered how they had met and if there was anything at all that they had in common.

I asked Tony how he knew Josh.

"I got Josh this job here at the mission," said Tony. "I told him that they were looking for a contractor and he should put his bid in, which he did, and before you could say baked beans, he had the contract!"

"Bid low," said Josh, and smiled. His eyes twinkled, and to my dismay I felt my heart leap. What was I thinking? He's not my type at all. He's not nearly as good looking as Tony. All he has is a beautiful smile and lovely eyes. He'll be good for Eva.

"Did you know Tony before you joined the church?" I asked, now feeling like the Spanish Inquisitor.

"No, not really. I had seen him around but didn't know who he was or anything. I moved my business to Bulawayo quite recently. There wasn't much going on in Fort Vic."

"Why didn't you go to Salisbury?"

"I had a few contract offers here. I thought I would go where work seemed the most likely. I'm also hoping to get the new school contract here at the mission."

I knew the mission was building a new boarding school; one that will allow children from outlying areas to attend.

"Well, I hope they'll keep you a while longer, then. I haven't made that many friends yet, and wouldn't want to start losing any."

"I'm pleased that you think of me as a friend. I'll try to stick around."

"Oh, yes, that would be lovely!"

It was towards the end of the evening that Tootie stood up and clapped her hands for silence. Someone tapped a glass with a teaspoon and the chattering in the hall faded to a low buzz.

"I have an announcement to make, ladies and gentlemen, that will surprise nobody, but I'll make it anyway!" There was a low murmur of amusement. Tootie pulled Avril and Neil towards her, her face aglow with delight and happiness.

"Dr. Neil Blanchard asked me to let you all know that he and Miss Avril St. Aubin are now formally engaged to be married." The buzz started up again only to be silenced with a glare from Tootie. "I hope you will all join me in drinking a toast to the happy couple." She raised her glass and people scrambled to find their glasses and to look for refills. Finally everyone raised their glasses and drank a toast to the couple. After the toast, Avril and Neil were mobbed by a congratulatory crowd of church people all talking at once.

"Congratulations, both of you," said Tony. "Holly and I hope that you will be happy!" Avril smiled and we kissed her and shook hands with Neil.

"Never thought I would ever get married," said Neil. "The mission has taken up so much of my time and energy; I felt I just couldn't expect a woman to compete. But Avril is a jewel. She has an amazing understanding of the mission and its demands and I know she'll be an enormous help to me."

Avril looked at him, her expression benevolent and understanding. A soft smile played around her lips.

"Darling, the mission will always be your first love. I accept that. Nothing will be much different than before, except that now we will be together."

"When will the wedding be?"

"We are thinking of a June wedding. The weather will be cool and dry—no mosquitoes—and *Maman* and *Pere* will be able to get away then. They live in Johannesburg, and *Maman* is not healthy. She finds the heat intolerable now and prefers to winter up here."

"I'm sorry to hear your mother is not in good health, but I do hear the winters are comfortable here."

"Can't beat them," said Tony. "They are perfect nearly all over the country. There are a few places where it never cools down enough to make a difference, but they are located mainly in the Zambezi valley and

Talk to the Moon

the Lowveld. Here on the escarpment, it can get quite cold, but never unpleasantly so."

"Then you haven't spent a winter in Gwelo!" laughed Neil. That is the coldest place in the country, with maybe the exception of the eastern highlands. The wind whistles over that highveld plain like you wouldn't believe. I've seen it knock strong men over. The days may be sunny and warm, but those nights will freeze the...well, will get below freezing."

"You mean they'll freeze the brass balls off a monkey!" exclaimed Tony and we all laughed, but Neil blushed and Avril looked amused at first, then seeing the expression on Neil's face, she looked down, her expression bashful.

"Well, I think it's time to say goodnight," said Neil frostily. "I have rounds to make early—before church, you know. Need to get some shut-eye, and so do you, my love."

Josh left too, and we watched as Avril and Neil walked down the path and got into the Wolseley.

"Neil's a good man, but he doesn't know much about women, that they're not as delicate as they look," said Tony, his face thoughtful. "I don't know how Avril is going to adjust to that. She's no hot house orchid even though she may look like one."

"No, she isn't, I've noticed. She speaks her mind, and she has an earthy sense of humor."

"Yes, you could say that. She was the one who taught me and Eric the facts of life, you know."

"What do you mean, the facts of life?"

"The things your parents are supposed to tell you." Tony laughed. "You know...where babies come from...or did you always think the stork brought them?"

"Of course not. I thought it was the cabbage patch. How did she teach you that?"

"We were about ten or eleven, and she was twelve or thirteen. She's two years older than me, you know. Well, she and her parents were at the farm one day, I think her Dad was buying cattle or something, and Eric and I were playing. She came over and wanted to play too, but we told her to get lost. She got this sly look on her face, and said that she would tell us a secret if we let her play with us. Well, we still weren't interested. What secrets could she possibly have that would interest two boys? We continued to ignore her. Then she said, "I'll bet you don't know how babies are made!" That got our attention! She proceeded to describe in vivid detail exactly how babies are made. We were so shocked; we didn't believe her at first. I couldn't imagine my parents doing it…I used to look at them and try to imagine it, and I thought she had to be lying."

"How long was it before you found out it was true?"

"I asked my mother if that was how babies were made and she washed my mouth out with soap. That's when I knew it must be true."

"Why?"

"My parents never told us the truth about anything. If they said something was black, I knew it would be white. They thought they could somehow protect us from the real world, but the real world always had a way of finding us without their help. They didn't tell us until we were teenagers that Father Christmas didn't exist but by then we already knew. We found out the truth from our friends at school."

"And Avril. That was the situation in my family too. My father would try and tell us where babies came from, in a roundabout way, but my mother would get all upset and scream at him. She would tell us to forget what he said to us, that he was drunk, and didn't know what he was saying. She called him 'an evil man.'"

Tony looked at me searchingly, and suddenly I realized what I had said. I hadn't meant to say anything…but now it was out. There was no way I could retract my words.

"I'm sorry; I didn't realize your father drank. I thought they were both in the church. You seemed to have such a sheltered upbringing."

"I did, my mother saw to that. But yes, my father's a drunk. He's a sick man at the moment, and so is Mom, in a different way. Eva and I were glad to leave that environment. I hope you never have to meet my parents."

Tony reached out and took my hand in his.

"It couldn't have been easy. My own mother was a bad one too. I remember her slightly. I don't know where she is now…no-one knows. She took off with a man when I was five. I don't know if it was my father—in fact, I don't even know who my real father is, or Eric's. I believe we have different fathers."

I never knew just how bad Tony's life had been, and here I was, feeling sorry for myself because of my family life! It was nothing….

"That must have been a shock for your parents—I mean your grandparents."

"No, call them my parents. I consider them my parents. They were quite devastated, being such upstanding church members and all, but she had been giving them trouble nearly all her life, I believe. She had me when she was only sixteen. I tell everyone who doesn't know the true situation that my parents died. I lied to you about that, and I'm sorry. I didn't want you thinking badly of me."

I felt I could forgive him for that lie under the circumstances. It was a relief that he thought enough of me to want to make an impression as I had with him. I hadn't lied about my parents but I hadn't told him the whole truth either.

I wanted to talk some more, but just then old man Swann and Aunt Lalie and Eric loomed out of the doorway of the hall.

"Let's go, Tony. Ma's tired and her back's giving her trouble. I don't know why they had to insist on staying until the end. We could have left hours ago."

Tony gave me a resigned look.

"I'll see you tomorrow, then. I'll stop by before I have to leave for Salisbury. Maybe after church. Goodnight!"

And that was the end of the weekend for me. It's so difficult sharing Tony with his family. Eva came out with the blonde girl and introduced her to me as Hattie Muller.

"She's a hairdresser in Bulawayo," said Eva, an excited lilt to her voice. Hattie laughed, a coarse braying laugh, and a wad of chewing gum appeared on her pink tongue in her open mouth.

"Eva told me about you trying to do her hair!" She shrieked. "I think that's so *funny*! I told her to stop by at the salon, *Tress Chic*, next time she's in town and I'll do her hair for *free*!" Hattie sprinkled exclamation marks, free and uninhibited, throughout her conversation. "I'll do yours, too, if you like!" They both giggled and walked off arm in arm into the night towards an old beat up Ford. I missed Josh's company, already. He had been so interesting.

"Want some company to walk you home?"

It was Faye.

"I'd love some. I was just beginning to feel lonely."

"That can happen quickly when you're in love. Oh, I'm sorry, I didn't mean to pry. I just noticed that Tony had left."

"Yes, he had to take his family home. Don't worry; it's not much of a secret. I am in love. It's so difficult, Faye. He's stationed so far away, and when he does make it to Bulawayo for the weekend I have to share him with his family. Not that there's something wrong with that—I just have a tough time dealing with it."

We started off down the dark road and it was a few minutes before Faye spoke again.

"When you're married, you think that you will finally have them all to yourself and that his family and friends have lost the battle and you will be getting the lion's share of your sweetheart's time. It's not like that at all. Instead, you find yourself spending much more time with the family and friends—almost as much as if you were married to them. Their problems become your problems, and their lives become inextricably entwined with yours. I think what I am trying to say here, is that you need to make sure you love his family and friends almost as much as you love him, because you will be seeing more of them in the future, not less."

"You're right, I know you are. Unfortunately, I don't feel that way about Tony's parents. They're harmless enough but I can't imagine having them around constantly. I don't know who his friends are, yet, but I do see exactly what you mean. They could be awful. But the fact remains; you can't dump someone because of their family. Mine are even worse, and I would hate for Tony to dump me because of them."

"You don't have to dump him. And I hope he doesn't do the same. What I meant was, adjust to the family now. Find what's good in them and focus on that. Be good to them and treat them as if they were your own, because they may be, someday."

It felt good talking to Faye. She's so sensible. She could have just agreed with me that it was terrible having to share someone, and left it at that, but she cared enough to share her opinions even if they may not have been what I wanted to hear. Hearing Faye say that someday Tony's family may be my family gives me hope, as if saying it will make it so.

Faye laughed.

"Here I am dispensing advice about families. Any poor bloke who met my lot would be well advised to head for the hills. I wouldn't think any the less of him for it."

"Your family couldn't possibly be that bad, Faye. You haven't seen mine yet!"

"Huh. You want to bet? I'll take you to meet them one day. They live in Bulawayo. I think you'll agree with me then."

Talk to the Moon

"I have my doubts. I'm not a betting person, but I'll wager you a malt milkshake that mine are worse."

We shook hands on it, and retired to our rooms.

CHAPTER 12

The Johnsons

Monday, 5th March

Two weeks ago we got news of the capture of Iwo Jima. Things look encouraging on the European front as well; the Americans are now in the Ruhr Valley and headed toward Cologne. The war will soon be over and Tony will leave the Air Force. I will see more of him and he may even settle down in Bulawayo. Perhaps he will get a job at the mission!

Eva and I have bought a radio—a second hand Majestic Zephyr—still in good shape, and an old Brownie box camera, amongst other items, from Mormons who are returning to their home in Salt Lake City. The radio makes our evenings more companionable. It's good to hear first-hand both the news of the war and the local news. It gives me a whole new perspective on the baffling politics of this country while Eva prefers the comedy shows and music. We've agreed not to argue about what to listen to, drawing up a list of our favorite programs and working out an acceptable schedule so that there will be no conflicts about who wants to listen to what.

I am proud of both myself and Eva. I never imagined that we could come to an agreement that actually worked about anything! We both sit quietly each night listening to each other's programs or our own; me writing in my diary or knitting, while Eva sprawls on her bed with a bagful of salted peanuts, munching contentedly. I find knitting calms my soul and focuses my mind.

Preparations for Avril's wedding are consuming the mission. Everyone wants to be involved and the competition is cut-throat. Tootie insists that the wedding reception be held in the hall, while Avril, since it's a June wedding in the middle of the cool, dry season—wants it outdoors. Tootie has begun to plan the wedding to the last hors de oeuvre and guest causing Faye to march over to the Parrish residence last week and confront Tootie about her 'interference.'

Talk to the Moon

"Avril is in tears every night because she doesn't want to hurt your feelings. This is her wedding, and if she wants it outside she should have it outside. Put that in your pipe and smoke it. Oh, and do let her make out her own guest list and menu while you're at it."

Word spread like an out of control bush fire about the confrontation. An angry Tootie was seen striding around the mission grounds, tight lipped and red faced, for several days afterwards. The mission servants and African employees, covering their mouths with their hands, giggled and turned away as she approached—they hated Tootie. Her reputation was equal to that of Heinrich Himmler, and she was unaffectionately referred to as Madam *Imvubu* or translated, Madam Hippopotamus.

I heard all of this from Esther. I have become fond of Esther, finding her a bright girl with a good sense of humor.

The problem of where Avril and Neil are to live on the mission compound came up briefly. There are only two married quarters that are currently occupied by the Parrish's and Van Breda's, but I have now heard that Avril has found a house to rent off the mission grounds. It's an old house but serviceable. The rental has been approved by the Mission Board and would be available on the 1st of June.

The wedding date has been set for the second Saturday in June.

Avril has asked four young girls from the Bulawayo congregation to be her bridesmaids. They are not particularly close to Avril—no-one is—but word has it they've been picked for their similar looks and svelte figures. The mission gossip is that Avril doesn't want any fat fairies in her bridal party. Neil asked Tony to be his best man, and Eric and Josh are to be ushers.

Josh has asked Robert Parrish if he could move in with Gerald into the single quarters when Neil moves out. The mission has approved this request since Josh is now as much a part of the mission as anyone. He told this to me when I stopped by the construction site as has become my daily habit.

"I'll probably be here for another year at least. The school is quite a big project."

"Well, it will be wonderful to have you here on the mission, Josh." I meant it. I like Josh, and I feel as if I could talk to him about almost anything. He is quiet and rather too serious, I think, but he listens carefully to everything I have to say as if it's the most important thing he has ever heard.

I wish Eva would forget Gerald and get interested in Josh. Eva is much happier now that she has Helium Hattie for a friend, as Tony refers to Hattie. Gerald has never asked Eva out again, and much to my relief, he has stopped pestering me for a date. Rumor has it that he is now dating Ayesha. Eva mentioned this one night to me.

"I don't know what it is about me, Holly. I can't seem to attract a man. Do you think I'm too fat? Am I ugly?"

"Of course you're not fat! What gave you that idea? And ugly? You're crazy, but not ugly!" We laughed, but I felt I had better make sure that Eva doesn't think of herself as unattractive. "There aren't too many single men here for you to meet, Eva. There's nothing wrong with you, it's the selection. You may just not be Gerald's type. I think he likes a certain type of woman, and you're just not it. Don't change yourself for a man, look for a man who likes you just as you are."

"Yes, you're right. Can you imagine going through life starving yourself to death because your husband likes skinny women? Or being serious all the time when you just want to laugh out loud? I wish I didn't fall for men who like the type of woman I'm not. It would be a lot easier."

"When you meet the right man you'll forget all about that stick insect. What about Josh?"

Eva laughed.

"Be serious! He wouldn't look at me in a hundred years. Besides, I don't think there's any spark there. He's not my type."

"Well I'm happy you can tell what your type is. Now don't blame yourself for the lack of talent around here. I was lucky that Tony came along. If he hadn't, I'd be in the same boat as you, so no more of this I'm too ugly talk! You have the de Villier's looks and they are not ugly people."

Saturday, 28th April, 1945

Tony has cancelled his scheduled visit to the mission again. Something has "come up," he says, and there is a chance of him being sent somewhere, but he can't say more than that over the phone. I am incensed. The war is almost over! What do they need Tony for? There is nothing but good news: the Soviets have captured Vienna and last week the U.S. 7th Army took Nuremberg. Now they want Tony?

This afternoon, while I was sitting in front of the radio knitting, there was a knock on the door and I thought I'd pretend I wasn't in. Eva had gone shopping with Helium Hattie and I wasn't expecting any visitors.

Talk to the Moon

The knocking persisted. I threw down my knitting and flung open the door. It was Faye.

"Hey, I'm sorry to bother you, but I was hoping you'd be here. I need some company, and remembering that you'd expressed an interest in meeting my family, I thought I would take you up on the offer. I have to go visit my folks this afternoon and could always use some moral support. Are you game?" I felt my anger evaporate. Of course I was game. It's impossible to be dreary around Faye. Her high spirits and cheerfulness shook me out of my blue funk and soon we were joking and laughing all the way in to town.

We drove to a suburb that Faye said consisted chiefly of blue collar Railway workers. The houses were small and crammed closely together, with identical red tin roofs, small front porches and yards littered with an assortment of rusted out vehicles on blocks. There were a few attempts made at gardens but the hardscrabble earth seemed unwilling to cooperate, supporting only the hardy and ever present milkweed tree, cactus and *khakibos*—an ugly weed that lived up to its name.

"This is where I grew up," said Faye, as we turned into a driveway. There had been a gate, once, but now it lay on an overgrown lawn, rusty and covered with weeds. A dispirited and mangy yellow dog sidled up to us.

"Hello, Shumba!" yelled Faye. "Shumba may mean 'lion', but he's been kicked one too many times for him to think he's a lion. Don't worry, he won't bite." I began to wonder if I'd made the right decision to come. This didn't look promising at all.

We picked our way down what had once been a path and Faye gave a loud knock on the door. "I don't know if they're awake yet. It's Saturday, and they would have had a blast last night. I'll bet the cops were here a few times!" I didn't know if I should laugh, so I just kept quiet.

The door opened suddenly, startling me. A heavy, gap-toothed woman stood there in a threadbare, chenille bathrobe.

"Whad're you doing here? I thought you weren't coming till tomorrow."

"No, it's today Mom, and I brought my friend with me. This is Holly. Can we come in?"

"Well, I'm not decent, but yes, you can come in. Maybe next time you'll give a person fair warning before you come bringing God knows who with you." I wanted to turn and run back to the car, but Faye had a death grip on my elbow, and I was propelled into the house before I could turn around.

"Since my daughter didn't introduce me—you would think she forgot her own mother's name—I'll do it myself. I'm Darlene. Sid!" She yelled. "Where is that no good son of a bitch? I'll kick his arse out of that bed if he's still there." She waddled down the hall to a door and kicked it hard with a large foot. "Get your stinking, lazy arse out of bed and come and greet your daughter!"

Faye's face was expressionless, as if this was just a normal family visit and nothing at all was out of the ordinary. We sat down on a sagging sofa that smelled like Shumba, and Darlene shook out a cigarette from a box of *Lucky Strikes* and lit up. She took a deep drag.

"Could use a beer now. I wonder if those leeches left me any. Faye, go look in the fridge for your mother. It's the least you can do. She's never here to do anything for her parents," she said as Faye got up and walked out of the room. "She walked out of here and never gave her family a backward glance. Joined that mission lot, what a bunch of hypocrites, when she could've had a perfectly decent job at Bulawayo General." She went on in this fashion, about how hard Sid worked to keep them out of the poorhouse, and how irresponsible Faye was turning down better paying jobs closer to home, *etcetera, etcetera.*

I was beginning to get a sense of *déjà vu* when Faye returned with an opened *Lion Lager* and handed it to her mother. There was a snorting sound in the passage and Sid shuffled in scratching his dirty undershirt and yawning. Tattoos covered his arms from wrist to shoulder.

"Get me a beer, Faye. So this is your friend, huh?" Faye seemed speechless in the presence of her parents. She scurried out towards the kitchen for another beer. Sid chortled.

"Can't say we didn't train her right, eh? You one of those mission people?"

By now I was feeling extremely uncomfortable and prayed Faye would not take too long looking for a beer. Sid was leaning against the wall, staring at me, paranoid suspicion glinting from small eyes. He reminds me of some of the men Dad keeps company with at the Gladstone: defensive men who perceive anyone they don't know as a threat; men who see others as either friend or foe. I was one of those "mission people" and in the Johnson eyes that made me foe.

Talk to the Moon

"Yes, I'm one of those mission people." I stared him straight in the eye. One couldn't show fear in front of his type. They were like hyenas, they'd move in for the kill if they detected weakness, although just what he could do to me I couldn't imagine. I felt safe enough, just uncomfortable. He broke off his gaze and reached for the box of Luckies. He was a bully, but a coward too. Faye came into the room carrying a tray with a beer and two bottles of Coke on it.

"Sorry about the bottles, Holly, all the glasses seem to be dirty." The Cokes were warm but I drank mine gratefully. My throat was dry and the cigarette smoke was making me sick. Darlene was continuing her whining litany where she had left off and Sid was sitting in sullen silence, sucking down his beer, interjecting every now and then with a snort or a "think they're better than ordinary folk, they do!"

Finally, the ordeal came to an end as Faye stood up and said it was about time they were going. She had barely said one word since they had arrived. Her parents had not asked her anything about her life, how she was or shown any concern for her welfare. They walked to the door with us, grasping their beers like life-lines in a stormy sea, a thick cloud of smoke enveloping them like a fog. I breathed deeply in the fresh air outside and we quickly walked to the car and got in.

"Phew! I'm glad that's over!" said Faye. "I'm sorry you had to see that. Maybe it wasn't a good idea to ask you to come with me. I'm used to their ways and forget what it does to normal people meeting them for the first time."

"Well, I never have considered my own family normal so I suppose that I also thought I was beyond being shocked. I really do think there are a lot of similarities, except my mother never liked alcohol, and she is an upstanding member of the church, but my father is often drunk. He does get nasty when he drinks which makes my mother worse in her own way."

"Well whatever your family do they can't be worse than mine."

I had to agree with this statement although I couldn't bring myself to say it.

"Why did you get those beers, Faye? If it were my parents, I wouldn't do it."

"Have you ever tried to get an alcoholic to stop drinking by depriving them of alcohol?" Faye asked. "It doesn't work. They will go through you and a legion of devils to get to that drink. I never did tell you how I got this glass eye."

"You said you had been in an accident."

"Yes, it was an accident, alright. My father was drunk, falling down, but he could still stand up enough to use his fists on my mother. I don't remember why, it really doesn't matter anymore. I was twelve years old. I saw him go for the bottle and I grabbed it before he did and started to run with it. He came after me—even drunk he is quick—and I ran to the kitchen and started to pour it down the sink. It was the only bottle left; I remember it was whiskey or something like that. The stores were closed and I knew he couldn't get another bottle until the next day. I was hoping he'd give up drinking for that night and sleep it off and leave my mother alone. When he saw that liquid go down the sink he howled like an animal and grabbed me by my hair. He picked up the empty bottle out of the sink where I had dropped it and I remember seeing it come down towards my face. That's all I remember. I woke up in the hospital, my face all bandaged up and I couldn't see. The nurses were so kind to me. That's when I decided I had to be a nurse."

"Oh, Geez, Faye, I never realized just what you went through. How awful! Is that when you got the glass eye?"

"Yes, although that was later. I wore a patch for a while."

"Did they send you back to your parents?"

"No, I was put into foster care until I left school. If that accident hadn't happened, Holly, I don't know where I would be now; probably sitting in that hovel with my parents with a bottle in one hand, a cigarette in the other, and ten kids hanging onto my skirt. It was the best thing that ever happened to me and I'm not sorry for it. My foster parents were the most wonderful people I have ever met, and they did more for me than you can imagine. They encouraged me to go to nursing school and they were the ones who brought me into the church."

"Where are they now?"

Faye looked sad.

"They were driving down to South Africa—Durban—to visit their daughter who was at university there, in '42. A bus lost its brakes coming in the opposite direction and hit them head on. They never stood a chance."

"I'm so sorry, Faye. How unfair."

Talk to the Moon

"No, I don't think so. They always told me that there is a purpose to everything, even the bad things, and that nothing in this universe is ever wasted. They believed that God's creation was perfect and that from our perspective we couldn't see the design but that God could. One day we would know the purpose of our lives and we should never regard any event as meaningless."

"What do you think was the meaning of their dying in an accident?"

"I don't know. I think about that every day. It's useless to speculate, but maybe one day I will have the answer. They're the only people who ever meant anything to me, so yes, it's easy to say it's unfair. But life never was fair and it's only our expectations that are unfair."

"You have a point. What did they do to your parents after you ended up in foster care?"

"Not much. They had a court case, but they both showed up as sober as the magistrate, Dad crying and saying how he would 'take the pledge' and never touch the stuff again, mom crying and promising things would be different—'just please don't take my baby away from me!' The magistrate felt they were sincere and put them on probation but officially removed me anyway. I hear they stopped in at a pub on the way home."

"Now that's not fair."

"That Dad should have been thrown into jail? No, their lives are hell anyway. I can't imagine a worse fate than to have to take responsibility for your own actions. Life kicks them in the arses every single day. There'll be no relief in sight for them until they change their ways. They are completely responsible for themselves; not some faceless institution. That's fair."

"You have your opinions and I have mine. I still think jail would have been right for him."

"Strange world, isn't it. I really do love them both although I can't say I like them at all. I still feel an obligation to visit them once in a while although the visits are not helpful to either them or me. I revisit a lot of bad memories and feel as if I am in need of an exorcism every time I go there."

"Oh Faye, look! There's a Dairy Den on the right up there. Please stop, I owe you a milkshake!"

CHAPTER 13

First Kiss

5th May, 1945

Avril has surprised everyone by handing in her resignation! We all thought she would remain in her job since Neil would be staying on at the mission, and they could drive in to work together, but she said that she has so much work to do in getting their house fit to live in that she wouldn't have her heart in her job. She said she wanted to devote her life to making Neil happy and comfortable and be a good wife to him and a job would take too much of her energy. Her resignation was accepted and a requisition put in for a replacement immediately.

19th May

Tony has returned, thinner and more sunburned, but intact. He told me over the phone that he didn't see any action but the desert was no fun and he'd come down with a bad case of dysentery. More than that, he couldn't say, and I didn't ask. He is over the dysentery now and for that I am grateful.

26th May

I've still not seen anything of Tony. He's due in Bulawayo this weekend. Hattie was shopping last Saturday morning in the city, and as she told Eva later, who then told me, she thought she saw Tony roar by on his motorcycle down Main Street, but she wasn't sure that it was him. The man was wearing a leather helmet and goggles, and the only thing that made her think it was Tony was the distinctive motorcycle, the '38 Norton. She knew what they looked like because her brother had owned one. There was also a woman sitting on the pillion who, even wearing a scarf and sunglasses, looked like Avril. She laughed about it, and said she couldn't imagine Avril on a motorcycle. But my heart did a sickening flip-flop and I can't stop thinking about it. I must be crazy. Why would Tony and Avril be seeing each other when Tony isn't even in Bulawayo? Why would they keep it a secret if they did? Avril is getting married in

Talk to the Moon

two weeks, there's nothing going on there, so Hattie must have just seen a couple who happened to look like them. That's all there is to it.

Saturday evening, late: June 2nd

I casually mentioned the motorcycle sighting to him today, while we were sitting on Faye's kopje with a picnic basket.

"Tony, you weren't in Bulawayo last weekend, were you?"

"Of course not. Why do you ask?"

"Well, this is really silly, and I wouldn't even mention it except that I did wonder if there was someone else who looked like you who had a Norton motorcycle? Hattie thought she saw you roar by on Main Street last Saturday morning with Avril on the pillion!" I giggled in a silly me fashion but watched Tony carefully.

"If there is, I'd like to meet this fellow. We'd have a lot in common. More, if she thought she'd seen you on the back!" He laughed and shrugged his shoulders. "I was on the Base in a stuffy room last Saturday getting debriefed. I wish I had been on my motorcycle in Bulawayo!"

He quickly pulled me towards him and kissed me hard on the mouth. I was so stunned that for a moment I didn't know what to do. We've been dating for so long and this is the first time he's kissed me! He stopped, looked at me and kissed me again, tenderly this time with a probing tongue on my lips, his arms wrapping me in an embrace. I relaxed and parted my mouth slightly. Was that what one was supposed to do? I had no idea. I've seen kisses and embraces on the movie screens, but short of being jammed together, lip to lip, I can't really tell what else goes on there.

It must have been the right thing to do, because I felt his tongue dart into my mouth and surprisingly enough, it didn't feel too bad! Was I supposed to put my tongue in his mouth too? I didn't think so, so I just let his tongue roam and I tried putting my arms around him too but couldn't quite manage it without it seeming awkward. He had me locked in a tight embrace. Finally it all came to an end and he slowly released me. I felt myself trembling with both fear and desire. This was all so different to what I had imagined. What should I say or do now?

"Time to be getting back, what do you say?"

I looked up at him in surprise. Is that what it felt like to him? A reminder of the time? I seldom even thought about time while I was with him and the kiss had erased the outside world. I felt as if we were the only two people left on the planet. Why should we be getting back just now?

"Well, okay. It'll be getting dark soon. I promised Eva I'd be there to help her with the dinner tonight."

We made our way back to the mission carrying the now much lighter picnic basket between us. Still, Tony said nothing about the kiss, and I wanted to say something—I wanted to hear how he felt when he kissed me, that he loved me, and I wanted to tell him how much I loved him—but I didn't want to be the one to initiate that kind of conversation.

I gave him frequent sidelong glances, hoping to see a small trace of what he was feeling on his face. Anything that would give his innermost thoughts away but I saw nothing. Just the same Tony I had seen before. Nothing had changed between us. It was as if the kiss had never happened.

Avril's replacement has arrived at the mission. Her name is Joan, and she is staying with the Parrish's until Avril moves out of the compound. She is a widow and much older than we are. I think she is somewhere in her late forties.

CHAPTER 14

John Blanchard

Saturday, 9th June, 1945

Unforgettable: a beautiful day. A large tent was set up for the reception in the empty field where camp meetings are held and the ceremony took place in the new church that has been completed just a week ago. It still smells of fresh paint.

Josh had come to the rescue of the choir by inspecting the organ and pronouncing it unfit for the new church.

"You don't want to put this into the new church," he told the Mission Inspectors from Salisbury. "It's riddled with termites and they'll spread into the woodwork in the new church in a few months. You'll have beams crashing down on the congregation."

We were elated at the news. The mission had approved a budget to buy a new organ, but in the meantime Gerald volunteered to play his guitar in lieu of the organ. The largely African choir needed no organ and their harmonization was beautiful and melodious even without the guitar.

Tootie was terrified that she wouldn't get to play the *Wedding March*. She had scoured Bulawayo looking for a replacement organ, but thanks to the wartime shortages, nothing seemed available. There were plenty of pianos though, and after much bargaining back and forth they finally procured a second hand upright with a reasonably good sound.

Tootie has practiced daily to get the *Wedding March* just right, and we had to admit that it sounds a lot better on the piano than on the old organ. The choir practiced the songs that Avril had requested for the ceremony, both *a cappella* and with the piano, and Eva, Faye, Gerald and I volunteered as a quartet for the reception.

Avril's parents arrived this week. Avril has prepared the house, making it comfortable enough for them to stay in.

Neil's father arrived a few days before the wedding too, staying with the elder Swanns in Bulawayo. He is a trim seventy-plus with white hair, mustache and a regal bearing.

Cars started arriving for the wedding at two p.m. and when we walked into the church it was already starting to fill up. Eric showed us to our seats in a row directly behind Avril's parents and Tony sat next to Neil in the front row. Tootie was playing softly on the piano and we all felt relieved that she wasn't giving it her usual pounding.

The African choir sat up front with Gerald; the proud choirmaster. They looked quite spiffy in their new robes of white with blue sashes. It had taken a great deal of effort but Gerald had fought tooth and nail to squeeze the funding from the budget for the robes and, to everyone's surprise, he won the battle. I have to admit that Gerald has done a great job with the choir. They look professional and they sound perfect.

The flowers were done by Avril the previous day. She received permission to cut as many of the mission garden flowers as she needed. The new paint smell had almost been drowned out with the smell of fresh bouquets of roses placed strategically around the church.

I had a chance to look more closely at Avril's mother now that I was sitting directly behind her. Mrs. St. Aubin was a petite but brittle, olive skinned woman. She wore a small pink hat with a spray of flowers and veil that, together with a silver fox jacket and pink linen dress, made her look chic and elegant. I could see where Avril got her looks and fashion sense. Once again I felt inadequate in my own brand new green velveteen dress which I felt I had paid way too much for, and a new hat. But then, I wasn't a part of the bridal party and no-one would be looking my way much, except Tony, I hoped.

I was surprised to see that neither Old Man Swann nor Pastor Van Breda would be conducting the ceremony. Instead, the regular Bulawayo pastor, Pastor Bennett, had stepped up. The Swann's were sitting on the other side of the aisle as friends of the groom, and so were the Van Breda's. There seemed to be a lot more people on that side of the church.

The church went quiet as voices from the back whispered "She's here, she's here!" and Tootie crashed out the first chords of the *Wedding March* as everyone rose to their feet, craning to see the bride. I didn't get to see her until she reached our row and I gasped. I had known that Avril would be stunning as usual but she had really outdone herself on her wedding day.

She wore a white satin dress with a full skirt and a long train. Her bodice and sleeves were lace over satin and she had a full, lacy veil that reached nearly to the floor. Her headpiece was a garland of pink roses and white baby's breath, as was her bouquet.

Walking beside her was her father. The ceremony was tasteful, with no overlong sermons or prayers, and the choir, conducted by Gerald, was masterful. There wasn't a dry eye in the church. Eva sat weeping next to me and I was fighting back a tear or two, myself. Why do weddings do that to people? I don't even like Avril!

The reception went as well as the ceremony. Tony gave a lively speech and everyone laughed in the right places, and then he proposed the toasts. Avril beamed but Neil looked like a sleep-walker—as if he wasn't sure what he was doing in the middle of all this hoopla. Eva, Faye and I sang *Till the End of Time* while Gerald strummed on the guitar, and all the old ladies cried and wiped their eyes.

The sun was setting behind the tall blue gums when Avril left to change into her 'going away' outfit. Everybody knew that it was going to be something exceptional, even for Avril, and she didn't disappoint us.

When it was time for her to throw her bouquet the young girls and women thronged about in front of her. I didn't want to go but Faye and Eva dragged me into the melee. Avril threw the bouquet and in the mad crush to get it, I couldn't at first see who actually did catch it, but to my surprise it turned out to be Eva. Eva waived the bouquet triumphantly aloft. Helium Hattie squealed in ecstasy whilst skipping and hopping around Eva.

"It's you next! Oh, who's the lucky guy? I hope I'm your bridesmaid!" They walked arm in arm through the throng, obligingly allowing their envious erstwhile competitors to examine the bouquet.

Neil and Avril got into the soaped up, tin-canned Wolsely and drove off into the sunset. They had been planning to leave on their honeymoon early the next morning driving down to Durban for a two-week stay. I wonder how much of a honeymoon night it would be with *Maman* and *Pere* in the house. Well, at least they can get away tomorrow and be alone. *Maman* and *Pere* were going to look after the house for them while they were gone.

I barely had a chance to talk to Tony during the reception. He was mobbed by people and wherever he went an entourage followed. I stayed with Faye and Josh, who provided back-up for me with the elder Swanns and other social mosquitoes, pulling me away under some pretext when it seemed they were settling in for the long haul. Faye, half-joking, said she didn't have that problem. "Most people avoid me. I just start talking politics and they fall over each other trying to get away from me!"

"Oh, so that's what you were doing when I first met you! Now that your secret's out, it won't work anymore."

The highlight of the wedding was meeting Neil's father. He is an interesting man, and I wonder how Neil is so different from his father. John Blanchard is not stuffy. The twinkle in his eyes makes him look ten years younger than his son in spite of his white hair. He laughs often and talks animatedly to everyone.

He has the distinction of being one of the original settlers in Rhodesia—trekking up from South Africa when he was only eighteen with the Pioneer Column. While he talked, I quietly took out my notebook and pencil that I always try to carry everywhere with me, and made quick, shorthand notes of nearly everything he said and that I will transcribe here:

"It was 56 years ago when I joined up at Kimberley. I was fresh off the boat from Southampton, come to seek my fortune in diamonds. The reality was different from the glowing reports I had heard and I was in trouble with some money lenders in Kimberley who were looking for me," he chuckled.

"I hated Kimberley. It was cold and miserable, and I wanted to go somewhere warm; I didn't care where. When I heard the rumor that there was an expedition leaving the next day for the northern territory I jumped at it. They didn't want me at first—they had enough people, they said, and I wasn't experienced enough. Well, I sweet-talked them into letting me tag along. I said if it got too much for me I'd drop out along the way, before we even left South Africa, so they let me come along. Met a great man by the name of Selous. Stayed with him as much as possible and the first time I felt like getting off the wagon was when we arrived in Fort Salisbury.

"I continued up to Mount Darwin, borrowed a horse and rode out my claim of 3,000 acres. I sold my 15 gold claims for eighty pounds and bought a horse, a bullock cart with two oxen, and a plough.

"That first year in Mashonaland was a nightmare. We had over 54 inches of rain that year and people were selling their land and claims left and right. I decided to stick it out. I was sitting in a small pole and daga hut trying to keep dry while the roof disintegrated over my head and termites chewed on the poles. I had no boots left, no food and the

Talk to the Moon

mosquitoes were eating me alive. One of my oxen was eaten by a leopard and my horse was sick. I came down with malaria and by then I was ready to pack it in.

"Christmas came and went and I had no idea it was Christmas. I woke up sometime in January, half dead and famished. I crawled out of my hut to find my horse gone and my last ox dead.

"One of my neighbors decided to ride over my land thinking I had left months ago and gone back to Fort Salisbury. He came upon me in the remains of my hut and nursed me back to health. I had to start all over again and the Company was asking fifty percent of all my earnings. What earnings? I had nothing! There was Mr. Rhodes, a millionaire, wanting what little I had left. I couldn't complain, however, they had given me the land to begin with—that they stole off the Mashonas and tricked Lobengula into letting them into the country. So unless I was willing to sell the land to a speculator for a song I had no choice.

"I went to Fort Salisbury, borrowed more money and bought more oxen, a horse, and some *mombies*—some strong Africander bulls and cows this time. I was in debt up to my eyebrows but this time I felt I was going to make it."

"And did you?" asked a wide-eyed Eva.

I had to stifle a laugh.

"Yes. It still wasn't easy, and for ten years I struggled to make a go of it—first with cattle, then when I saw how successful tobacco was growing on other farms, I branched out into that. I still have some *mombies*, but tobacco is my main cash crop now."

"How did you meet your wife? It doesn't sound as if there were many women around with the Pioneers."

Mr. Blanchard laughed.

"I was too sick at first to worry about women and then I was too concerned with my survival to look around.

"In 1900, I was twenty-nine and convinced I was going to die a bachelor. I had to go into Fort Salisbury for supplies one Christmas and was invited to a Christmas ball. I was surprised to see how many women were at the ball, most of them unattached. I almost didn't know how to behave around them. I felt as if every word I uttered was coarse and ungentlemanly.

"I thought the ladies were laughing at me, so I stepped outside and was ready to leave and go back to the farm. I felt a tug on my sleeve, and turned around and looked into a pair of sparkling eyes. The young lady said that she had not danced with me yet and would I please be so kind as to escort her back into the ballroom. Well, what could I say? We danced the whole night with each other, and I found out her name was Moira Kelly, from Dublin. The rest is history, as you say, and we were married in 1902. Neil was born in 1904.

"She was not a strong person, and she died in childbirth with our second child, a daughter, in 1907, who was stillborn. I never remarried. Neil has been my whole life, and I am really happy to see him marry such a beautiful and kind woman who reminds me a lot of my own dear wife. I know of her family, of course, although we did not socialize being from different parts, but she comes from good stock. I am sure they are going to be happy and I look forward to seeing grandchildren before I die. I had nearly given up on that hope, but now my spirits have been lifted once more, and John and I will have some heirs to leave Greystones to."

"Greystones is the name of your farm?"

"Yes, my wife named it. She was from a town near Dublin in County Wicklow called Greystones and the stones the house is built from reminded her of the granite rocks her town was built on."

Eva and I, together with Martha, Merry, Cephus and Esther helped Tootie clean up and clear away the debris of the wedding. The St. Aubins disappeared, and Faye remained, talking with Mr. Blanchard about politics until the Swanns pulled him into their car still arguing with Faye about the Land Apportionment Act. They seemed to get along well, and he looked almost disappointed when the Swanns said it was time to leave. Faye helped us clear things away.

"What's the matter, Faye? He didn't run away? The Swanns had to pull him away."

"Yes, he must be lonely. I have to admit that he's interesting. I hope I can get to split hairs with him again before he leaves. Did Tony leave already?"

"Yes, he had to return to the Base tonight. It takes him at least four hours to get there. He had to put in for a special pass for the wedding. I do wish this war will stop dragging on so he can become a normal person again."

I returned to the compound tonight feeling somewhat deflated. It has been an exciting day, and the eagerly awaited wedding is over. I had been envisioning a different day than how it has actually turned out. In my mind's eye I saw myself and Tony, arm in arm, chatting happily with wedding guests who would ask us, slyly, if we were going to be next. I'd see Tony look at me from under his long lashes, a lock of his hair falling over his forehead, saying: "I certainly hope so, don't you, Holly?" and I would look at him with an enigmatic smile and say nothing.

Ravaged by doubt and uncertainty, he'd wait until the last guest had left, pull me behind the tent, drop down on one knee and pop the question. Then he'd jump up and pull me into his arms and we'd kiss as passionately—no, more passionately—as our first kiss a week ago.

What I had not foreseen was being left on my own for most of the day, and a brief peck on the cheek and a "See ya!" when it came time for him to leave.

I will cry later tonight, when Eva can't hear me.

CHAPTER 15

Suspicion

Saturday, 16th June
Tony has dropped off the planet again calling me only once this week to tell me he won't be able to see me for several weeks. His motorcycle has developed a problem and he is having trouble finding the right spare part. I wonder why he can't get a ride with someone. People are always sharing rides now that petrol is scarce, and that is how he has visited Bulawayo before. I wish Avril and Neil had offered him one of their two cars, but they haven't, and it is too late now. Gerald is driving the Wolseley and the MG is being used by Avril's parents.

Joan has moved in with Faye. Room Two looks less cluttered already. I have noticed with great delight that Joan's brought a large collection of books, mostly mysteries, and what Mom calls *penny dreadfuls*—cheap gothic romances and thrillers. We have spent companionable evenings sitting in the lounge, cozily wrapped in blankets, reading.

We are now sure Gerald is seeing Ayesha. Eva tells me he often comes into the office and calls Ayesha out into the hallway where they have whispered conversations. I try to mumble some words of comfort and sympathy but Eva shrugs it off and acts as if she doesn't really care.

"I'm glad he's seeing Ayesha. I like her and she's probably the right one for him. I've decided to forget about him and to just enjoy myself. I'm teaching Hattie to ride now. I'm still trying to get her to the point where she doesn't scare the horses. She's too loud sometimes and they don't like that. She also forgets and walks behind them…" The conversation then goes to horses and riding lessons and I don't have the heart to mention Gerald again.

Tootie, on the other hand, doesn't have the same problem. She is scandalized by the news.

"Nanny-chaser!" she spat. "I always knew he was that type. I told Eva that Gerald would break her heart—worthless scum—and she agreed with me!"

Talk to the Moon

I asked her what she meant by nanny-chaser, and she explained that it was a description of men who chased women of color, but she did not use those words. To her, all women who are not white are by definition nannies, fit only to watch white women's children. This description must have included Indian girls.

"Told Robert, I did, they shouldn't hire nannies. Unfortunately she was hired by our predecessor and he had nothing to do with it. That Mrs. Ncuma thinks she's something too. Just because she was one of the first black women to be educated up to high school she thinks she is better than all of us now. Never smiles. Sits there in her office lording it over the white girls. A Reserve nanny," she spat.

I stated in a low, but shocked voice that the only white girl in there, Eva, didn't seem to mind. In fact, she and Mrs. Ncuma got along well, by all accounts. She also happened to like Ayesha.

"Eva's a poor judge of character. Can't see through people, like I do. She won't get far in life with that attitude. Mark my words."

Monday, 25th June

Neil has returned to work from his honeymoon. He looks rested and happy, or as happy as Neil can look. I feel relief—I don't know why—Avril can't have made him miserable already, but I am glad to see he looks well. He asked me to visit Avril at their home. He would take me and Eva there and bring us back again anytime we wanted.

"I don't want my sweetie becoming lonely," he said. "She's used to having people around her and its isolated out there. Her parents returned to Johannesburg today and it won't be long before the isolation becomes too much."

"We would love to and I would also love to hear about your honeymoon!" I blushed immediately. "I-I mean, uh, you know, how Durban was…"

Neil laughed. "I know what you mean. How about this Saturday evening? I'll pick you both up at six then?" I hesitated. What if Tony called me and wanted to see me? Well, then I'd wangle an invitation for him too. No problem.

"Okay, Saturday it is!"

Wednesday 27th June

Tony hasn't called. It's been two weeks since I last heard from him. I am frantic. I don't know how to get hold of him. He has no telephone where he can be reached. I saw Aunt Lalie and Malachi at a prayer meeting this evening, and I asked them if Tony had called them.

"No, my dear, we're not on the phone, you know," said Aunt Lalie, "We really should get a phone, Malachi. Its so awkward being without one. They have party lines available now for our area, you know…" I gripped Lalie's arm and squeezed it, impatient. "But he does send us a postcard every now and then. The last one we got…when was it, Malachi…? Yes, this Monday! From Cape Town, I believe. Or was it Durban…? You know, that place that has those Ricksha boys with the Zulu headwear, the beads and stuff, pulling those carts like donkeys…"

I didn't hear anymore. The world had faded into a whiteout and there was a roaring noise in my head. I took a deep breath and steadied myself on the back of a wooden pew.

What is Tony doing in Durban, for God's sake? Why hadn't he told me he was going? It couldn't possibly have been just a coincidence—the same time Avril was there—something would have been mentioned if it had all been just a hilarious coincidence. And it must have been Durban. Durban was the only place on the whole continent that was famous for its brightly attired Zulu Ricksha's. Then I got a mental grip on myself.

Maybe it was a secret mission for the Air Force. Like the one he had been on in North Africa. Maybe he hadn't had time to tell anyone, and maybe he wasn't supposed to send anyone a card, but he had. His parents after all would worry if they didn't hear from him, wouldn't they? Maybe it would have been too risky to send her one too. And the biggest maybe of all, it was all maybe a grand coincidence that Avril had been on her honeymoon in Durban at the same time.

I laughed at myself with a sense of relief. What was I thinking? That Avril would find time to slip away from her husband of less than a week to see a man who had shown no interest in her; whom she had shown no previous interest in? There has to be an explanation and I am going to find it. Like that motorcycle thing Hattie had seen. How silly!

Saturday, June 30

Avril greeted us like old friends. She showed no signs of loneliness, and took us from room to room to show us all the improvements she had made. We had to admit that she'd done a masterful job in the short week she'd been back. She has begun to paint each room and it already looks quite different to the modest place it had been a few weeks ago. She bought new furniture before the wedding and it's now in place. I thought

Talk to the Moon

it all looked quite expensive but has definitely been worth it. Avril obviously has a talent for decorating. Neil laughed and said he would've been happy with a few cinder blocks and orange crates, but he knew how happy it made Avril to decorate and beautify her surroundings, so he told her to literally 'go to town.' It was well into dinner before the conversation turned to the honeymoon.

"...And we just loved the hotel! They gave us the honeymoon suite and we could step right out of our door onto the beach!"

"Yes, I think I still have sand in my shorts," laughed Neil. "I'm not one for the beach. Too much sand. I'd rather swim in a pool or a lake."

"But you do look rested, both of you," said Eva. "I agree with you about the beach though. It's not for me either."

"Oh, I love the beach," I said, thinking this was the perfect time to do some digging in the sand. "I have always wanted to go to Durban. I hear the beaches are beautiful. In fact, did you know Tony was down there? Did you happen to see him while you were there?" I didn't want them to know that he hadn't told me of his plans and I scrutinized Avril's face as she spoke. Avril smiled as she passed the beans to Eva.

"No, we didn't. What a surprise it would have been. Well, if he was in Durban it was unlikely we would have run into him since we spent the whole two weeks in Umhlanga Rocks—about fifteen miles from Durban. Do you know where he stayed?"

I felt my face grow hot in embarrassment. I hadn't counted on the interrogation turning in this direction.

"Uh, no, he didn't tell me."

Avril smiled.

"Did Tony mention anything to you Neil, about being in Durban?" she purred.

Neil shook his head and looked mystified.

"No. What would he be doing in Durban?" He looked at me.

"I-I don't know. Aunt Lalie told me he was there," I added, my embarrassment growing by the second. I may as well admit I was shooting in the dark, now.

"Well, I wish he had told us!" exclaimed Avril. "We could have all got together for dinner or something."

"Maybe he didn't want to disturb you on your honeymoon," said Eva. "You didn't tell me he was down there, Holly?"

"I-I only just found out," I said, thinking that things now could not possibly get worse even if Avril came out and said that she had secretly met him every day on the beach. I didn't know which was worse—Tony obsessively following Avril or me having to admit he didn't let me in on his plans.

"Well, I'll definitely talk to him about it," said Neil. "We can't have him running all over the place and not letting anyone know. We're all family here and he needs to know that. He's too used to being the bachelor and doing things independently of others. Well, I can relate to that, but I'm learning, aren't I, darling?"

Avril smiled and winked at me.

"Don't be hard on him, *ma Cherie*. He's a sweet boy and I'm sure he thought he was doing the right thing by not telling anybody. Except his parents of course; he did right there. Maybe he thought you'd be too upset if he told you he was going so far away. We know how you feel about Tony and you would have been terribly distressed, my dear."

"Not any more than I am now."

"Well give him hell, then!" laughed Neil. "Sounds like he's been getting away with far too much and is taking you for granted."

"I have to agree with you both," I said. "He does take me for granted, but it's also my fault. He probably thought I would be upset if he told me and he would've been right. But I do wish he'd told me anyway."

The dinner ended on pleasanter conversation and no more was spoken of Tony. I feel a little better and wish I had spoken to Neil privately about the matter instead of bringing up the subject at the dinner table. I am now certain that nothing untoward occurred in Durban between Tony and Avril. He had gone down on a whim and been too afraid to tell me. Am I that bad a person? Did he expect me to sulk and cry? I was quiet as Neil drove us home. I have a lot to think about. My biggest nightmare is turning into my mother. I must watch that.

Sunday, 1st July

The sun has come out in my life again. Today, I walked into church, and who should be sitting in the front row but Tony. I chose a seat right behind him. The emotion I felt was anger; white hot and scorching. I did not hear a word of the sermon and I filled my lungs to capacity with air as I sang, the oxygen fueling the fire I felt within. Tony turned around once during the hymn and looked at me. I didn't miss a note and continued to belt out the words as loud as I could. Tony grimaced and turned around.

Talk to the Moon

He didn't look at me again and I felt the anger continue to rise. I wasn't going to be the genteel lady today. I was going to let him have it; I couldn't wait.

After what felt like hours, the service was over. I pushed my way through the crowd, and out of the door. I wanted to be waiting outside for him. I walked over to a low brick wall surrounding the church and sat down. One by one the congregation filed out until Tony emerged in the rear. He was dressed in his uniform today and looked as good as ever, suntanned and healthy. He spotted me and walked over like a man going to the guillotine.

"Holly! I need to talk to you."

"That's a good looking sun tan, Tony. I can never tan myself. I just turn red like a lobster and then I peel."

"Yeah, well, listen. I'm sorry I didn't tell you about going to Durban. Mom told me she told you I had gone and Neil collared me this morning when I got here. He gave me a real dressing down. Told me I don't deserve you, and he's right. I treat you like shit, Holly..."

I didn't give him a chance to finish. I was going to have my say if I had to gag him to do it. "Tony, if I mean nothing to you, please let me know now and end this farce. You humiliated me beyond what I can describe. Now everyone knows that you didn't tell me you were going to Durban and I can only imagine what they think. 'What kind of person is she that he didn't tell her where he was going and for how long? Why does he need to lie to her?' That's what I want to ask you. Why did you lie? You told me your motorbike was broken and that's why I wouldn't be seeing you for a couple of weeks. I believed you, Tony. What else is there about you I believe and I shouldn't? Can you correct me now if there is anything I believe about you that isn't the truth?"

Tony looked down at his feet, his face reddening as I came to the end of my tirade. I felt a lightening of the body, as if a huge boulder had been lifted off my shoulders. It didn't matter now what he said to me, what ungodly truths came out of his mouth. I had told him the way I felt about his duplicity and suddenly that was all that mattered. He could tell me anything. I couldn't possibly be any angrier than I had been a few minutes ago. He shifted around for a few seconds, put his hands in his pockets, and cleared his throat.

Holly, you're right, absolutely right. I had no right to go off like that and to lie about it. The truth is," he looked up at me, pleading. "The truth is that I did it all on the spur of the moment. A pal of mine was driving down there that weekend and I wanted to get away from the Base for a bit. I thought he was only going for the weekend but when we got there he decided to stay on for a whole week. I had no idea…" I felt a surge of disappointment as he spoke. This feeling was not as pleasant as the anger. I tried to get the anger back but it had already dissipated.

"Tony! You told me when you called that you would not see me for a couple of weeks. Don't you remember? You're tripping yourself up in a web of lies. You knew you would be gone for two weeks. Why didn't you just tell me you were going to Durban and be done with it? Why the lies?"

"I don't know, Holly. I honestly don't know! I've been lying since I was a kid. It comes naturally to me now, and I don't even stop to think about it. My mother catches me out in lies and she gets angry with me but she never could stop me either. I don't need a reason to lie. It just seems the easiest way out of a situation, at the time, and there I go. White lies, big lies, lies of omission, it doesn't matter. I'm sorry that I lied to you. I see now that it has consequences. I don't do it because of the kind of person you are, Holly. You are the kindest, most gentle woman I have ever met. I have no reason to lie to you. I know you would understand if I told you I wanted to go somewhere for some reason. You have a heart on you that other women only wish they had. It hurts me to know how much I hurt you. It wasn't my intention, believe me! Oh, I do wish I could make you believe me. Now that you know I'm a compulsive liar you won't ever believe me again. Holly, please give me another chance. Don't break up with me. I will make a solemn promise now never to lie to you again. If I break it, you can do whatever you like with me. Break up with me, hit me, anything. I won't blame you. Please, just give me another chance."

There was nothing I wanted more in the whole wide world than to give him another chance, but I wasn't going to let him know that. I looked away and pretended to think about it. Let him squirm for a few minutes.

"Take all the time you need, Holly, just don't let me suffer too long. Okay?"

"Well, I suppose we can give it another try. But this time I want some changes, okay?"

"Definitely okay with me!"

"Please call me at least once a week. Tell me exactly what your plans are that involve me. If they don't involve me, such as the Durban trip, then tell me that you are doing something that doesn't involve me and set

Talk to the Moon

my mind at rest so that I am not embarrassed again in front of our friends and your family. You don't need to go into detail but don't let me feel you are hiding something from me. Tony, I don't want to run your life like a drill sergeant. I just want to know that you think enough of me to clue me in once in a while. Okay?"

He nodded. "Yes, that's not unreasonable. I don't know what I was thinking of before. I probably wasn't thinking. It won't happen again, I promise! *Man*, can you sing loudly. I thought my eardrums were going to burst!" We laughed and I felt a warm glow course through my body. I wish Tony had told me he loved me and couldn't bear to lose me, but he hadn't. Maybe it was better that he hadn't since I still can't be sure if he is lying or telling the truth. Only time will tell.

We spent the afternoon together at the mission, talking and laughing. He told me about his trip. He spent the whole time in Durban taking Ricksha rides and sitting on the beach and swimming in the surf. His friend, a fellow officer in the Air Force, had let him share a room and they had done nothing but laze around and eat a lot. He had not seen Avril and Neil, he said, and didn't know where they were staying.

"It's a big place, you know, and I wouldn't have known where to look. Besides, they were on their honeymoon, and three's such a crowd." I laughed and wondered why I had ever thought those terrible things about Tony and Avril. I had such a suspicious nature. Avril was nasty sometimes but she was not capable of the ugly things I had thought about her.

I would make it up to both of them, somehow. I have begun to realize just how much I care for all the people here at the mission, Avril included.

CHAPTER 16

The Ghosh's

4th August, 1945

The end of the war is imminent. Germany surrendered months ago but Japan is still tauntingly tenacious in the Pacific and intent on collective suicide. I'm not worried about Tony anymore. He is talking about leaving the Air Force as soon as peace becomes official and he is looking for an alternate career. We've had many discussions on this subject: I hoped that he would join the mission. I broached the subject once but he wasn't enthusiastic.

"Not enough money in it for me," he said, with a dismissive shrug. "I want something that will pay well with the least amount of effort on my part. True, being a missionary doesn't take that much effort but the pay is equal to the job. What do you think I could do? Sit in an office with Gerald and listen to his drivel, or take up preaching like my Dad and act the hypocrite like he does? No thanks, I'd rather be a sinner and proud of it than be like any of them."

I had no answer for him. He sees all Christians as hypocrites and I wonder if that includes me. I wonder if, as far as I am concerned, he could be right. I do feel as if I have been living a lie all my life—doing what other people expect of me and never because it is something I want to do. I live in fear of inadvertently committing a terrible sin. Why can't I enjoy life like Tony does? Nothing ever seems to weigh on his conscience and I can't imagine him losing sleep over a few drinks or a lie here and there.

He is right about the mission: he'd never fit in. It just isn't his style. Perhaps he'll find a job in Bulawayo and I'll still see him more often.

7th August

This morning we were awakened by a loud banging on the door.

"They've just dropped a bomb on Hiroshima!" Faye yelled, as I opened the door.

"They? Who?"

Talk to the Moon

"The Americans! They have this huge bomb that wiped the whole city out! Can you imagine that? The war will soon be over. The Japanese will never get over this. It's the end of them!"

17th August

It has taken another bomb and another city in Japan to end the war, and today a peace holiday has been declared. We have been given the day off. I have this very strange let down feeling. I have prayed so long for the war to be over so that Tony and I can be together and now it feels anticlimactic. I am a lot less excited than I imagined I would be. Nothing seems to be different. Except for the unexpected holiday its business as usual at the mission.

I am taking the extra time to work on a new dress I bought the material for in June.

15th September

I have not been writing much in my diary lately.

Tony left the Air Force immediately after Japan signed the *Instrument of Surrender* two weeks ago. He said he didn't feel right leaving before that since one never knew what might happen and things might start up again. Now he feels he has done his duty for his country and he can freely become a civilian. He's returned to the farm in Fort Victoria.

I am sad about this although I know there's no chance of him remaining there. He hates farming and calls Fort Vic a hick town. He said it was for business reasons only that he had returned: to encourage Eric to buy him out.

3rd October

Eric has scraped together enough money to buy Tony's share of the farm.

Tony has returned to Bulawayo and seems in no hurry to find a job. He is staying with the elder Swanns and spends a lot of time at the mission with me. When he isn't at the mission, he is over at Avril and Neil's. I am not complaining because I know now that Tony and Neil are good friends. He has every right to spend as much time as he needs winding down from the war. The four of us frequently go out to the movies—Tony now calls them movies like the Americans do and insists we drop the old fashioned word *flicks*--and dinner on the weekends.

I am feeling something approaching respect for Avril, if not love. Avril is a complicated woman and I was so wrong in my first impressions. I feel shame when I think of the suspicions I harbored about Avril and

Tony's relationship. I will do my utmost to make it up to Avril and Tony, and by extension, Neil.

There is one dark cloud in our sky, and that is Eva. She is lonely. Hattie has unexpectedly eloped with a young man no-one knows and who isn't a church member. Eva is devastated.

"Holly, I only met him once, but I already feel as if Hattie has done the wrong thing. I can't imagine what she sees in this boy. He's immature and he drinks. I think she may be pregnant!"

I have misgivings too. Hattie is immature herself and now there are two children bringing another child into the world. I hope that things aren't as bad as they look, but that still doesn't solve the problem of Eva.

Gerald is openly dating Ayesha. No one but Tootie seems to care. Eva confided to me once that she still loves Gerald, but, she said, when you love someone, you only want what is good for them and she felt Ayesha would be good for Gerald. We have both made a point of including Ayesha in all plans that include Gerald. I have never spoken to Ayesha much, and now I am finding hidden depths to this girl I had never noticed.

Ayesha's parents are Hindu, but they have been in Rhodesia for many years, coming over with their own parents as children. Her father's store supplies the Native Reserves with various consumer goods from food basics to clothing and textiles. Eva and I often shop there and speak frequently with the elder Ghosh's. They are a friendly, outgoing couple and they give us both a lot of breaks in prices. They are proud that their daughter works at the mission. It isn't easy for Indian women to get white collar jobs in a European dominated job market. Unless you own your own business, as the Ghosh's do, the job pickings are slim.

Ayesha does not want to help run the store. She feels that her older brother does well in that area and will eventually take over the business from their parents. I wonder if the Ghosh's approve of Ayesha's choice in a boyfriend. I wonder if they even know. Surely they must. Indian women aren't free to date men as they choose. I heard this from Faye. Generally their marriages are arranged.

Saturday morning, 6th October

Today we made our weekly bicycle trip to the store so that Eva could buy some material for a new dress I have offered to make for her. Mr. Ghosh was not in the store, but Mrs. Ghosh was there. She greeted us warmly and offered us each a Coke from the cooler. We accepted it

Talk to the Moon

gratefully. The October sun was warm and our throats were parched with dust from the road.

"Thanks," said Eva. "What do you think of your daughter's new boyfriend?"

It was all I could do not to choke on my Coke in mid-swallow.

"Eva!" I was horrified and embarrassed at Eva's appalling lack of manners. "I'm so sorry, Mrs. Ghosh. Eva didn't mean to say that. It's none of our business. Please just forget anything was said."

Eva looked befuddled.

"Did I say something wrong? I just meant to ask how Mrs. Ghosh liked Gerald. He is my friend too, you know, Mrs. Ghosh. If I said something wrong, please forgive me."

Mrs. Ghosh looked down at her feet and didn't say anything for a long time. I hoped the floor would open up and swallow the lot of us. I glared at Eva.

"No, it's alright. Don't worry about it," Mrs. Ghosh finally replied. She sighed. "I will speak to you about it, but please, never mention it to my husband or son. They are, as I, not happy about the whole business. Unfortunately, Ayesha is strong willed and she has made up her mind. I say let her marry the man if that is what will make her happy. We don't live in India anymore. We must acclimate ourselves to the European customs now and accept that these things can happen. At least we still have our son who is going to marry an Indian girl who is also a Hindu. For that, we can be thankful. If Ayesha wants to marry a Christian, then she must convert to her husband's religion and live as he sees fit. But I don't know that things will ever be the same in our family again."

I was mortified to notice tears slowly making their way down Mrs. Ghosh's cheeks. "Now look what you've done, Eva!" I put my hand over Mrs. Ghosh's.

"I'm so sorry we brought this up. I don't think Eva had any idea of the pain it would cause you." I gave Eva another look that would have pierced a tank, and Eva hung her head.

"Oh, it's not Eva's fault. I am glad I can confide in you. I haven't been able to talk to anyone about this and it's been wearing me down. The subject always causes my husband to get angry and my son refuses to mention it. I've been a buffer between Ayesha and her father and I don't think I can stand it anymore." The tears now flowed freely, and I searched in my bag for a handkerchief. Fortunately, I had one.

Eva shot me a triumphant look.

"Well, you can talk about it with us any time, Mrs. Ghosh. Can't she, Holly?"

I gave her the back of my shoulder. We stayed with Mrs. Ghosh much longer than we had planned on being at the store but finally the tears ended and we were able to make our purchases and leave.

As soon as we were out of earshot I launched into a tirade. I told Eva what I thought of her tactlessness and rudeness. Eva responded loudly that she was the kind of person who said what was on her mind and there was nothing wrong with that. The argument got more heated as we pedaled back to King's Kraal. By the time we reached the compound we weren't speaking. We put away our bikes in silence, and I dumped the material Eva had picked out on the table, saying, "Make your own dress," and then sat down on my bed and pretended to read. Eva gave a snort and marched out, slamming the door behind her.

This evening, after I had cooled off in the rondavel, Eva and I made up and are speaking to each other again. I realize that I've been the childish one. Eva is blunt and tactless to be sure but she is not malicious. I feel I ought to recognize that by now but it is so embarrassing to be caught flat footed like that. My own anger, I feel, arises from a desire not to offend; to never stir the pot. Eva habitually stirs things up and seems oblivious to any emotional turbulence in her wake. I am always careful with my words, weighing each one before parting with them. Eva just opens her mouth and allows whatever is rattling around inside her head to tumble out. Eva was forgiving, though, and when I apologized to her at dinner, she genuinely seemed surprised that an apology was needed.

"What for? Oh, that! Never mind, Holly. You had your say and I can appreciate that. You are still going to make my dress, aren't you?"

I laughed, and we both ended up laughing—snorting loudly, as Merry, a disapproving and head shaking presence, hovered in the doorway.

CHAPTER 17
Majozi

Late evening, 13th October
Another bomb shell has fallen on the mission. Tony broke the news to me today over a plate of stuffed grape leaves and a bottle of *retsina* at Nick's café.

"Did Avril tell you that she and Neil are moving to Greystones?"

"What! You must be joking."

"Oh no, my dear, as serious as a heart attack. Neil has put his resignation in to the mission. They're leaving the end of November."

"B-but Neil…! He loves the mission! It's just inconceivable he would want to return to Greystones. What brought this on?"

Tony shrugged.

"It's Avril. She's bored and she won't return to the mission. Says that she never did enjoy working there and she's not going to spend the rest of her life in this hell hole. Can't blame her. So she gave Neil an ultimatum. She's pregnant, by the way. Told him she wasn't going to raise any child of hers in the middle of nowhere. It was Salisbury or she was leaving. So he compromised and said they could return to the farm. She accepted."

The double bombshell has left me feeling confused. Avril pregnant? Avril and Neil leaving? I don't know whether to be happy or sad. I also feel disappointment that Avril has not told me the news herself. We have become quite good friends lately and I have confided many things to Avril that only Faye and Tony know about. It has now occurred to me that Avril rarely, if ever, confides in anyone. She's always a good, sympathetic listener, asking just the right questions and always knowing what to say, but she never reveals her own innermost feelings or fears. She never discusses her family or her past, and now, she has not discussed the pregnancy or the move with anyone other than Tony.

"Well, I'm thrilled Avril's going to have a baby but really sad they are leaving. I just got used to having them around and I know I'll miss them."

"Oh, you'll go up to Greystones to visit. If I know Avril she'll have a lot of visitors coming and going. She needs people around her. Not the mission types, but you're an exception: you, Faye and Eva. We'll go up there for a visit once they get settled."

"What about Mr. Blanchard? How will he feel about the move?"

"He's thrilled, apparently. He's wanted Neil to do this for years now and Avril is the only one who has been successful in convincing him it's the right thing. He'll be as happy as a pig in a mud puddle."

I didn't care for that metaphor—I feel Neil's father deserving of more respect but as usual I didn't say anything.

"As for Neil," continued Tony, "He'll miss the doctoring and the mission, I'm sure, but he'll get used to the life. Avril will make sure of that."

"Yes, I know how much he loves this mission. It's going to be hard on him." Then I smiled. "Maybe once the baby comes he'll be too busy to think about King's Kraal. Maybe he'll open up his own clinic at Greystones. That would be wonderful!" I was briefly lost in a daydream of Neil's African Clinic—farm laborers bringing their wives and children in for treatment, Avril smilingly assisting as a fat cheeked boy gurgled happily from a nearby crib…

"Penny for your thoughts!" laughed Tony.

"Oh, you don't want to know!" We changed the subject to Tony's hunt for a job.

"I applied for a job today. It looks promising."

"Where?"

"It's an Import-Export firm, importing mainly farm equipment and exporting grain and so on. They seemed interested in my farming background and asked me to come back for another interview with the Big Cheese next week. What interests me in this job is that I will be traveling a lot—going overseas. That's if I get it. They're looking for someone single who likes to travel. That's me!" He grinned.

I once again felt the sensation of my heart making its now familiar way down to my shoes. This time it did not seem to want to come back up. I looked down at my plate and my eyes began to blur. *Bloody hell*! Did I always have to tear up! He hadn't got the job yet, and with luck, he wouldn't get it. Perhaps I could call them and tell them he wasn't suitable…no, that wasn't the kind of thing I could do. I stuffed a mouthful of rice and lamb into my mouth and chewed. It tasted like cotton. I continued to stuff and chew until the lump in my throat went away.

"Well, what do you have to say?" asked Tony, not appearing to notice my sudden preoccupation with my food.

"I think that's wonderful, Tony. I wish you luck."

He smiled and picked up his glass of *retsina*.

"Here's to me, then. Bottoms up!"

I forced a smile and picked up my cup of tea and drank.

2nd November

Faye has remarked that the brouhaha at King's Kraal over the resignation of Neil was Edward and Wallis Simpson all over again. She hadn't seen anything like it since the abdication. Tootie is shaken. Face pale, she slumps around the mission like a slowly deflating balloon. Everyone is sure that the real problem lies in the fact that Avril had not informed her, either, of the news. She heard it third hand from her husband who heard it from the Church Board in Salisbury.

A requisition has been put in for a new doctor. The official statement was that "for personal reasons" Dr. Blanchard would be resigning his post at King's Kraal to return to Salisbury. The more unofficial version is the rumor circulating around the mission that Blanchard senior is ailing and needs Neil to take over the farm as soon as possible. I know this is not true but I have kept quiet about what I feel is the truth: the pregnancy and that it had all been Avril's decision from the start.

Some good news: A dispirited Tony called this week and he did not get the Import-Export job. I did my best to keep the joy out of my voice:

"I am so sorry, Tony," I lied. "Maybe that job was not meant for you, but I just know that you will get something. You will find the job that you are looking for." I felt like a hypocrite. He said he was still looking and had several more prospects lined up. I wished him luck and truly meant it that time.

"I'm driving into the Reserve next week to see the Native Commissioner. I hear he has a job opening for a Field Officer to serve a 100,000 hectare tribal area that isn't too far from the mission."

My heart did a somersault and I made a small exclamation of delight.

"Tony! That is wonderful! I do hope you get it."

"Yeah," he said, but his voice was lacked energy. "I don't know if I have the right qualifications. It depends how desperate they are, and of course, how desperate I am. Inspecting cattle for tsetse fly infestation is not what I had in mind. But I'll go and talk to him. It couldn't hurt."

I didn't think it would hurt at all and neither would a prayer or two as insurance. I don't care if he finds a job picking fat ticks off cattle; I just want him to be nearby.

I saw Avril at the mission shortly after hearing the news about the move from Tony. Unable to hold my curiosity in any longer I decided to broach the subject.

"I hear you're pregnant?"

There was something to be said for imitating Eva's blunt approach—it worked. Avril didn't look surprised or offended, however. She smiled.

"Well, news gets around quickly! I wasn't planning on telling everyone just yet, but yes, I am!"

"Oh Avril, I'm so thrilled for you!" We spent the next hour talking about babies, what we hoped it would be—Avril wanted a boy—and thinking up names. I almost forgot to ask Avril about the move.

"So I hear you and Neil are going to Greystones?"

"I would rather we brought a child up there than here," said Avril. "Our house is so remote and I have no nearby neighbors that I can ask for help if anything happens. I don't even have a phone, for God's sake." I thought this made sense, but then I wondered how many people would be at hand on Greystones—young mothers with children, for example. I decided not to pursue the thought and let it drop. Avril and Neil had their reasons and they should remain private.

Bulawayo and its surroundings are not the most exciting places; especially for someone like Avril. There is a joke circulating that Bulawayo is half the size of a New York City graveyard but twice as dead. Perhaps a thriving tobacco farm would attract more interesting people than a mission. I am not surprised to feel a fleeting stab of envy. I too wonder how it would be to live in a place where interesting people came and went all the time, where money was not a problem and where you could entertain and be entertained by the cream of society on a regular basis. I think Avril knows exactly what she is doing. It has nothing to do with the child. If I was honest about my own feelings I think I would want the same thing for myself.

It's all very well to say that I will be happy anywhere as long as I am with the one I love but things have a way of changing. Soon, I would want more, and solitude would no longer be as attractive as it had once seemed.

Talk to the Moon

Monday, 5th November

Tony came to pick me up on his motorcycle today to go to the Reserve. I had taken the afternoon off and was looking forward to meeting the Native Commissioner. I am now used to riding on Gloria's back pillion and no longer feel the terror I first experienced. I also dressed better for the occasion, wearing a scarf around my head and sunglasses instead of the goggles.

The afternoon was sultry; the gun-metal sky an incubator for dark, looming storm clouds. A small breeze carried from far horizons the promise of raindrops falling on a distant and dusty plain.

"Don't worry, it won't rain on us today!" yelled Tony above Gloria's roar. I don't know how he could tell, but he has a knack for reading the weather. If he says it isn't going to rain then I can rest assured that it won't. The rainy season is threatening in its closeness.

We rode for what seemed like endless miles over a road that was little more than a track. The motorcycle had to slow down to a crawl in many places and when we came to washed out, dry gullies across the road we had to dismount, pushing Gloria through on foot. Potholes and broken tree branches impeded our progress in other places but we finally arrived at a small African village.

Our arrival had been telegraphed and we found most of the villagers had gathered outside their huts and I felt curious eyes examining our every move. Small children thronged excitedly around Gloria as we dismounted. They laughed and chattered with delight as they dared each other to touch her shiny chrome work. I felt quite excited myself. This was the first time I have been in a native village off the mission. I have seen many of them from a distance as we sped past on the main road to Bulawayo or insulated within the wood and metal confines of a train. I have always wanted to stop and visit but it has never been possible for me to do so. Now I was here, in a real village with real people forming curious clusters around me. I wished I could speak their language. Why, oh why, hadn't I learned? Tony had no problem: he is fluent in several African dialects including Shona and Sindebele. He talked with an old man who drew directions in the sand with a long stick.

"That was the head man," he explained as we got back on Gloria. "He was showing me how far it was to the Native Commissioner's Office. It's not far to go now, we're almost there."

"Thank God, My bum aches!"

Soon a white building appeared, nestled in a small hollow between two kopjes, then another. A signpost read Native Commissioner. A Land Rover and a rusty, ancient Overland lorrie were parked outside. We dismounted and walked up a small path between carefully planted hibiscus shrubs. The soft scent of a nearby frangipani tree wafted towards me and I stopped and plucked a waxy white flower and put it in my buttonhole. Tony opened the door to the small building and we found ourselves in a cramped office lined with bookcases, framed photographs and faded diplomas. A desk overflowing with papers and books stood in the center of the room. Behind the desk sat a man dressed in a khaki shirt and shorts. He stood up as we entered and stuck out his hand.

"Mr. Swann?"

Tony nodded. "Yes, sir, I am Tony Swann. I hope I am not late. The road was worse than I had thought. This is my friend, Holly Morgan from King's Kraal Mission."

"Aah! Pleased to meet you Miss Morgan. I'm Nigel Withers, the Native Commissioner—obviously! Have a seat, have a seat. Would you like some tea?" Without waiting for an answer, he yelled "Julius! Three cups, Julius. Now…yes…let's see." He shuffled through some papers on his desk.

He was a plump man in his middle years with graying salt and pepper hair, and I noticed his gooseberry-eyed gaze traveling up and down my legs, lingering at my waist, and coming to rest on my chest area. I felt clammy and shivered as if cold eels had slithered over my body. My face went hot and I looked down.

"Well, Mr. Swann," he finally said. "Tell me about yourself."

Tony launched into a lengthy description of his previous employment experience: a lifetime of hands-on experience in farming—cattle in particular—and how knowledgeable he was about growing crops like maize, millet and wheat. I thought he made it sound as if farming was really his first love.

He then went on to describe his Air Force employment, how invaluable he had been in the administrative field, and his skill at keeping track of every piece of equipment that had come his way. I was impressed. I was sure I would have hired him on the spot!

He went into great detail about how, during the war, he had been sent to Birmingham for training and later to North Africa to move equipment and supplies and, although he had enjoyed his year in Birmingham, the

Talk to the Moon

desert had been another story. He told Withers amazing stories that I hadn't even heard yet.

Withers and I were spellbound as he related anecdote after anecdote about the difficulties he had personally experienced—the unrelenting heat, the Bristol Blenheim that had almost crashed with him in it, the sand getting into every piece of equipment and machinery, and men down with dysentery. Withers seemed impressed. He asked a lot of questions and made notes on a sheet of paper, and by then we had each drunk a cup of weak, luke-warm tea and the interview was over.

"I'm pleased to see you are still single," he said, as we stood up to leave. "This job doesn't offer much in the way of amenities for the married man. We have single quarters nearby, where I stay—I'm also single by the way"—and his gaze came to rest on my chest again—"But if you and the young lady did decide to tie the knot I am sure something could be arranged." I felt my face turn red again.

"We're just friends," muttered Tony, almost under his breath. My throat tightened. So that's all he thought about me? Just a friend? And he couldn't even say that with any passion! Mr. Withers looked pleased. At last we were saying our good-byes and Withers told Tony that he would be hearing from the Native Department shortly.

"I'll put in a word, you know. That will go a long way."

Tony looked as if he didn't care.

Silent, I climbed back onto the motorcycle. I wondered if I had a right to expect anything more than friendship from Tony. He had, after all, made no promises or given me any reason to think that I could ever be more than a friend. I was lost in thought as we pulled into the native village once more, stopping under the shade of a large mahobahoba tree.

"There's an old *nganga*—witchdoctor to you—named Majozi I want to see. I hear he's a wiz on the bone throwing stuff. Perhaps he can give me some ideas where to look for a job."

I was intrigued. I had always secretly been fascinated with mysticism and the occult but this tendency had been vigorously discouraged and suppressed by Mom and the church. Anna had rooted out and destroyed every book she could find that contained any mention of the occult in my possession. She had forbidden the subject to be discussed in our home, calling it 'the devil's work.'

We walked through the village, escorted by the headman, toward a hut set back from the rest of the village in a thicket of acacia trees. The hut was much like the others, square, with a thatched roof and brown and ochre pole and *daga* walls. Drying herbs hung under the eaves of the roof and bleached skulls of various animals lay here and there on the ground in front of the hut. A neat, stone lined path led up to a door hung with animal skins. The headman clapped his hands outside the door and upon receiving a reply from the unseen occupant within stuck his head respectfully through the doorway, saying something in Sindebele. Then he motioned for Tony to go in and disappeared back down the path to the village.

"You wait out here," said Tony. "I won't be long."

"Oh, Tony, please ask him if he will throw the bones for me too!"

Tony looked surprised, but said "Ok, I will," and disappeared into the blackness of the hut. I waited for what seemed like ages, but was probably only ten minutes, until Tony reappeared. He didn't look pleased.

"Ugly old fake!" he spat. "You're next."

"Does he speak English? What if he doesn't?"

"Oh, he speaks English well. He was probably educated at Oxford."

I laughed and pulled the skins aside. The hut's interior was dark after the bright sunlight. It smelled smoky and there was an odor of what could have been herbs. A small fire surrounded by stones glowed dimly in the center of the hut. There seemed to be nowhere for the smoke to go except out a small window, and I felt my eyes tearing up.

On a large zebra skin in a dark corner sat an old man in an animal skin loincloth and a necklace of what looked like bones or teeth. His feet were bare. He motioned for me to sit on a low, hand-hewn wooden stool nearby. It didn't look as if it would take my weight but I sat down carefully. I felt awkward and didn't know where to put my feet so stuck them straight out in front of me.

"Good afternoon," I said.

Majozi ignored my greeting and picked up an animal skin pouch.

"Was that your friend that just came in?"

"Yes." I was surprised to hear how good Majozi's English was.

"He called me some names, I suppose."

I smiled. I didn't know what to say.

"What is your question?" he asked.

I was taken aback. I didn't know I was supposed to have a question. I had just thought he would throw bones, tell me something general, and that would be that.

Talk to the Moon

"Oh! Uh, well, okay then....ah...I suppose all I want to know is how my friend out there feels about me!" I had not prepared myself to confide to a strange old Ndebele healer my innermost desires, but he did not react in anyway and neither did he look surprised. He merely shook out from within the bag some flat bones intricately carved with twisted whorls and animal shapes onto the zebra skin. After a minute he silently gathered them up and put them back into the bag. He threw the bones a second time, and a third. Finally, he spoke.

"Your question has been answered."

I waited.

"Yes?"

"That is all."

"You aren't going to tell me what the answer is?"

"No."

"Why?"

"You will know soon enough. If I tell you now, you will not believe me. I will tell you one thing. Be careful of those around you. You cannot trust everyone. The one you thought was a good friend is not a friend. That one is a crocodile. That is all I will tell you."

I looked at him in disbelief. Who was the friend? It couldn't be Tony, could it? No, he had refused to say anything about Tony. I couldn't just leave with more questions than I had arrived with. I tried again.

"Can you tell me who the friend is?"

"It's a woman."

"Can you tell me more?"

"No. Go now."

I sighed and slowly rose.

"Should I pay you?"

He looked up. His wizened face was expressionless. His eyes were cloudy white. It was only then I realized that the old man was as blind as an earthworm. Of course...that's why Tony had called him a fake. How could he possibly have seen the bones? He was just guessing! I felt relieved. Now I wouldn't have to worry about an unknown, traitorous friend.

"Give the children some money or sweets," he said.

"I will be happy to do that," I replied, and meant it. At least he wasn't extorting money from gullible people. I came out of the hut blinking in the bright sunlight. Tony was sitting on a nearby rock waiting for me.

"Well, how did it go?"

"Just as you said, he's an old fake alright. Had me going for a while though!"

Tony chuckled.

"Me too, until I realized he couldn't see those bloody bones! What a waste of our time. I can't believe there are some people around here who think he's the greatest thing since Houdini. He's a trickster, alright, but nowhere near Houdini's league." We laughed, and I felt in my pockets for some coins I had taken with me just in case. As the children gathered around, I gave them each sixpence or a *tickie*—threepence—and their cries of delight followed us down the dirt track as they ran after us until they were lost in Gloria's dust.

"What did you go and do that for!" yelled Tony. "Now they'll mob me every time I go through that damn village!"

Tonight, I told Faye about the old *nganga*. As I came to the part about his blind eyes, Faye smiled.

"Yes, I know old Majozi. He's had cataracts for years now and refuses all treatment. He could see quite well up to a few years ago but now he's completely lost all sight. I've had him throw the bones for me several times."

"Why, if he can't see?"

"It doesn't matter. You see, this is what he told me. He said that he never used his eyesight anyway. Eyes are for nonbelievers, he said, and so are the bones. He said that he always knows what the bones are saying because the *amadlozi*, the ancestors, tell him. He says he sees more without his eyes than we see with ours."

"What do you think he meant about me not being able to trust a certain woman? Do you think I should believe that?"

"I can't tell you what you should or shouldn't believe. I just know that everything he has told me has been right on the money. He's a strange old man and it's difficult to tell just what is happening inside his head. He's definitely in another world, one that we don't understand. Don't discount that world. It works for his people and they think highly of him."

"I do wish I knew why he wouldn't tell me about Tony!"

Faye smiled. I think he wants you to figure it out yourself. Like he said, would you have believed him if he had?

I laughed.

"You've got a point. He seems to understand people well. I wonder what he told Tony."

"Somehow, I don't think you will ever know," said Faye.

CHAPTER 18

Greystones

10th November
The Christmas holidays are coming up and Mom wants us to come home for Christmas. We feel as if we ought to but we don't want to. We still remember the last Christmas we spent at home. The train trip is long and the fares much more than we can afford right now.

Avril and Neil have left for Greystones. Tootie got over her snit long enough to organize a huge going away party and the whole mission and nearly everyone in the Bulawayo congregation turned out. Everyone helped with the food and there were more guests than anyone had seen at the mission since the wedding. Every person seemed genuinely sad that Neil was leaving. I am not surprised to find that not too many people wept at Avril's departure but I know that I will miss Avril.

Avril has received a lot of help from mission people in packing up. They couldn't afford a packing company so packed their own things and had it freighted by train to Salisbury where they would use a farm truck to take everything to Greystones. Avril was very excited before they left:

"We'll be using the guest house for now," she told us as we wrapped kitchen utensils, pots, pans and dishes in newspaper and then placed them in big cardboard boxes. "You would think he would have given us the big house, wouldn't you? But it's in terrible shape so it's just as well. It will take years to fix up the main house. I never realized just how far he had let it go." By he I assumed she meant Neil's father.

"Well he's a widower, Avril. Have you ever seen a man who knows how to decorate? I think if we just left them to their own devices they'd all still be living in caves."

We spent a cheerful afternoon sharing amusing stories about men as we packed, as Faye and I watched Avril to make sure she didn't lift anything heavier than a teacup. I felt I couldn't have cared more if it had been me having the baby.

12th November

Talk to the Moon

Gerald and Ayesha have announced their engagement. Gerald has bought Avril's car and it is rumored Gerald is teaching Ayesha to drive. Eva and Ayesha have become closer friends now that Hattie is not available. She and her new husband, 'Speedy' Scheepers, have moved to Queen's Mine where he has a job. No one knows what Speedy's real name is but it is obvious to me now how he arrived at that name.

The last time we saw Hattie was shortly after she and Speedy eloped. She had persuaded Speedy to make a trip to the mission while they were in Bulawayo visiting her parents. He is a sullen and inarticulate boy with spotty skin. In spite of a liberal application of *Brylcream* his colorless hair spikes, defiant, from a scarred skull that looks as if it had once been used as a battering ram. He sat silently in the car while she visited with Eva and honked his horn impatiently when he decided she had visited long enough. She looked happy; her skin was glowing and she hadn't lost any of her bubbly nature. If anything, it seemed more pronounced, as if to make up for the lack of *joie de vivre* in her husband.

3rd December

Tony called to tell me the news: he has been accepted for the Field Officer job. My prayers have been answered. God must not be punishing me for anything lately!

He did not sound as enthusiastic about it as I but he said it would tide him over until he could find something better. The only dark cloud on my horizon is that he has to return to Salisbury for training before he actually starts the job. He will be gone over the holidays! Since Eva and I haven't made any plans, perhaps we'll be able to get together for Christmas or New Year's.

7th December

Today I received an unexpected phone call from Avril.

"*Ma Cherie*! I miss you all so much! I have invited Tony over to the farm for Christmas and he mentioned that you and Eva don't have plans yet. Darling, this farm is enormous. The main house, although falling down, can accommodate plenty of guests. Please, please say you and Eva will come to Greystones for Christmas and the New Year?"

I feel that God is outdoing himself. Tony and I would be together for the holidays. I enthusiastically accepted and we are making plans to take the train to Salisbury on the Saturday morning of December 22nd returning on the 5th of January. Eva is just as excited as I am. She has not been looking forward to staying at the mission and has been thinking of postponing her leave until something interesting came along. She has already taken her suitcase out and begun packing. It's frustrating since I'm always falling over the thing planted in the middle of the floor. Clothes are strewn across her bed and she's constantly emptying drawers looking for items she wants to pack.

"For heaven's sake, Eva, we still have two more weeks! I can't imagine why you've started packing already."

"I'm trying to get organized," answers Eva, "How else can I tell what I'm going to take with me?"

"I pack one day before I go anywhere. That's all the time anyone needs."

"Yes, but you know exactly where everything is and what you've got. I don't have a clue."

That is the truth. Eva's drawers and closets are a mess. Esther tries her best but she can't keep up with Eva's haphazard lifestyle. The neat clothes, so carefully ironed and folded by Esther, are now crumpled and squashed back into drawers this way and that. Esther cries and asks me to please ask her to be more careful, and Eva promises that it will never happen again, but the next day the drawers are pulled out again with even more clothes lying on the floor.

20th December

Esther is moping a lot lately. It isn't just Eva's disorganized ways. Martha has left with Avril and Faye has found another maid from the Reserves who is much older than Martha and recently been widowed. Rather than join the family of her brother-in-law with diminished wifely status she decided to find employment and support herself and her children. Faye, impressed with her independence, hired her on the spot.

I wonder if we should take Esther with us to visit her sister. We can afford the train ticket if Esther travels third class. I feel bad about that but know that we can't afford the price of another second class fare. I will call Avril to ask her opinion.

21st December

I called Avril today to ask if I could bring Esther with us tomorrow.

"I think it's a wonderful idea, Holly. Yes, please bring Esther. I notice Martha has been down in the mouth herself since we got here. She doesn't speak any Shona and she hasn't made any friends. She keeps to herself a lot. I brought her with me because we are so used to each other. It takes a long time to train another maid to Martha's capabilities. Esther can stay with her in the servant's quarters. There's plenty of room. It would cheer them both up."

We asked Esther if she wanted to go and visit Martha at Greystones and she was overcome with joy. She has rarely been outside of the reserve, never further than Bulawayo, and she has never traveled by train before. She has no comprehension of the distance that is now between herself and her sister and she must feel as if they're separated from each other by an infinite gulf—almost as if her sister has been removed from the surface of the earth. To her, Salisbury is a big city somewhere far away and it has no more geographical meaning to her than London or Tokyo.

She has now begun to help Eva sort through her clothes instead of complaining that Eva is undoing her work. She and Eva spend hours going through each item of clothing; discussing each one in detail as to its merits and drawbacks.

"No, Miss Eva, this is not good for Salisbury. It's good for Bulawayo, yes, but you must have something better. How about this dress here? I will pack it for you myself." Esther knows how it would look if Eva packed it.

"I think this blouse is fine for Christmas. No, not that one. It's too small for you. It will fit me! Oh, thank you, Miss Eva! I will wear it on Christmas…" And so it goes. The bedroom now looks tidier with clothing put away and suitcases stacked out of the way. Everyone is happy.

Everyone, that is, except Tootie. The mission is emptying out over Christmas. Her daughter has arrived to spend the Christmas holidays at home. I have met the daughter, Regan, a couple of times when she has been home for the school holidays. She is a sulky looking ten year old. Her mother dotes on her, buying her all the best dresses and toys. Once, she had proudly shown Eva and I Regan's room. Dolls and stuffed animals sit on every available surface. One can barely see the floor for toys, puzzles and games. This child has more possessions than Marie Antoinette. She is an only child and Tootie has no-one else to lavish her maternal feelings on. Regan is right in the path of runaway, unadulterated adoration. It must be difficult: almost as bad as its opposite—extreme neglect.

Tootie is not happy that she will not be able to invite all of her favorite people over for Christmas. She doesn't think of Faye and Gerald as people. I suggested Joan and Josh. Tootie didn't look enthusiastic, but apparently she couldn't think of any reason not to ask them. They may not thank me for my suggestion. I hope they have already planned something else.

I stopped by the school site this afternoon to see how it was coming along. Most of the walls are up and rafters being laid for the roof. Josh came over as soon as he saw me. He always looks happy to stop whatever he is doing and talk to me. I told him of my plans for Christmas and asked what he was doing.

"I'll spend Christmas here. It's too far for me to go home. I don't know anyone in Fort Vic who'd want to invite me and South Africa is a long ways away. My mother has remarried some old chap I've never met—my parents were divorced long before my father died—and my brothers and sisters all have their own families and lives."

"How many brothers and sisters do you have?"

"Two sisters and four brothers," he replied.

"Wow. A big family. It must have been interesting to have all those brothers and sisters!"

"Well, I don't really know. My parents divorced when I was young and we were farmed out to various relatives as children. I don't even know my brothers and sisters that well. My mother worked like a galley-slave just to make enough money to send to the relatives for our upkeep. My father was a drunk. He was no use at all. I left my aunt and uncle's farm at sixteen and joined the mines as an apprentice. They taught me all I know about carpentry and building, then I got my Master Builder's license at age nineteen, and that's when I married. My wife and I had a son by the time I was twenty and we were divorced the following year. It wasn't a marriage made in heaven. Now you know all there is to know about me."

I didn't know what to say. I have never heard him discuss his private life at all and know nothing about his background. This is an entirely unexpected development and all I asked was what he was doing for Christmas!

Nevertheless, I feel pleased that Josh thinks enough of me to confide in me. I never realized what a hard life he must have had. In fact, a year ago I thought Eva and I were the only people in the world with an unpleasant family situation. Now I wonder if there is anyone who comes from a normal family, whatever a normal family is.

"Tell me about your son," I asked. At least that was safe ground.

Talk to the Moon

"His name is Ian. He turned four in November but I haven't seen much of him. I saw him briefly when I went home for Dad's funeral, but the wife didn't let him stay long. I believe her parents take care of him most of the time, but she still gets the money."

"Oh, that's too bad. Well, I hope Ian is benefiting from it in spite of your misgivings. Maybe his grandparents are seeing to that."

"I doubt it," sniffed Josh. "They spoiled Jillian and now they're probably spoiling my son. They are more than likely paying for his upkeep out of their own pockets while she spends my money on jewelry and clothes."

"Well, as long as someone is doing it, and he's safe and healthy, that's what matters."

"Yes, you're right. I still worry about him though. What choice did I have? I couldn't bring him with me even if I had custody. I have to work every day and wouldn't feel right leaving him with servants all the time. No, a child needs its mother even if the mother isn't perfect."

"I actually stopped by to warn you—you will more than likely be getting a royal summons to the Parrish residence for Christmas dinner. If you want to go, fine, but if you don't, you will now have time to think up a likely excuse."

Josh smiled. "I do appreciate that. Hell, I might just go. Our cook will have the day off and I don't care for my own cooking much. But it wouldn't be the first time I've had bully-beef and baked beans on Christmas day!"

I don't think Avril will be serving bully-beef or baked beans and I wish we could take Josh with us. I feel so sad that he will be spending Christmas either alone or at the Parrish's—which adds up to the same thing.

I feel bad for Faye too. Gerald at least has Ayesha, even if he isn't going to be invited to her home since they didn't celebrate Christmas, but Faye and Josh have no one. There was nothing I can do about it now. I will think about them on Christmas day but it will be difficult to enjoy myself knowing my friends are alone.

Saturday a.m. 22nd December

Faye took us to the station and we are now on the train. The train is slow. It's hard to stay awake as it groans and creaks down the track, stopping lengthily at hamlets with names like Shangani, Somabula, and Que Que. Eva is sleeping.

Later this evening:
Neil was at the station, alone, to meet us.

"Avril sends her apologies for not coming into Salisbury with me to meet you, but I don't think it's advisable for her to make long trips at this stage of her pregnancy. We had a scare a few days ago, but everything is fine now."

We are relieved to hear that. It would have been difficult cramming the five of us and the luggage into the car anyway.

"My father sends his apologies too, he's in Salisbury on farm business but he'll be back at Greystones by tomorrow evening. We're also expecting Tony tomorrow, so you girls will only be alone for one night in that big house."

We drove down a long dirt road after getting off the main road from Salisbury, going through several gates, over a bridge and down a dark avenue of large shady trees before stopping in front of a bright-lit house. Like many houses in this part of the world it is a solid, granite stone house with a thatch roof and an enormous stone columned verandah that runs down three sides. Avril came out of the house and hugged us both.

"It's so good to see you again! It hasn't been long, I know, but it feels like months already. Please forgive me for not driving into Salisbury with Neil. He wouldn't allow me to do it. He's so protective he won't even let me ride horses anymore!"

"Well we don't blame him! We're just happy to see you and we'll have plenty of time to talk."

I have never seen Avril look more beautiful. Her skin glows and her figure, although slightly rounded at the waist, is as slim as ever. She isn't even wearing maternity clothes yet. Neil brought our suitcases up the front verandah stairs and led us into the house.

"The guest house is too small for everyone so we're bunking all our guests in the main house with Dad. I hope the roof doesn't leak on you! This house needs a lot of work."

It's a charming yet unaffected house with red polished cement floors and heavy black rafters. The house is lit with paraffin *Tillie* lamps that hiss and sputter as insects of all shapes and sizes fly pell-mell into the glowing wicks. Large, cobwebby metal chandeliers still holding ancient candle remnants hang from the rafters. In the living room, there's an enormous stone fireplace that looks big enough to roast an ox on a spit and kudu and impala horns hang here and there on the white-washed stone walls. This must be exactly how the house looked when Neil's mother was still alive.

Esther and Martha are elated to see each other again and I feel happy that we have brought Esther. Avril and Neil led us down a long corridor, down one wing, that seems to go on forever. Spooky shadows fell onto the walls, making us look like a party of hobgoblins skulking our way around darkened, rock-walled catacombs.

Eva and I each have a room to ourselves. We've never had that luxury before. Even at college we always shared our rooms with at least one other person. The rooms are large and airy with big French doors leading onto the verandah. There are no lamps in the rooms but there are plenty of candles. It is difficult to write by candlelight but I am getting used to it.

The bathroom is at the end of a long sooty hall and the guttering candles flicker like faint fireflies as we walk back and forth down the tunnel. The bath water trickles out of antiquated taps, rust-brown and tepid.

I don't know how I'll sleep tonight. When I blow out the candles, as I will have to do soon, I know it will be as black as the inside of a tar-barrel and the unfamiliar creaks, squeaks and rustles along the rafters and in the thatch make me wonder just what is creeping around up there.

CHAPTER 19

Avril has Plans and Tony Dreams

Sunday, 23rd December
During the daylight everything looks much different. The house is friendlier but I can now see what Avril means by falling down. Pinholes of sunlight pierce the thatch in many places, and the concrete floors are cracked and sunk, making walking hazardous. Eva and I are sitting in the living room by a crackling fire. Earlier, we ate breakfast from a mahogany sideboard that held large silver serving platters and chafing dishes of bacon, kidneys, scrambled eggs, grilled tomatoes and toast. We're overwhelmed. This is all just for us? It's enough to feed ten people! We tried to do justice to the food, but it was too much, and we don't like kidneys anyway.

The fire is warm and friendly and although it looks like it is going to be a warm day outside the interior of the house is still chilly. There is no sign of Avril, Neil or Tony, so we have decided to look around the house and grounds for ourselves.

After Lunch:

This morning as we began our exploration, two large brown dogs with ridges down their backs got up lazily from the verandah and followed us.

Steps from the long verandah lead to a circular driveway and a weedy, overgrown area with rocks and haphazard bricks that mark what looks like the remains of old pathways. Wild rosebushes peek out from between the waist-high weeds, competing with bushes of red-spined seed pods and large lobed leaves that seem to flourish nearly everywhere here. I recognize them as the ever-present African Castor Bean plant.

As we walked down the driveway we noticed a rectangular depression down what may have been the center of the garden.

"That used to be a fish pond."

Startled, we turned. Avril was right behind us.

"Good morning!" she chirped. "It's good to see you up and about already. Yes, that hole in the ground was a pond, filled with tropical water lilies and carp. This used to be a beautiful place. Neil's mother did it all and he said it was the most talked about garden in the area. I'm going to restore it as it used to be.... *Get the hell out of here!*"

We both jumped as Avril aimed a kick at one of the dogs and it bared its teeth. "I hate them. They're Rhodesian Ridgebacks and very unfriendly."

"I didn't think so," said Eva. "They seemed to like us."

"Well don't let them near me. They aren't crazy about me for some reason."

"What are their names?"

"Shit and Shinola. How should I know?"

The old Avril has put in an appearance. Perhaps it is possible that I can love both versions. She told us of her plans to restore not just the garden but to modernize and improve on the house as well.

"It's going to take a lot of work but I'm determined to do it. The old man isn't keen on the idea. He said he's the one living in it and he's happy with it the way it is, an anachronism, without electricity or modern plumbing. I think he just doesn't want to spend the money. We told him it's unsafe with the roof falling in and the floor like it is, and in that respect only he has conceded we are right. We can start fixing the floor and roof but it's going to be difficult to get him to allow me to do what I want here."

We walked around the house and the garden—Avril pointing out what she was going to change and how she was going to do it. I wish I can stay and help. It all sounds so exciting and challenging.

It was while we were inspecting the overgrown back yard and vegetable garden that I heard a familiar sound that made my heart do cartwheels. It was Gloria! I kept my excitement in check and waited until Avril had finished talking before saying, "Oh, I thought I heard somebody arrive, didn't you?" Avril smiled and we walked around the house to the driveway. It was Tony.

He hugged us each in turn and I wished he'd reserve a special greeting just for me but he seems to treat me exactly the same way as he treats Eva and Avril. My brief disappointment gave way to an overwhelming joy. He is here at last. That is all that matters. We are going to have a wonderful Christmas. We spent the rest of the morning sitting on the long verandah, the dogs staying close to Eva, talking and laughing and later, taking a long walk down the tree lined road to the tobacco curing barns. Avril told us that the tobacco had recently been harvested and the delicate leaves of the Virginia tobacco have been brought to the sheds to flue cure before being sold.

"That's where Neil's father is right now, at the auction," she said. She added that Neil had left for Salisbury early that morning to help his father at the auction and learn how to market the crops. "He hasn't had that much experience yet, even though he grew up with tobacco."

"Well I imagine it won't take him long to pick it up," said Tony. I wish I had a tobacco farm myself. They're money makers, especially now the war is over. I'll bet every country in the world will be clamoring to buy good old Rhodesian tobacco!"

"It's supposed to be one of the best, I hear," I said, "but I don't smoke so I wouldn't know."

Tony laughed. "Well, don't tell anyone, but I do!" He took out a pack of cigarettes and shook one out, lighting it with an expensive looking gold lighter and dragging deeply.

I was astounded. I never knew he smoked! I wasn't shocked, but I wonder why he has waited so long to reveal that fact? Did he think I would preach at him? I don't mind him smoking. It's his life and I would no more think of trying to stop him from smoking than I would try to stop him from drinking. I tried to ignore this new development and changed the subject.

"We haven't seen your house yet, Avril. Are you going to show it to us?"

"We can do that after lunch. Let's go back to the house and get something to eat. I told the cook to have lunch ready at noon."

After lunch Avril said she needed a nap so Eva, Tony and I are lazing on the cool verandah. Tony is smoking and drinking beer while Eva has fallen asleep in a comfortable chair. The sun is hot and shimmering heat waves rise off the driveway and road. I feel half asleep myself but I am making myself write in my journal. I don't want to forget any detail, no matter how small, about this weekend.

A little while ago, Tony gave a big sigh and said:

"Ah, this is the life! I can see myself on a farm like this one day. Sitting on the verandah with my feet up just like this and drinking beer."

"Didn't you just sell your farm?" It was all I could think of to say.

"*That*! That wasn't a farm—that was a nightmare. It's hard scrabble on that kind of farm! Up before dawn and working like a *kaffir* until dark.

Talk to the Moon

Just barely making the payroll each month then one drought and you're dead in the water. No, that's more Eric's style. He rolls with the punches and keeps coming back—like one of those dolls you see with the center of gravity in their feet. What do you call them?"

"I don't know, but I know what you mean. Tony, I think this farm must be an awful lot of work too. I don't see Neil or his father sitting on the porch all day."

"You've been here less than a day. How can you say? Anyway, in my opinion, they do more than they need to. They're afraid to relax and just enjoy life. Perhaps one would need to put in some hard work a few days out of the month but the rest of the time you're a gentleman of leisure. That's what you've got the darkies—the old Black Magic—for my dear. Find a good farm manager and your troubles are over." He giggled and began to hum something that sounded vaguely like *Old Man River*.

Do I really love this man? A bottle of Castle Lager tilts to his mouth; the lips that I always think of as so beautiful now look sucking and greedy, like those of a new-born baby looking for its mother's breast. Beads of sweat shine wet on his upper lip and he makes loud swallowing noises as the golden liquid sloshes down his throat. Is this all there is to Tony, a man who wants the world on a silver platter? No, I have to be wrong.

Don't I also have dreams of living a life of leisure and comfort? Maybe Tony is one of those rare, visionary dreamers destined for better things. Maybe he feels, quite accurately, that life has more to offer than drudgery. I can't fault him for that. Of course I love him: more than I can say. I love him, *I love him*!

The dogs are snoring and so is Eva.

Late, Christmas Eve:

Avril showed us her cottage today. It's tiny and uncomfortable and I am not surprised she wants to fix up the big house soon. It looks the right size for Tom Thumb to live comfortably and their furniture is crammed in and boxes are everywhere. Avril said she doesn't have the strength to finish unpacking.

"I've left most of the things in the boxes and taken out only what we need. I'll get to the other stuff when we move into the big house after it's fixed up. It's been difficult and Neil says I've done too much already. Martha has been doing most of it anyway, but it's the stress, you know; trying to find a place for everything."

"Well at least you know it's not permanent," said Tony. "Get that old monstrosity down the road habitable and you'll feel like yourself again."

"Tell that to the old man," said Avril, and smiled. "Now you can see why I couldn't ask you to stay here."

"Well, as long as it doesn't rain, we'll be alright!" laughed Tony.

But, of course, it did rain. We had just returned to the big house when the sky darkened and there was a rumble of thunder. A few minutes later it was coming down in sheets, as Cuthbert the cook, and Esther and Martha ran through the house with buckets, beakers, bowls and jam jars. When they found spots where the water was pouring or dribbling through the holes in the thatch they placed a receptacle under it, attempting to stem the flow of water as much as possible with what they had.

We all helped by looking in the kitchen for suitable crockery and pots and when we found them, Tony would look for a spot that Cuthbert and Martha had missed and place it under the leak. Lucky for us, there are no leaks in the bedrooms. They are on the one side of the house where it is either more sheltered from the rain or the roof is in better condition. Most of the leaks are in the living room, kitchen, hallway and dining room.

We sat in the driest area we could find listening to the musical pings, splats and tings of the raindrops falling into buckets, bowls, jars and pots. It began to get dark and Martha brought a *Tillie* lamp into the room. Cuthbert found some dry wood and he lit a fire in the fireplace. It was cozy and wonderful, and we all huddled together around the fire and sang Christmas carols and told stories about Christmas's long past but not forgotten.

Avril told of the Christmas when she got a pony, and I remembered that one we spent at *Ouma* and *Oupa's* farm, before Mom and Dad fought so much. Tony told a very long story. It went something like this:

"I was stationed at RAF Litchfield in '42, which is an air base not far from Birmingham. Christmas was on a Friday, that year, and me and some of my mates had a long weekend pass. There was nothing going on in Birmingham and we had some money to burn so we decided to hitch a ride down to London. We got there on Christmas Eve and it was blacker than a nun's habit thanks to the blackout, but if you knew where to go, there was plenty going on!

"One of the chaps was from London and he knew every dance hall in the city. We weren't wearing fifty bob suits like some of the patrons, and it cost five bob apiece to get in these halls, but we managed to hit nearly every dance hall in a ten mile radius. The women just went mad over our uniforms and we never sat down for one minute. They were literally fighting to dance with us!"

He shook another cigarette out of his box and lit it. He inhaled deep into his lungs and continued. "Everything shut down at 1 a.m. by the latest and there was no place to go after that. We were still in the party mood and we had hooked up with some girls—and I don't mean one girl each—looking for some action. The pubs were closed but one of the chaps we were with had a bottle of *Pym's* under his jacket, so we were on our way to the park when all of a sudden the air raid siren goes off. We were going to ignore it, but the girls start panicking—they had been through the Blitz, after all—and they start running towards the nearest shelter, which in that area was the underground. We go in there after them and people are pouring into the shelter by the hundreds. We lost the girls, but we finally found a corner where we could sit and have a drink.

You know how you feel when you know someone is looking at you? Well, I had that feeling and I turned around and there's this kid, oh, about five years old, sitting there looking at us. Bill, the other guy, says, 'What you looking at, eh?' and the kid—I swear I am not making this up—says, 'How will Father Christmas know I'm here?'

'Where's your Mom and Dad kid?' asks Jeff.

He points back to some shapes in the shadows.

'My Mum is there,' he says. 'My Dad's gone.'

"We didn't know what he meant by that, but I am getting this big lump in my throat. I am thinking about all those kids down there that hadn't been evacuated and were wondering if Father Christmas would make it this year or if Hitler would beat him to it, and how many of them didn't have a father anymore. We put our heads together and came up with a plan. We walked the length of the platform asking every damn person if they had a certain article of clothing on them. Finally we got together what we were looking for—a reddish bathrobe for starters, a red scarf and hat, and we tied a white handkerchief around his chin and in the dark, if you were half blind, you would think that just maybe that was Father Christmas on a bad day.

"The kid's sitting there half asleep by now, but Bill touches him on the shoulder, making sure he's staying in the shadows.

"'*Ho! Ho! Ho!*' says our intrepid Bill. 'Are you the kid wot's worried Father Christmas ain't goin' to make it this year?' The kid is all bug-eyed now and he nods his head in excitement. 'Are you Father Christmas?' He squeaks. Bill says, 'I am. Wot's your name, eh?' The kid tells him, I forget now what it is, but let's say it was Jimmie—they're always Jimmie, eh? 'Well, Jimmie, let's see,' he takes out his little black book with all his girlfriends' phone numbers and pretends to search through it. 'Jimmie, Jimmie…*aaah*, yes, here you are. Yes Jimmie, I'm scheduled to make a stop at your house next. Got a special shipment for you, I 'ave. Well, I'd better get going. It's getting late and the reindeers're impatient, they are.' And with that he melts back into the shadows, and that kid is so happy you can see it coming off him in waves.

"Some people around us start clapping, and soon the whole shelter is full of people shaking our hands and then someone starts singing *Silent Night*. I can tell you, there wasn't a dry eye in the shelter that night, even the girls—who have by now found us—are crying."

Eva wiped her nose with her sleeve and I gave her a handkerchief. I felt close to tears myself but it wasn't young Jimmie who was responsible. Girls, indeed! Why did he have to bring that in to an otherwise beautiful story? Avril snorted.

"Oh, how sweet."

We couldn't miss the sarcasm in Avril's voice.

"Avril, It was beautiful!" said Eva. "I've never heard such a lovely story. It must have been a special Christmas to know you and your friends did such a kind thing for a child."

Tony shrugged.

"I don't care whether anyone believes me or not." He glanced at Avril. "It happened just as I said. We didn't get an air raid that night and the all clear sounded shortly after that, but I think of that kid often and hope Father Christmas really did make it to his home that night and didn't make a liar out of poor old Bill."

The rain had eased and just as Eva was telling her story we saw car headlights in the driveway.

"That must be Neil and Dad," said Avril. "It's about time. I was just starting to get worried."

"How sweet!" Tony snorted, and Avril shot him a filthy look.

John Blanchard hasn't changed since we last saw him. He is as cheerful and talkative as ever and after apologizing for his absence he changed for dinner and we all gathered around the huge dining table. Avril managed the preparation for the Christmas Eve dinner with

Talk to the Moon

Cuthbert to the minutest detail. She did no actual work herself, but she organized it like a general in a war room planning an invasion.

Two chickens from the coop were slaughtered and roasted to a golden perfection surrounded by crisp potatoes and colorful vegetables. The table had been decorated with green sprays of cedar and yew and a cluster of the reddish castor bush pods made a splash of red in the cedar centerpiece on the table.

"Avril was working on the decorations all day yesterday," said John Blanchard. "It's so good to have a woman's touch around the place again. It reminds me of when my lovely Moira was alive and we'd have Christmases like these every year. Unfortunately, there weren't too many of them, but I will never forget those we did have. The house would be full of people and I always thought she cooked enough to feed a Zulu Impi!"

"Eat up, we're having leftovers on Christmas day," said Avril. "I gave Cuthbert and Martha the day off tomorrow."

John Blanchard looked so happy. His merry eyes sparkled and his face glowed.

"If the pantry is going to be bare tomorrow," he said, "I'll do what Moira and I used to do in this kind of weather. I'll go mushroom hunting!"

"Can we come too?" asked Eva.

"If you can get up by six a.m. The best mushrooms are those gathered early in the morning."

"Be careful, Dad, you haven't done it in a while, and you know how poisonous some of those mushrooms are. They look alright, but they'll kill you."

"Don't worry, Neil, it's true that I haven't done it in a while, but I still know my mushrooms: never had an accident yet!"

I hope he knows his mushrooms. I'm not sure I want to eat any wild mushrooms. Maybe I should go along with Eva too; I can make sure they pick nothing that looks suspicious. What does a poisonous mushroom look like, anyway?

"Had a good day at the auction, huh?" asked Tony, changing the subject. He must have noticed how happy Mr. Blanchard looked.

"Dad had a successful day," said Neil. "I've never seen the price of tobacco go up so fast."

"It seems the whole world wants to buy our tobacco now," Mr. Blanchard agreed. "They're tired of the wartime shortages. American tobacco is doing well and their exports are picking up but the Rhodesian blends are gaining in popularity. England and the other colonies will import a lot of our tobacco, wait and see!"

We toasted to the continued success of tobacco sales. Avril had supplied wine for Mr. Blanchard and Tony while the rest of us raised our apple juice glasses.

Dessert arrived—a Christmas pudding flambéed in a rich brandy sauce.

"Don't worry, the alcohol burns out," said Avril, noticing the alarm on my face. "Such a shame!" said Tony, and we all laughed with him.

We spent the rest of the evening playing Monopoly by lamplight. Avril won after a close battle with Mr. Blanchard. Tony had lost early in the game and sat and watched us, sipping a glass of red wine and smoking cigarettes. He seems to be smoking quite a lot for someone who has just picked up the habit but I didn't comment on it. It is none of my business.

CHAPTER 20

Kaitano and Tatenda

Christmas Day
I awoke early this morning with a rapping at the door. It was Eva.
"Aren't you awake yet? Its time to go mushroom picking!"
I didn't know if I wanted to go mushroom picking. I still wanted to sleep. It was dark and I could hear a cock crowing in the distance. I snuggled under my covers and tried to ignore Eva, but she persisted.
"C'mon, sleepy! It's nearly six, and Mr. Blanchard is up already."
I gave up. I walked out onto the verandah just as the sun was peaking over the horizon.
"Merry Christmas! It's going to be a beautiful day." Mr. Blanchard was sitting on the verandah drinking coffee. "Have a cup of coffee. You look like you need waking up!" I did, and soon we were walking down the driveway with the dogs bounding alongside and ahead as Eva threw sticks for them.
"The dog's names are Livingstone and Stanley. Mr. Blanchard says they're always exploring, just like their namesakes!" I feel that, for the vast majority of dogs, exploring consists of sticking their snouts where they don't belong. I was more interested in listening to a chorus of warbling and twittering birds in the treetops and noticing how the early morning sun touched the branches and leaves with a gentle light that filtered down through the canopy in golden shafts. Everything was green and wild flowers bloomed along our path. I could smell the fertile, mushroom odor and see bright colored toadstools in amongst the brushwood and ferns in the deep recesses of the forest.
"Those colorful fellows are not what we are looking for," explained Mr. Blanchard. "We are looking for these," he said, and stooped to pick a plain looking brown mushroom. "This is a mushroom, and those are toadstools. You can mostly tell what is poisonous by the frill here," pointing to a skirt on the stem of the toadstool, "and the gills." He placed the mushroom in the basket he was carrying.

"Watch out for these grayish white toadstools," he said. "They are deadly—you can tell them apart from the others quite easily." He pointed out the various distinguishing marks of the poisonous mushroom and I felt my earlier misgivings beginning to dissipate. He does seem to know his mushrooms well.

"What will happen if you eat a poisonous mushroom by mistake?" asked Eva.

"Depends on the mushroom. Sometimes you'll just get a stomach ache and be sick for a few days, and sometimes nothing will happen. But this one is a species that can kill, especially if you're not treated right away. They will kill cattle."

"How did you learn so much about mushrooms?" asked Eva.

"The Shona taught me a few years after I got here. I was nearly always short on food at first; I had a lot to learn about growing my own. They showed me how to survive in the bushveld on berries and mushrooms and also how to hunt wild animals. There weren't many grocery stores around in those days!"

"I don't see too many around here, now," I said. "I notice you are self-sufficient."

"I never did enjoy those shopping excursions into Salisbury. If it weren't for the basics that everyone seems to need now, you'd still find me living off the land and what the farm can provide. Cuthbert is used to the white-man's staples, like flour, sugar and that kind of thing. He gets irritated when we run low. I still have to make monthly trips. I usually take Cuthbert in with me. I haven't needed to do it for some time now since Avril insists on making the purchases. She's good at it, you know."

I did know.

Eva piped up:

"She's doing a wonderful job, or will, when she isn't so tired. You should let her fix up your house, Mr. Blanchard, she'll make it so beautiful—not that it's not beautiful now," she added hastily, as my face darkened, "But it will certainly be a lot different."

"You're right; she is a talented woman. I have been mule-headed, I know. I've had time to think about that. I think it's because I felt that the only woman who had any right to make changes was Moira. That's unreasonable, since Moira Jean has been gone for many years and the place is deteriorating much faster than I can keep up. I don't even have the energy anymore to hire people to do the job. That is why I was so happy when Neil said they were coming back to Greystones.

"I am starting to feel my age now and I didn't think I could carry on much longer with all the responsibilities. I'm overjoyed that I'll soon have a grandchild. Greystones could have gone to the auction block if Neil had not expressed an interest in returning. The Blanchard's are here to stay!"

I feel such empathy for Mr. Blanchard. I am trying to imagine how he would feel, having worked all his life on something, to have no one to leave it to who could take care of it. To lose your life's labor and dreams to the auction block! It doesn't bear thinking about.

I knew Avril would be pleased to hear the news and thought that Mr. Blanchard would tell her himself when we got back. It was after all, Christmas day, and that would make a good gift for Avril.

The sun was getting higher and we decided to return and make breakfast before it got too late. We arrived at the house just as Avril and Neil walked up with armloads of wrapped Christmas gifts. Eva and I went to our rooms to get our gifts and returned to the living room where a sleepy Tony waited for us.

"Jesus, I don't know how you can stand all this light in here," he muttered. "Can someone please close the curtains?" His face was unshaven, eyes red and hair uncombed. I haven't seen him look this bad since I've known him.

"Are you sick, Tony?"

"Nothing that a good cup of coffee won't fix," laughed Neil. "Had a few *Shumbas* too many, last night, eh?"

"No, it was the wine, actually," smiled Tony. "I'm not used to that variety. Not the kind I usually buy. It's probably a bad vintage."

"Can't be. It's the best I could find," sniffed Avril.

"I've volunteered to make breakfast this morning," said Mr. Blanchard. We'll have some of my mushroom omelets. You'll feel much better after you eat."

Eva and I offered to help and Mr. Blanchard accepted our offer with a smile.

We began to open gifts. Eva and I had done what we could with what we had. Mine were a blue and white cable vee-neck cardigan for Tony, a cotton maternity blouse for Avril, a present for Mr. Blanchard—a bottle of after-shave, and some perfume for Eva since I knew Eva hated knitted gifts.

Eva has been busy all year pressing flowers, both wild and cultivated, and she has turned them into beautiful pictures by arranging and gluing them onto rectangular sheets of white cardboard. She took them into Bulawayo to be matted and framed. She made one for each person. Avril was delighted with hers.

"You have a real talent Eva," she said. "You know just what colors and flowers look good together. I know exactly where I am going to put this."

"As long as it's not the trash!" Eva laughed.

Avril and Neil had given Eva and I each a large pack of bath salts. Mr. Blanchard had obviously asked Avril to pick out his gifts for us: a variety of cosmetics—lipstick, blush and powder—from Helena Rubenstein. I know this is not a cheap brand and still difficult to come by. Tony got a shaving brush and soap from Avril and Neil, and a tie from Mr. Blanchard. To my delight, he was especially touched by my gift.

"You made this yourself? It's just what I need."

"Does it fit? I had to guess at your size."

He tried it on. "It fits well. You're clever; I don't know how you do these things!"

I felt the dreaded blush. I didn't think it was that brilliant. If Mom could do it…I must have picked it up from her.

Tony reached down behind the chair where he was sitting.

"I didn't have time to wrap your gifts," he explained. "I feel really rotten now that I've seen all the lovely presents I've received but I hope you'll understand. They're small and had to be easily transportable but they were picked out with great care." He handed a string of red and black African mahogany-seed beads to me and a small wooden carving of a giraffe to Eva. I felt a deep stab of disappointment. Was this a joke? I looked at the beads and at Tony's face, but he was looking at me, expectantly. I forced a smile. I have seen these beads sold at roadside stands and they are cheap indeed. I already had a few in my drawer.

"Oh, don't worry, Tony. It's beautiful. Thank you!"

Eva thanked Tony for her gift. She didn't look at all disappointed.

He relaxed and handed a box to Avril.

"This is for both you and Neil; you have been so good to me this past year. I couldn't think of any way to thank you."

The box was about ten inches long and I wondered what it could be. A wooden carving, maybe? Avril opened it.

Talk to the Moon

"Oh! Oh my God, Tony! You know how much I love these things!" She exclaimed. "*Maman* had a whole collection of them! Where did you find it?" I could hardly wait. Avril lifted it out of the box and we all gasped. It was a porcelain figurine of a woman holding a baby, exquisite in every detail, down to the subtly rendered expression of tenderness on the woman's face.

"It took me some time to find it," said a modest Tony, "but I managed to find an antique shop owner in Salisbury who went to a lot of trouble to locate one of these babies. It's a Royal Doulton, you know," he explained to my frozen face. "It's named *Contentment*, and if you turn it over you can see the seal of authenticity on the bottom."

Avril turned it over so they could see the blue lion mark.

"It's also got a number," she said. "That's so you know it's the genuine article."

We admired the figurine in turn. I was happy that Avril and Neil had received such a beautiful gift from Tony but I also felt an agonizing pain in my chest that didn't seem to want to go away. It wasn't the disparity in the prices of the two gifts: it was the obvious fact that he had taken so much more trouble over Avril's gift—for surely it was Avril's gift more than Neil's—than my own. It couldn't have taken him more than a minute or two to pick out my gift—an afterthought, even? He would have spent more time picking out Eva's gift. I even wore my own beads once when we went out somewhere. He couldn't be that obtuse—and then to flaunt the more expensive of the two gifts in front of me!

I felt anger, but then I remembered how our parent's anger had spoiled holiday after holiday for me and Eva. I did not want to be like them. I would say nothing. At least we all received gifts and for that I need to be grateful. There are many people in this postwar world who will receive no gifts today and who will never spend Christmas with a loved one again. I have much to be thankful for. No-one seemed to notice my disappointment and anger. I helped Avril clean up the wrappings and we went to the kitchen with Mr. Blanchard to begin the breakfast.

We set the table while Mr. Blanchard cooked mushroom omelets with eggs from the chicken coop. Avril came into the kitchen wearing a frilly and festive apron with huge pockets. She made the coffee and toast and by 11 a.m. we were all sitting down at the long table as Neil said the blessing.

I took a bite of the omelet. It was the most delicious thing I have ever eaten. I had no idea mushrooms could taste like this. Mr. Blanchard looked pleased as we all complimented him on his cooking. Only Avril didn't eat the mushrooms.

"I don't want to risk anything with my baby. Neil says it's possible for just one wrong mushroom to harm the child at this stage. It may not do anything to an adult, but I can't take that chance." Mr. Blanchard agreed with her whole heartedly and didn't seem at all offended by her choice. She ate another omelet he had especially prepared for her with cheese instead.

Avril got up from the table and went into the kitchen. A few minutes later she came into the dining room carrying a silver tray with the poured coffee. She graciously handed a cup to each of us and we sat around the table talking and laughing and drinking the coffee. I can't remember when last I felt so relaxed and at peace.

After breakfast, we all got into the Wolsely, with the exception of Avril who said she needed to rest and the car would be too small for us all anyway. Neil drove us around the farm. The farm seems endless with fields, both fallow and planted, everywhere. The crop is mostly tobacco but there are fields of maize and millet too. Mr. Blanchard explained:

"We grow only Virginia tobacco—that is by far the most popular and it does well in the light, sandy soils of this area. We transplanted this crop from the seedbeds in late October, always after the first rains, and these plants will be ready for the first harvest by next month.

"You need to harvest before the plant goes to seed, and we do it in several stages: the first pick on the bottom leaves and a few weeks later, on the second pick, we take leaves up to nearly the top of the plant. This pick is our most valuable, in terms of quality. The final pick gets the rest of the leaves."

"Why don't you grow only tobacco? I notice you have some other crops too," asked Eva.

"Well, the problem with tobacco is that it's susceptible to certain diseases and pests. The first year in a field is always the best, producing the highest yields, but after that production falls off—lost to fungus, white-fly and nematodes to mention a few. I have found that leaving a field fallow for a few years is the best method. I'm diversifying my crops as much as possible until I can see which way the wind is blowing on the tobacco market. So far, it looks promising."

Talk to the Moon

We visited the now empty seedbeds and Mr. Blanchard explained how the tiny tobacco seeds were planted in the late winter season. Too small to be hand planted they were mixed into watering cans and 'watered' onto the seedbed. This was by far the hardest part of tobacco growing, he said, since they needed constant thinning, watering twice a day and checking for diseases. About ten days before transplanting they need to be toughened up by cutting back on the watering so that they would survive the shock of being transplanted into the field.

I wondered if Tony had noticed that tobacco farming was not the cake walk he seemed to think it was. He remained mostly silent, sitting next to me and Eva in the back seat, smoking his cigarette. I thought of the toil and labor that had gone into the pleasure he so casually enjoyed. The smoke made me sick, but since no one else said anything, I decided not to mention it. He suddenly spoke.

"How many laborers do you employ?"

"Oh, roughly two hundred and fifty, off the top of my head. I could use more, but that's all we can afford right now." The laborers planted, harvested and watered when necessary, he explained. "I separate my workforce into gangs: one measures the distance with a stick, and the next one digs a hole with a *budza*—that's a hoe, Holly—big enough to plant the small seedling; the next one places the small plant into the hole; the fourth one waters it to make sure there is good root-soil contact, covers the hole, and tamps the soil down around the plant.

"We also have fetchers and carriers, bearers and various camp followers all milling about at the same time. It gets hectic and you need your wits about you to coordinate the whole operation. I have some excellent boss boys assisting me, so I'm lucky."

Eva asked where the workers lived.

"They live mostly on the farm," said Neil. "We have several villages on Greystones where nearly everyone living on them is employed by us. A few come in from neighboring areas but most of them are taken care of by the farm."

I thought I would like to visit the villages and said so, remembering my visit to the old *nganga* over a month ago and wondering how a Shona village would compare to an Ndebele one.

Tony looked at me, incredulous.

"Of course," said Neil, "We're near one of them right now." He turned down a small road—a track—and Tony sighed.

"Haven't you seen enough of them yet?" he asked. "You're acting like a silly tourist. Where's your camera?"

"Now, it's no trouble at all, Tony," said Mr. Blanchard. "Holly and Eva haven't seen how we live on farms yet so let's be good hosts. They'll be pleased to see us. I don't get to the villages often enough myself."

I felt better when Eva said she'd love to see the village too, but I wonder why Tony is so dead set against visiting Africans. He's been brought up around them, and understands their language. One would think he'd be the one to feel more comfortable around Africans. I haven't been brought up around them at all. Where we lived it was mostly white and whites seldom venture into Native areas or mix with the colored population: they are workers or servants. I feel I never can really get to know them on an equal basis as I do with whites.

Even Esther seems uncomfortable when we try to talk with her as an equal. All the deference and the "yes madam, no madam" attitude make me feel as if I am being humored: that as soon as the girls returned home, safe in their own environment, they'd be laughing uproariously at the madam and her airs. Wouldn't I, if the tables were turned? I know now without a doubt that I'll make a real effort to learn the language. I don't know if it will be the Ndebele language or the Shona language, but it will be one of them.

I don't want to pick up the mission *Chilapalapa*—the mixed pidgin of English and Ndebele or Shona that passes as a common means of communication between white master and black servant. It is easy but demeaning to both parties. I know I can learn another language. After all, don't I already speak two?

In a few minutes we arrived at the village. An excited crowd of men, women and children gathered around us as soon as we stepped out of the car.

"*Masikati*, boss, madam!" We were greeted by the hand clapping group.

"*Masikati!*" Replied Tony, Neil and Mr. Blanchard. I noticed that the men greeted the white men with an open palm-to-fingers slap, while the women clapped their own hands together.

"*Masikati* means 'good afternoon'," Tony translated. "You must say it and clap back now." I did so, and the women smiled and laughed out loud.

Talk to the Moon

"They're not laughing at you," said Neil, smiling, "that just means they're pleased." I felt pleased, too. I have learned my first Shona word. "These are traditional people here on the farm. They place great emphasis on politeness and customs, unlike many of their counterparts in the cities who are losing their traditional values. These people would now be considered country bumpkins by their more westernized kin in Salisbury."

"No, you don't experience the traditional greetings much anymore in Salisbury," agreed Mr. Blanchard. "You will see it still from African to African, but never between white and black. It's unheard of. That's our fault—we never bothered to learn their ways or customs. Now we are teaching them ours and that has become the preferred way."

"But I notice you have learned the African ways—and the language. That's quite admirable."

"Not enough of us are prepared to do that," he replied. "It's too much trouble for most of the white population when the African is prepared to speak English instead."

"Or *Chilapalapa!*" laughed Eva.

A man—probably the headman, arrived to lead us to a large Marula tree where low stools were brought from other huts to seat us. Mr. Blanchard lowered himself stiffly onto a stool with the help of Neil.

"A few years ago I could do this quite easily," he laughed, "Now it's getting past me." A motley group of scanty-clad small children eyed us with suspicion. "This is my boss boy, Kaitano," said Mr. Blanchard, indicating the man who had led us to the tree.

"Does he speak English?"

Kaitano answered, "I speak it well, madam. I went to a mission school nearby and completed Standard 3."

Mr. Blanchard, Neil and Tony spoke with Kaitano for a while, in Shona, as Eva and I looked around us. The children wear loincloths and little else—some with knitted tops—in spite of the hot day—and here and there a raggedy pair of cotton shorts; but for the most part they are nearly naked. The barefoot women in cotton dresses, some carrying babies on their backs wrapped in cotton toweling. All wear bright colored cotton scarves around their heads. The village is clean and well kept. The grounds around the pole and *daga* huts with their conical thatched roofs are swept free of clutter, and chickens run amongst the huts, clucking and scolding. I noticed a few goats on the perimeter of the village chewing contentedly from sparse, thorny bushes. I wished I could take a peek inside the huts.

The women were giving me and Eva sidelong glances, pretending not to notice anything, but I am sure they were making mental notes of every detail. I wondered if any of them spoke English and felt frustrated that I didn't know their language yet. I wanted to be able to understand the conversation between the men even if it only concerned boring things like farm matters. I waited for a lull in the conversation and soon there was one.

"Do you think the women would be able to show me and Eva the huts?"

"Certainly!" answered Kaitano and he clapped his hands and shouted at one of the women carrying a baby on her back. "This is my wife, Tatenda. She will take you to her hut and serve you tea. She does not speak any English, unfortunately."

Tatenda smiled and we got up and followed her. She led us into a nearby hut and the group of children followed, standing in a curious knot by the door. She indicated that we sit on a narrow, mud plastered platform that ran around the interior wall of the hut. In the center of the hut a small fire smoldered.

Tatenda shouted at one of the small boys standing by the door, and he ran off. I noticed a wooden stool sitting near the hearthstones. On the other side of the hut was a larger shelf that held pots, tin dishes of varying sizes, and large, orange clay pots decorated with black zigzags. The child returned with a bundle of sticks and wood, and Tatenda put them on the fire and then placed a pot of water on the fire. She sat down on the floor with legs straight in front of her, undid the cloth holding the baby and brought it to her front. We watched, fascinated as she breast fed her baby.

The mother and baby looked so contented that I felt something approaching envy. I thought of Avril's *Contentment* and wished that Tony had bought it for me. It would have always reminded me of this moment. Eva seemed just as spellbound in the moment as I was. I wished I had brought my camera, but don't think the camera could have captured what I felt.

Soon Tatenda had finished feeding her child and she tied it once more onto her back. The water was bubbling on the fire and Tatenda busied herself making us tea. The tea was heavy on both milk and sugar, and served in tin cups, but it was full of body and flavor, and we thanked Tatenda in English and hoped she would understand.

Soon the visit was over and we rode back to the farmhouse, the sun setting the horizon on fire; the trees etched in a fiery glow.

"Happy now?" asked Tony.

"Yes, very."

"Did you notice the stool by the fireplace?" asked Neil.

"Oh yes, no one sat on it though."

"That's for Kaitano, the husband," said Neil. "She would have made it for him herself."

"How did you like the tea?" asked Tony. "Did you accept it with both hands?"

"The tea was good, but why both hands?"

Tony laughed; a nasty laugh. "Well, you must have insulted her, then. If you accept something with one hand it means it's not good enough."

"I don't think she looked insulted. She'd know we wouldn't know, surely?"

"Don't worry Holly," said Neil. "Tony's playing with you. Tatenda is not so stupid. I think she was flattered you were both interested enough in visiting her and taking tea. It's a compliment to be offered tea so you both did well."

We were quiet as we drove back. So was Mr. Blanchard. I noticed he looked pale and wondered if he was tired. It must have been a long day for him and he wasn't young anymore. I thought he needed, as we all did, an early night. Avril didn't seem to notice. When I mentioned it, she just shrugged it off and said, "Oh, I am sure he's just not used to visitors. Don't worry about it." I did, though, and went to bed feeling as if there was something wrong but I wasn't quite sure what.

CHAPTER 21

John Blanchard

Wednesday, 26th December

It has rained *guti*—a fine misty rain—the whole day. Mr. Blanchard does not look well today, either, and by this time Neil has noticed it too. We wrapped him in blankets and he sat in front of the fire while everyone fussed over him. He said he couldn't eat anything so I made some broth from the leftover chicken and tried to get him to drink liquids.

Avril said, "He must be getting the flu. Neil thinks he's been doing too much lately. He needs to rest more."

I am sitting by the fire with him, writing. There is so much to catch up on. Tony and Eva are restless.

Tony: "I'm not used to being cooped up in the house like this all day."

Eva: "I know what you mean. Avril, can we play your Monopoly game again?"

Its noon now, and Mr. Blanchard looks decidedly worse. Neil looks alarmed.

"I am going to have to take him to Mt. Darwin, I think. There's a hospital of sorts there. I know a few of the doctors. Maybe we can run some tests and monitor him."

"No, no, I don't want to go to the hospital," Mr. Blanchard said. His voice sounded so weak. "I've never been in one of those places in my life and I don't plan on going now. I'll go to bed and I'll be alright by this evening."

Wednesday evening, late:

He is not alright.

"He's vomiting now with diarrhea and I don't like his pulse," Neil said about 7:30 this evening. "It could be a bad case of the stomach flu, but I'm not going to take any chances. I'm taking him to the hospital."

"Would you like one of us to go with you?" I asked.

"No, I'll just lay him on the back seat and put a blanket over him and have a bucket handy. It's going to be messy, I'm afraid."

Talk to the Moon

"I'll go with you," said Tony, and I, for the first time in quite a while, felt proud of him. They left as soon as they had bundled Mr. Blanchard into the car. We sat in the house together, trying to figure out why he was so sick and yet none of us were feeling ill.

"It couldn't be the mushrooms," said Eva. "We all ate them and we feel just fine!"

"I think Neil is right, it's the flu or something."

"He was in Salisbury, recently," said Avril. "Maybe he picked up something there or ate something bad."

I feel that in a few hours Neil and Tony will walk in smiling, with Mr. Blanchard weak but much improved; that it's all a case of food poisoning and now that it's out of his system he will be fine. By tomorrow, everything will be back to normal.

27th December, morning:

At midnight the phone rang. Avril had gone to bed and Eva and I were still up waiting for the men to return.

"Oh, Tony, thank God. We've been so worried! What's going on?"

"It's not good, I'm afraid. They're going to keep him here for a while. We thought we had lost him on the way in. It seems he's gone into some kind of coma or something."

"D-do you think he'll make it, Tony?"

"I don't know. No one seems to know anything. Just keep your fingers crossed, it's all we can do right now."

"Should I tell Avril? She's gone to bed."

"No, leave it till the morning. We don't want to worry her unnecessarily. There's nothing she or anyone else can do. You go to bed too, my darling. Don't wait up. We'll probably be here all night."

I scarcely heard the word *darling*, I was so upset—a small comfort, I thought later, as I tossed sleepless in my bed.

This morning we still hadn't heard anything, but it seems as if every person in a hundred miles has heard. Cars and farm lorries are pulling up in front of the farmhouse in droves—every farmer in the vicinity, their wives bearing steaming dishes of food, armloads of vegetables or just plain comforting talk—pour up the verandah steps.

"Bush telegraph," said a cynical Avril. "The party phone line. Those old biddies sit and listen in on everyone's conversation. They know everything that's going on in the area."

"Well, I can't say I'm not glad they do!" said Eva. "They've brought some really good stuff to eat."

The white farmers are not the only people utilizing the bush telegraph—the African workers on Greystones have received the news too, and they are congregating outside the farmhouse, sitting on steps and waiting patiently for news. I recognized Tatenda and Kaitano in the crowd and I asked them to come inside. They stood, awkward, just inside the living room door, and when I invited them to have a seat they sat straight-legged on the floor by the door. Avril snorted.

"Are you going to serve them tea too?" she asked. I couldn't miss the sarcasm in her tone. I smiled the sweetest smile I could muster.

"Yes, Avril, that's a good idea. I'll make it myself." I needed something to occupy myself with and making tea would focus my mind on something other than Mr. Blanchard. It didn't seem to work.

As I made the tea, I thought of—was it just yesterday—how he had been standing—right there—making the mushroom omelets. It seemed more real now that I was actually in the kitchen. I saw Eva and myself coming in and out, getting plates and cutlery to put on the table from the cabinet right over there, and Avril—what had Avril been doing? Oh yes, she had been making coffee.

She had also dished up individual servings from the pans onto each plate—to cut down on washing up later, she said. Eva and I had carried the plates to the table. I remembered carrying Neil's and Tony's plates, but not Mr. Blanchard's. Eva must have taken his and Avril had taken in the coffee. "Why is this important anyway?" I thought. We already decided that it isn't the mushrooms that made him sick: they had all been cooked and dished up out of the same pan. It just isn't possible. A bad one in there would have sickened us all at the very least.

I took the tea tray into the living room and sat down on the settee and poured the tea for Tatenda and Kaitano, whom, I noticed, clapped their hands gently and then took their cups with both hands, palms up. So Tony had been right! Tatenda did not have her baby with her today.

"Where is your baby, Kaitano?"

"He is with his little mother at the village," he responded, then seeing my look of confusion as I looked at Tatenda, he smiled. "Our children have many mothers and fathers. His little mother is an auntie, my sister, and she is fourteen." I thought that children brought up this way would never be lonely. There would always be someone to take care of them no matter what.

"What is his name, and how many children do you have?"

"Tichagwa is the youngest of four children, two girls and two boys. We have been blessed by the *midzimu* madam."

"What is the *midzimu*, Kaitano?"

"They are our ancestors, the spirits of my grandfather and my father. They are my *mutupo*—I do not know how to say this in English—totem I think. My clan totem is the *nzou*, or the elephant totem. Since we add our praise name or *chidawo* to the totem name, I am Kaitano Sororenzou."

I wonder if I will ever understand this complicated system of naming. I have so much to learn.

Kaitano and Tatenda left quickly after drinking their tea. Tatenda needed to get back to her baby and Kaitano had work to attend to on the farm "now the boss is sick."

Later this evening

It was nearly dark before we saw headlights approaching the farmhouse. We ran out onto the verandah with Avril and watched as an exhausted looking Tony and Neil climbed up the stairs. We did not want to ask questions. The men's faces said enough. They walked into the house and I made more tea and brought it into the living room. It wasn't until they had each drunk a cup that Neil spoke.

"We left him there. There is nothing that anyone can do. I think it won't be long now. They said they'll call if his condition changes one way or the other."

"Did he ever come around?" asked Avril.

"Yes, for brief periods, but he doesn't seem to recognize anyone. I will go back first thing in the morning. They are talking about moving him to the hospital in Salisbury if his condition stabilizes."

"What is wrong? Do they know?"

"The symptoms are nonspecific but there are several possibilities they are looking at from hepatitis to a staphylococcal infection and perhaps other pathogens. I told them about the mushrooms yesterday, but they don't seem to think it's that since no one else got sick, but they haven't ruled it out. Mushroom poisoning of the most deadly variety would be consistent with the symptoms. It is possible, I suppose."

"I wish we hadn't let him do it!" exclaimed Eva. "I couldn't bear it if it was one of the mushrooms we picked." She looked so terrified and unhappy that I drew her towards me and hugged her.

"Don't worry Eva, it's just an outside chance, and they have to look at all possibilities. Avril and I think he ate something when he was in Salisbury."

"Like bad meat," said Avril.

"I don't think its hepatitis or mushroom poisoning myself, but it could be viral," said Neil. "Maybe a virus that wouldn't kill anyone younger but deadly in an older person. Difficult to diagnose."

"How about the urine and blood tests," asked Avril? "Didn't they show anything?" She and Neil discussed the tests, using language that only the two of them would understand, but from what I could piece together, they had revealed nothing either.

"Well, he's not dead yet," said Tony. "Let's not give up on him. He's got a lot of fight in him and I wouldn't be surprised if he's not back in a few days." We all smiled weak smiles and Avril suggested we eat and go to bed. I asked if Eva and I should return to Bulawayo but Avril and Neil wouldn't hear of it.

"If you can stand our long faces until all this is over we would appreciate your company," said Neil. "We're just sorry your holidays have been spoiled."

"No, they haven't! We've had a wonderful time anyway and no matter what happens from here on we'll understand. Besides, we'd love to stay and help in whatever way we can." So it was decided we would stay until after New Year's when we were originally scheduled to return to Bulawayo. Tony decided he would stay too.

"Got nothing better to do anywhere else. Training won't start again until after New Year's. I know I can be of some help too." I wondered why I had ever thought of him as being lazy and selfish.

Friday, 28th December

This morning early, I heard the phone ring. I bounded out of bed, grabbing my robe and slippers, and ran down the hallway but Tony had already picked up the phone when I got there. I noticed he had slept on the sofa all night.

"Yes," he said into the phone, then "No, this is his friend Tony Swann, I was there yesterday? Yes, that one. He's not able to come to the phone at this moment. Oh, yes, yes, I will be sure to tell him. We'll be

Talk to the Moon

there as soon as we can." He put down the phone and turned to me. Eva had also arrived by this time and her brown eyes were round and questioning. "He's much worse," he said. "They think Neil should get there as soon as he can." I felt such sadness. I didn't know what to say. I put my arm around Eva and we returned to our rooms to change while Tony delivered the message to Neil. When we returned to the living room Martha and Cuthbert were there. Cuthbert's eyes were teary and, his voice breaking, he said:

"I didn't hear until today, the news. I went to see my father in Bindura and got back early this morning." Martha quietly wept—lamenting in her language something I did not understand. We talked with Cuthbert for a while, telling him as much as we knew.

"*Aaah*! Those mushrooms! I tell him many, *many* times—do not eat the mushrooms. They have killed cattle!" He walked away, shaking his head and muttering, "I go make breakfast for the young madams." We ate breakfast in silence. Tony and Neil had already left. Avril wasn't feeling well either and she had decided to sleep in. Another thing for Neil to worry about. I hoped Avril hadn't caught what Mr. Blanchard had. What if it was something contagious? I felt a stab of fear. The old people and pregnant women would get it first—then the younger, stronger ones like us. We were all going to die! I mentally slapped myself. I was being just like Mom, again.

Avril came over later looking rather pale.

"I didn't sleep well last night," was all she said. I didn't think that any of us had slept well.

"You'd better rest today, then. Eva and I will do anything that needs to be done. Cuthbert is back, so he can be a big help."

Later, Friday evening:

At noon today, the phone rang. Avril answered it. She returned to the verandah where we had been sitting, her face white and her hands trembling.

"He's dead!"

I swallowed back my tears but Eva didn't. I tried to comfort both of them as much as I could without breaking down myself. Cuthbert came out, wailing.

"*Ah, ahhh, my boss*! What will I do? What will I do? He took good care of us. I wasn't even here. *Ah, ahh!*"

"Shut up, Cuthbert!" snapped Avril. "Enough of the wailing. You'll be taken care of. See that the farm workers get the news. We'll need to make some plans. We don't need any of your blubbering and whimpering."

I felt anger at Avril's callousness but it helped to keep me from disintegrating like Eva and Cuthbert. It was all I could do to stay on an even keel with everyone else crying.

Today, I saw Avril at her best. Her tiredness and dispiritedness have left, replaced by a strong woman who knows exactly what to do. I stopped worrying that Avril has taken ill. She was tireless, and stayed on the phone all day calling people and making arrangements for the funeral. We began to make food for the masses of people who would arrive as soon as the bush telegraph had made the rounds. She had also called for Esther and Martha to help, cutting short their leave, to clean the house and make it presentable. It hadn't been given a good clean in years, she said, and the living room was a disgrace. Neil's cousins would be arriving from Salisbury and they needed to get some rooms ready. We helped as much as we could but Avril had everything so well organized we felt as if we were getting underfoot. By the time Neil and Tony returned the house was in an uproar.

"I really don't know what I'd do without her," said Neil. "She's a gem. Doesn't let anything get the better of her." We all agreed. Neil looked pale but other than that I thought he was holding up well. At least the suspense was over; the inertia that had everyone in its grip of the previous day had left and action was restored. Tony helped Neil go through his father's papers and find what was important and what wasn't.

They discovered the name of his solicitor in Mt. Darwin and made arrangements for the will to be read after the funeral. The funeral had been arranged for Monday, the 31st. Avril said they did not want the body to be kept in the mortuary over New Year's so she made arrangements with the mortician to collect the body as soon as the hospital could release it. She called the hospital and asked to speak to the attending physician. She had a long conversation with him and slammed down the phone.

"He says he can't release the body until they've signed a death certificate, and he can't sign a death certificate, because he doesn't have a cause of death!"

"Can't they just guess?"

Talk to the Moon

"No, they can't. Now they want to do an autopsy immediately. That means they have to send the body to Salisbury and it will delay the funeral indefinitely. That just won't do!" She marched off to tell Neil the latest development, and he got on the phone to the mortuary. After ten minutes, he returned.

"Bart Sinclair agreed to sign the death certificate without an autopsy. He and I went to medical school together and we also grew up together so I know him well. I asked him what difference it would make to have an accurate cause of death and he admitted it wouldn't be any skin off his nose. He feels confident the death is not suspicious so he's putting the death down to natural causes, more specifically acute liver failure. That's the best we can hope for, I suppose."

"Well, as long as it doesn't mean an autopsy," said Avril. "That would hold up things no end."

"I would like to know what caused my father's death," said Neil, "But you're right. We can't drag our feet forever on this. It's traumatic to all of us here and we need to get it all over with as soon as we can."

The relatives arrived this evening.

There is a family and two unmarried aunts of indeterminate age dressed in black crepe, each carrying a bird-cage containing a traumatized budgerigar.

"Cousins on Neil's mother's side," said Avril. They arrived with John and Lydia Kelly who were also related to Moira Jean, and their children. The children, ranging in ages from four to twelve, never sat still long enough for us to count them. I thought there were three but it sounds at times like there are five. They run unfettered around the house screaming and yelling like banshees. Eva has attempted to corral them into some kind of order but it would be easier to subdue a bucket of live eels.

James and Lydia sit like placid statues in the living room, while their offspring systematically wage a scorched earth policy war throughout the house. The aunts also sit stone-faced, fingering worn rosary beads, only showing signs of animation when a budgie squawks.

Tony's parents and Eric have called to say they will be arriving Sunday evening for the funeral. They will drive back to Bulawayo on Tuesday and Eva and I have decided to return with them. We feel that a longer stay will put too much strain on Neil and Avril who already have more guests than they can handle. Over Avril's protests I offered my room to the Swanns and moved my belongings in with Eva.

New Year's Eve:

This weekend has been the longest two days I can ever remember experiencing. The children barely slow down long enough to eat and slept in shifts. They are perpetual motion contraptions, needing only a nudge to send them rocketing off on the path of least resistance. I tried to talk to them, my questions slyly designed to elicit introspection, but I may as well have been asking questions of a troop of baboons.

"Quite puts you off having kids, doesn't it?" said Eva. Her normal patience with children had reached its zenith. "Mind you, I can't see any of my hypothetical children behaving like that!"

"No, nor mine. I wonder what's wrong with those parents. You think they're deaf?"

"Dead, probably," said Tony. "Just haven't been buried yet. What's with the two old maiden aunts? They look like they've been dead quite a while."

"They sit there all day talking to those birds like they're people."

The dogs hid from the children too. Eva thought the dogs were grieving the loss of their master, but Tony scoffed at that idea.

"They don't know he's gone. He could be off on another trip for all they know. By the time they realize he's gone they'll have forgotten him altogether."

"That's so illogical," said Eva. "Of course they know."

Today was a beautiful, sunny day. The farm hands dug a grave in a fenced off area about a hundred yards from the house that also contains the graves of Moira Jean and Mary Rose. The elder Swanns and Eric arrived the Sunday night. I never thought that I would be glad to see them but I am. They are a lifeboat in a storm and I feel relief we're returning with them tomorrow. Lalie and Malachi looked somewhat askance at the maiden aunts and their rosaries and they were given the evil eye in return.

At least one representative from every farm in the area, and even some people from Salisbury, arrived for the funeral. The African farm workers were all there too. The men stand silent, holding their hats in their hands, while the women weep loudly and ululate. This was a sign of respect, said Tony. Old Man Swann conducted the funeral service at the gravesite. It seemed to go on endlessly, but at last it was over and we returned to the house for the wake.

Avril had done a tremendous job organizing the food and many of the farmer's wives had also contributed to the feast. The African workers were served tea and sandwiches: no small feat, since there were a few hundred of them. Martha and Esther helped serve and Tatenda and Kaitano had enlisted the help of the village to serve food to the workers. Not a soul went without and I thought I could never have organized anything on this large a scale but Avril looked as if it was merely routine to her. She still managed to look beautiful, her skin glowing with her pregnancy and her eyes clear and untroubled. I knew that if I had been in Avril's shoes it would not have been that easy. I would have shown signs of strain and things would surely have gone wrong.

When the last guest had left, and the servants had begun the cleanup, the solicitor, a Mr. Goodfellow, led us into the living room for the will reading. I wondered if we should be there but Avril told us to please come in. The family would not object to our presence.

The reading was predictable. After the usual legal mumbo jumbo, I gathered from what ensued that the farm went to Neil. The cousins got nothing. Their placid faces betrayed nothing and the bead clicking of the aunts did not miss a beat. I thought it unlikely that they expected to benefit from Mr. Blanchard's death as long as Neil was alive. While I was sitting thinking about this I remembered what John Blanchard had told us the morning of the mushroom picking. I had forgotten all about it! I waited until Avril and I were alone in the kitchen later this evening to tell her.

"Avril, do you know what your father-in-law said to Eva and me before he got sick? I meant to tell you earlier but I forgot."

"What did he say?"

"Eva and I mentioned something about the house needing repairs, and he said he had been reluctant to allow you to do what you wanted but that he'd reconsidered and thought you should be free to do anything you liked to the house and grounds. I think he felt it was going to be yours anyway one day so you should be able to act as if it was yours now."

Avril didn't say anything for a while. She continued putting food away in the old paraffin fridge, making sure each dish of leftovers was covered, before I noticed that her shoulders were shaking. I dropped what I was doing and went over and put my arms around Avril's shoulders.

"Now I've done it," I thought. "I'm as tactless as Eva. This hasn't made her feel better, only sadder." Then Avril turned around. There were no tears, but her eyes were bright, and, to my amazement, I saw that she had been laughing!

"Too little, too late!" said Avril, chuckling. Then seeing the incredulous look in my eyes, she stopped and her face got very solemn.

"I'm sorry, dear. These past few days have been a terrible strain on me. I cry when I should laugh and laugh when I should cry. I feel so guilty that I allowed my anger and impatience with the old man to show. I wish I had known that sooner, we could have been such good friends, but he never told me what his intentions were. I don't know why he told you."

"Well, maybe he had just decided," I said, still shocked at Avril's reaction.

"But it doesn't matter now," said Avril. What's done is done." She went on putting food away, and I wondered what she meant by what is done is done. Avril made no sense this evening. Perhaps the strain has been too much. It would have been for me, too, had I been in Avril's place, but Avril's words echoed through my thoughts all evening: what's done is done.

CHAPTER 22

1992

Gabe

    Gabe had come to the end of a pile of diaries and couldn't read anymore for today. He felt as if his head was spinning in confusion. As far as he was concerned there was still nothing in the diaries that would implicate anyone—let alone his mother—in something ugly. He agreed with Aunt Holly; that the strain on his mother had been too much. He also realized that for all the years he had known Aunt Holly, Aunt Eva and the others, that he hadn't known them at all. So much had happened since these diaries were written. So much that it would take another set of diaries just like these, or more, to catch up to present times.

    He knew that there had been a time when his mother had been estranged from his godmother, but that they had settled their differences and, up until Aunt Holly's death, had been close friends.

    He had heard of some suspicions about his mother in 1962 when something else had happened: something involving Tony. He had not wanted to think about that either.

    His curiosity overcame his fear. He picked up the next book.

CHAPTER 23

The Ring

Friday evening, 11th January, 1946

Something unexpected happened today. I have not written in my diary since returning from Greystones. I still can't believe the events of the last month and Eva and I seldom speak of them. I told Faye I never wanted to look at the diaries again, but the numbness from Christmas has worn off and life is once more magical.

This is how it happened:

Tony started his Field Officer job shortly after New Year's. To my surprise, he seems to like it:

"It's the easiest job I've ever had. I only wish it pays better."

He gets along well with the Native Commissioner and is already referring to him as Nigel. I feel he and Mr. Withers are spending way too much time together. A lot of this time, according to Tony, involves drinking copious amounts of beer in the single quarters at Tshabanda.

I am also tired of tsetse fly infestation lectures from Tony. He now acts as if he is the world's leading expert on tsetse fly and thinks he is destined to single-handedly solve one of Africa's most daunting problems if only the higher ups could hear his knowledgeable suggestions.

In my spare time I type up long reports for Tony that I suspect no one ever reads. I think Tony has been hard at work supervising the dipping of cattle and setting up screens and ground bait that trap any flies that might be in the vicinity. So far he has come up empty but he says the cattle are as tick and pest free as they'd ever been. I now know more about *glossina morsitans* now than I ever cared about knowing. The fly's bite is responsible for the incurable *trypanosomiasis*—called *nagana* in horses or cattle and sleeping sickness in humans. It is so good to see Tony enthusiastic about something again. I willingly sit up nights helping him with his reports. Tony's written style consists of run-on sentences and misspellings and I polish his reports so that they sound professional and well thought out.

Talk to the Moon

"I didn't pay much attention at school," he confessed during one of our more brutal editing sessions, this evening. "English was my least favorite subject: I really preferred sports to academics, and I just barely squeaked through with an "O" level."

"Don't worry, Tony, I loved English and always got good marks. I enjoy this so please don't feel guilty."

We were sitting at the dining room table working and it was getting late. Eva had gone to bed and Faye had gone to the hospital on an emergency call. Joan was in Bulawayo with Josh to see a new release movie. Tony seemed restless tonight. He was shifting around on his chair and running his hands through his hair so it stuck up comically. I smiled and smoothed his hair flat with my hand. I was startled when he took my hand in his and turned a bright red. I have never seen Tony blush before.

"*Lordie*, Holly, I feel exactly like Gerald right now."

"What do you mean, Tony?"

"I know he was always after you. He got beet red around you, his pimples glowed—I can feel my face is hot, it must look like Times Square on New Year's Eve—and I'm sorry but I just don't know how else to say this. Will you marry me?"

I thought that if I hadn't already been sitting I would have fallen. My body went weak from shock and I knew my heart was making plans to break out of my chest and escape through the door. I have imagined this moment a thousand times before but it had never been like this.

In my day dreams, Tony has always been on his knees while I, calm under an ethereal moon, would tell him that although I had never given the idea much thought, I would consider his proposal and let him know sometime next month. I had never been dressed in an old pair of khakis and faded cotton shirt either. My hair was a mess. Why, oh why hadn't I seen this coming? Finally I found my voice. My heart was still AWOL.

"Tony, I never expected this. I thought we were just friends?" I remembered the sting of those words last year and thought, "*touché*"!

"Well, I've never had a friend like you before, Holly. I think it's important for a man and wife to be friends, too. But all that aside, I do love you. I know I haven't shown it before. It's really difficult for me. I haven't even had that many girlfriends before. All I know is I want to spend the rest of my life with you."

The words I have always longed to hear were said, maybe not as romantically as I hoped, but I will take them. I did not want to appear too eager, so I said:

"I love you too, Tony, I always have. But I can't say what I want to do right now. Will you give me some time to think it over? I haven't had many boyfriends either and I don't know how to respond just yet."

"Okay, love, I will. Just don't take too long to decide. I've been looking at a ring and it won't be there forever."

That surprised me even more. I wonder if it had been in a pawn shop. I hope it isn't like my Christmas gift. We stayed up late tonight.

My first real kiss!

19th January

The reactions to our engagement have been varied.

Today, the morning after the proposal, Eva awoke first.

"You stayed out late last night! Must have been a good one." She winked.

"Oh Eva, I wanted to wake you up when I came in but I thought it could wait until this morning. Tony proposed to me last night!" I waited for Eva's thrilled response, but Eva didn't look as happy as I thought she'd be.

"Oh! Well, what did you say? Or should I even bother to ask? You said yes, I presume?"

"No, no of course not. You presume wrong. I just asked for more time. What's wrong Eva; don't you like the thought of me getting married?"

"It's not that. Well, okay then, yes, it is that." And Eva burst into tears. "Oh damn! I never thought I'd be this upset, either," she sniffed. "I think I am jealous and frightened at the same time. What'll I do without you, Holly? I'm so used to having you around. Now, I'll be on my own!"

"You won't be alone, silly! I'll still be here! Nothing'll change. I'll ask Tony if you can come and live with us, if you like."

We spent the rest of the day speculating about this unexpected future. It was Saturday, and I asked Eva not to tell anyone about the proposal just yet, although I did feel tempted to run straight to Tootie to ensure the news would spread as fast as possible. How could I not share my joy with anyone? But then I realized that I hadn't yet said yes, and it wouldn't be right to discuss it with anyone other than Eva, or Faye. Yes, I would talk to Faye about it.

Talk to the Moon

Faye didn't look thrilled either. I was beginning to feel paranoid. Why? Didn't anyone want me married? Then I remembered Eva's words and thought that Faye must have felt the same way. Well, we can't have Faye living with us too. It would be too much. No one had felt this way about Avril's marriage. I thought I would tell Tony the next time I saw him that I had accepted. That way I could see just how the news would be received by all.

Tonight we had another mission get-together. Tony was there, and I was reminded of the first social function I had attended at the mission. It was just the same, only Tony and I are now the item. Everyone could see that, the way we held hands, the way we looked into each other's eyes. The old Tony was back, and I liked this Tony.

Gerald and Ayesha were there, acting just the way Tony and I were, and Joshua was there too. I wished that Avril and Neil were there. I couldn't wait to telephone Avril and tell her the news! Later, after the social had ended, Tony and I went for a walk. The moon was bright and a warm breeze caressed the air, carrying smoky odors from the nearby villages and native quarters. It wasn't the enchanted moon I had visualized, but it would do.

"So? What's the verdict?"

"You call this enough time? It's been less than twenty four hours!"

"Sorry, I just can't wait. Please tell me now and put me out of my misery."

"Well, okay. The answer is yes. Yes, *yes!*" I couldn't contain myself any longer, either. Tony kissed me again and again, and we walked down the road arm in arm, talking and laughing, and making plans.

20th January

Today at church, the elder Swanns were there, and so were Tony and Eric. Tony confessed that he had asked Eric to come down for the weekend just in case I had refused his proposal and he would need some support. I felt flattered that he had thought that far ahead. At least it hadn't been a spur of the moment decision for him. The Swanns were delighted with the news. They hadn't known in advance, apparently, but the news had not been a surprise to them. They fussed over me as if I had been their own daughter. Aunt Lalie never let go of me for one second, pulling me around like a child with a rag doll and telling the news to everyone we bumped into. I was disappointed. I had wanted to tell people but Lalie had taken it upon herself to be the Town Crier. If I had felt any paranoia before it was now gone. People were thrilled to hear the news and no one seemed unhappy about it. Even Gerald looked happy for me.

"I'm so glad you have found happiness, Holly," he said as he shook my hand. "Perhaps we can make it a double wedding!" I didn't think so, but I smiled anyway.

"Well, it sounds like you and Ayesha are now 'official', too."

"Yes, I popped the question over Christmas. We'll be getting married soon."

"Why isn't she coming to church with you?" sniffed Aunt Lalie. She didn't look at all happy about the news.

"She would like to, but she wants to wait a while. She's not sure how people will treat her."

"Well please tell her to come," I said, ignoring Lalie's malicious glance. "She has nothing to worry about. I'll take care of her myself and so will Eva and Faye."

Gerald gave me a grateful look as Aunt Lalie pulled me away. Not everyone had heard the news yet. There was much to do.

The minute Tootie heard the news she hurried over.

"Why haven't I heard this yet?" she thundered. "I had to hear it from Gerald, of all people!"

"Oh Tootie, we were just coming to see you," simpered Lalie. "Instead, we got waylaid by that Gerald too. He's such a simpleton. I can't imagine why anyone, even an Indian woman, would want to marry him."

I was appalled. I knew Aunt Lalie was malevolent but I had never heard her say such a terrible thing about anyone—except Avril, of course. She didn't even know Gerald or Ayesha that well! But I couldn't say anything, Lalie and Tootie were off and running, each trying to outdo the other one in verbose hate. I tuned them out and tried to wander off and leave them to it, but Lalie had a death grip on my arm, her talons digging into my skin. I endured more of the conversation until Tony arrived to extricate me from his mother's grip.

"Let me have my fiancée for a minute, mother. You've been hogging her way too long." I felt relief, and a strange, new feeling. I felt…tangible. I am no longer a non-entity…a person without substance. I am now a fiancée. I felt a sense of belonging, a sense of reality that I have never experienced before.

"I suppose that makes you my fiancé now? I'll have to get used to it."

Talk to the Moon

"Well don't sound so thrilled. You make it sound like a disease." We laughed and I felt like Lalie, clutching Tony's arm so tight it hurt my hand. I wished he was still wearing his uniform but he would never wear it again. I loved him so much in that uniform.

Still January, 1946

It wasn't until this Saturday that we went into Bulawayo to buy the ring. Tony led me to a jeweler's store, iron bars across the windows, in a seedy part of town.

"I know the jeweler. His name is Harry, and he offered me a good deal on a diamond," explained Tony. "Don't worry, he won't cheat us."

That wasn't what I had been worrying about. Harry emerged from the back of his shop, a bell having rung somewhere in the rear as we opened the door. The shop was a dark, dusty and fly spotted hole-in-the-wall. It smelled of damp and mold. Harry looked as if he farmed goats for a living and smelled like one too. He looked blankly at us and didn't seem to remember Tony having been there before. When Tony explained that he had kept a diamond for him his sallow face twitched and he went back into the rear of the shop and reemerged with a box.

"Is this it?" he asked. He opened the box and I could see a small diamond lying on a wad of cotton.

"Yes, that's it. Can we look?" He picked up the diamond and handed it to me. "It's what they call a round brilliant. It's cut to show the fire of the diamond."

"Fifty eight facets. All perfectly cut," said Harry.

I wished I could see it better. It was so dark in the store and I couldn't see the fire they were talking about. I also wished I had asked Avril for advice on diamonds when I called her this week. Avril knew about the engagement. She said that Tony had told her a week ago he was planning to propose. I felt surprise and more disappointment. Then, I wondered, perhaps he had told Avril about the engagement so she could advise him on the ring? Perhaps she had suggested this jeweler? But I didn't think so. Avril's own engagement ring had been beautiful—flawless, according to her. They had bought it at a jeweler on Fife. Not here, near the railway station.

"How many carats is this?" I asked at last. I couldn't think of anything else to say.

Harry tried, unsuccessfully, to hide a smirk. "It's point oh five one."

"That means it's not a full carat," explained Tony, "but it's not the size that's important when you are buying diamonds. You have to look at the clarity. Big diamonds can be really flawed. This one is quite clear."

Harry smirked again.

"Well, it looks okay I suppose. What about the ring?"

"Harry has one, don't you Harry?"

Harry reached down and pulled out a shoe-box from under the counter. Inside was an assortment of gold rings, missing their stones or containing what looked like cheap stones in the setting.

"Pick one."

We looked at each ring and I tried some on for size. Finally I picked one that Harry said was white gold. I didn't know what that was, but I liked the look of it and thought the stone would look good in its setting. Harry measured my ring finger, took the ring and diamond and disappeared into the back of his shop again. After what seemed like an eternity (there was nothing worth looking at in the store) he reappeared with the diamond ring in a velvet box. He opened it and I took out the ring and tried it on. It fit me perfectly. He made out an invoice for the sale while Tony dug around in his pockets, pulling out a wallet, then slowly counted out the money, one bill at a time. I tried not to look. I didn't want to know what it cost. I didn't think it cost much but it isn't the price of the ring that's important or the size of the stone. They are merely symbols. Tony isn't making a huge salary and I don't want him spending a lot of money on a ring anyway. I would feel guilty if he had. This way I can feel good about the ring. It is the most expensive thing I have ever owned and I am not about to ruin it by quibbling over the price. Tony wouldn't let me wear it just yet.

"Let's go to Nick's," he suggested. "I want to put in on your finger myself." I agreed that Harry's shop was not the most romantic setting. Nick's was a better suggestion. Both Nick and Pete were there and they celebrated our news of the engagement with a bottle of wine and some wonderful *hors de oeuvres*, on the house. I broke my rule about wine and had some. Tony placed the ring on my finger and Nick and Pete laughed and clapped. I had never been this happy.

It was then, that an awful thought occurred to me. I have not yet told Mom and Dad! I had been putting the letter off for another day, and now, I realized, I had not done it at all. I resolved to do it as soon as I got back to the mission.

Talk to the Moon

I wondered what Mom would say.

The news would surely come as a shock but she would get over it and who could not love Tony? Dad would approve of him. Maybe Tony wouldn't think he was strange in any way. Tony drank too and didn't shock easily. I hoped it would all turn out right.

11th February

I received a letter from Mom today. She's not in shock: she's outraged. She let me know in plain language that she took to her bed after receiving my letter and the doctor had been called. He had put her on a nerve tonic and diagnosed her as hysterical, but what did he know?

She is certain that I am making a huge mistake and this man was only after one thing, in her opinion, and I should know what that thing was although she was too ladylike to say it. When he had got it he would leave me and I would be a marked woman. I wonder how I would look, marked. A big scarlet letter, perhaps?

She then went on to say that she and Leolin would take the train up and meet this unscrupulous young man face to face. I translated that as, "We're coming, ready or not". Eva and I decided to wire them the train fare. We may as well get it over with.

28th February

Mom and Dad are arriving on March 6th, a week before my birthday. Pastor van Breda has volunteered to pick them up at the station in his larger car. Faye wanted to do it, but she couldn't fit both of us and our parents with their luggage, in her car. The van Breda's car was adequate for the job but it would be a squeeze. Tootie had volunteered to put up Anna and Leolin in her house for the duration of their visit. Regan is back at school and she has plenty of room for them both. We are grateful for the offer, but feel somewhat apprehensive.

What if Dad misbehaves? Can he stay off the booze for a few weeks? We don't think so. There may be an incident. We consulted Faye and put our heads together to come up with an alternate plan. The mission hasn't found a resident doctor yet. One from Bulawayo comes in every day and Neil's room in the men's quarters is still open. We explained to Tootie in the most tactful way possible that our father snores terribly and he will keep everyone in the house awake. Tootie agreed that her Robert needed his sleep (he is such a busy man!) so the Morgan's would take Neil's room. It is furnished and in easy walking distance to our compound, and they could eat with us or use the kitchen facilities in the men's quarters. Gerald was only too happy to share his house.

"I am looking forward to meeting your parents, Holly. I am sure we'll all have so much fun." I tried to hide a smile. I hope things won't get too out of hand.

CHAPTER 24

Anna and Leolin

6th March, 1946

This morning we rose early and made a final check of the room in the men's quarters. It's Spartan but comfortable. Gerald's room is on the opposite side of the house so he won't hear or observe much—we hope. We both took the day off from work and were ready when Pastor Van Breda arrived to pick us up.

"We're really grateful that you took the time off to pick up our parents, pastor. We know you're busy with the new school." Pastor van Breda has been put in charge of finding staff and procuring supplies for the new boarding school that is now almost complete. There are still a few buildings that needed completion, and Josh is working overtime to get everything in shape before the official opening in June.

"*Ja*, it's been a busy time for me wearing two hats but this is what I came here to do. Preaching is not my only skill." His face assembled itself into a modest look.

"How many teachers are there going to be?" asked Eva. "I would love to teach."

"Well, why don't you apply? We still have plenty of openings, and it would solve one of my problems."

Eva looked astounded. "Me? Are you sure…I mean, I don't have a teaching certificate or anything, but I have been to college…"

"That's all you'll need. You have a certificate in stenography, right?"

"Yes, I do."

"So don't worry then. That's more than a lot of the applicants I've seen so far."

Eva was jubilant. She had almost forgotten her anxiety about Mom and Dad's arrival. She sang in the back seat as the pastor and I discussed the new school.

We got to the track just as the train from Cape Town chuffed into the station. I could see Dad's pale face and Mom's black straw hat at a window.

Dad got off first, helping Mom as she stepped, tremulous, off the high metal steps onto the platform. Mom acts more like an eighty year old than someone who's only forty-nine. She seems to have aged even more, her face etched with newer and deeper lines around her mouth and nose. She hugged us, feebly, and looked at Pastor Van Breda.

"Is this the young man?"

"Oh no, Mom! This is our Pastor Van Breda who is also the principal of the school."

Introductions were made and her face relaxed into something that may have been a smile. Dad looked sober and alert. It must have taken a supreme effort on his part to stay away from the call of the bottle on this trip, but however it had happened I am relieved he is sober.

Mom and the pastor hit it off immediately. She sat up front with him talking with animation as he pointed out all the landmarks they passed. Dad, in turn, seemed interested in everything we had to say and asked questions and made jokes almost non-stop.

This is our old Dad! Maybe I have exaggerated his condition. Maybe he is just going through a phase in his life and now that he is out of his depression from the war things will be better. This is all that they need—a break from Cape Town and new horizons. I noticed his hands shook when I took hold of them, but I held onto his hand and Eva did the same.

When we arrived at the mission it felt as if we were seeing it again for the first time through the eyes of our parents. We could tell they were impressed. I wasn't sure what they had expected but I could see it had been nothing like the actuality. It's the first time Mom has been out of the country and Dad has not left South Africa since his arrival as a child. I thought I knew how they must feel. We took them to their room first to drop off their luggage and when the pastor had been thanked again and left we walked to our own compound.

"So, where is this man you are so determined to marry?"

"He's working today but he'll be here tonight to meet you. He's having dinner with us."

"I'm looking forward to meeting him," said Dad. "I hope he has a good sense of humor. I've been saving up some good jokes to tell him."

"Oh, he has the best sense of humor!"

Talk to the Moon

"Is he a church-goer?" persisted Mom.

Maybe Mom had time to get used to the idea: she doesn't seem so rabidly opposed to the marriage anymore. A few minutes later I got my chance to talk to Dad alone. Eva had gone to show Mom the bathroom facilities. They were no sooner out of the door when Dad spoke up first.

"Your mother had a terrible time with the news but she's over it now so don't worry about it too much. She won't oppose the wedding."

"I was so worried, Dad! I got a letter from her. She sounded so sick and I didn't know what to do about it."

"There's nothing anyone can do about it. When it comes to your mother she'll always be exactly what she is. She's a sick woman but her sickness is all in the mind. Don't allow her to spoil your life. She's not used to being crossed and fights back with unfair weapons. If she were a man I'd know how to handle her but she uses passive weapons of tears and illness and I can't fight those." He leaned back and closed his eyes.

"The trip was hell. I promised myself I wouldn't drink on the trip so I wouldn't shame you when we arrived in Bulawayo, but, my dear, I don't know how long I can hold out. You must have noticed my hands shaking. It's been three days of torture. I'd rather have three days of interrogation with the Nazi SS. They'd have put me out of my misery sooner. She prayed and read the Bible all the way here. She told me over and over how selfish you were to abandon her for a job and now a man. She said you were a sinner too, just like your father.

"Don't tell her I told you all this. She'll have another breakdown. I made her promise she would treat your intended like he was her own son. I told her that I intended to stay sober while we were here but if I heard anything out of her that I didn't like I would find a shotgun and blow her head off. I have no intention of blowing her head off but she doesn't need to know that."

I was relieved, but at the same time, depressed. Our parents are still sick, both of them. Their problems have only made a temporary retreat. I feel desperately sorry for Dad. He looks so tired and pathetic. I can see now the strain around his eyes and the tremor in his hands. He is still thin and his skin looks yellowish. I hope this self-enforced dry period will build him up enough so he can fight his demons. He has put on a wonderful show so far and I will do my best to help him through their planned two week stay.

The dinner went perfectly. Tony was on his best behavior too. We included Faye and Joan in the dinner invitation and Mom took to Joan as a kindred soul but looked askance at Faye every time Faye opened her mouth. I remember how I first felt about Faye and am not surprised. Faye is not the type of woman Mom approves of.

On the other hand, Dad liked Faye. He laughed uproariously at all of Faye's witticisms, slapping his knee and trying to outdo her in bad jokes. Mom looked disgusted and pointedly turned her back to them—talking only to Joan, Eva and me. She paid no attention to Tony, treating him with polite disdain, as if he had been a stranger who had just happened to be sitting at their table.

I walked out with Tony to where Gloria was parked. It was a cool night and he pulled me towards him, covering me with his jacket as we kissed.

"Your parents aren't as bad as you made them out to be," he said as we came up for air.

"They were on their best behavior tonight. I had a talk with my Dad today and he's going to try to stay dry while he's here. I don't know if he can do it. Whatever you do, Tony, please don't offer him a drink while he's here. He won't have the strength to resist it."

"I was hoping to share a few Lagers, but if you say so, I'll respect that."

"Thanks, Tony. You don't know how much that means to me. All hell will break loose if he drinks."

"Well, I like him. He's the jolly sort. I don't know about your mother though. She looks like the Grim Reaper. I think she and my mother would like each other." We chuckled and said goodnight. Tony is right. Aunt Lalie and Malachi Swann would love Mom.

Saturday, 9th March

Faye took us into Bulawayo today and we visited the park. Mom loved the park and even Dad looked happy and rested. His hands no longer shake and he seems stronger. Tootie invited us over for dinner and the other guests were Tony, the elder Swanns, and Eric, who was up for the weekend again.

Lalie and Mom hit it off like soul mates. They only stopped talking once and that was during the dessert when Tootie turned to Dad and said, loudly, "I have some good remedies for snoring, I do. Remind me to tell

Talk to the Moon

you about them." Dad looked mystified and all conversation at the table stopped.

We have decided to have the engagement party coincide with my 23rd birthday on the 13th. It's short notice but the mission thrives on short notice and everyone has pitched in. Since my birthday is on a Wednesday, we decided to have the party on the 16th, which is a Saturday, instead.

Friday, 15th March

I left work early today and as I cycled down the road towards the compound I heard the beep of a horn behind me and almost fell off my bicycle. A familiar Wolsely pulled up alongside. It was Avril and Neil.

"I didn't know you were coming! Oh, it's so wonderful to see you again! Go on up to the compound, my parents are over there. I want you to meet them." I reached the compound a few minutes later and rushed inside the common room to find them already seated and talking with Mom and Dad. Avril looks huge. Her face is bloated and it's the first time I have seen her look anything but beautiful. Her eyes are puffy and her ankles thick. I wonder if she's having twins. It's hard to believe two months of pregnancy could make such a difference.

"When are you due, Avril?"

"Neil says he thinks it's going to be around the middle of May. I'm of course hoping its sooner. I never knew pregnancy could be this bad. I've been sick since you left in January. My back hurts, everything is swollen and I haven't seen my feet in ages. Oh Holly, don't do this too soon, its hell!"

"It wouldn't be so bad if you did less," said Neil with a frown. "She never stops. I have to beg her to stop and rest. I've never seen such a workaholic."

"You'd love the house! It's all worth it, even though we're far from finished. Actually, we've only just started, but I can see it coming together every day. The new roof has been completed. It's a beautiful thatch and we found the best thatcher in the area to do it. The floors are next. I found terracotta Italian tiles for the living room—can you believe it—and there's enough for the dining room, kitchen and main bedroom. The other rooms will be re-cemented…" Avril continued talking until Neil interrupted.

"Let's see your ring, Holly!"

"Oh, I've been so wrapped up in what I am doing I clean forgot to ask," said Avril, looking shame-faced. "We were really thrilled to hear the news. Let's see that ring."

I held out my hand.

"Where did you get it?"

I told her and Avril clucked her tongue.

"I told Tony to go to the same place we did. He never listens! Buying anything in that part of town is risky. Isn't that right, Neil?" Neil gave her a blank look, but agreed. "Where's the certificate of authentication?" I confessed I didn't know I was supposed to get one. Avril looked at me as if I had just sprouted three heads. "I wish you'd spoken to me first." I wished I had too. "I would have told you where to go and what to look for. This is a, well, a nice ring, sweetie, but just look at it. I can tell you without being an expert that there are imperfections here." She held my hand up to the light. "Just look at that—a yellow shine to it! It's not even clear!" I felt as if Tony had bought the Brooklyn Bridge. I pulled my hand away and twisted the ring around until the diamond was hidden in the palm of my hand. Neil spoke up.

"That's enough, Avril. It's a beautiful ring. If Tony and Holly picked it out that's all that matters. No one except you is going to examine it under a microscope."

"Well, *mon cherie*, no one needs a microscope to see it's flawed. That's my whole point. I was just trying to be helpful. Maybe they could still get it changed."

"No, Avril, I love the ring and I don't really care about the flaws." Even though Avril's remarks had stung me—they were too close to what I had actually felt in that dark and dusty store—I knew I would never change the ring. What it stood for meant more to me than the price, carat, or flaws. "I appreciate your advice, Avril, but we'll keep it. At least I won't need a microscope to see the diamond."

Avril and Neil were staying with Tootie, of course. She had let them know about the party and they decided to make a weekend trip of it. Neil said it had been the only way to remove Avril from the renovations and he hoped she would take the opportunity to stay off her feet. We all agreed.

After they had left Mom looked at me. "I like this Neil chap but I don't think much of her. She's got her nose so high in the air she's in danger of getting altitude sickness. How dare she criticize your ring like that! What was all that nonsense about floor tiles and hand carved damask chairs? Who does she think she is, the Queen of Sheba? A woman in her condition should be taking care of herself more instead of worrying about tiles and houses."

Mom continued with her tirade and Eva and Dad decided to go for a walk. I wanted to go too but Mom was still talking. I couldn't just get up and leave, so I sat.

Sunday, 17th March

The party was a tremendous success last night and everyone enjoyed it—even Mom and Dad. Mom acted like a young girl again and she even began to look younger. Dad was the perfect gentleman and did his best to charm every woman in the place. I was the only one who noticed the wistful glances at the lemonade punch bowl on the table. He nursed the glass in his hand and I knew he was pretending it was something stronger. He didn't drink it, but caressed the glass as he spoke or waved it around as if to punctuate a sentence. I knew that he would sell his soul at the moment for a bottle of good Scotch. It must have taken a Herculean act of will for him not to give in to his cravings, although I wondered, if he didn't bring anything with him, where he would get it. There is no alcohol on the mission and none of the Native stores sell it. The Africans make their own home brew from millet but, as a white man and a stranger, he wouldn't know how to go about getting it. I relaxed.

Monday, 18th March

All hell has broken loose.

Tony took Dad this afternoon for a spin on Gloria. I thought they would be gone for half an hour, at the most, but by sundown they were still not back. At 9:00 p.m. we heard Gloria's roar approaching the compound. We ran outside, apprehension on our faces but also relief that the men had finally made it home.

Our worst fears were sitting, or rather slouching, over Gloria as she weaved into the compound.

"*Hey girlsh*! We had fun today!"

It was evident they had. Mom's mouth clamped shut like a steel trap and she turned around and marched into our room, slamming the door shut behind her. Eva sighed, "*Oh no!*" We could smell the rancid liquor fumes from where we were standing above the oily odor of Gloria. Tony unsteadily got off the bike, leaving Dad to fall off. They were both laughing as Tony tried to help Dad up off the ground and almost falling himself. They drunkenly dusted themselves down.

"What's wrong, love?" asked Tony, pretending that he had only now noticed my expression.

"She's trying to make us feel guilty for having a good time, Tony. Just like her mother. Can't a man go out once in a while and enjoy himself? If you want to keep a man happy, young lady, you'd better remember that he needs a long rope once in a while."

"Yes, so he can hang himself," said Eva. I was still too angry to speak. After I had asked Tony…explained it all to him…and he still…. I turned around and went into my room, forgetting Mom was there. Eva followed.

"I can't believe they rode on the motorcycle from wherever they were, in that condition," said Eva. "How they never managed to kill themselves…."

"I asked Tony not to give him anything to drink. How could he have done that?"

"Don't blame him. Maybe he didn't. Maybe Dad just did it himself and Tony joined in."

"And maybe pigs fly," said Mom. She was sitting on the chair by the desk. "We need to pray, girls. The devil has your father in his grip and won't let go. Let us all kneel."

"Oh Mom!" said Eva. "I don't think praying is going to help sober them up. Let them sleep it off. We may as well too. You can sleep here if you like. I'll take the couch in the living room. Use my bed. They can do whatever they want to."

Tuesday, 19th March

Tony was nowhere to be found this morning. Dad was asleep, snoring loudly, in his bed. We searched the room. If he had brought anything back with him, we wanted to find it, but we found nothing. Mom looked in the toilet tank in the bathroom.

"His favorite spot."

It wasn't there either. We gave up and left. Avril and Neil were waiting for us at the compound. They were taking us on a picnic.

"Are you ready to leave? Where's your Dad?"

"Dad's not well," I said. No one contradicted me. Avril knew of Dad's problems. I had told her briefly once before, but I did not feel like going into it all again today.

"Should I take a look at him?" asked Neil.

"No, he's fine, he just has a migraine. He says he needs a day to rest. He's been overdoing things too."

Talk to the Moon

They accepted that and there were no more questions. We got into the Wolsely and drove to the Matopos. Mom and Avril ignored each other as much as possible, giving each other wary, sidelong glances when they thought no one was watching.

We sat under some shady trees on a blanket and I wished I could just stay here, under this tree, and never return to the compound until it was time for Mom and Dad to leave. I didn't want to go back and face Tony or Dad.

I wished Josh were here, now. I could talk to him and he would understand how I felt. His father is an alcoholic, too. I wanted to talk to somebody. Mom and Eva were prattling on about nothing in particular, and I wanted to scream at them and tell them to stop pretending everything was normal, but it was the exact same thing I was doing myself, so I kept quiet as I twisted my engagement ring around and around on my finger. I love Tony. Why does he do these things to me? Why does he always know how to make me angry, and how to disappoint me?

Avril got up.

"I need to use the facilities: one of the joys of being pregnant. Do you want to come with me, Holly?"

I got up and we walked towards the primitive toilets near the picnic area.

"Ok, so what's bothering you? And don't say 'nothing' because I know there's something wrong. You've had this lemon-sucking expression on your face all day!"

"You're right, Avril. I've so wanted to talk but it's too difficult with my mom around. She's not the easiest person."

Avril smiled. "You can say that again. Is it her?"

"No, it's Tony and my father." I explained what had happened and how I felt about it.

"Tony, Tony, Tony," she clucked. "He only thinks of himself sometimes. I bet he wanted to have a drink and thought your Dad could sit and watch him throw back a few without being tempted. What an arse he is. I would kick him where it hurts, dear. If you don't mind, I'll talk to Neil and see if he can suggest something. There must be something we can do for your father."

"I don't mind you talking to Neil, just don't do it in front of Eva and mom. No knowing how they'll react when the subject comes up."

Avril promised she wouldn't. I felt lighter, as if sharing my problems halved them, and I managed to relax and enjoy the picnic and the rest of the day.

We got back to the mission later this afternoon. Tony and Dad were at the compound waiting for us. They both looked sober although Dad looked shaky and weak. Tony looked shamefaced. Before I or anyone could say anything, he stood up.

"I know you all know about my behavior last night," he said. "I can see it in your faces." Neil looked puzzled. "I just wanted to apologize to everyone here, especially you, Mrs. Morgan. I did you a great disservice. If you are going to be my mother-in-law, I need to learn how to behave better around you. Please don't hold this against me. It will never happen again." Mom's mouth opened then closed. She didn't say anything.

"What's going on here?" asked Neil.

"I haven't told you yet, darling," said Avril. "Holly told me earlier but asked me not to say anything yet. Now that it's all out, Tony can fill you in."

Tony did. He didn't spare himself either. According to him, they had planned on driving just a short distance but had ended up at Tshabanda where they had found Nigel Withers well into his own solitary party. He insisted they stay and have a drink. Dad had declined but Tony hadn't. He thought he would have a quick one and they'd be back on the track again before it got dark. Unfortunately, one turned into two, and by that time Dad had joined them.

When it got dark they had decided that they may as well be hung for twenty as for one and they continued to drink. Fortified by whiskey and full of false bravado, they decided to risk the treacherous track back to the mission in the dark.

"I can't believe I was so stupid," acknowledged Tony. "We could have both died out there in the dark. No one would have found us for a while."

They discussed the situation for a while longer as a thoughtful Neil rubbed his temples and forehead.

"How badly do you want to get better?" he asked Dad.

"I don't know," he muttered. "I thought I could do it. I really did. But it was too much for me."

"There's a program out in America for alcoholics. It's been out since the thirties and I don't know what it's about but I hear it has been successful in treating alcoholism. The bad news is that it's not here yet, as far as I know. I will talk to a friend of mine at the Bulawayo General Hospital. He gets involved in this kind of stuff and will know what to do. I'll make a phone call. Wait here."

Neil disappeared. The nearest phone was at the mission hospital, so I presume that's where he was. We all sat around making awkward small talk until Neil returned.

"I couldn't locate him, but I spoke to the Matron. She knows what it's all about and told me to bring him in."

"What, now!" exclaimed Dad. "We don't have money for hospital visits. I'm not sick, or an alcoholic! I just don't know my limits, sometimes!"

"Don't worry about the money. We'll cross that bridge when we come to it. Get in the car. Who wants to come with me?" Tony and I volunteered and Avril and Eva stayed with Mom. Dad got in the car, muttering about it all being a lot of hoopla about nothing and that he was no alcoholic, it was just that he overdid it sometimes, but he was ignored.

Bulawayo General is a genteel white building with shady verandah's set in the middle of well-tended gardens. Everything in this city looks so park-like. The sun was setting and turning the white walls into an orange glow as we walked up towards the entrance. Neil asked for the Matron when we arrived at admissions, and she helped us check Dad into a private ward. He looked so forlorn I felt like crying. I hated to leave him there but we had no choice. The doctor explained that there was a danger of him going into DT's if not treated properly. He was in good hands, I felt.

CHAPTER 25

Gabriel Blanchard

23rd March
The drying out process has kept Dad in the hospital for three days. Avril and Neil returned to Mt. Darwin but Faye offered to take us into Bulawayo every night to visit with Dad. He told us that he had spoken to a doctor who had diagnosed him with later stage alcoholism.

"A bloody psychiatrist. Why they think I need a head doctor I don't know. I drink, I'm not crazy."

No one knew what to say about this, so we kept quiet. He was on medication and he looked less shaky than the last time we saw him. He picked up the Bulawayo *Chronicle* and waved it at us.

"Been looking through the job section. May as well. I think your mother and I need a change and a new start will help me to stop drinking. If we go back to Cape Town, I know I'll drink. I like it here, anyway."

Eva and I looked at each other. We didn't know what to say. Mom's face brightened. "I hope they don't check your past employment too thoroughly," was all she said.

"My father works on the Railways," said Faye. "I can ask him if there are any job openings." She shot me an apologetic look. "He's not the best person for your Dad, but he seems to know what's going on there."

"I'll take anything," said Dad.

26th March
Dad, with Mom's approval and encouragement, has applied for a Railway job. Faye's father told her there were plenty of job openings and he should apply as soon as possible. He gave us the name of a man to see.

1st April
Dad has a job. Mom has made arrangements to return to Cape Town by train so she can pack up their belongings and freight them to Bulawayo while Dad and I search for a house.

The Railways offered them a house in the same area as the Johnson's, but Mom, to my relief, flatly refuses to live there. She doesn't want to be

Talk to the Moon

surrounded by railway people, as she put it. Eva offered to go back with her, taking her annual leave, so she could help with the packing. I don't know which I feel more: gratitude or compassion towards Eva for volunteering to return with Mom. I also feel guilt—that I wasn't the one to volunteer, but I can't leave Tony for a month! A month with Mom would be hell. Without Tony by my side, hell would be an improvement.

Dad has a week's grace before starting his job. We scanned the paper to see what houses were available for rent and Faye drove us to the houses we circled.

Most are beyond what they can afford but we did find one in Bellevue, a sprawling suburb on the western outskirts of the city. It's a semi-detached house, shared by a retired couple, and it has a large garden in a quiet street. Best of all it's on a main bus route which will be convenient. Dad says he wants to buy a motorcycle like Tony's as soon as he can. He doesn't want to be dependent on public transportation to get to work although the bus will be perfect for Mom.

They had not needed their own transportation in Cape Town. The public transportation had been more than adequate and there had been no need to drive. We were told the house will be ready for occupancy on 15th April.

4th April

Hattie has a son! Weighs 8 pounds 7 ounces and his name is David John. Must let Eva know. Hattie's mother had called the office looking for Eva, but when she was told Eva was not there she had asked to speak to me instead. I sent a telegram to Eva immediately. I know Eva will be thrilled at the news. They are due back on the 17th.

I have begun to feel close to Dad again. I realize that it's the drink that changes him and when he's sober he's a different person. I have told him everything that has happened to me since arriving in Bulawayo over a year ago. He listened without comment but I could tell he is happy that I am able to confide in him. When I finished, he said:

"I think Tony is a fine man, Holly, and I like him a lot, but I'll be honest with you. He likes the bottle nearly as much as I do. Don't marry a man just like me!" He smiled to take the sting out of his words but I feel disheartened. I don't want to marry an alcoholic. Tony isn't an alcoholic, surely? He's still young and wants to have fun; to escape the rigid upbringing he'd had and the strictness of the church and its narrow minded views of everything. I can understand that. The first time I saw him drunk was a few weeks ago. Dad has been drunk every night for many years. Tony isn't like him at all. I wonder if Dad thinks that everyone who drinks is like him. I didn't say anything but I smiled and kissed his cheek. I will marry Tony; I am sure of that.

17th April

Anna and Eva have returned. A week later the freight arrived and I took a guilt-week off work to help them move it all into the house. I will be staying with them in Bellevue, sleeping on a foldout bed in the living room.

25th April

I feel so far from Tony in Tshabanda. He hasn't been to see me. He is obviously afraid of Mom.

The old couple in the other half of the house are delighted to have Mom for companionship. They're Afrikaners and treat Mom like a gift from heaven. Perhaps their move to Rhodesia isn't such a bad idea after all.

Dad has so far kept his promise. He gets up at 4:00 a.m. to start his 6:00 a.m. shift, taking two buses to get to work. He arrives home at 4:00 p.m. every afternoon talking about his new job and his fellow shift workers. Mom has a meal of meatballs, rice and cabbage prepared, alternating it every other day with her shepherd's pie. I don't attempt to relieve Mom of her penal servitude in the kitchen. I eat the meals and don't complain. I remember there were times at the mission when I longed for Mom's burned meatballs and watery shepherd's pies.

Eva and I have helped them out financially as well. They have run into many expenses from the move and they can scarcely make the first month's rent on the house. We drew on our savings. We have been saving up ever since we got to King's Kraal, and although to someone else it's not a lot of money, to us it is. Eva said she had been saving to buy a horse, and I had been thinking about having a big wedding, like Avril's, knowing I would have to pay for it myself. I can still have a wedding but it will have to be smaller. I will find ways to cut costs. Eva said the horse could wait.

Tony and I have still not decided on a date. He has said that he wants to see how much our housing allowance will be. Nigel has promised him a considerable raise in salary—dependent on his marital status—before deciding. I wonder if this carrot had been dangled in front of him prior to his unexpected proposal, but I shouldn't be thinking that way. No one could be that avaricious. I am getting paranoid. Why can't I just accept that Tony loves me? I always doubt, suspecting ulterior motives in everything he does.

19th May

The news today is the birth of Gabriel St. Aubin Blanchard. He is a small baby, weighing just over 7 pounds, but, according to Neil, who had called with the news, Avril said it still felt as if she had given birth to a heifer. They are both doing well, he said, and would be leaving the hospital in a few days.

"I got her there just in time," he said. "She began her contractions after going to bed and we reached the hospital a few minutes before Gabriel arrived. We'll bring the baby down to Bulawayo soon. Avril can't wait to show him off, and I am as proud as she is. Her parents are arriving in a few days. I just wish my father had been here to see his grandson."

I wished too that Mr. Blanchard could have been there. How unfair that he had to die months before the event that would have made him so happy. Then Neil dropped the bombshell.

"I know Avril wants to ask you this herself but I thought I'd better prepare you. Would you consider being godmother to Gabriel? It would make us both so happy to know someone responsible like you will be around as he grows up. We have discussed this and, besides Faye, you are the only one Avril trusts enough to take care of her son if anything happens to us. Would you think about it?"

"Oh, Neil, there is nothing to think about! I would love to be godmother to Gabriel! Please let Avril know that I am honored to be asked and I will do everything I can to be the best godmother a boy can have." I called Tony right away with the news. I am right, he is pleased.

"That's such an honor; they must think a lot of you, Holly. I know they do anyway, but this is really confirmation." He laughed. "I don't think they think as much of me as they do of you, but together we'll make fine godparents."

6th July

It's been so long since I last wrote in my diary.

Tony and I have decided that we'll be married in July, '47. It's a long time to wait but we both need to save more money because Tony wants to buy a house. He says he doesn't want to be a renter. I think it's a good idea, since he is talking about being transferred to the Bulawayo office. I am going to miss the mission!

Eva has been accepted for the position of teacher. The school's opening is scheduled for August and it already has enrolled many students, both boarders and day scholars, from the surrounding reserves. Josh showed us around the school. There are several low, tin roof whitewashed buildings and five classrooms. The other buildings are dormitories, one for boys and one for girls. Teacher's quarters have been built nearby and Eva will be moving in soon. I will miss her.

A requisition has been put in for replacements for Eva and Ayesha. Gerald has insisted that after their wedding in November, Ayesha will stay at home.

"No wife of mine will ever need to work," he told me. He gave me a sidelong glance as he had said this, and I wondered if he thought he still had a chance. I hope not. Ayesha deserves more than that. I hope Ayesha doesn't feel having a job is important. Since the war ended there are more women in the market for jobs and staying at home is no longer the only option. I know I would like to keep my job after the wedding but if we buy a house in Bulawayo it may not be advisable. I don't want to drive back and forth every day to the mission.

I wonder who my new roommate will be.

17th July

Eva's replacement has been announced. She is Paula Redman, from Bulawayo, and all of eighteen years old. She will be sharing Room One with me during the week and returning home for the weekends. She knows how to type and take shorthand. I only hope we will get along in such close quarters.

Ayesha's job has been eliminated. The church has embarked on a cost cutting crusade and jobs are the first to go. The school has taken much of available funds, and postwar donations are down to a trickle. Boarders need to eat and they do not come from African families who can afford private boarding school fees. They pay what they can afford but it won't be nearly enough to pay costs of board and tuition. For that, donations are essential. I make sure I tithe regularly, putting in as much as I can afford, and I asked Tony to do the same. He is not open to it.

"I work hard for my money. I don't know why I should be expected to throw it away on educating *kaffirs* who will only go back to the reserve and drink beer. If they want free education there's plenty of government schools that will do that. I don't know why the mission got into this school thing to begin with."

"That's because there aren't enough government schools to accommodate every child. The distances to travel are too far for many children so they don't bother. Esther told me that she used to get up at 3:00 a.m. to be at school on time. She'd also have to do chores first. If we can give some children a chance for a complete education then I feel a few pounds a month from my own salary is worth it. What time did you have to get up in the morning to get to school?"

Tony looked ashamed.

"Well, the old man threw us out of bed at 5:00 a.m. and I thought he was being a tyrant. I never thought that I had it easy compared to others. Shows how wrong you can be. I'll be a good Christian boy and tithe in the future if it will make you happy."

CHAPTER 26

Paula

Sunday, 28th July

Avril and Tony are here this weekend for the Christening. Avril has regained her youthful, svelte figure and the puffiness around her face has disappeared, replaced by an apricot blush of smooth, velvety cheeks. Gabriel is still tiny but everyone agrees on one thing: he is the most beautiful baby we have seen. His dark hair is thick and wavy and his eyes are bright blue. Even though it's difficult to ascribe intelligence or personality to a child so young I feel that my godson has a remarkable look of awareness to him that defies logic. I love him so much already!

I stepped up to the podium today with Gabriel's parents to receive the blessing. Avril's parents stayed for the Christening and then left for South Africa. I do wonder why Avril did not asked Faye to be Gabriel's godmother. She has always seemed much closer to Faye than me, and had known Faye longer. Perhaps it's because Faye has no intention of getting married. Maybe they want a couple as godparents rather than a single woman. Faye's feelings don't seem to be hurt. She fusses over Gabriel as much as anyone.

The only person I am concerned about is Neil. He looks thoughtful, and didn't say much, even for Neil. I mentioned it to Tony, but he said he hadn't noticed anything different: Neil was always like that; he was probably overwhelmed with the baby and that was that. I don't think so. There's a look to Neil that's different. I can't nail it down it but it's there. Sadness, perhaps? Not an emotion one would expect from a new father. He holds the baby like a new father, proud and gentle, but the eyes betray something—something different. Since I am the only one who has noticed this I will put it down to my overactive imagination and general paranoia.

Josh has left the mission. It isn't unexpected—his job is complete and it's time for him to move on, he said. He has been offered a job in the reserves, in the northwest part of the country, building a government clinic. He told me that he will also be doing a lot of hunting in that area.

There are no butchers or stores nearby and he will have to shoot Impalas or Kudus for his work force.

I will miss him.

I've also noticed Eric has been visiting the mission rather a lot in the past few months. At first I thought he was visiting Tony, but he doesn't seem to spend much time with Tony and me, yet he's always taking Eva somewhere. The last weekend he visited they went to the movies. I don't think Eva thought of it as a date: he had been way too awkward asking her to go with him, so we both assumed that he merely wanted company since Tony and I had made other plans. But then he had taken her out again the next weekend he was visiting, and the next, until I realized that his trips were not to see Tony or his parents, but Eva! I asked Eva if she and Eric were now officially dating.

"I don't know! I suppose we are. He's not a bad person at all, Holly," she said, noticing the expression on my face. "He's really sweet and shy. He hasn't any idea how to do things and he says he's never had a girlfriend before. I took him to meet mom and Dad last week and they both like him." I didn't see this coming, but I didn't say anything. It's far better to see Eva dating Eric than to see her lonely and dateless. She has made new friends after the departure of Hattie but she's not as close to any of them as she was to Hattie.

Things on the home front in Bellevue continue to look good. Dad has not had a drink since the Tshabanda incident and even Mom seems more cheerful during my visits. She has made friends in the Bulawayo congregation and attends Sunday services faithfully. Some church members live nearby and they pick her up every Sunday so she won't have to take two buses. Dad continues to refuse to attend church, saying he will certainly drink if he is forced to go. Mom has never mentioned it again.

Zebras do not change their stripes, and Mom is still a whiner. She will keep after Dad about something until he snaps and begins to shout back at her. Mom did not bring Dad's shotgun up with them. She sold it in Somerset West and we thought it a wise move.

The fights are not as turbulent as they were when Dad drank but they are disturbing. Sometimes he will grab his pack of cigarettes and his hat and stride out of the house, slamming the front door behind him. Where he goes we don't know, but he always comes back, still sober. I think he walks off his rage. There are many paths through the savannah in front of the house and Eva and I or Mom and I sometimes take long walks through the dry scrubby veldt to the railway tracks. These are the tracks that go to Plumtree, on the border of Bechuanaland—the same tracks Eva and I had traveled on.

Mom will walk along the path slowly, picking up every scrap of shiny foil she can find—usually from cigarette packs. She squeezes it into a small ball, and when she finds the next paper, whether from cigarettes or a sweet she will wrap that around the first piece, and so on, until she has a large ball of shiny papers. We asked her what she planned on doing with this ball.

"Oh, it's for the blind. They can reuse them—they make things, you know?" We haven't heard of this but it seems to calm her. She does the same thing with string. Any piece of string, no matter what its condition or length, gets wound around a ball that gets bigger each day. It's for the blind too, she explains. We wonder what the blind are going to do with this trash but we never say anything. We silently collect shiny papers and pieces of string as we walk. It has become such a ritual and its fun to see who has the most string or the biggest ball of papers at the end of the walk.

Saturday, 3rd August

The school opened today. Pastor van Breda officiated at the ceremony with the proud teachers sitting in rows behind him. With the exception of Eva, they are all Ndebele and Jesuit trained. There are many young children enrolled in the lower classes, while there are as yet only two forms represented in the high school and those are not filled to capacity. Some of the classes have to double up with one teacher. Eva has been assigned the youngest children, from ages 6 through 8, many of whom cannot speak English.

She's nervous.

"I know I'm going to make a mess of this, Holly!" she exclaimed in desperation hours before the opening. "Do you think they'll be able to find someone else at short notice if I tell them I can't do it?"

"Don't be silly, Eva, you'll do fine. I'll help you, I promise, and it's a good opportunity for us both to learn some Sindebele. Take my books, you should start immediately. And don't worry about the children; they'll pick up English quickly." I feel exasperated with Eva. Did she think the children would arrive at school fluent in English? She's had time to think about it and plenty of time to begin her language lessons. The books I bought and am now studying make it easy and I had encouraged Eva to learn but Eva was too preoccupied with other things. Eva took the books. I hope she can fake it for the first few weeks.

1st August

I miss the bear's den that used to be Eva's side of the room. Gone is the clutter and disorder—it is now replaced by a nihilism and slovenliness that takes my breath away. Compared to Paula, Eva is merely an apprentice anarchist. Her possessions fill her own side of the room and spill over onto my turf. She has more clothes than Avril and her makeup lies on every surface in untidy piles. She doesn't read, unless it's a comic book, but she has brought her own wind up gramophone and what seems to be every record ever made by Frank Sinatra, Bing Crosby and a duo I have never heard of.

10th August

I am entertaining dark and homicidal thoughts every time I hear the talentless duo screeching *Someday I'll Find You*. The smell of stale foot odor permeates the room.

"It isn't my fault," she shrugs, when I ask her to put her shoes outside. "My Mom has it too and we can wash and use foot powder all we like, it doesn't help." Bathing every other day seems to be her norm, and even though it's still winter the warm days bring on a light perspiration that could become offensive in a few hours. She also wears cheap lisle stockings every day, sometimes more than once, before laundering them. When she does launder them they hang dripping in the bathroom until Faye tells her to hang them somewhere else. She doesn't want wet things flapping in her face when she takes a bath. Faye is sympathetic but there doesn't seem to be an alternative to the problem of Paula.

Esther tries her best to clean up after her but Paula nit-picks and blames Esther for things that I know she is not responsible for. Yesterday I came across Paula chastising Esther for losing an item of clothing. Esther insisted she had not seen the item and I believed her. When I took sides with Esther, a sulky Paula retreated, and we haven't spoken since. Paula is a beautiful girl. She has a cute upturned nose and odd, amber eyes, like a cat. I think she is pleasant and sweet faced in company but sullen and vain in private. I hope she will grow out of her piques and mature soon.

Tony doesn't seem impressed with Paula, much to my relief.

"Never liked blondes much," he said. "I prefer someone more sophisticated." I agreed but at the same time wondered if I would ever meet Tony's criteria of sophisticated. I don't think so, but at least I am a smidgeon ahead of Paula on the proverbial trip around the block.

Eva loves her new job. All doubts have vanished and she tells me that she has found her true profession. She adores the children and they have no trouble communicating. She is making an effort to learn Sindebele and has picked up enough to make the children laugh. Quite often Pastor van Breda has to come and see what the noise is about. He finds Eva's class in paroxysms of laughter, shrieking and leaping around the classroom with Eva leading the riot in a game they have just invented. He then pulls Eva out of the classroom and sternly tells her that this is a school, not a nursery, and he expects her to control the children and to act in a dignified way. She agrees and says that she has no idea what happened, but she won't do it again, and a few days later the same scenario is repeated. He has begun to ignore the clamor, only intervening during the worst fracases when it's likely the other classes will be disturbed. The children idolize her and she does seem to be teaching them something in spite of her haphazard methods.

Ayesha and Gerald have set their wedding day for 16th November. Since Tootie has declined to offer her services—much to everyone's relief—Faye, Eva and I are helping Ayesha and her family organize things. The Ghoshes have accepted Ayesha's choice of a husband and are even willing to have the wedding at the mission church instead of the traditional Hindu ceremony at their temple.

Ayesha has converted to Christianity and was baptized during the annual baptism at the camp meeting. She is now a member of the church. There are a handful of those who cannot, or will not, accept her, an Indian woman, into their social circle. However, and I find this just as true as it's opposite—there are just as many if not more who accept her completely and without reservation, not just in church services, but into their homes and hearts.

Tony is Gerald's best man and Faye and Eva are Ayesha's bridesmaids. Tony jokingly said to me, "always the best man, never the groom!" while I wondered why I have never been chosen for a bridesmaid. I don't begrudge Faye or Eva—Eva is so excited—but I have always been the bystander. Then I remembered I had been chosen to be a godmother to Gabriel and my pity party came to an end.

CHAPTER 27
Ayesha

16th November
The wedding was beautiful. It poured this morning but as soon as Tootie struck up the wedding march on the piano the sun came out and a beam of light came through a window bathing everyone in a golden glow. I thought that was a good omen.

Tony is his usual handsome self, and not for the first time, I imagined myself standing in Ayesha's spot next year, with Tony by my side. The Ghosh's had outdone themselves in preparations, holding the reception at their home a few miles from the mission on a damp lawn under scarlet Flamboyant trees. They served Indian food with a sit down dinner and punch bowls of non-alcoholic punches. They knew Gerald and the church did not approve of alcohol and decided to respect that wish. It was also cheaper, Ayesha told us, laughing.

Tootie and Robert Parrish behaved like human beings toward the Ghosh's, and Gerald and Ayesha, much to my relief. I didn't think Mr. Parrish would be rude or insensitive but it's Tootie we had been concerned about. My boss has never seemed to be color conscious in any way and always conducts his life in the same way—bland and inoffensive. He has no opinions about anything that do not involve accounting or administrative matters. After working closely with him for nearly two years I feel no more enlightened about him than I was on my first day of work at the mission. He is the perfect politician at social events, doing what's expected and no more.

Tootie was the queen by his side playing peasant for the day with the riff-raff and laughing out loud when Ro-bert, red in the face with effort, attempted a joke. Tony, on the other hand, was the life of the party. All—Indian, Ndebele and white—enjoyed his jokes. They were clever and obviously well-rehearsed, and his speech and toasts went over well.

The elder Swann's did not make it to the wedding. Tony said his mother hadn't been feeling well and I didn't ask questions. I would rather not know if there had been any other motivation for not attending the wedding. Eric attended, and he stuck to Eva like a thorn to a rosebush, not taking his eyes off her once. The writing is on the wall. Eva, still rebounding from Gerald's indifference, can't resist this kind of attention. She has pretended for a long time she's happy but I can always see through the sham.

Today, Eva's eyes were overly bright and I know she was making a real effort to be vivacious, but it looked contrived—more like a manic spell. Eric doesn't seem to notice Eva's not-so-subtle nuances of moods and this worries me. He grins like a hyena as he shambles alongside her.

I had a good time in spite of the fact that Tony had brought along his own supply of liquor and surreptitiously added it to the punch. Everyone else had a wonderful time too, and no one ever found out who the culprit was. I knew it was something only Tony could do. He denied it, but the twinkle in his eyes told me otherwise.

Christmas Day, 1946

Last night, Eva and Eric announced their engagement. Predictably, both sets of parents are delighted.

"We couldn't be happier that our sons are marrying two such wonderful sisters," exclaimed Aunt Lalie to me at the Christmas service today. "We also think highly of your mother, dear, and we know she's as happy as we are." I didn't pause to wonder why Dad hadn't been mentioned—word has leaked out about his weakness and as far as Aunt Lalie and Malachi Swann are concerned, his status is deceased.

The deceased is also pleased.

"He'll take care of our Eva. He seems the steady type—not like me, eh! I think he'll calm her down and she'll be too busy on the farm to worry about us. She'll also be away from her mother's influence. I don't think that fact has occurred to your mother yet." I didn't think so, either, and I didn't bring it up. Mom had no idea of the distances involved. Bulawayo is a considerable drive from the farm in Fort Victoria. Eric did it often, but once he and Eva are married, there won't be any reason for him to visit Bulawayo quite so frequently. I hope Dad is right.

Tony also seems to think they're a good match.

"Now she'll stop mooning over Gerald. Eric's twice the man Gerald is anyway. There're a lot of women in Fort Vic who would be happy to get Eric. I know he's no Einstein, but he's solid and a hard worker. She won't want for anything."

Talk to the Moon

I don't feel Tony's opinions of his brother's marital assets sound very attractive. I know Eva wants more out of life than hard work; she also wants some romance and fun. She won't find much of this with Eric. The bright spot on the horizon is that she loves animals. Now she can have all the horses, cats and dogs she can handle. It is, in my estimation, the only way Eva can be happy with this arrangement.

We are thinking of a double wedding to save costs and to make it easier on both sets of parents. I'm not sure yet if that is a good idea. Dreams about my wedding have never included another couple even if one of those people happens to be my sister. Tony says he doesn't mind one way or another. I have decided to nix this proposal.

CHAPTER 28

Peaches

4 January, 1947

We spent New Year's day with Mom and Dad. Mom said the double wedding was an excellent idea, and she can't imagine why I wouldn't want to do it. She asked if I want to hog it all to myself. Perhaps Mom is right: I can't even share my wedding day with my own sister. She has already informed Eva that I have agreed to a double wedding. Eva looked so happy that I couldn't tell her it hadn't been my idea. I have decided to be at peace with this decision. It has been made and there is no going back. I may as well enjoy it.

I can't help but think of our last New Year at Greystones. I know Eva is trying to forget about it. She has refused to discuss it at all. She blames herself for Mr. Blanchard's death—convinced it was she who picked a bad mushroom by mistake and that somehow it found its way into his omelet. I have tried to convince her that it wasn't the mushrooms and that even if it was, anyone could have picked it, including Mr. Blanchard but she refuses to be comforted. She says she will go to her grave knowing she killed someone and that is all she will ever say about it. I wonder too if perhaps Eva is right. Not that she picked the mushroom—no one will ever know that—but perhaps that his death was caused by a poisonous mushroom that found its way into his food.

But then, why had Avril said what she had said? It doesn't make any sense…only…if she had done something herself. I just cannot believe it. Won't believe it! Avril had been as upset as any of us! It was either a horrible accident or his death had been natural. I must accept that. I have decided to take a leaf out of Eva's book and never think about it again. Avril is my friend and nothing will ever change that, I am sure.

6th January

Avril called today.

"*Ma Cherie*! I am so lonely here on the farm. It's so good to hear an adult voice again. The reason I called is to ask, no—beg—you to come up

Talk to the Moon

and spend a few days with me, or as long as you want. I do miss my friends so much."

"I'd love to, dear. As a matter of fact, I was just thinking it would be a good idea to go somewhere for a few days. I would like to see my godson again!"

"Oh, he's getting so big now, you won't believe it. He's seven months old and as big as a sack of mielie-meal. I struggle to pick him up, and he's crawling everywhere. It won't be long before he's walking. Maybe Tony can bring you up?"

"What, four hours on Gloria's back pillion? No, I don't think so. I'll take the train."

"I've just had an idea. Why don't you ask Faye if she would like to drive up? I would like to see Faye; it's been so long since we talked. Maybe she can get some time off too?" I thought that was a wonderful idea. It would save me a slow train trip and I will enjoy Faye's company. I wonder if Faye's Austin will be able to make the journey. It looks more decrepit by the day. I decided to ask Faye.

"But of course she can make it!" Faye exclaimed "I've just had her in for some repairs. I even got her front seat fixed. And I'd love to go. I want to see that dear, sweet baby again before he goes off to medical school." We've decided to go the end of January when we can both get some time off work. I was concerned that Tony might feel left out that I didn't ask him to take me, but he was pleased that Faye and I were going.

"I would like to be going with you, of course," he said, "but I have some end of the month projects that are important so I'll let you go and enjoy yourself with Faye and Avril. Just don't have too much of a good time without me." I'm sure I won't.

Wednesday, 29th January

Faye and I left early this morning, stopping briefly in Gwelo for some breakfast, and arrived at Greystones around noon.

Even before we got out of the car I noticed things looked different. The garden with the rectangular fish pond has been cleared and the once straggly bushes are now pruned and clipped. The flowerbeds have been replanted and there is even a green lawn. The pond's flat leafed water lilies shelter carp and goldfish swimming in an emerald green bed. The driveway has been paved with stone to match the outside walls of the house. The house itself looked different to me too—the old, thinning, darkened thatch that had been there a year ago was now thick and lush.

Avril came out to meet us.

"You've no idea how good it is to see you two again. I'm so happy you could come!" An African woman in a starched white uniform walked out of the house holding Gabriel. I eagerly took him from her and Faye and I took turns holding him and exclaiming over and over how much he'd grown.

"I told you," said Avril. "He's enormous. He's really made up for his earlier weight. Okay, Violetta, you can take him in now. It's time for his bottle. Make sure you warm it up right this time, then give him his bath and put him to bed."

Violetta said "Yes, madam," and silently disappeared.

We walked up the verandah stairs into the house. I never would have recognized it if I had been blindfolded and taken into the house. Avril watched for our reactions and we didn't disappoint her.

Avril told us the house had been gutted. Where the interior walls between the living room and dining room had once been there are now architectural curving partial walls painted stark white with huge blackened beams of wood rising to rough-hewn rafters under the thatch in one large space.

The fireplace is still there, its stone hearth the piece de resistance while the old Victoriana has disappeared and is now replaced with artful antiques. A large Zebra skin rug on the shiny, terracotta floor adds to an atmosphere of effortless African gentility.

"So, what do you think?"

"Oh, it's the most beautiful house I have ever seen! I think when you described it, I couldn't quite visualize it, but now I see what you mean. You've done a magnificent job, Avril!" Even Faye was impressed.

"I don't know what it looked like before, but I like it."

"Look!" said Avril, pleased with our reactions. She reached for a wall switch and clicked it on. A metal chandelier hanging from the rafters glowed with a yellow light. "Electricity! Let me take you to your rooms, and I'll also show you the rest of the house."

The long passageway now glows warm with accent lights until it reaches the second leg of the verandah where it opens up into airy French doors. My old room had changed significantly, as well, but the French doors are the only feature that has remained intact from the old design. The old cotton curtains have been replaced with matchstick blinds and gauzy panels that flutter gently in soft zephyrs of air blowing through the open doors. Faye's room is similar except hers has large windows overlooking the back garden instead of French doors.

Avril wanted to show us the nursery too, and I recalled that the room, built into the verandah, had previously been a storeroom of some kind. Now, it's a cheerful room painted in soft yellow and stenciled borders of colorful balloons. A lace covered crib stands in one corner.

"I painted this room myself," said Avril, her voice betraying her pride. I did it before Gabriel was born. Almost cost me a miscarriage."

Avril led us back up the passageway to the office. The untidy desk with papers and heaps of books on the floor are gone. Floor to ceiling bookshelves line the room and what looks like an antique roll top desk stands in the corner. Above the desk is a gun rack with some kind of old rifle hanging on it. I noticed the old party line phone has been moved in there.

"That was the only contraption I couldn't get rid of," Avril laughed. "But at least now it doesn't bring the conversation to a grinding halt every time it rings."

Avril and Neil's room, the master bedroom, is just across from the office. It too is a thing of beauty. We stood transfixed in the doorway. The walls had been painted a pale peach with black rafter beams that contrasted stark against the delicate tint.

"How does Neil like all this?"

Avril rolled her eyes.

"Don't ask. He was rather unpleasant while all this was going on. I didn't dare ask his advice on anything. He didn't want to know. Basically, he told me to do what I wanted to do and not bother him with details." Just then Martha walked into the room with an armload of ironed clothes. She greeted Faye like a long lost sister and we talked with her for a while as she put clothes away in drawers and a long, built-in closet. As we left the room, I asked, "Where's Cuthbert? I haven't seen him yet." Avril snorted.

"I have a new cook. I fired Cuthbert not too long ago. I noticed him making eyes at Martha one day. Does he think a proud Ndebele woman is going to look at him? Her family would disown her! Not only that, he was getting increasingly insolent and rude towards me.

"One day, we came home after a trip to Salisbury and discovered there was money missing from the drawer in the desk where I had placed it myself before we left. I had locked the drawer and it had been forced open. Cuthbert was the only person here the whole day since I had given Martha the day off. When we confronted Cuthbert, he became angry and belligerent and threatened us. We called the police—there's a BSAP post about ten miles from here—and he ran off before they got here, but they searched his quarters and found the money under the mattress. They caught up with him down the road and he spent two months in jail. The constable who caught him also told us he had threatened us and that he said he would 'get' us."

"Where are the dogs—what are their names—Livingstone, and I forget the other one?"

"Stanley. I got rid of them too. Gave them to a local farmer who was looking for hunting dogs. Nasty creatures. They growled every time I came near them. Fat lot of good they would do if Cuthbert came back. They'd help him do us in."

"How are you going to protect yourself, Avril?" asked Faye. "You're practically alone here all day."

"Don't worry. Neil's father kept a shotgun and I know how to use it. It's the one hanging over the desk in the office. *Pere* used to take me hunting on our ranch. We'd shoot rabbits and fowl, stuff like that, and I was always a good shot. The shotgun is always in the library, loaded."

I felt sad. I liked Cuthbert and I wondered why Cuthbert had not taken the money with him when he fled. I can't imagine Cuthbert being either a thief or a vengeful killer. He had soft, gentle eyes and I remember how he had cried at the funeral. I looked at Faye, and I could tell Faye was concerned too.

We didn't see Neil until supper this evening. He came in just as the sun was setting, dirty and exhausted, and greeted us. He seemed genuinely glad to see us and his face lit up into a happy smile. He changed for dinner, joining us in the dining room just as we were sitting down.

Faye commented on how tired he looked. "Is the baby keeping you awake at nights, Doctor?" she joked.

I noticed a quick, contemptuous glance towards Avril before he replied.

"No, not the baby. The nanny sleeps with the baby on the other side of the house. We wouldn't hear him if he was choking to death and neither would she, I am sure. She sleeps like a rock."

Talk to the Moon

"If you want to get out of bed at 5 a.m. after two hours of sleep because you were up all night with a screaming baby, then you're welcome. Just let me know and I'll move his crib into the room and fire Violetta. I had my own room all my life and I'm not any the worse for it. *Maman* said she wasn't going to get prematurely old from a lack of sleep. I had an *ayah* who slept in my room until I was five!"

"*Ayah-schmaya*! They're called nannies in this part of the world. What kind of a mother leaves her baby alone all night with a stranger?"

"Violetta's not a stranger. We've had her for seven months now and she's done a good job. She loves Gaby like she was his own mother!"

"She may as well be," muttered Neil.

My face burned. I mechanically chewed my food, head down, pretending I hadn't noticed anything was amiss. Faye looked uncomfortable, too.

"I didn't mean to hit any sore spots with you two. How's the farm coming along, Neil?" They discussed farm business and other generalities for the rest of the meal and they carefully steered clear of any conversation regarding the baby. I wonder what's happening?

During dinner, I noticed that Neil rarely looks at Avril. I remember how besotted he was with her a year ago, unable to take his eyes off her, adoration pouring from every pore. Surely the bloom hasn't faded from their marriage already? They should still be in love! They're behaving much like Mom and Dad behave. Can a baby alter marriage dynamics so quickly? No, it can't be the baby. No one would be happy if babies were responsible. It must be that he's stressed out over the farm. He isn't a farmer—he's a doctor. Perhaps he's having trouble with the farm and taking it out on Avril. That must be it. Things will improve once he gets used to farming.

We retired to the living room for coffee, and Neil and Avril had a brandy. It's the first time I have seen Neil drink alcohol. He excused himself early and went to bed. He had to be up at five, he said. I think farming must be hard work. I feel sorry for Neil.

30 January, late evening

Today, after lunch, we sat in the cool shade of the verandah and talked. Gabriel gurgled happily in a playpen nearby as Violetta sat on the cement floor, watching him. Sleepy, I watched as a small cloud of dust—a car in its center—made its way down the long road towards the farmhouse. The car honked a little tune as it approached.

"Oh dear, that must be Peaches. I told her to come and meet you but I didn't think she'd be here today. Brace yourselves. She's quite a character. Violetta, take Gaby into the house and feed him and then let him take his nap." The car screeched to a halt in the driveway. The door opened and a peroxide-blonde with a Betty Grable hairdo and a cigarette sticking to her red lips got out.

"*Whoo-ee*!" She trilled, as she negotiated her way up the verandah steps. "I see you've started the party without me." She had a voice that could strip paint off the side of a barn. "*Hey, hey, hey*, girls! Where's the boys?" She stuck out a liver spotted claw.

Peaches was drunk.

Avril introduced Peaches as if she had been the visiting Duchess of York. I admired her *sang-froid*. Peaches sat heavily in an empty chair next to me. She wore enough makeup to sink a battleship.

I thought she might have been lovely at one time, but now she looked, and smelled, like a melon that had been left out in the sun too long. Peaches waved a hand and lit another cigarette with the old one, throwing the butt over the verandah wall, and taking a deep drag of smoke.

"*Phew*! It's hot, isn't it? My pool is getting cleaned today so a girl can't even swim." As she talked, the smoke came out of both of her nostrils, dragon-like, in a series of puffs. "Where's Gaby? Hidden him away again, have you? She always hides the little tyke when I get here." She looked at Faye and me conspiratorially. "What does she think I'll do to him? I've lived here all my life. Knew young Neil—he's slightly younger than me, although you'd never guess it—all his life!" She gave me a coy look. "How old would you say I am?" I jumped as a sharp elbow dug me in the ribs.

"Uh, well, thirty-five?"

Peaches shrieked.

"Oh, honey, no, but don't worry. No one ever guesses right. I'm actually fifty-five, can you believe it? *Goddammit*, what kind of a hostess are you? I've been sitting here for three cigarettes already and you haven't offered us a drink. You'll have to get with it, deary, if you want to be the hostess with the mostest!" Avril meekly picked up a small brass bell on the table next to her chair and rang it. Peaches continued to talk. A few seconds later a white-uniformed African appeared silently, with a tray.

"Bring two beers and some tea for the madams." He disappeared.

Talk to the Moon

"So, as I was saying: I've known the Blanchard's for many years. We live just over on the next farm, you know. I was quite a looker in my day. Had half the farmers in the area after me—the other half were too old—cocks always at half past five. Not for me, although I married one. Now, John Blanchard, I should have married him instead. I wasn't here for his funeral," she sniffed and wiped a tear from a bleary eye. "Me and Ralph were in South Africa when it happened. Couldn't believe the news when we got back. He always looked so healthy." She took another deep drag on her cigarette and the smoke made its way down to her feet and exited back up through her nostrils in a steady stream.

The beer arrived, and so did the tea, and Peaches talked and talked. More beer and more tea arrived and still Peaches talked. I kept drinking tea until my hands shook. I felt the caffeine would at least keep me awake. Faye finally got up and asked to be excused. She was tired, she said, and thought she would take a nap. "The trip is catching up with me, I think." I wished I could do the same but thought it might look rude if both of us left. I stayed put. Avril did too, and I wondered how she did it. If this woman was my neighbor, I'd move.

The sun began to sink towards the horizon but Peaches stayed glued to her seat. I wondered if she had a cast iron bladder. I heard a tractor pulling up into the shed nearby and a few minutes later Neil walked up the verandah steps.

"Hello Peaches."

"*Neil*! Dear, *dear* Neil! Come and join the party! We're having a wonderful time. I hardly ever see you anymore. You must come and sit down and tell me what you've been up to."

"I think it's time you got on home, Peaches, before it gets too dark. You don't look like you're in any shape to be driving. Avril, why don't you run her home in her car and I'll call Ralph to drive you back."

"Okay, hon. Come on sweetie, we don't want you wrapping yourself around a tree. You can bring that beer with you." She assisted a wobbly Peaches to the car and Neil went in to make the call. I remained on the verandah. I wanted to clear my head. I felt as if I had been mentally raped. A few minutes later, Neil came out and sat down in the chair Peaches had been sitting in.

"I hate that woman," he said.

I wasn't surprised.

"Yes, she is rather hard to take. I can't imagine how Avril puts up with her. They are so different!"

"I wasn't talking about Peaches."

Time stopped. The frogs that were croaking in the dusk fell silent for a split second; then restarted as I found my voice.

"Then, who?" Maybe it was Faye? But I knew.

Neil looked at me and sighed. "I wasn't going to say anything Holly, but for some reason you seem easy to talk to, and God knows I need someone to talk to. I've been holding everything in for way too long now and I feel like a dam that is about to burst. I know you're Avril's friend, probably her best friend, and I hate to put a burden like this on you, but I don't know who else to talk to."

"What about Faye?" I asked. "She's known Avril for much longer than I have."

"I would like to talk to Faye, but I'm sure she would go to the authorities. You, I don't think so. You can keep a secret, I feel."

"Well, yes, certainly, Neil, but what secret? And why would anyone need to go to the authorities? You are still talking about Avril, right?"

Neil got up and walked to the verandah wall. He leaned over it and picked something off a bush growing against the verandah wall, a bush with reddish brown flowers, lobed leaves and bright red-spined seedpods. "Do you know what this is?" He asked.

"A castor bean seedpod?"

He broke it open and placed three speckled seeds that looked like large ticks in my hand. "These three seeds are enough to kill you and me." I dropped them on the table, alarmed. "Don't worry, you have to crush them and ingest them before they have any effect. I suspect that's what my father died from."

I was aghast. I suspected something myself, but it had never taken any concrete shape before and I had not thought of castor beans. An unfortunate accident, perhaps…

"Do you think someone…Avril…did it on purpose? Murder? Couldn't it have been an accident? Maybe one of these things fell in his food—there were some on the table as decorations. Maybe it was the mushrooms…?"

"A whole seed will pass through his system harmlessly, and I've ruled out mushrooms. It doesn't add up. The tests may have picked up something too. But these castor beans—I just can't rule them out. True, I have no real proof. Avril made sure of that when she didn't want an autopsy done, but to be honest, I doubt that the poison in these beans, ricin, would have shown up at all. The local police department doesn't have a sophisticated forensics laboratory. The most they get in way of foul play is the occasional stabbing from a drunken brawl. Avril would know that. She would also know how to extract the poison and add it to someone's food. She's had the basics in chemistry and pharmacology and she's not unfamiliar with certain procedures. The more I think about it the more it makes sense to me."

"But why…? Your father was getting on in years. If she had wanted an inheritance, couldn't she have waited?" I felt embarrassed talking about Avril this way, like she was a criminal. It didn't feel right. But hadn't I also had my own suspicions?

"He wasn't that old. He could have easily lived another ten, twenty years if he continued in good health. His side of the family does tend to live beyond the normal span.

"You've seen yourself how things have changed around here. Dad would have been dead set against all of this. True, he conceded a few changes were necessary, but he would have cut off the funding after the roof and perhaps a few smaller changes. Avril has spent thousands of pounds—way beyond the budget that this farm can support—already, and she's not finished. I'm slaving out in the fields every day, trying to increase our yields so that I can pay off our accumulating debts, but it's like a tidal wave. It keeps coming and it keeps getting bigger."

"Can't you just tell her to stop? She really shouldn't be doing all this if you are unhappy about it."

Neil laughed.

"I may as well tell the sun to stop rising. I didn't see this coming when I married her. True, I knew she loved to spend but it had never amounted to anything so ridiculous before. Now, it seems like it's an obsession with her. She won't stop until we're broke. It's what her parents did to their ranches; they went broke from runaway shopping."

"She may be a spendthrift, Neil, but a murderess? I don't want to believe it."

"I didn't think you would. I wouldn't have a year ago, either."

"What aroused your suspicions?"

"I was looking for something one day, back in the cottage we lived in before moving here, some papers, or something, and I was going through an old shoe box that had been pushed to the back of the closet. I found these beans," he pointed at them, "in the bottom of the box. Some of them had been broken open but others were intact. I knew what they were immediately. My father had warned me about them many times and told me not to play with them under any circumstances. I did, of course, so I knew exactly what they were.

"I confronted Avril with the beans and asked her what they were doing in her box. She denied ever putting them there and said they must have found their way into the house, accidentally. But she looked frightened, Holly. Under that smooth face of hers, there was fear. I could see it. I still didn't want to believe she had anything to do with my father's death, but it gnawed at me, and the more I thought about it, the more sense it made. His symptoms were all indicative of ricin poisoning. It could have been a text book case."

Neil continued to talk about the medical aspects of ricin poisoning but I didn't understand much of the terminology. There are different symptoms from ingesting ricin to getting it in your blood stream, but both can kill. That much I understood. It did make sense.

"Why don't you go to the authorities, then, Neil? If you feel she did it, then isn't that the right thing to do?"

"I've asked myself, a hundred times, that exact question. If we didn't have Gaby, perhaps that is what I would do. At the very least, I'd divorce her. But when I think of my son growing up without a mother, or knowing his own mother is a murderess, I find I can't do it. I don't want him to grow up like I did, not having a complete family. I always feel I've missed something by not having a mother."

"Yes, I see. But now that you know she may have been responsible, I am sure she would be willing to do everything you told her, wouldn't she? In exchange for you not going to the authorities?"

"You mean blackmail?" Neil smiled a bitter smile. "Yes, it may work. If she's guilty, she won't know how much I know. I might even have proof. I can get off this farm: sell it to pay our debts. I can return to the mission and tell her to be happy with the deal and raise Gaby like a real mother. We may even learn to be happy, after a while. Perhaps she'll get all this decorating nonsense out of her head. A mission house won't cost that much to redecorate."

I didn't know if the plan would work or not. I had a bad feeling in the pit of my stomach. Something didn't sit right.

Talk to the Moon

It's too dangerous and many things can go wrong, but Neil looks a lot happier than I have seen him in a long while and I feel I have extended a lifeline towards him. I don't want to reel it back in. If the plan doesn't work at least he will have tried.

Neil laughed again.

"I had so many suspicions about Avril before I married her," he said. "I wish I had listened to my instincts, even if some of them were wrong."

"What suspicions?"

"I thought she and Tony had something going. No," he said, seeing the alarm on my face, "that was the one thing that turned out to be wrong. The reason I had suspicions in the first place was that Tony warned me off her right from the start. He told me she wasn't the right person for me. I asked him if he thought she was right for him, then, and he didn't answer.

"I felt angry for a long time but one day we talked again and he told me how he had grown up with her and that she felt just like a sister to him. He knew and understood her and loved her in spite of her ways, but as a brother, not a lover. He said he had felt a duty towards me, as a friend, to inform me of his opinions. I appreciated his candor and we became closer but he didn't change my mind about marrying her.

"I think I wanted to show him that someone like Avril could be attracted to an old bore like me. I conned myself into thinking it was me she loved, not my farm."

"She was rather eager to move here," I said, feeling like a betrayer. "To be honest, I also thought at one time Tony loved her more than he was saying. I had my suspicions, too, but like yours, they turned out to be wrong. After all, Tony wouldn't marry me if he didn't love me, would he?"

Just then, Faye stepped out onto the verandah.

"You're still out here? What happened to the guest? Where's Avril?"

We brought her up to date on Peaches but we didn't tell her what we'd been talking about. I badly wanted to confide in Faye. The burden that Neil had passed to me was sitting heavy on my mind but I promised Neil I wouldn't say anything to anyone. I always keep my promises.

2nd February

The rest of our visit at Greystones passed uneventfully but I feel as if my life has been tainted. I will never feel the same way about Avril again, or Neil. I have always looked up to him as a strong, father-like figure, and now I see he is as vulnerable as the rest of us. I love him more, but now pity is part of the mixture.

I'm not sure how I feel towards Avril. Angry, yes, but there's still doubt in my mind. Neil could be mistaken: after all, hadn't he been mistaken about Avril and Tony? Doctors make incorrect diagnosis all the time, and he has nothing concrete, no evidence, to back it up. It's poisoning his marriage.

Since I got back from Greystones, I feel as if I am able to analyze the situation more lucidly. I was wrong to tell him to blackmail Avril. I am going to talk to him at the earliest opportunity and tell him to reconsider his suspicions: to make peace with Avril. It's important for their marriage and for Gaby. Maybe I could talk to Avril and tell her that her spending is out of control. Maybe Tony can help her. After all, she respects both of us enough to listen, won't she?

CHAPTER 29

Neil

5th February

I have been so preoccupied with Avril and Neil's problems that I forgot to mention Paula wrecked the rondavel in my absence.

Joan told me the first day I arrived back that there had been a lot of noisy goings-on while they were away. Loud music and talking were not all, she hinted, and she felt that Paula had been entertaining young men. I was furious. Esther was at her wits end.

"I cannot clean in that room anymore." She was close to tears. "The madam Paula is mean to me and shouts at me when I go in there."

Merrie isn't pleased with the young madam either.

"*Ahh*! She complains about the food always and she does not come to breakfast on time."

I went to Robert Parrish. I didn't tell him what I suspected had been going on—Paula could be fired for that—but I did tell him that I felt that Paula and I are not compatible room-mates and asked him if there was anything he could do to remedy the situation. He listened to me in silence, only nodding, and then saying, "Leave it to me."

Today, the solution was proposed. Paula came home to the rondavel after work, in tears.

"Thanks to you, I'm going to be miserable. My life has been ruined!" she exclaimed, her voice dripping with drama.

I didn't say anything.

"Well? Aren't you going to say something?"

"Say what? What am I supposed to say? I don't even know what you're talking about."

"Oh, you know alright. You planned it this way, didn't you? You wanted this room to yourself, and now you're getting it. In the meanwhile, I am being shunted over to the Parrish's! I hate those people! They're worse than my parents. I'd rather go home than live with that awful old

Tootie woman and her moronic daughter. What's more, I'll be in the same house as my boss. Do you think that's going to be fun?"

I couldn't help myself—I started to laugh, which infuriated Paula even more.

"I'll get even with you, just wait and see!" were the last words I heard from her.

For the first time I feel gratitude towards Robert Parish and Tootie. It couldn't be easy for them to open their home to an obnoxious teenage girl, a virtual stranger. Paula is immature. Given freedom she blew it. She has no idea how to behave in a responsible way. I am naïve too, certainly, but irresponsible, no. I was paying my own college tuition at that age and I'd no time for boyfriends.

Maybe I should ask Tony to sleep with me now that Paula and Eva are out of the room and I have it to myself. Would he lose respect for me? Maybe I should ask him: see how much he really loves me. I wonder why Tony has never tried to make love to me? Do I repulse him? Or maybe he just has respect for my wishes since I explained my views about sex before marriage one night as we kissed.

I have decided not to think about it anymore. These thoughts are taking me places I don't want to go. I can wait another five months and I don't want to end up like Paula, talked about and judged by others. The mission will not put up with that kind of behavior.

Eva, at least, is happy. All she can talk about is the wedding. I am going along with Eva, looking over invitation lists, debating the merits of a buffet reception against a sit down dinner, and whether or not it should be outdoors or indoors. Patterns of wedding dresses are strewn all over Eva's room and samples of satins, laces and taffeta lie on top of them. I find all of this confusing. If the wedding was only about me and Tony I would wait another month before thinking about the arrangements. Tony agrees with me.

"Maybe we should just elope. Save everyone including ourselves a lot of trouble." But I can't bring myself to do this either. I have always dreamed of a fairytale wedding, and I want mine to be like Avril's, but not my married life!

This makes me think of my resolution to speak to Neil. I don't know how I am going to do it. I can't call on the phone and ask to speak to Neil. The phone at Greystones is constantly monitored by party-line busybodies, and besides, Avril will certainly be nearby. I'll have to wait for them to visit again and hope that an opportunity will present itself. I hope it won't be too long. I still have that bad feeling in my gut. I haven't mentioned a word to anyone about anything, not even Tony. I haven't even told Eva that she wasn't responsible for Mr. Blanchard's death. That would raise too many questions. I know I'll have to do it: take that burden of guilt from Eva, but I need to find the right way to do it without implicating Avril.

7th February

Paula has moved into the Parrish's home and I am relishing the peace and quiet of my rondavel. Now it really is all mine! Paula was right. I can now listen to what I want on my radio without having to move outside or into the communal room because I can't hear anything over Paula's music. I hope Tootie and Robert enjoy the singing duo. Joan and Faye can also visit unmolested by the sullen aura from the other side of the room.

It's also easier to write in my diary. I can think easier in the quietness of a mission evening when the only noises are choruses of croaking frogs and the call of a night owl.

Friday, 14th February

Avril called me today.

"Angel, I really need to talk to you. I am so frightened," she gave a sob that was quickly cut short. "But I can't talk now. You know what these lines are like. I wish you lived closer."

"Are you alright, Avril? Is it Gaby? Is Neil okay?"

"I can't say much, dear, but yes, we are all fine. Remember what we were discussing when you were here, about Cuthbert?"

"Yes."

"He's back. Violetta saw him on the farm just yesterday. I am so scared, I just know he's here to do some harm to us."

"Did you call the police? Do they know he's here?"

"Oh yes, it's the first thing I did, but all they said was that they can get him for trespassing, and they can't stop him if he wants to come back. They don't have the manpower to keep hauling him off. I think he has to do something first before they'll take action."

"What, like kill you? Oh Avril, do take care!"

"I told Neil to be especially careful while he is out in the fields. I know he'll try to harm Neil. He is angry with him for allowing me to fire him."

We discussed the Cuthbert situation a little longer and then I asked Avril how the house renovation was coming along. I wanted to find out if Neil had put an end to it yet.

"Oh fine, just fine. I will be doing more in a few weeks. Right now I am taking a break. Gaby needs some attention and I've moved him into our room for the time being. How are you doing, my dear?"

I now know without a doubt that Neil has drawn the first line in the sand. There is no more decorating and renovating going on. Avril would have talked about it if there had been, and moving Gaby into their bedroom was another sign that Neil had begun to get his own way in things. I feel a great disappointment. It seems to indicate that Neil was right: Avril is guilty and she is afraid. I wish that I had never suggested the blackmail to Neil, but like Avril said, what's done is done. There is no going back now, and maybe it will work just the way we thought.

24th February

Tony told me that he has spoken to Neil over the phone, and Neil told him they will be returning to the mission, soon.

"I can't believe Avril is letting him do this without a murmur," exclaimed Tony. "Selling the farm? That's her life now! She hates the mission."

"So you're sure he's selling the farm?"

"That's what he said. He's going into Salisbury next week to put it on the market and then they're packing up and coming back here as soon as it's sold. He's going to ask for his old job back. I know they'll take him. They've wanted him back ever since he left."

I have no doubts either. I wondered why Avril didn't mention this to me on the phone. Maybe she didn't want the old busybodies finding out. The plan is working. That bad feeling is also lifting. I will have my friend back, be near my godchild, and everything will be the way it always has been.

Or will it? We'd be closer, yes, but closer to a killer. I still can't believe it. There just has to be some other explanation.

Tuesday, 25th February

Last night, as I was sitting writing in my diary, there was a frantic knocking on the door. It was Tony. He looked as if he had been crying. Shocked, I let him in.

"What's the matter, Tony?"

Talk to the Moon

"Sit down, Holly, I have some bad news." I didn't like how this was sounding but I sat.

"I drove all the way from Tshabanda in the dark. I'm surprised I didn't take a spill. I just had to see you...this is all so terrible!"

"Please, Tony, tell me what's going on! Is it your parents? Are they ok?"

"It's Neil," he finally said, stifling a sob. I felt the energy drain from my body. I knew, even before he spoke, what had happened.

"Is he alright? Is he hurt? Was it Cuthbert?"

"How did you know? Yes, of course, and no, he's not alright. Holly, he's dead!"

I had to wait for the shock wave to travel through me before I could speak. I felt no grief as yet; I couldn't believe it. Neil dead? It couldn't be. Cuthbert would never kill him. I would surely have seen something in his demeanor...something...there had to be a mistake. He was hurt, but not dead. Tony had jumped to conclusions.

"Avril! Gaby....?" I hadn't thought of them yet but if Neil had been hurt...killed...maybe Avril had been killed too or hurt, too.

"No, as far as I can tell, they're both fine."

He went on to tell me how he had heard the news. Avril called Nigel Withers a few hours ago, he said. Nigel found him in his room, almost asleep, and told him that there was a hysterical woman on the phone who wanted to speak to him. Avril was so overcome with emotion she had hardly been able to speak but she told him the police had been called and while she was waiting for them she had to speak to someone. Neil had just been shot by Cuthbert, and she had practically witnessed it. She was terrified that he would return to kill her and the baby. He finally got the whole story from her, in bits and pieces:

Cuthbert had returned earlier that evening just before it got dark. There was a thunderstorm and the electricity went out so Neil lit some lamps. He went out on the porch to see what Cuthbert wanted and Avril was in their bedroom with Gaby, putting him to sleep. She said she called out to Neil to ask him what Cuthbert wanted. He replied that Cuthbert claimed that they owed him two weeks back pay and they were going to the library to sort it out on the payroll sheets she kept in the desk.

"She said she had locked the door to their bedroom, just in case there was trouble, but listening at the door she heard Cuthbert's voice rising in anger and Neil's voice, calm and soothing, then getting louder, more urgent; hearing him shout "*No, no! Stop!*" She thought she heard a shot but it had occurred the same time as a peal of thunder so she hadn't been sure.

"She remained in her room for a few minutes, straining to hear the sound of a voice or a movement, but there had been no further sounds.

"Carefully, she unlocked her bedroom door. The lamp light still shone out of the door but everything was silent. The storm was subsiding and she could hear the soft pitter-patter of raindrops on the windows. It was then that she noticed the muddy footprints that led into the library also came out of the library, back towards the front door.

"Since Neil had not been outside during the storm they could only belong to Cuthbert. Leaving the safety of her room she went towards the open library door. She mustered up all her courage and walked into the library. That was when she discovered Neil lying face up on the floor in a pool of blood with nearly half his head blown away. She screamed hysterically, cradling him in her lap and covering herself with blood in the process.

"She ran to the phone and called Peaches, who fortunately, was sober enough to call the police. Peaches and her husband were on their way over, she said. She was completely alone. Martha, Violetta and the other servants had left for the day. There was no sign of Cuthbert but when she calmed down she noticed that John Blanchard's shotgun that she had always kept loaded and ready to fire was missing from its rack on the library wall."

After Tony stopped talking, we remained silent for a minute, deep in our own thoughts. It still felt to me like something Tony had made up, but even he couldn't make up something like that. It had to be true. Avril had been right all along. Cuthbert was the criminal. Maybe it had been he who had poisoned John Blanchard! Why hadn't I thought of this before? Maybe he had been going to fire Cuthbert or maybe Cuthbert was angry with him for some reason that no one else had known about. I dismissed this thought before it could leave my mouth. He hadn't been there on Christmas or the day after. I tried to recall his face but it was blurry and indistinct. All I could remember were soft, gentle eyes. That didn't mean anything. Even a murderer could look like an angel.

"I'll have to go to Greystones," said Tony. "Avril needs some help. Do you want to go too?"

"Oh yes, of course. I'll talk to Mr. Parrish first thing in the morning. We can leave after that. I don't have anything urgent to do and Gerald can cover for me for a while."

26th February

Gerald has offered us the use of the red MG and we accepted. We arrived at Greystones this evening, around dusk, and found the driveway full of cars and the house full of people. Every neighbor from miles around had heard the news and, as with Mr. Blanchard's death, they were there to offer their support, food, help or just a comforting presence.

The Kelly's were there, and to everyone's eternal gratitude, minus their children. Avril is once again in her element, organizing and bidding, like a Hollywood film director with a crowd of extras. I am surprised that Avril is not prostrate with grief, but then, Avril is not the type to allow her emotions to dictate her actions. I feel sure that, in spite of the problems in their marriage, Avril loved Neil but sees emotional outbursts as a sign of weakness and keeps any display of grief in check by staying busy and occupied. Tony accepted Avril's composure with admiration.

"What a woman!" was all he said. I had to agree.

28th February

Today was the funeral, and things have begun to settle down. Neil was buried on the farm. It has been the saddest day of my life, even sadder than the day his father died. Neil had been a good friend and I still can't believe he's gone.

Many people from the mission and the Bulawayo congregation drove up for the funeral and back again, the same day. Eva came up with Eric, Gerald and Ayesha and the elder Swann's and Tootie had driven up together. Nearly everyone in the area attended and so had all the farm hands and villagers from the district that knew and loved Neil.

There were so many people that the local police were brought in for crowd control. I felt sure they were scanning the crowd, looking for Cuthbert. I don't think he would be stupid enough to show up but sometimes murderers do return. I have read enough mystery novels to know that the police always attend the funerals when there's an unsolved murder to see if the murderer would attend.

Peaches didn't get tipsy until the wake began. She glued herself to Avril, sobbing loudly throughout the funeral service, while Avril remained stoic and calm.

Marc and Gabriella St. Aubin arrived from Johannesburg earlier and they're staying awhile, Avril said, to help her with the farm and business matters. At the wake I noticed Gabriella sending Peaches looks that could freeze a polar bear. I felt for Peaches.

Gabriella is an older version of her daughter, but with less warmth.

The library door has been sealed with tape. I have not been into the library and neither have I wanted to since my arrival. I noticed that many guests peer curiously into the hallway or stop briefly at the door as they pass it. I am sure there has been much speculation about the murder but everyone it seems has accepted Cuthbert as the killer.

There's a manhunt on for him: every farmer in the area on the lookout and every farm hand alerted to report his whereabouts if he is seen. I am sure Cuthbert would not stand a chance. Everyone loved Neil and he was popular with the workers on the farm. The autopsy revealed he died instantaneously from a shotgun blast to the head. There is no mystery to solve. We know how he died and who did it. The young widow is the chief witness and there is no reason to disbelieve her especially in light of the missing murder weapon. The police have thoroughly searched the surrounding areas and found no trace of it. Avril would not have had time to dispose of the weapon if she had been the killer.

Peaches and Ralph arrived shortly after the murder. Avril had not left the house. The time of death was confirmed by autopsy. None of the servants saw anything: they were cooking their dinners in their quarters, a hundred yards at least, from the house. A farm hand informed the police he had seen Cuthbert walking up the road to the farmhouse about fifteen minutes before the murder had taken place. He had exchanged greetings with him, he said, and he had not appeared to be angry or murderous. He had, in fact, seemed rather happy, saying that a great injustice was about to be corrected. He had not elaborated any further on this, merely saying he had an appointment to keep. All who heard this took it to mean that Cuthbert had been bent on revenge.

To make things even worse for Cuthbert another witness has come forward to say they saw him running in a state of panic away from the farm after the rainstorm with the shotgun in his hands. I feel that with all these witnesses there's no doubt in my mind to the identity of the killer. I still feel it had to be more of an accident, though, than a deliberate, premeditated murder.

Talk to the Moon

Avril filled us in on what had occurred in more detail. Her story does not differ from what she had told Tony on the phone, only that she had no idea what had killed her husband since the shotgun was missing. She had come into the library to find him lying on the floor between the desk and the door, blood everywhere, the strongbox with the money open on the desk, and the money missing. There had been about one hundred pounds in there, she told us; the money for the following week's wages.

She lifted his head in her arms, screaming uncontrollably when she saw that half his head was missing and pieces of brain and bone had been blown onto the surrounding furniture and carpet. The police and the autopsy had confirmed that he had been shot at close range.

"How would Cuthbert know that the shotgun was loaded?" I asked.

"The shotgun was always loaded. We kept it there, on the wall, in-case we needed it in a hurry. I don't know how Cuthbert knew it was loaded, maybe he grabbed it thinking to scare Neil and it went off. It has a bit of a hair trigger. Neil's father was always cleaning it. He said it was old and he used it to hunt with or scare away jackals after the chickens. We didn't think it dangerous but at close range it's deadly...." Avril's voice trailed away and she began to tear up. We didn't talk about the murder anymore.

It was not until the funeral that I noticed something odd about Martha. She seems to be preoccupied; not her usual jolly self and not even asking me for news about her sister. I have put it down to grief over the murder. Avril has noticed it too and I overheard her telling Martha to get with it, to stay focused on her job, and did she want to be fired, too?

Mr. Goodfellow arrived for the will reading shortly after the funeral. Tony and I made an excuse to leave the house. We didn't want to intrude on personal matters. When we returned, Avril looked happier than she has looked since we got here. The Kelly's had left and the house was quiet. Gabriella and Marc looked pleased.

"It's as I expected," said Avril. "Neil left the farm to me and to Gabriel when he is twenty-one. Only then will the farm officially be his. Mr. Goodfellow has taken care of all the legalities. The farm's mine!"

I wondered why Neil hadn't changed his will. But then, he had been expecting to sell the farm, not to die. Perhaps he didn't think it necessary. It was just as well now that Avril, in my mind, has been exonerated from both deaths. It would have been unfair to Avril had Neil changed his will and left her nothing. Perhaps the courts would have given her the farm anyway since she was his wife, but perhaps not. Someone had to take care of the farm until Gabriel came of age and it should be Avril. She loved the farm dearly. She would take excellent care of it.

I feel that, all things considered, everything has turned out for the best. Tony and I can return to Bulawayo and know that Avril and Gaby will be alright. We will leave in the morning.

1st March

Cuthbert has been captured! The BSAP called this morning before we left and informed Avril she was out of danger, Cuthbert is in custody. He was picked up in Bindura trying to sell the shotgun to a local gun dealer. He obviously needed the money: he was tattered and ragged, hungry and tired, as if he had been sleeping in the bush and living on whatever he could find to eat. I wondered why he hadn't gotten rid of the gun. Perhaps he knew its value, since it was an antique, and would be sought after by gun collectors. His case will be an open and shut one, and he'll probably hang unless he gets some decent legal help. We left Greystones feeling even more relief. Life will soon return to normal. All's well!

CHAPTER 30

Cuthbert

15th March

The trial of Cuthbert is the talk of the country. Everyone by now has heard the story of the brutal murder and the trial has been moved to the High Court in Salisbury since the small local magistrate's court is not equipped to handle the intense publicity and crowds that the trial will attract.

I speak regularly to Avril by telephone, receiving updates on the preparations and the developments of the case. Avril tells me she is working closely with the prosecutor's office and will be the chief witness at the trial. *The Rhodesian Herald* and every minor paper in the country have pressed her for an interview but she's holding out until after the trial.

"I'm going to be famous!" she trilled, in one conversation. "Already, I have more social engagements than I can handle and reporters are driving out here every day taking pictures of the house. I can't let them in until after the trial, but when it's all over, I am going to let them in so people can see how beautiful my house is. Oh darling, you should see it! It looks like something out of a magazine. The neighbors are so jealous."

I felt heavy-hearted. There was no trace of even the slightest bit of grief or sadness in Avril's voice. I have been more than willing to give her the benefit of the doubt but it's difficult to ignore this level of callousness.

"Avril, your house is not the reason why people are interested in you. I admit it's the most beautiful house I have ever seen in or out of a magazine, but Neil lost his life in it, quite brutally, and it's surprising that you're not feeling a lot more sadness and less concern with appearances. I know you must be grieving, I can't think otherwise, but why so taken up with the house and the social scene now? It doesn't seem respectful to Neil's memory."

There was a long silence on the other end of the phone. "Now I've gone too far," I thought. I was about to speak again but Avril finally spoke.

"Darling, you are so right. I just never allowed myself to grieve properly over Neil. I have done everything in my power to forget that terrible night and perhaps I have gone crazy. I never do things halfway, do I? Please don't think badly of me. It would hurt me so much and it's not how things really are. I have been throwing myself into the house and the social scene because, honestly, I am terrified of the upcoming trial. Everyone's eyes will be on me and I am afraid. I have to convince myself that there is a positive side to this and it has manifested in what you see as callousness. I don't mean it that way. Please forgive me!"

I felt immediate remorse. I judged Avril and came up short myself. I should have seen that Avril was only trying to hide her true feelings behind a thick wall of pseudo-happiness. I apologized for thinking the worst and Avril went back to discussing the trial and the events it had generated.

The High Court has scheduled the start of the trial in May when jury selection will take place. From everything I have heard about the justice system, in this country as in others, the jury will be comprised of white men. I think the outcome is a forgone conclusion. Cuthbert is as good as hanged. I feel the sadness again and wonder, for the millionth time, why Cuthbert would kill Neil. He had known Neil for many years and they were the same age. They would have been sure to work out their differences in a less violent way, surely? What had possessed him to pick up that gun? And according to Avril the lock-box with the money had been opened and robbed. Why would he have shot Neil and robbed the box when it was apparent that Neil was going to pay him anyway? If Neil had no intention of paying him anything he would have not opened the box to begin with.

I imagined Neil walking to the back of the desk to open the drawer where the lock-box had been kept. I can see him opening the drawer and taking the box out. I have been in the library many times, and now I remember something I hadn't thought of before: the shotgun rack's behind the desk—Cuthbert would have had to elbow Neil out of the way to reach the gun. An awkward movement indeed and one that Neil would have seen coming long before Cuthbert had reached the gun. I hope Cuthbert's defense have noticed this.

But why am I defending Cuthbert? He had, after all, killed Neil. I don't know why I think up reasons he couldn't have done it. The police will have thought of these things too, surely, and if so, it's obvious they still feel he could have done it, especially if Neil had not been standing by the desk. His body had been discovered closer to the door.

I also pondered the meaning of Cuthbert's words when Silas had encountered him on the driveway: "A great injustice would be corrected." He was going to the house expecting something. His back-pay? What led him to believe he would be getting the money owed to him? Why would he think killing someone would correct an injustice when it was already in the process of being corrected?

All these questions confuse me more. It is accepted generally, that the murder was not premeditated, although the prosecution is getting ready to prove that his words indicate he was planning something. I feel, like most, that he lost his head and killed on an impulse. I hope the courts will be more lenient if they could accept that he had not premeditated the killing and will give him a prison sentence instead of hanging him. Two wrongs will not correct the situation. Hanging a man cannot bring Neil back.

I can't waste any more time thinking about the trial. The wedding is to take place on 26th July and there is so much planning to do. We have of course decided on the mission chapel for the ceremony and Tootie insists on holding the reception in her garden. As with Avril's wedding she has taken over the planning and Eva and I are too intimidated by her to refuse.

I have asked Faye to be a bridesmaid and Eva has asked Hattie to be her maid of honor and two girls from the Bulawayo congregation she was friendly with, to be her bridesmaids. It's going to be a big wedding party.

We have picked out the material and patterns and Mrs. Ghosh insists on sewing nearly everything since we found many of the materials in their store, but I want to sew my own wedding dress. I found a beautiful pattern in Bulawayo that I have fallen in love with but I am still looking for the right materials. Eva has already found hers and Mrs. Ghosh has begun sewing.

Mom and Dad are still living as happily as it's possible for them to be happy in their small duplex in Belleview. Dad has kept his word and he's as dry as the Limpopo River in winter. The battles have not stopped but the worst is in check since Dad's a better person when sober and he bears Mom's nagging and whining with admirable fortitude. We do wonder how long it will last before the self-medication begins and things return to the way they had been.

Dad enjoys his job and, thankfully, seldom comes into contact with Faye's father on the job. Mom also has better things to occupy herself with now that wedding plans are afoot.

I, however, have problems involving Tony in the wedding plans. He doesn't seem interested. He hasn't even chosen his best man. I've had to ask him several times to apply for a license and help with other matters that I don't have time for. He agrees and promptly forgets about it. I feel that I'm turning into a younger version of Mom when I have to remind him, more than once, of what he has promised.

18th April

Cuthbert has escaped. I heard it on the news today. A massive manhunt is on for him, and it wouldn't be long before he'll be recaptured.

24th April

Cuthbert has disappeared like a mist on a hot morning. He has not returned to his old haunts—that would be stupid—since they're all a-crawl now with police and their informants. He has gone to ground elsewhere.

An investigation into his escape has been launched but the cause isn't complicated: a young police constable was careless while transporting him from the local lockup to the prison in Salisbury. Halfway to Salisbury, on a lonely stretch of road, Cuthbert began moaning and complaining of violent stomach cramps and he needed to stop urgently. The young police constable, who was both compassionately and pragmatic, had allowed him to leave the van and even unshackled him to make it easier for Cuthbert to squat behind a bush. He thought that training his rifle on him would be enough to prevent an escape. It didn't. Cuthbert was fast, and before the lad knew what had happened he was without his weapon and Cuthbert locking him in the van instead. When he was finally found and rescued, Cuthbert was nowhere to be seen and the constable in a lot of trouble with his superiors.

The media have not had so much fun since the war. Headlines scream the inadequacies of the police and the justice system. Avril is telling reporters that she fears for her life. Cuthbert escaped in order to silence her, the chief witness, and they play it well in the papers: *"Young Widow Fears for Life"* and *"Killer Loose—Out for Revenge"*. I wonder if she has relented and let the reporters into the house. The house isn't mentioned.

25th April

Talk to the Moon

Today has been a nightmare. I don't want to write it down. I don't even know where to start, but I must.

Tony was anxious. I put it down to normal pre-wedding jitters. He called me from Tshabanda to tell me that he's going to Greystones for the weekend. He's concerned about Avril.

"Should I go too?"

"No, if Cuthbert is on the loose, I don't want you there. I think it's better if I go alone."

"But Tony, there's so much to do here that I need your help with. Avril will be fine, she says she has a police guard twenty four hours a day. They're as thick as flies on mombies at Greystones. Cuthbert wouldn't dare return!"

But he insisted, and I became so angry I hung up on him. When I looked up, I noticed Paula standing in my office door, smiling. How long had she been there?

"What do you want Paula?"

"Having boyfriend troubles, hmm?"

"It's none of your business. If you don't have anything better to do than eavesdrop then please go do it somewhere else. I'm busy."

Paula sidled into the office, closing the door behind her.

"Not so fast. I have something to tell you that I think you'll want to hear. I've wanted to tell you for a while now, but Alan stopped me. He said it wasn't any of my business." Alan is her current boyfriend. She has gone through several since arriving at the mission.

"Well, I'm sure Alan is right. Why don't you take his advice?"

Paula smiled. She had a look on her face that resembled the one-point focus of a cat stalking a bird. She sat down on the sagging mustard chair next to my desk and crossed her long, lithe legs. Her smooth-shaved upper leg moved in a rhythmical tap to a beat that only she could hear. Her spike-heeled shoe dangled from a toe, and she seemed to be listening to a song in her head that pleased her—*Someday I'll Find [Get] You,* perhaps? Then, as if remembering why she had come in the first place she looked up. Her cat's eyes glittered.

"Alan and Tony are friends, did you know?" So this was the big news. I smiled. What did I care if Alan and Tony were friends! I shrugged.

"What about it?"

"He knew Tony in the Air Force."

"So?"

Paula hummed something under her breath and continued to rock her foot up and down, inspecting her shoe dangling on the end of a toe, as if she had forgotten again what she was talking about. She was obviously relishing this, whatever this was, I thought. I wanted to throw her out, bodily, but something stopped me, a morbid curiosity that I knew, deep down, I did oh-so-badly want to know what the big news item was. I looked through some paper work on my desk, pretending I had forgotten Paula's presence. Finally Paula looked up.

"Do you remember when Tony was in the Air Force, he used to go away a lot, to North Africa?"

"Yes. It was once, I believe."

"Maybe. Well, he never went."

"What do you mean, he never went?"

"Oh no, he never went at all! He told Alan he was going to tell you that he was in North Africa, on a top secret mission and all that rubbish, but really, he was here, in Bulawayo." I stared at Paula. I didn't know what to say. I felt as if all the air had been sucked out of the room and my legs felt weak. I was glad I was sitting down. I looked down at my paperwork again and pretended once more to find something of interest there. Paula continued as if I had asked her to.

"Yes. He stayed with Alan sometimes, but most of the time he found a hotel room somewhere and he and Avril and Alan and his girlfriend then—I forget her name—used to go out. Avril stayed in the hotel with him, pretending like they were married!" Paula giggled and covered her mouth with her hand, scandalized. "The poor doctor who got killed didn't know that Avril and Tony were still seeing each other. He thought it was all over, poor man. She married him because she thought he was rich, you know, and Tony let her do it. He encouraged her, Alan said, because I think he wants the money too. I don't know. Sometimes," her head tilted to one side as she looked up at the ceiling, as if trying to remember, "sometimes they would come to the mission and have parties. No, not here, silly," she said, noticing my openly disbelieving look, "but in the bush. On the kopje, you know, that one that ugly old Faye is always going on about, with the cave? They'd go to the cave and drink beer and do stuff. Him and Avril. Tony told Alan about it afterwards, like he was bragging, you know? He even laughed once and said you had told him about the cave!"

Talk to the Moon

"Get. Out. Of. My office." I couldn't think of anything else to say. The anger was white hot. My legs and her hands were shaking and I clasped my hands together and kept my legs under the desk. There was no way I was going to let this trashy tramp see how shaken I was. I wanted to slap the fatuous face in front of me but I deliberately held my hands in my lap. My face was frozen in an expressionless mask.

"*Okay, okay*! Don't get your knickers all knotted. I thought you would be grateful to hear it. I'm not the skunk. Now you can dump the bloke before it's too late and get someone decent." She stood up and it seemed as if she was about to say more but she looked again at my face and left silently, leaving the door wide open. I got up and closed it.

It was all lies. It had to be. This girl had it in for me from the day we met. She had said she was going to get even and now she had. That's all it was. Stupid, stupid revenge. There was no truth at all to it. I would talk to Tony about it and he would tell me too how stupid it all was. He'd produce proof that he had in fact been where he said he had been. No one could be that duplicitous. Going to such lengths! Why would he want to marry me when he could have had Avril? It didn't make sense.

Somehow this girl had found out my most vulnerable spot and she had struck. Somehow she had found out that I had once suspected Tony of having an affair with Avril—how? I didn't know, but I had. Maybe she had read my diaries. Yes, that was it! She had read the diaries that I had hidden in my suitcase on top of the wardrobe while I visited with Avril and Neil. That's how she knew! I felt so much better even if the vision of Paula snickering over my diaries made me ill. I took several deep breaths and the shaking began to subside. It was careless to leave my diaries where Paula could find them. I should have known but I always had been too trusting. It wouldn't happen again.

The phone on my desk rang. I mechanically picked it up.

"Holly! Are you still angry with me? I didn't want to leave things the way they were. Perhaps we can talk."

"Yes, Tony, let's talk. In fact, make it tonight will you?" I hung up quietly without waiting for a response. I felt like such a fool. Even if Paula had been lying, it made no difference, someone was playing me for an idiot and I wasn't going to stand for it anymore. I sat at my desk in silence for the rest of the afternoon. I didn't get any work done.

"Penny for your thoughts?"

"They're not worth a penny, Ger. Is that all?" He left, rebuffed. Gerald had always cared about my feelings and I treated him like a dog. Ayesha is a lucky woman to have him. Why, oh why, was I attracted to men who were not meant for me? It was evident to me now that I needed to rethink my relationship with Tony and men in general.

I remembered Majozi, the old nganga in the village—what had he said? Something about someone close to me being a crocodile—a woman. It had to be Avril, assuming if what Paula said was true. I was assuming no such thing, yet. I had to be careful; I was always so quick to jump to conclusions. I would hear Tony's side of the story and then decide. All was not over yet. I felt better.

Tonight, Tony showed up bright and early for a change. I had just pushed away an uneaten supper. Faye had gone back to the hospital and we were alone in the living room. I felt nervous. I had been so eager to confront him earlier but now that his twinkling blue eyes were in front of me begging forgiveness for our earlier spat I didn't feel quite so brash. Then I remembered Paula's words and my resolve hardened.

"Tony, I had a bit of a confrontation with Paula today. I wouldn't be mentioning it but it involved you—us."

He gave me a quizzical look.

"Do you remember Paula's boyfriend, Alan?"

"Yes, why?" He didn't blink.

"You were in the Air Force together, weren't you?"

"Yes, we were. What's all this about?"

"Apparently, Alan told Paula about you and Avril, and she came and told me."

Tony's voice became quiet.

"What about me and Avril?" His eyes now looked steel hard.

I decided not to beat about the bushes anymore and the whole story poured out. I repeated, as best I could, word for word, everything Paula had told me. Tony didn't flinch and he remained poker faced throughout. When I finished, I looked at him and pleaded, "Please tell me this is not true, Tony."

He sighed and there was a long silence. He at last spoke.

"I wish I could, Holly, but I've been doing some thinking too, lately, and I don't want to live a lie any more than you do. It's not fair to either of us. Yes, I know that I asked you to marry me, and I shouldn't have done that, but at the time I thought it was the best thing for me. In fact,

Avril encouraged me to marry you. She thought she was going to be married for the rest of her life to Neil and she didn't want to see me left alone." He pretended not to notice the tears that began to trickle down my cheeks.

"I liked you and felt we were good friends and we understood each other. My mother said that was always the best basis for a marriage: respect and friendship; romantic love never lasts. But Avril and I have been in love since we were children."

I listened as I dabbed at my eyes with my handkerchief. I didn't want to interrupt him. He was talking now, as if purging an old wound, and I wanted to know the truth—the whole truth, no matter how painful it was.

"Avril decided she was going to marry a rich man. This was something we always knew, even as kids, that she would never consider marrying anyone for love unless he had money too. She made no bones about it. I accepted it. What choice did I have? My folks hated her, they didn't want me marrying her anyway, but I was a fool and I thought maybe she would change her mind when we got older, my parents would come around—stuff like that. That's why I'm always hustling to get rich fast. I wanted Avril to see that I could make a life for her; that I'm not such a big loser.

"Then she met Neil. She'd just graduated from the Tech in Johannesburg and, hell, I introduced them! He told her about the new laboratory they were installing at the mission and how they needed someone with her qualifications. She jumped at it. Avril is no missionary. She had no intention of converting heathens or wiping baby's arses.

"Her parents came into the church years ago but she never showed much interest in being a part of it. She says it's all a bunch of hypocrites running around telling other people what to do and sticking their noses in everywhere and I'm inclined to agree, but besides that, it doesn't even pay much. She told me the pay-off would come later. I knew what she was up to. Anyone who knows Avril would have seen it but she's good. She's damn good. No one even suspected. She made friends with that old hell-hag Tootie and played the role to perfection of the devoted servant of God come to minister to the less fortunate.

"Within months she'd snagged poor old Neil and he was a goner. She worked him like a virtuoso on a Stradivarius. I am—was—fond of Neil, don't get me wrong. I tried to tell him several times what she was up to but each time I choked. I couldn't do it. I think, eventually, he knew, but by then it was too late. She had snared him well and he was in the honey trap. Besides, I knew if I had told him everything she would never have looked at me again.

"I stayed around her like a love-sick fool. She enjoyed the attention she was getting from me and still does. When you came along she told me to date you. She felt guilty that she was 'having all the fun' as she put it, and I agreed. I wanted to make her jealous. I agreed to date you on the condition I could still see her every now and then. I couldn't go cold turkey. She agreed and we met fairly often whenever and wherever the opportunity presented itself. By the way, I wasn't lying about going to North Africa. I did go—put that in your pipe and smoke it, Paula—but I came back a week earlier than I said I did. I booked into a hotel—not even my parents knew—and we had a blast.

"Unfortunately that goose Hattie saw us but luckily she didn't get a good look. I knew she'd run to you but I was ready for it if she did. I was more afraid of Neil finding out, if you must know. All along, I felt as if I was betraying Neil, not you. I justified it by telling myself that I couldn't betray someone I didn't really love. We had never slept together and for that I was grateful.

"I wasn't looking forward to the wedding but I knew I could do it. I still have so much respect for you, Holly, I want you to know that, and in many ways I do love you but I could never love you in the same way I love Avril.

"I must go to her now, she needs me. Please don't think too badly of me. I hope we can always stay friends but I know you are going to need time and I won't intrude on your anger and grief if you need to express it."

He got up and walked to the door. He turned around.

"Please keep the ring. I don't want it back."

I wrenched the ring off my finger and threw it at him with all my might. It bounced off his cheek, cutting him slightly, and fell to the floor. He stooped and picked it up, putting it in his pocket.

"Take your cheap ring. I never want to see you again!"

He left, quietly closing the door behind him.

CHAPTER 31

Majozi

28th April

The news has spread like an out of control brush fire that I have been jilted two months before the wedding. It's impossible to avoid the gossip. Paula walks around the office with a self-satisfied smirk on her face. She stays out of my way and I will never speak to her again.

There has been an outpouring of emotional support from the mission people but none of it can heal the gaping wound in my heart. Eva wants to cancel the wedding altogether but I have insisted she go ahead as planned.

The old wedding invitations had been at the printers, ready to print, and only a quick phone call saved us from financial disaster. Mrs. Ghosh said she would take the wedding materials back that I had bought and give me a refund. Mom's appalled but not surprised. I gave her a watered down version of why I had broken off the engagement.

"I knew he was no good from the moment I saw him! He did just what I expected—used you and dropped you like an old rag. The acorn doesn't fall far from the tree. I heard about his mother from Lalie. Such a good, Christian woman to have spawned the devil's child! At least Eric seems a Christian young man and I'm glad one of you is making a good marriage. I don't know who's going to want you after this—you're spoiled goods now!"

Dad was philosophical.

"And I really liked him! Well, rather you found out what he's made of now than later."

I did not give anyone, except Eva and Faye, the full story. All anyone knows is that the engagement's off and so is the wedding. Paula and Ian know, of course, and I also know that the real reason will be served, bit by salacious bit, in strictest confidence to sundry friends and acquaintances as a source of entertainment and titillation.

Faye is disappointed and saddened. She, like me, always considered Avril a good friend even though she was under no illusions as to Avril's character.

"I knew she was ambitious but I didn't think she had it in her to be that shameless. She'd have to be as hard as granite to marry a man under such pretenses and at the same time put on such an act! She had me convinced it was the real thing and I don't consider myself to be naïve!"

I do wonder if I am still Gaby's godmother. I love Gaby dearly and the thought of never seeing him again makes me cry. Can godmothers be fired? I don't know, but I don't think it's possible to play that role anymore considering the circumstances.

30th April

I got a surprise phone call today from Nigel Withers.

"Where's that young man of yours? He never showed up for work on Monday and I've heard nothing from him since he left on Friday!"

"He's not my young man and I've heard nothing from him either and neither do I expect to. If you do hear from him I don't want to know about it."

"Oh? So it's like that, eh?" He *harrumphed*. "I'm sorry to hear it. He must be off licking his wounds somewhere. Well, if you do see him tell him to give me a tinkle won't you? I can only cover his absence for so long." I didn't respond and hung up. I didn't care at all. I also received a weepy phone call from Aunt Lalie.

"Your mother told me what had happened, my dear. I can't tell you how much it has affected Malachi and me. We're just devastated! We were so looking forward to having you as our daughter-in-law!" I feel there is a good side to this mess after all.

Aunt Lalie didn't give me a chance to respond. "The young scoundrel didn't even have the decency to tell us himself; we had to hear it from others. And now he's gone off to Greystones, throwing himself at that *strumpet*! It's her fault that our dear Neil is no longer with us. If she hadn't angered that murdering swine of a cook he'd still be here. Eric is so angry with him he says he never wants to speak to him again. Now our family is even more estranged than before. Oh dear! I did so hope that he would make something of himself and settle down with a decent girl, like you."

Lalie went on and on endlessly, until I shoe-horned in between the sobs and the wailing monologue to mutter a few meaningless phrases and make some soothing noises, then I hung up after saying I was really busy and would talk to her later.

I wonder if Lalie and Malachi would ever know, or already did know, the whole truth. I won't be the one to tell them. I feel exhausted. How long will I have to field questions, expressions of sympathy and waffling platitudes from others before life returns to normal again? I hate being the object of pity. Eva's wedding will be an ordeal but it's one I'll have to bear with fortitude.

5th June

Tony has not returned to Tshabanda. I heard this from Josh who came to see me today at the mission.

"He's gone AWOL. I heard it from Withers and now he's been fired. He didn't even call and tell him he wasn't going to be back. It's going to be tough for him to find another job." I am relieved that Josh spared me the sympathy routine. He made no comment other than, "I'm sorry. These things happen. I know." And that was that.

He mentioned he had received an invitation to Eva's wedding. "Would you like me to be your escort? You won't get quite as many pitiful stares if you look like you're having a good time. Just pretend I'm Clark Gable and you'll have no trouble." I laughed and accepted. I am determined to enjoy the wedding and finally kill the misconception that my heart has been broken. Somehow, I don't feel as bad as I thought I would. Angry—yes, but sad, no. I feel betrayed and used. I don't understand my feelings and I wonder if the sadness will come later.

3rd July

I have been so wrapped up in myself and my problems that it was only today I noticed all is not well with Esther. She is normally such a high-spirited girl, laughing and talking constantly with me. I now realize she has been this way since returning from the annual leave she had spent recently at Greystones visiting Martha.

"What's wrong, Esther? Is there a problem?"

Esther continued to iron. She kept her head down. It seemed as if she wanted to cry and talking would precipitate a flood of tears. I waited. Finally Esther spoke.

"Yes, there is a problem. But I can't tell you what it is. I will be in big trouble if I do!" The tears flowed freely, now, and I handed her one of my own embroidered handkerchiefs that she had just ironed. I waited until the sobs quieted down before speaking.

"Esther, you must tell me. Whatever it is, it can't be so bad that I won't be able to help you. If you don't tell me, then I can't help you at all."

"If I tell you, you will go to the police, and it will all be much worse." I felt icy cold. What had Esther done that she would have to go to the police about? She's such a good, Christian girl, honest to a fault. I couldn't imagine Esther doing anything illegal. I thought for a bit.

"Esther, whatever you tell me, I promise I won't go to the police. I won't tell anyone, if I don't have to. I *promise!*" I felt quite safe. Esther would never have done anything criminal. She probably pinched some sugar or something and was suffering pangs of guilt.

Esther looked at me with hope in her eyes, but then began to cry again.

"There is nothing you can do!" I had to wait for the tears to stop, again.

"We won't know that until you tell me," I persisted. Esther relented and I led her out of the kitchen and we sat on the doorstep in the weak, winter sun and talked.

Esther told me the whole story: how she had left two weeks ago for Greystones, and when she arrived, she noticed that Martha was in much the same state she was in at this moment. She also noticed that young master Tony was there, at Greystones, and that Martha told her he and Miss Avril were sharing a bed. She thought this must be why Martha was so upset. She tried to set Martha's mind at rest, saying he and Miss Holly were no longer to be married, but Martha remained upset and cried every night.

She finally made Martha tell her what was wrong, much as Miss Holly had done with her, today. Martha said she was pregnant, about six months already, and she didn't know what to do. She had hidden her pregnancy rather well, since Esther hadn't noticed it, and neither had Miss Avril, apparently. She asked Martha who the father was. Would he be prepared to marry her? They were Christians now, and it was the Christian custom to marry the father of the child.

Martha told her that she was in big trouble. The father would never be able to marry her—he was wanted by the police! And if Miss Avril found out who the father was, she'd be fired, without a doubt.

"Who's the father, Esther?" I asked, but I already knew the answer to that.

"It is Cuthbert!" and the sobs began again. Martha and Cuthbert had fallen in love in spite of being from two different tribes. He had not returned to Martha after his prison escape, but Martha knew where he was hiding, and she had been taking him food. Cuthbert had told her the whole story of what had happened the night Neil had died but Martha had been sworn to secrecy. All she could say was that Cuthbert was innocent.

"Why was she sworn to secrecy? If she knows something, anything, that can prove Cuthbert's innocence she must come forward, now."

"Oh, no, you don't understand. If she told what really happened that night her own life would be in danger. The police, they would not believe her anyway. It is her and Cuthbert's words against that of the madam Avril. They will take Cuthbert and hang him and Martha will be dead too. He told Martha that and she is too afraid to even tell me. My life could be in danger too! But now her child's father—he is not able to live like a normal man. His own people will turn him in to the police so he lives like a jackal—going out at night and feeding on carrion. What is she to do?" Esther sat and sniffed, her head bobbing up and down and her shoulders shaking. I was stymied.

I know that Esther is right, I have a moral obligation to reveal what I heard here today to the police, but I don't feel right about doing it. Something is wrong, terribly wrong with the official picture and now my gut screams to me that Cuthbert is innocent. But what can I do? I feel as helpless as Esther. We sat for a while on the steps, saying nothing, each lost in our own thoughts.

Saturday, 4th July

After a sleepless night I came up with a plan.

I arose early this morning, borrowed Eva's bicycle and as soon as Esther arrived for work I told her what we were going to do and we set off for the village. Since it's the dry season, the road is in better shape than the last time I was on it, with Tony. We made good time, arriving in the village before ten.

We were surrounded by the usual gang of small boys and girls, and I was prepared with a bag of sweets. I also brought some gifts for Majozi. Esther had told me that *nganga's* liked tobacco and we first made a stop at the Ghosh's store to buy the tobacco and some sugar and tea.

The headman came out of his hut—blinking in surprise at the strange sight before his eyes of the brown skinned girl and the white girl riding bicycles. Esther explained that we wanted to talk to the *nganga*, and after showing the headman the gifts, he nodded his head and made his way to Majozi's hut, as he had before. Clapping at the door he entered. We could hear low voices inside and a minute later he came out and motioned for us to enter.

Esther was terrified—I could tell. Her face was a shade paler and she trembled and shook. I held her arm to steady her and also to propel her inside before she could lose her nerve. Esther had not been keen on my idea at first. She has been brought up a Christian and she is sure God will smite her for seeing the witchdoctor whose heathen ways she and her family have irrevocably renounced. I explained that he isn't the devil's pawn but merely an herbalist. Besides, we weren't planning on consulting him in a professional capacity anyway: no ancestral spirits or throwing of the bones or spells—he is only someone I feel can get things done. I gave Esther a slight push and we were inside.

The hut looked exactly the same as before. Majozi sat on the same zebra skin and the same smoky fire burned in the center of the hut. Now that I know he's blind I am no longer afraid of him but I respect his abilities. He was close to the mark before and I couldn't put that down to chance. He seems wise. He seems like someone who would have answers to all things—that is why I want to talk to him: I trust him. We clapped our hands in greeting and I explained who we were. Esther seemed to have been struck mute.

"I remember you," said Majozi. "I don't know this Esther, but no matter. What is your question?"

"I don't have a question for you, this time. We need help and you were the only person I could think of to come to." Majozi motioned us to sit. I didn't know if I should give him the gifts now or wait until later. Why was Esther so useless? She was leaving it all up to me! I thought I would wait.

We sat with legs out straight and feet crossed on the bare dirt floor in the African custom and I began to speak, telling Majozi everything that had happened since I had last visited his hut, even to how accurate he had been in the bone throwing and everything that had transpired up until then. He interrupted a few times with questions but mostly let me talk, listening carefully. Esther interrupted too, in Sindebele, when she wanted

Talk to the Moon

to be sure that Majozi got the point or when she felt that I wasn't being clear enough. She was regaining her composure. When we had finished, he sat for a while, saying nothing, seemingly asleep. Then he got up and, sticking his head out the door, shouted something. The headman appeared as if by magic. It was likely he'd been sitting outside the door the whole time, listening. Majozi spoke rapidly in Sindebele and the headman nodded, grunting, as he listened. Then he left.

"I had to tell him," said Majozi, "we will need his help too."

"So you're going to help us, then?"

"We will try. This man, who is falsely accused, is in Mashonaland. It will be difficult but I know a Shona *nganga* up that way who might help us. If he doesn't, there is not much I can do. But don't worry," he added sensing tension, "he won't tell anyone of your sister's boyfriend's whereabouts. He is not friendly with the police due to a misunderstanding some years back. You might need to pay him some money. I will send the headman up there—he is the son of a regional chief, and wise too, so you have nothing to worry about. You will need to give us some money to proceed. I will find out how much money for the bus fare and expenses for the headman and let you know. Come back tomorrow." With that, the consultation was over. I placed the gifts close to Majozi and we left. I felt somewhat deflated. I had hoped for something more concrete—like the outline of a definite plan.

Esther was not as optimistic as I.

"He will not help Cuthbert. He will take the money for himself and say the Shona *nganga* has it. These *nganga's* are not to be trusted!" I didn't know what to say. I hoped it wasn't too much money—more than I could afford. But I began this process and now I must see it through. We cycled back to the mission.

"Where did you and Esther go?" asked Eva.

"Uh, just to the store. I wanted her to help me carry some stuff and I knew you'd be busy." Eva seemed satisfied with this explanation. I told myself that, in a small way, I am relieved to be out of the loop in this wedding. I am still actively helping Eva, but I no longer feel the pressure I was feeling before, when Tony and I were still engaged. Now it will be wholly Eva's day and I will do everything in my power to make it beautiful. I am not going to drape myself like a wet blanket over the festivities.

Sunday, 6th July

After church I cycled back to the village. I am getting good at this, becoming almost familiar with each pothole and gully in the road. The headman said the money I brought wasn't enough but he will be able to get there and back and will get the rest of the money from me the following week.

Saturday, 12th July

I again rose early and left before Esther arrived for work. I didn't want Esther's pessimism spoiling the negotiations. I no longer felt nervous cycling to the village by myself and now enjoyed the solitude of the ride. The sky, just after dawn on a winter morning, was a deep rose-pink as I rode out of the mission gates. It slowly brightened to an aquamarine and I breathed deep in the crisp air and felt it rush through my body into the dark corners of my soul. I imagined all the old hurts and disappointments evaporating, now replaced with a crystal-clarity of mind—as if the child Holly had died and an older person had taken her place.

As I pedaled I vowed to myself that I would never give anyone power over me again, neither man or woman, and that included Mom and Dad. I would also get to the truth of the matter regarding Cuthbert if it took me a lifetime. I had stood by helplessly when John Blanchard died, and then said nothing about my suspicions regarding Neil's death, but I would not stand by impotently as another innocent man was led to his death.

I am under no illusions to the futility of attempting to place the guilt where it belongs—I have no evidence other than what I have been told—it's all hearsay. I know that if I ever voice my suspicions it will only be assumed I am the jilted lover out for revenge. I am out for revenge, but the sense of outrage I felt for my betrayal by the man I thought I once loved is nothing compared to the death of two men I admired deeply. The desire for revenge is what I feel for John and Neil Blanchard, not for myself, and I want justice for Cuthbert. I can live with the anger and hurt. It has taught me something and for that I will be eternally grateful.

I brought some more money with me—what I thought might be a reasonable fee for the *nganga*, and the outstanding balance on what I owed the headman—hoping it would not be more. Now that I no longer have the financial responsibility of the wedding I feel able to spare some of my own savings to help Cuthbert. I felt the apprehension return as I pushed my bike up to the *nganga's* doorway and leaned it up against the hut. I clapped my hands loudly, identifying myself.

"Come in! Come in!"

Talk to the Moon

Majozi was not on his zebra skin this time. He was sitting on a stool and a woman was giving him a breakfast of *sadza*. It smelled delicious but I was embarrassed.

"I could come back later. I didn't know you were eating."

"Please come in. Sit!" he commanded. The woman ladled out a heap of the steaming porridge onto a tin plate, surrounding it with greens, and a mug of tea sat on a low table nearby. Majozi said something to the woman and she took another plate from a shelf and dished out another ladle of *sadza*, handing it to me.

"Oh, no, I couldn't..." I began to say, but Majozi interrupted.

"Never refuse a gift of food from an Ndebele. It is insulting." I blushed, and gently clapped my hands before taking the plate.

"Thank you." I noticed I had not been handed any cutlery but Majozi broke off a small portion of the *sadza* with his fingers, rolled it around with one hand until it was a small, round ball, dipped it into the green stew-like mixture and popped it into his mouth. I did the same. It was good! We ate quietly until we had finished everything on our plates. I hadn't realized how hungry I was. The woman gave me a cup of sweet, milky tea and then left with the dishes.

Majozi spoke of the weather, the prices of tea and mealie meal, and of just about everything except the matter I had come for. I was beginning to wonder if he wasn't going to help me and didn't know how to get around to saying it, but as if he had read my mind, he said:

"White people are too impatient. They want everything done yesterday, and then they want it over with. The Ndebele are different. When business is to be discussed, you don't leap into it right away. You eat first; you talk, have some tea or beer, and then discuss what needs to be discussed for however long it takes. I see you are trying to learn our ways and that is why I tell you this. If you were not I would not mention it. One can only help those who want to learn.

"Our headman returned late last night so he is still asleep." I felt so impatient now I knew it must show. I couldn't help it, I was white, and I had been waiting all week for the news. Now I would have to wait for the headman to awaken. We drank some more tea, talked, and the sun rose higher in the sky.

A clap came from outside the door and the headman entered. He greeted me and poured himself some tea. Would this tea ceremony never end? Then the headman began to talk, but I couldn't understand him since it was all in Sindebele and my own Sindebele was not good enough for conversations yet. When he finished, he produced some ticket stubs and a scrap of paper from his pocket, handing them to me. They were bus ticket stubs. I looked at the scrap of paper and on it was written some amounts that had been added up to a total.

"Is this what I owe?" It wasn't bad. I had brought enough to cover it.

"Yes," said the headman. "Expenses, bus ticket and for *nganga*. Maybe more." My heart sank.

"How much more?"

The headman shrugged. "Depend on *nganga*."

Then he left.

"What happened? Please tell me!"

Majozi smiled.

"The *nganga* knows of the case. He visited with Martha and persuaded her to tell him where Cuthbert was hidden. She did, and they took him away to a safer place. Don't worry—no one will find him. There are some places in the highlands of Mashonaland that no white man knows about where they have hidden him. Caves and ravines that never see sunlight. When it is safe, they will take him somewhere else. Maybe out of the country, I don't know. The less we know the better.

"Martha is leaving her employer. She said that she cannot feel safe there anymore and she will return to her village here. She will have her baby here and family to take care of her. She thanks you for all you have done."

I sighed with relief. I felt I had compensated for much of my past stupidity. I hoped Martha would be alright. I felt light and carefree as I stepped out of the hut after profusely thanking both the headman and Majozi. The air was once again the champagne elixir it used to be—before death and dishonesty had stunk it up. I would gladly have given every penny I had to free Cuthbert. The money I would have spent on the wedding has now been put to better use.

CHAPTER 32

Eva

26th July, Eva's wedding

I awoke this morning with a strange, sinking feeling in my chest. The dreadful day had arrived, as I knew it would. I would have to get through it as best I could. I felt as alone as the day I had arrived at the mission, but then, I'd had Eva as a companion.

My stomach was doing slow flips. I knew that in spite of it being Eva's special day, every eye would be on me, Holly. Curious, probing eyes, and after the wedding was over, I would be verbally dissected, like a biology class experiment: how I had looked, what I had worn, my every word and expression analyzed for signs of grief—everyone knew that this was to have been my day too. I would be as conspicuous by my presence as Tony and Avril would be conspicuous by their absence. They did not receive an invitation. Eva said that Eric had no desire for his brother to be there, and, as far as he was concerned, he could stay in Mashonaland.

I went over to Eva's room at the school to help her prepare and do some last minute packing. They are going to the Eastern Highlands for their honeymoon—a brief one, since Eric can't be absent from the farm for too long. Eva is so looking forward to being a farmer's wife. She has been to Fort Victoria several times since the engagement to see the farm and she tells me it already feels like home to her. She has so many plans. None of them involve redecorating, she tells everyone, laughing. The house could stay just as it was for all she cares. I believe her.

Eva looked radiant in her white satin wedding gown and carrying a bouquet of white and yellow daisies. I had rushed back to my room at the last minute, putting on the same dress I wore to Avril's wedding and running a brush through my hair. Like Rhett Butler, I really didn't give a damn. I had just applied some powder and lipstick when there was a knock on the door. It was Josh. He was not Clark Gable and I am no Vivian Leigh but we both looked presentable. We arrived at the church just in time.

The ceremony went without a hitch. We sat next to Mom in the front row and Mom sobbed audibly as Eva walked down the aisle with Dad at her side. I was glad Mom was crying; she could do the crying for the both of us. I wasn't going to give the old biddies the satisfaction of seeing me cry. I bit my lip, face frozen in a stiff simulation of happiness. It reminded me of that game Eva and I used to play called *Statues*. The one who twitched first was the loser.

Aunt Lalie, in the front row across the aisle was sobbing even louder than Mom, and I wanted to laugh, but I had been good at *Statues* so I bit my lip even harder.

I did wonder why Mom couldn't have picked a better outfit for the wedding. I gave her money to buy a new dress and hat and she found the cheapest looking and ugliest cotton dress in Bulawayo, and then topped that off with another shiny black straw hat—a bilious bird perched on its flat brim.

I felt relief that Tony and Avril hadn't been invited. I could only imagine the cynical comments that would have been made about the outfits later, and the sidelong glances I'd have received, but I knew that would be trivial compared to how they themselves would be treated by the good church-folk. Everyone had been unanimously vocal in expressing horror and disgust at Tony's defection: *"...and her husband not even cold in his grave yet!"* I thought it just as well they didn't know the rest of the story. Eric looked proud and red in the face as he boomed out his vows. Eva said hers quietly. No one was able to hear her except for those of us in the front rows.

The reception was rather dull, but I endured it. I pasted the same stiff grin on my face and laughed too loudly at all the jokes. I now understood how Eva must have felt at Gerald's wedding. Tootie was the perfect hostess. She had been tenderly solicitous toward me; hovering over me like a mother cat over a hurt kitten. She expressed loud outrage at Avril and Tony's behavior and had informed everyone in earshot that they would no longer be welcome in her house. She also told everyone who would listen that she had known all along that Avril was 'a sly one' and that she hadn't been fooled for a minute.

If it hadn't been for Josh, I would not have made it through this day. He has a quiet strength about him that I am only now beginning to notice. I don't know why I have been so dismissive of him in the past—always comparing him to Tony. He is nothing like Tony, and that is his strength.

Talk to the Moon

He's almost as good a storyteller as Tony: losing himself in the story and forgetting his shyness as he makes us laugh out loud and gasp in horror or surprise. I realize the differences between Josh and Tony are many but when Josh tells a story it is not to glorify himself but is more of an attempt to convey what he feels when alone in the bushveldt, or *bundu* as he calls it.

CHAPTER 33

GABE

1992

Gabe scanned the entries in the diary after the wedding. They consisted mostly of day to day trivialities:

Aunt Eva had invited her family down to the farm for Christmas. Aunt Holly wrote that she felt neither happy nor unhappy: merely neutral, doing her job, going out with friends and generally trying to put the year's events behind her.

He wondered if there was anything more about the murders; anything that could shed some light on what had happened to *Maman* during the bush war in the '70's. He felt sure there was a connection.

He found some entries that may or may not have been what he was looking for:

Martha had not returned to the mission as Aunt Holly and Esther had expected. Another visit to the *nganga* confirmed what they had surmised: she did not want to return to Bulawayo defeated and dependent upon her family for help. She had made the decision to disappear along with Cuthbert. Majozi guessed that they were both out of the country with new identities and for all he knew they were happy. Martha had likely given birth by now.

Aunt Holly stayed in touch with Majozi; visiting him frequently for advice and sometimes just to talk. According to her, he had become a close friend. He said he had no idea of Cuthbert's exact whereabouts but Aunt Holly felt he did know. She thought he was keeping quiet to protect her.

Uncle Josh had left again to build a bridge somewhere in the bush. He would stop by the mission on his infrequent trips to Bulawayo for supplies, staying for a few hours, then disappearing like a leopard in the noonday sun into the shadows of the wilderness.

When he stayed overnight at the mission, they'd sit out in the garden and sip lemonade as they watched the bright stars overhead. Aunt Holly

Talk to the Moon

would try not to think about how she and Tony used to sit and watch the same stars and kiss and talk about their future. Uncle Josh knew the names of the stars and constellations and said he found his way in the *bundu* at night by looking at the position of the stars; the Southern Cross in particular. He'd go on long hunting trips in areas where there were no roads and where a man could easily get lost by day as well as by night.

Aunt Holly wrote too about Uncle Josh's paintings: he painted bush scenes in beautiful oils on small canvases that he brought to show her on one of his flesh pot trips. She was surprised at the quality of the paintings. His sunsets were delicate and understated. He told her that if he actually used the brilliant oranges and reds he saw every evening or dawn the paintings would be too gaudy. Animals would appear in some of them—a shy kudu peering between the butterfly-shaped leaves of a mopani tree, or a dusty gray elephant drinking at the dried up hole that now only contained a few puddles of dirty brown water. She wished she could see the animals he saw. His world was fascinating to her.

Uncle Josh asked Aunt Holly if he could write to her.

"I get lonely out in the bundu and I often wish I had someone to talk to. There are no phones where I am but the post does come once a week. Aunt Holly said she couldn't think of any reason why she shouldn't write: she loved to write and she felt she expressed herself far better with her pen than with her tongue. She compensated by keeping her diary current. There was not so much description anymore since things were no longer new to her but she often wrote down her daily thoughts and feelings. She would be happy to share a few of them with someone. Yes, she would write to him.

Gabe felt like an intruder, reading these entries that were so personal to his godmother, yet he was afraid that if he did not read it all he would miss an important detail about his own mother: something that would shed some light on what had really occurred all those years ago, so he continued to read.

CHAPTER 34

Holly

4th December, 1947

Josh wrote to me that he will be staying in the bush for Christmas since he has nowhere else to go. I feel bad for him. I wonder if Eva would extend the invitation to Josh. I called her immediately.

"Of course he can come too," said Eva. "We have lots of room. I'm putting mom and Dad in the biggest guest room and we have another smaller one for you and I can clear out a room I use as storage now for Josh. The house is not Greystones, but it's livable."

17th December

I got the word to Josh and he has written back saying he will be happy to accept an invitation since he had been angling for one anyway, or, if that was how it had sounded he may as well not attempt to deny it. He said he will drive to Fort Vic and will be happy to give me a lift if I didn't want to travel with Eva, Eric and my parents. The plan was that Eva and Eric would be taking them all down and back again.

It is at times like this that I keenly feel my inability to drive. Lacking a car is a handicap. I should have bought Avril's car when I'd the chance but I hadn't seen the need; and, hadn't I been just a bit afraid? Eva told me she has learned to drive already on the farm and now she feels quite confident behind a wheel. Mom had never learned to drive. Her upbringing was that it was unladylike not to mention downright dangerous for women to drive and she had conveyed this nonsense to us. That would be another resolution for 1948: I will buy a car and learn to drive.

24th December

Josh and I drove down a day after Eva and Eric had arrived to pick up Mom and Dad. The road is strip tarmac most of the way but sometimes rutted dirt. The lorry bounced around all the way to Fort Victoria, its suspension even worse than Faye's car.

Talk to the Moon

Fort Victoria, or Fort Vic as it's known to locals, is the proverbial one-horse town. There is a wide main street and an old Fort that has given the town its name. It was settled early in the country's history and the pioneer column had stopped here en-route to Mashonaland in 1898. The tribes in this area, Josh told me, are mostly Shona, Shangaan and Karanga. He can speak their language well and says he feels more at home here than in Matabeleland.

We arrived at the farmhouse in the midst of what seemed to be a pack of barking, yelping dogs of every size and color. Turkeys gobbled and fluttered in panic at the new arrival and cats slunk into deep shadows under the nearby tractor shed.

We fought our way through the dogs that were just as happy to see us and made it up the steps and into the shade of yet another of the traditional verandah's that often surrounded Rhodesian farmhouses on two sides.

So this was the house that Tony had grown up in? I felt strange—like an interloper—I shouldn't be here. Mom and Dad were sitting on chairs on the verandah, A peevish Mom swatted at the dogs.

"Get away from me you filthy mongrels! I don't know why you have so many dogs, Eva; I certainly didn't bring you up this way. They stink and they won't leave a person alone."

Dad laughed and hugged me.

"It's good to see you. At last we'll have some sanity around here. Your mother has been verging on hysteria ever since she got here and Eva's ready to send her packing. Maybe you can calm things down. Good to see you too, Josh." They shook hands and I felt that Dad liked Josh. He had liked Tony too but for the wrong reasons. Josh is only a friend but it seems important to me that they like him. I couldn't tell how Mom felt about him. She always acts guarded around him and less than friendly but she does that with any man she doesn't know. Josh looked uncomfortable around Mom too but that doesn't surprise me either.

The house is not as large as Greystones but it's considerably larger than I imagined it to be. Airy French doors lead into a living room furnished with old fashioned mahogany carved armchairs and threadbare, sprung sofas. It's rather dark and dusty and reminds me of Greystones before Avril improved upon it. There's no fireplace, however, and no surprises—just more rooms leading off another long hallway.

"It's Spartan, I know," said Eva, "but it will take us some time to get things organized. Eric isn't big on furniture and his parents left most of their old stuff here when they moved to Bulawayo. We have what they left."

Eric and Eva's room was across the hall from Holly's, a large, room with French doors that led out onto the verandah. Mom and Dad had the guest room next to theirs and Josh had been put in a room off the verandah used as a store room for miscellaneous items.

The kitchen is rather primitive with an ancient wood stove. Blackened pots hang from the rafters under the tin roof. A large work table stands in the middle of the room, and an African cook was working at it making what looked to me like meatballs. Flies buzzed around the kitchen, settling unmolested on the meatballs as the cook passively mixed and shaped. I had been hungry but my appetite was disappearing. Perhaps I'd just have some bread for dinner. The cook looked up as I turned to go, his expression sullen and resentful. He probably wasn't used to all this company giving him extra work and around Christmas too. Maybe I can help in the kitchen while I'm here, lighten his load and clean up while I was at it.

I was surprised Mom hadn't taken over the kitchen yet. I knew a sight such as this would have her issuing orders like a general at the Battle of the Bulge.

The reason for Anna's uncharacteristic neutrality became apparent when I mentioned my willingness to help out in the kitchen to Eva.

"Oh no, don't do that, please! Mom did the same thing this morning, went in there like a panzer division and Eric blew his top. He said that no guests of his would work while we had *kaff*…uh, servants, to do the job. He said that's what we pay them for and he ordered Mom out of the kitchen. She looked quite scared. Eric can get angry at times." I was surprised. He seemed so mild mannered. But then, I didn't know him well either. I hope he doesn't blow too often.

25th December

I have to reluctantly admit today has been the most pleasant Christmas I have spent since that first unforgettable one with Tony, Neil and Avril at Greystones. This one, fortunately, lacked the drama and angst of that Christmas, passing in a peaceable and cheerful way for all. Gibson, the cook, had made a beautiful lamb roast for dinner and I tried not to think of the kitchen while I ate.

Talk to the Moon

Flies buzzed around the dining room table as dogs sprawled, panting and drooling, under the table as Eva fed them scraps. Mom wisely kept her mouth shut while Eric glowered at Eva from the head of the table as he ate. She chattered brightly; unconsciously swatting at flies as she talked. Once, she caught one—single-handedly—killing it with a swift squeeze and dropping it onto the floor where a curious dog thinking it was another scrap ate it.

I don't know which family Eva comes from. It isn't mine, I am sure. She must be a changeling. Living on a farm has brought out everything alien and disparate in her; everything that Mom and I are not. I felt embarrassed that Josh had to witness this inelegant breach of good manners and taste but he didn't seem to notice. He was enjoying himself. He ate everything that was put in front of him and asked for more. He was probably used to flies and dogs, being a bush man. I relaxed and decided to enjoy myself, too.

2nd January, 1948

We all survived the meals, the dogs and the yard full of assorted animal and bird droppings and returned to Bulawayo after New Year. I feel more relaxed now that I have finally put the year behind me and that I can get on with my life with hope and, if not with the heady, fiery feelings of love, then at least something that resembled happiness but that feels quieter and more obedient to my will.

I have decided to forget about Avril and Tony until I am able to approach the subject with less emotion and more objectivity. I can't accuse Avril of a double murder at this time in my life. I don't know, without a shadow of a doubt, that Avril killed anyone. Maybe I only want to believe it. Revenge would be sweet but it is not how I want to clear Cuthbert's name or restore peace to my own life. Besides, what evidence do I have: the words of a dead man? I wasn't even there the night he was killed. Cuthbert had not murdered anyone, but if not Cuthbert, then who? It could only have been Avril. Yet I still feel reluctant to believe that Avril would—could—kill her own husband so cold-bloodedly.

It's difficult to believe she would have killed her husband's father, either, by poisoning him. She would have known how to do it, certainly, but it still would have been tricky. And without an autopsy proof will be difficult if not impossible to obtain. I could go to the authorities with my suspicions but they have already made up their minds about their suspect. Why would they believe me? I would be branded as a vengeful, scorned woman, and the scales of sympathy would swing once more to Avril's side.

Perhaps they would investigate my charges—they could not ignore such an accusation—but the evidence needed for conviction, even a suspicion, would be long gone. I am pleased that I have written everything down in my diary. Every detail of both those nights and the events that led up to the murders are written down. One day justice will be done. Nothing goes unpunished and even if Avril has literally pulled off two perfect crimes she will not get away with it. I feel as certain about this as the sun rising in the morning. It is not up to me to dispense justice and point fingers at another. I will leave that up to God, and the universe, which has a way of balancing things out. In the meantime I will be there for Gaby if and when he ever needs me. That is all I can do.

CHAPTER 35
Maman

1992

The sun had set and the first diamonds of the evening studded a deep violet tropical dome. Gabe now knew all of Aunt Holly's suspicions about his mother. He felt confused and tired. He had read the diaries almost to the end. There was no reason to read any further—he had made his decision. He had to do it. He had to find out for himself what had happened. He was the only one who could do that. Perhaps he didn't really want to know but he couldn't live the rest of his life not knowing. Would she tell him? In spite of her severe spinal cord injuries her speech had not been severely affected. The traumas inflicted were both physical and psychological.

He thought back to that catastrophic day in 1972: the day he had left his mother alone with only the servants for protection. He had not forgiven himself for that even though he knew there wasn't much he could have done had he been there. They had breached the security fence—not difficult for a determined Freedom Fighter, and the band of guerillas armed with AK47's had moved quickly towards the farmhouse looking for anyone unlucky enough to still be there.

The servants fled as soon as the alarm on the fence alerted them to the presence of danger but his mother had not gone with them. She had instead grabbed the shotgun she always kept loaded and with her at all times during those war years and come out onto the verandah firing, surprising the group and even dropping one before they could regroup. But regroup they did: her shotgun taking more time to reload than it took to fire an AK47. She tried to take shelter behind the verandah wall but she was not quick enough. She fell as the first round of machine gun fire strafed the wall. The bullets entered her body at an angle, but close enough to her sixth cervical vertebra to severely injure the spinal cord.

The rag tag group could have finished her off then and there but they took their time and using an enormous machete one of them slowly carved at her neck and face, laughing, as she lay helpless on the cold concrete of the verandah. Fortunately, their machetes were dull and they found it difficult to sever the carotid artery. It was then that an Alouette—or K-Car—the helicopter gun ship that had been pursuing the terrorist group arrived and the battle was over. But not for *Maman*.

She was air-lifted by the same helicopter to the hospital in Mt. Darwin but all the surgery the small hospital was capable of could not make her walk or move her limbs again or remove the mutilation to her once beautiful face and neck. Her will to live was enormous, he felt. Anyone else would have given up a long time ago.

Her scars, although painfully visible, were also psychological; the trauma causing her to go into places where no one could follow. He knew how humiliating it must be for her to have no control over her bodily functions and not even able to feed herself. This evening she sat in the dining room as Violetta fed her dinner. Gabe took the plate and spoon from Violetta.

"You look tired, Gabe. What have you been doing?" Avril asked.

"Reading, *Maman*." He wiped her mouth with her napkin and continued to feed her. She seemed quite lucid this evening. She did not ask him what he had been reading and he did not know how to broach the subject. He felt awkward. This would not have been easy at the best of times. Was there ever a good time to ask your mother if she had murdered your father and grandfather?

"I went over to Aunt Holly's place last week when I was in Salisbury." Avril did not respond. "Her daughter, Allegra—you remember her—had some diaries she wanted me to read."

His mother still did not respond. He wondered if she had even heard him or if her mind had gone again into the distant void where no one could follow. He decided to continue.

"They were Aunt Holly's diaries from the '40's. I finished reading them today. They're interesting. I read how Aunt Holly thought you'd killed my father and my grandfather."

There. It was out. There was no going back now. But had she heard him? She was still eating, chewing her food as if that was the most important thing on her mind right now; her eyes reflecting once more the blankness of the familiar void. Then she smiled: a crooked smile, since only half of her mouth was cooperating. She swallowed with difficulty and she slowly spoke.

Talk to the Moon

"So that's what was eating at her all these years, and all this time I thought it was about Tony."

"Well, is it true? Did you kill my father and grandfather?" Gabe felt he got his directness from his mother. She did not respond and he loaded up another spoonful. A few minutes went by and he thought that she had forgotten the question and what they had been discussing, even that she'd been eating, and he'd have to start all over, but then she spoke again.

"Did she guess how it was done?"

His hand froze halfway to her mouth. After a second's hesitation he put the spoon down on the plate. He looked at his mother and she had that faraway look in her eyes again. So that was where she had been all those times when she seemed unreachable. He used to say "penny for your thoughts" and she'd just smile.

"How was it done, *Maman*?" He thought he knew, but he wanted to hear it from her.

She attempted to shrug. It wasn't easy for her but her shoulder did twitch.

"I didn't think she'd guessed. Who would have thought…she was so, ah…naïve. Ah well, what can they do to me now?" Her eyes sharpened again and he knew the old Avril was back. She began to talk, slowly yet confidently, the words forming then tumbling out of her mouth as he sat back and listened.

"You weren't there—you weren't born yet or you were just a baby, so how can I explain how things were so you'll understand? I did it all for you, Gabe: all of it. Even before you were born I knew that you and I must get control of this farm at all costs. The old man was standing in my way, blocking me at every turn. If I had not done something we'd have been in the stone ages for God knows how long.

"I had been planning it for weeks; collecting those seeds and going into the kitchen when everyone was gone and Neil asleep. I'd heard something about ricin but didn't know an awful lot about it, how to extract it for example, so I just sort of crushed them up. I thought I'd try it out on one of the dogs but he refused to eat the food I gave him so that didn't work. I'd heard about cattle dying after ingesting the seeds so I crushed the seeds, making an elixir of a sort and kept it for an opportune time.

"It came that Christmas when Aunt Holly and Aunt Eva were here and we were all in the kitchen making breakfast. I was making the coffee and

I had the vial in my apron pocket. It seemed to be the right opportunity for me to wear that apron and a good place to put the vial so no one would see it. I didn't know how much to put in his coffee so I just guessed. No one noticed but it worked. Even I was surprised! Unless the old man had something else going…but I doubt it, it had to have been the seeds." She laughed and said, "It could have been one of the mushrooms too, you know. And here I am thinking it was me that killed him when it might have been a bad mushroom! I thought the game might be up when they wanted to do an autopsy but we managed to convince them not to do one. Neil was a help in that, wasn't he?"

Maman now had a look of pride on her face, as if she had just pulled off something quite brilliant, thought Gabe. He couldn't tell at this point whether he felt hate, disgust or both, for his mother. He thought of the horrible death his grandfather had suffered and he fought the tears now stinging behind his eyelids. He must not weep now—not when she was about to tell him the whole story. She'd see it as a sign of weakness and she'd go into that place again where reality did not exist and maybe he'd never know the whole truth. There was more to come.

"However it was that he died the farm really came to life after he was gone," she continued. "I fixed up this old ramshackle place and for the first time ever it looked like something I would be proud to call home. It reminded me of our sugar farm back in Mauritius and our ranch in the Lowveld. They were both really something, you know…" Gabe could not allow her to go off on a tangent. He gently steered her back to the subject at hand.

"So why kill my father?" he asked. "What had he done to deserve that?" But he felt he already knew.

"Don't think of him as '*your father*'," she snapped. "He was not! Oh, don't look so surprised, darling, you must have known! Everyone was talking about it all the time. I didn't bring it up because I thought it didn't really matter. Tony was your father in more ways than one; he was your biological father too. Can't you see how much you look like him? You are a love child, dear, conceived that cold August night on a blanket in that dark and smelly cave of Faye's. He wanted to see me one last time. Where else could we go? I had told him that our affair would of necessity come to an end because I was going to tell Neil to return to Greystones. He never used protection like he normally did and I never stopped him. Perhaps I wanted a reminder of Tony in the form of a child—you. I never loved Neil as I loved Tony. But, as you know, even Tony disappointed me after a while."

"The murder, *Maman*. Please tell me. Why?"

"Neil realized what I had done to his father. That's why. He found those damn seeds! Why didn't I get rid of them? Well, even I make mistakes sometimes. He made my life so miserable: angry and cold, and then blackmailing me and refusing to allow me to continue with the renovations, threatening me with divorce, and then he told me he was going to cut me out of his will! I simply had to do it. I did not enjoy it one bit, but I had no choice. It was terrible for me. The aftermath was traumatic: that part required no acting. Luckily for me I had already put the plan into action some time ago anticipating that something just like this might happen.

"Cuthbert and I did not get along. He was insolent and disloyal. I had also found out that he had managed to get Martha over on his side—can you imagine—an Ndebele woman like her! That meant she was no longer loyal to me either and she was pregnant too. Even I could see that. I felt I might have to arrange something for her too if she couldn't stay loyal, but she disappeared soon after Cuthbert disappeared and I never heard from her again, and neither did the police.

"I arranged the theft, breaking into the money box myself and putting the money under his mattress one day when he was out. I also removed a pair of his shoes from his quarters. That part was easy. I then fired him, and that was that. He had to go anyway. He was too protective of Neil and it would be difficult for me to do anything with him around, always watching. Then I put the word out via Martha that I had second thoughts about the way I'd treated him and that Neil would give him the back pay we owed him. I told Martha to tell him to be at the farm that day and he'd get what was owed to him, maybe even his old job back.

"It was raining that day and I had given all the servants the day off. That evening, I saw Cuthbert walking up the road towards the house and I quickly put on the wet shoes that I had kept out on the steps and I went into the office and took the shotgun off the rack. I then called for Neil. He asked me what I was doing with the shotgun and I said I needed to get rid of a rat. He said that wasn't the way one got rid of rats; it was better to use poison. I answered that it was only one rat and that the shotgun would be good enough. At that point, he knew what I was going to do. He froze, and that is when he got it, point blank in the face. I never expected such a mess. Blood everywhere and all over me too!

"I quickly left, and just as I got back to the verandah still holding the shotgun, Cuthbert appeared. You should have seen his face! I thought he would cut and run right there, but I said to him, 'stop, or I'll shoot!'" He looked at me still wearing his shoes, covered in blood and holding the gun, and said to me, '*Ay*! What do you want? Will you kill me too?' I said to him, 'Cuthbert, you take the shotgun and these shoes and get as far away from here as you can. *Run*! If you don't, I'll kill Martha too and your unborn child.' I had emptied the shotgun of bullets so he couldn't shoot me, and he was so terrified he was incapable of thinking anyway. He took the shotgun and shoes and ran, as if devils were chasing him down the road, and I watched him until he disappeared. I went into the house and called the police. And I'm sure you know the rest."

"How did you know that Cuthbert wouldn't tell the police what he saw?"

"So what if he did? It was his word against mine. No one would believe that he'd actually take the murder weapon and shoes just because I told him to or threatened him about Martha. They wouldn't know just how frightened he was; so frightened he would obey me to the letter. Up until that moment I didn't know myself if he'd actually do what I told him to do: he could have just as easily refused and walked away and then I'd have had to get rid of the shotgun and shoes. But there are plenty of places on the farm to do that; it just would have been inconvenient. The plan went off without a hitch and he was even seen running away from the farm with the shotgun. It couldn't have been more perfect!"

Gabe had seen enough TV shows and movies to know that the gunshot residue test was usually one of the first tests performed during a murder investigation, but he also knew that it would not have been around in the 1940's. He wondered what the forensics had been like during this time although he couldn't think what tests they had available in those days that would have proved anything. Blood spatter on his mother's clothes may have fingered her as the shooter, but these were local cops. Fingerprints would have been useless. The murder weapon was no longer at the scene, and besides, it would not have been strange to find his mother's prints all over the shotgun. It did belong to her, after all. There seemed to be no solid proof implicating his mother. He asked if the police had questioned her thoroughly or done any tests of any kind on her.

"You must remember that I am good at what I do, Gabe. I was blood soaked and hysterical when they arrived and the last thing any of them wanted to do was question a hysterical woman and conduct tests on me.

You must remember too they were rural and unsophisticated—unaccustomed to complicated murder investigations. They took my word for it that I had been in my room when the murder took place and then cradled my dead husband in my arms covering myself with blood in the process. I even smeared more blood on me to cover the spatter.

Peaches was helpful; she had arrived by that time, peppering them with questions, asking when did they think they were going to find the murderer while they were standing there wasting their time questioning her dear friend Mrs. Blanchard, and how the murderer was already probably halfway to the border. I think they were so brain-addled by that time they really did a sloppy investigation. For that, I was grateful to Peaches."

Gabe felt as if he had heard enough. He put the now forgotten plate of food down and stood up.

"Are you going to turn me in?" asked Avril, her voice quiet.

Gabe did not answer. He wanted to do just that. He knew the local police well and he knew the case was not yet closed. But did he have enough evidence? The confession was enough for him, but would she deny the whole thing or go into one of her fugues when they questioned her, playing the part of a sick woman in a wheelchair to perfection who was unable to answer questions? No jury would ever convict a woman based on hearsay and witnesses were no longer there. He knew his mother had planned it all well and luck had been on her side too. It seemed it was true the devil took care of his own. At last he answered his mother.

"No, I won't turn you in. I think you have suffered much since the attack and you will certainly suffer more. I will take care of you as much as I can but know that I no longer consider you my mother. You are dead to me." He turned around and began to walk away but his mother was not finished yet.

"There is something else."

He stopped, and slowly turned around to look at her. He didn't know what other bombshells she could drop on him but it was obvious she had one. Her face was even whiter than before and her mouth moved several times before she could get the words out. It had to be something painful—so terrible that even he could not begin to guess at what it was.

"This is difficult for me," she continued, "and I've never told anyone this. No one at all. I am telling you now because I want you to know that even though I did not go to prison or get hung for those murders I would have preferred that. It would have been bad but it would have been preferable to living like this: wearing a baby's nappy all day and unable to take a pee by myself. No, Gabe, you may not consider me your mother anymore. I understand that. But justice has been done. It was done by Cuthbert."

Gabe looked puzzled.

"What do you mean, by Cuthbert? You haven't seen him since he disappeared."

"Oh, not by him personally, but he had escaped along with Martha, and Martha was pregnant. It's my guess that they left the country and went to Zambia. As you already know Zambia was a prime recruiting spot for terrorists. The gang who attacked the farm and shot me were all killed by the government forces that arrived in the helicopter, but before they arrived…" here *Maman* stopped, her eyes filling up with tears and her mouth working. Gabe did not move to comfort her even though he knew the memories of that day must have been extremely painful for her. He waited. Eventually she regained her composure and continued.

"I was still conscious although in terrible pain. One of them, the one who was cutting my face with the machete, bent down and whispered something in my ear. He said, 'This is for my father Cuthbert and my mother Martha.' That was all he needed to say. I knew I was a dead woman then. I wish he had killed me that day and I will not ever forget the look on his face as he cut me. I knew he did not fear death either. We both wanted to die and unfortunately it was I who did not. There, I'm finished. Now you can do with me what you like. Turn me in. Tell everyone what I did. I feel relief now that you know and there is nothing in this world or the next that can punish me anymore than I have already been punished."

Gabe was quiet. She had stated what he was already thinking and he would leave it at that. He knew that no matter what she had said here today he would still love her but that he could not ever forgive her and neither could he ever again admire her as he once had. As a mother to him, she was dead, and nothing could change that now. He turned and walked out the door. He needed fresh air again and sat on the verandah thinking of all his mother had said.

Talk to the Moon

He had always thought of Neil as his father even though *Maman* and Tony had married when he was still a baby. He had heard how people spoke admiringly of the Blanchard's and he felt sadness that he was not the son of such an upstanding family; that instead, he was the bastard offspring of a ne'er-do-well drunkard. Perhaps she was wrong? Perhaps he was not Tony's son. How would she really know? Yes, he did have Tony's eyes and dark hair, but his mother had dark hair too and the Blanchard's also had blue eyes. Maybe it was wishful thinking on his mother's part that he was Tony's son. That is what he would believe. It was easier for him. He refused to accept what his mother had just told him.

He wished Aunt Holly was here. He so badly wanted to confide in her as he always did. He had loved Aunt Holly; she had been his godmother and he had spent more time with her and her family than he had with his own. Cancer had taken her from them all and he wished it had been his mother instead of her. He had never felt close to Tony either and Tony had left them some time ago anyway. He seldom saw him anymore and he had remarried several times since he and his mother parted ways.

He looked out at the pool, moon sparkles on dark water, and thought about the diaries again. He knew how the last one would end. He could have written that part himself, he knew it so well. Aunt Holly had often told him the story of how she had married Uncle Josh a few years after Tony jilted her. She used to laugh and say he had caught her on the rebound, but he knew that she had really loved Uncle Josh, and when he died too just a few years ago she had been heartbroken. They'd had their problems as most married couples do, but they had always seemed so happy and loving towards each other, unlike his own parents who constantly fought and bickered.

They had been married in 1949 immediately after Uncle Josh had signed a contract for a job in the city. He felt that he could ask a woman to marry him now that he was finally living in a civilized place. Gabe smiled, remembering how short-lived that was; the job had come to an end and the only other jobs Uncle Josh could get had been out in the *bundu* again, and how Aunt Holly and her babies had gone with him and all the adventures they'd had in wild places where few white people ventured.

He used to love to listen to their stories: Uncle Josh told the most amazing tales of the bushveldt. He wondered if Aunt Holly had written about them. She probably had. There had been more diaries. He would ask Allegra tomorrow what she would do with those. She was an aspiring writer and they would make a good book. He hoped she wouldn't turn the diaries he had just read into a book. Some things needed to stay a secret.

THE END

Glossary

Afrikaans: a dialect of Dutch with a smattering of English, French, and Malay spoken exclusively in South Africa.

Bundu: See Bushveldt.

Bushveldt or Veldt: Alternative spelling: Veld. Wide open, rural spaces of Southern Africa; or Savannah. Also: *Bundu*

Daga huts: not to be confused with "Dagga", which is marijuana; daga was a process of hut building using mud clay and sticks.

Doilies (Doily) and Tea Cozy's: Very British. One did not serve tea without the ubiquitous doily, which was a lacy round, beaded cover used for the milk jug to keep out the flies. The tea cozy was often knitted or crocheted, and it's purpose was to keep the tea warm since it fitted snugly over the tea pot. There were no tea bags used, ever. You brewed your tea from loose leaves in a proper tea pot and served it with a small jug of milk and a bowl of sugar; lumps preferably to indicate you weren't totally uncivilized.

Flicks: old fashioned slang from the 1940's for movies.

Karos: an animal skin blanket, usually rabbit; pronounced "kah-**ross**".

Karoo, Little or Greater: a semi-desert region of South Africa where sheep farming is the economic backbone of the area.

Kopje: (pronounced KOP-pee) usually large granite outcroppings that come in various sizes and shapes; from enormous domed hills to smaller piles of rock formations that balance precariously on top of one another. Kopjes are found all over Zimbabwe.

Kraal: traditional southern African rural village surrounded by a stockade.

Lowveld: an area of Zimbabwe where elevation is below 2,000 ft. or another name for "Bushveldt"

Mealies: An Afrikaans word for corn or maize.

Mombi: a cow, in a pigeon Bantu language known locally as "*Chilapalapa* that is used mainly in Zimbabwe. Chilapalapa stems from the Matabele/Ndebele languages and was often a language bridge between English speakers and Ndebele or Shona speakers.

Ndebele or Matabele: The northern **Ndebele** (Northern Ndebele: amaNdebele) are a nation and ethnic group in Southern Africa, who share a common Ndebele culture and Ndebele language. Their history began when a Zulu chiefdom split from King Shaka in the early 19th century under the leadership of Mzilikazi, a former chief in his kingdom and ally. Under his command the disgruntled Zulus went on to conquer and rule the chiefdoms of the Southern Ndebele. This was where the name and identity of the eventual kingdom was adopted.

Nganga: an African tribal medicine man, or herbalist. Not a "witch doctor".

Rondavel: a round hut with a conical, thatched roof in southern Africa; originally from "*Rondawel*", an Afrikaans word.

Rooibos tea (pronounced "ROY-bos" or Red Bush tea: a tea that is not actually "tea"; it is made from a broom-like member of the legume family, also called "Fynbos" (pronounced "FAYN-bos") in South Africa.

Sadza: a maize meal porridge; a staple in southern Africa.

Shona or Ma'Shona: the Shona are actually a conglomerate of different groups and tribes of people who live in the eastern and southern portions of Zimbabwe. These tribes are all the original inhabitants of the country but speak different dialects depending upon where they originated.

Strip Road: Asphalt strip roads were built in Southern Rhodesia (now Zimbabwe) from 1933 onwards as an inexpensive way of opening up the country for development. They consisted of two strips of tarmac, car-width wheels apart over a dirt road. When cars approached, both would need to keep one wheel on each strip and the other on an often sandy or rough verge to go by each other: a nail-biting experience that required a strong-nerved driver to keep the vehicle on the road!

Veldskoen or Veldtskoen: (pronounced FELT-skoon). Afrikaans word for tough leather boots made specifically for the Veldt. Rumored to protect one from snake bites to the feet!

About the Author

Katlynn Brooke was born in Zimbabwe, or Rhodesia, as it was then known. She grew up in remote bush veldt areas and both her and her mother's experiences at a Christian mission in the 1940's inspired her to write about a country that no longer exists as it once did. Talk to the Moon is a fictional work as are the characters and situations. She now resides permanently in the US.

Talk to the Moon is Katlynn Brooke's debut novel. She has also written young adult fantasy fiction, *The Six and the Crystals of Ialana* and it's sequel, *The Six and the Gardener's of Ialana.* She is currently working on a fourth novel.

Printed in Great Britain
by Amazon